The Golden Lynx

A FIVE DIRECTIONS PRESS BOOK

The Golden Lynx

A NOVEL

C. P. LESLEY

LEGENDS OF THE FIVE DIRECTIONS 1: WEST

This is a work of historical fiction. Apart from the well-known historical personages, events, and locales mentioned in the novel, all names, characters, places, and incidents are products of the author's imagination or are used fictitiously. Any resemblance to current situations or to living persons is purely coincidental.

ISBN-13 978-1947044203
ISBN-10 1947044206

Published in the United States of America. Revised 2018.

A Five Directions Press book

Cover photographs: Young woman riding at sunset © Vera Volkova/Shutterstock; Eurasian lynx © Reidl/Shutterstock; birch tree forest in fog © bazucha2/ Photos.com. Map on page ii adapted from "Map of the Volga River System," © Karl Musser (reused under Creative Commons Attribution-Share Alike 2.5 Generic license).

Book and cover design by Five Directions Press
Five Directions Press logo designed by Colleen Kelley

FIVE DIRECTIONS PRESS

CONTENTS

MORE BY C. P. LESLEY

Legends of the Five Directions
The Golden Lynx (1: West)
The Winged Horse (2: East)
The Swan Princess (3: North)
The Vermilion Bird (4: South)
The Shattered Drum (5: Center)

The Not Exactly Scarlet Pimpernel

Tarkei Chronicles
Desert Flower
Kingdom of the Shades

Why a Second Edition?

WHEN I BEGAN THE LEGENDS OF THE FIVE DIRECTIONS SERIES in 2008, I had certain rough ideas about how it would develop. I wanted to focus on the years of Ivan the Terrible's minority, a particularly troubled time in Russian history. I also wanted to present, in a way that nonspecialists could access, the research conducted by my fellow Muscovite historians into the social, political, and cultural system of that distant world. As I went farther into the story, I became increasingly fascinated by the complex and evolving relationship between Tatars and Russians in that period when the Juchid *ulus*—usually and incorrectly called the Golden Horde—disintegrated into a small group of successor states over which the Russians eventually triumphed. I learned a great deal more about both Tatar culture and the political infighting of the 1530s, revealing a few historical errors, as well as additional insights into the craft of writing fiction. I created new characters with their own stories based on the needs of individual books. And I received useful feedback from readers.

As the series drew to its end, it became clear to me that *The Golden Lynx*, in particular, would benefit from an update. The appearance of the last book in the series and the decision to publish the e-books in box sets made this the perfect time to spruce up and reissue Nasan's first adventure. While revising, I also removed certain scenes that kept young adult readers who might otherwise embrace the idea of a sixteen-year-old warrior heroine from feeling comfortable tackling the book. The changes are more at the level of nuance than of fundamental shifts, but I hope they will increase readers' enjoyment.

Central Russia and Tataria, 1530s

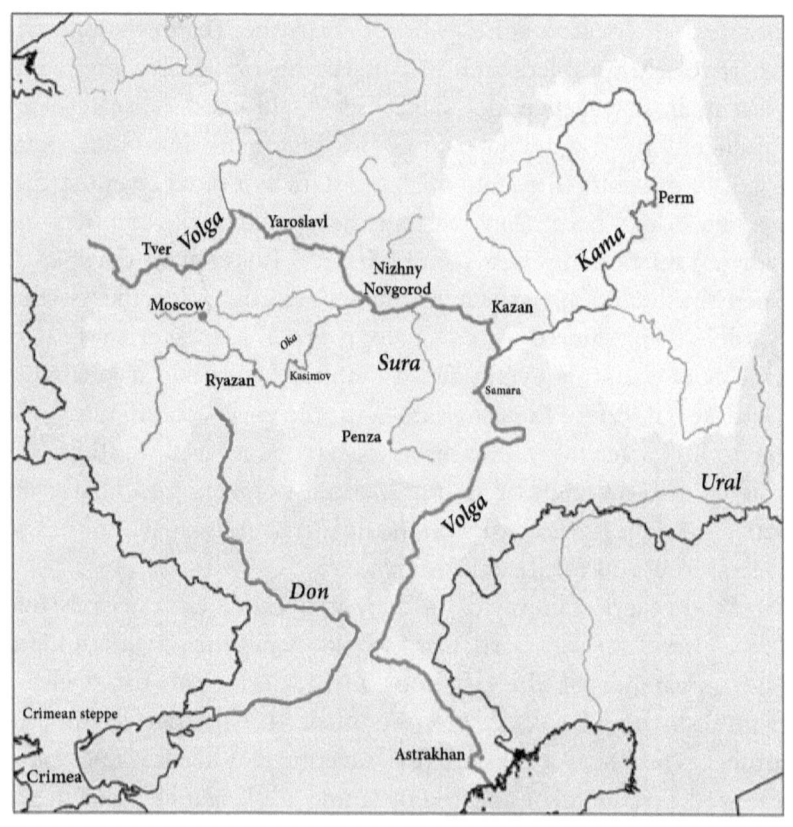

Cast of Characters

FICTIONAL CHARACTERS

Tatars

THE WORDS FOLLOWING THESE TATAR NAMES ARE TITLES, NOT surnames: *khan* (ruler, descendant of Genghis Khan); *khatun* (wife of a khan); *sultan* (son of a khan); and *khanim* (daughter of a khan).

Bulat Khan: Fictional half-brother (by a lesser wife) of the historical Shah-Ali and Jan-Ali—who alternated as khans of Kasimov, a subject principality of Moscow, and Kazan, an independent Tatar khanate in whose internal politics Moscow often interfered. In 1534, when *The Golden Lynx* opens, Shah-Ali has been imprisoned, and Bulat is governing Kasimov.

 Sumbeka Khatun: Bulat's chief and favorite wife; niece of the Crimean khan; mother of three children who survived to adulthood, as well as several more who did not.

 Ogodai Sultan: At eighteen Bulat's heir; sworn brother of Daniil Kolychev.

 Nasan Khanim: Heroine of *The Golden Lynx*, forced at sixteen to confront the vast disparity between her dreams and her society's expectations of women; baptized Irina Bulatovna immediately before her arranged marriage to Daniil Kolychev. Her maidservant, *Tanya*, also makes a brief appearance in the novel.

Girei Sultan: Nasan's younger brother and closest companion, a few months away from manhood (fifteen) when Semyon Kolychev crosses his path.

Kolychevs
Senior Branch

Nikolai Borisovich: Head of the clan, boyar (the highest rank below royalty in the Russian political hierarchy).

Natalya Vasilyevna: Nikolai's wife. They have two sons who survived to adulthood, as well as other children who did not.

Boris Nikolaevich: Nikolai's older son, aged twenty-four; Maria's husband.

Daniil Nikolaevich: Nikolai's younger son, aged nineteen; his first wife, *Anastasia,* died in childbirth within a year of their marriage; Ogodai's sworn brother, although the vendetta undermines their friendship.

Maria Fyodorovna: Boris's wife, aged seventeen; eldest daughter of Fyodor Koshkin, Nikolai's political opponent.

The Kolychevs run a large household consisting of enslaved domestic servants and support themselves with a collection of rural villages scattered across Russia. Only two of their servants play an important role in the story.

Grusha: An eighteen-year-old slave; Daniil's love interest of the moment until he meets Nasan.

Father Job: The household chaplain; married, like all Orthodox priests (except monastic priests), and the father of a large family.

The Kolychevs' next-door neighbors, who are not related to them, are *Pyotr Sheremetev* and his younger daughter, *Darya.* Pyotr hopes to arrange a marriage between Daniil and Darya before a series of revenge killings forces a change of plans.

Junior Branch

Pavel Borisovich: Nikolai's younger brother; died of dysentery contracted during army service five years before the story begins, leaving two sons.

Semyon Pavlovich: Pavel's older son, the same age as Boris and his cousin's look-alike; unhappily married to *Solomonida*, Pyotr Sheremetev's older daughter. She and Semyon have a baby girl, Anna, born in 1531.

Dmitry Pavlovich: Pavel's younger son, killed by Bulat's nephews at the age of twenty-one, before the story begins. Dmitry leaves no children, and his widow has retired to a convent.

The junior branch of the Kolychevs runs its own household, a few blocks away from Nikolai's compound, and has its own landholdings.

Other

Fyodor Mikhailovich Koshkin: A nobleman linked by marriage to the senior branch of the Kolychevs; Maria's father; a hidden supporter of Prince Yuri Ivanovich (see below).

Stenka: A guardsman in Koshkin's service, attracted to Grusha.

Timoshka: Another of Semyon's men.

HISTORICAL CHARACTERS

Grand Prince Vasily III: The death of Vasily (1479–1533; r. 1505–1533) a few months before the story opens has thrown Russia into turmoil, because he leaves two sons below the age of four, a young widow desperate to protect them, and two adult brothers with their own principalities and courts who can challenge the children's right to rule.

Grand Princess Elena Glinskaya: Member (1508/1510–1538) of a Lithuanian princely family that transferred its allegiance to Moscow in 1508; married Vasily in 1526 after he divorced his first wife for barrenness; mother of his two sons. Despite her husband's plans to the contrary, Elena has steadily increased her authority at court since his death and by the summer of 1534 can bypass the appointed council of guardians and rule on behalf of her son Ivan. Gossip links her to *Prince Ivan Fyodorovich Ovchina Telepnev*

Obolensky, a court favorite whose sister, *Agrafena Cheliadnina*, serves as the young princes' nanny.

Grand Prince Ivan Vasilyevich: The future Ivan IV the Terrible (1530–1584; r. 1533–1584; crowned tsar 1547), at three much too young to stabilize the political hierarchy through marriage.

Prince Yuri Vasilyevich: Ivan's infant brother (1532–1563), next in line for the throne.

Prince Yuri Ivanovich of Dmitrov: The elder (1480–1536) of Grand Prince Vasily's surviving brothers, second in line for the throne, never allowed to marry. Under arrest when the story begins. The younger brother, *Prince Andrei Ivanovich of Staritsa* (1490–1537), remains free in his own principality.

Shah-Ali Khan (1505–1567): Ruler of Kasimov, under arrest in 1534; aged twenty-eight or twenty-nine at the time of Nasan's wedding but already famously fat. His younger brother, *Jan-Ali Khan*, is the ruler of Kazan.

Sahib-Girei Khan: Ruler of Crimea, 1532–1551; an enemy of Bulat's lineage. Sahib-Girei has many nephews, two of whom receive repeated mention in this series: *Safa-Girei Khan*, former and future ruler of Kazan; and *Islam-Girei Sultan*, who often challenges Sahib for his throne. In the spring of 1534, the two nephews command a joint raid on the Ryazan region, threatening Kasimov. The Girei dynasty ruled Crimea for centuries; the name is often spelled Giray.

Elements

NORTH, SOUTH, EAST, WEST, CENTER—FIVE DIRECTIONS, FIVE colors, five elements brought into harmony by the World Tree. Rooted in the nether realms of the dead, the great trunk of the World Tree passes through the middle lands of earth and water and links them with the heavens.

In the west the earth goddess Umai reigns, with the trees sacred to her and the animals that inhabit those trees—which, like all animals, have multiple souls that let them communicate, even with humans.

Usually they do not bother. Perhaps we are not as interesting as we like to believe. But once—long ago, when the steppes rang with the cries of riderless horses and the tiger prowled never considering the hunter's snare—the Great Blue Wolf Ashina, at the very base of the World Tree, rescued and suckled a boy. Where he came from, no one knows. Why, she did not say. But when he grew into First Man, she bore him a litter that gave rise to the peoples— Turks, Tatars, Mongols. She taught her cubs to hunt and fish, to build felt tents against the cold, to control vast herds of grazing animals, to respect the natural world and their own pack but fight others of their kind without restraint. To honor the grandmothers—ancestral spirits like herself—who watch over the dead and the unborn and direct the living. To worship Tengri, Lord of the Eternal Blue Sky, and Umai his consort. To recognize the sacred animals that Tengri sent to guide them—wolf, bear, tiger, turtle, swan, lynx.

Ashina's children cherished their wolfish heritage. They applied the lessons of the hunt—preying on their neighbors, vanquishing the settled peoples beyond the grasslands. Genghis subdued much of Eurasia. Batu burned his way from *the Volga to the Danube and ground Russia under the heel of his felt boot. Timur piled pyramids of skulls outside Damascus and slew war elephants before the gates of Delhi. Babur took Afghanistan; Akbar, Hindustan. Mahmet breached the massive walls of Constantinople. Grandsons of Genghis ruled the plum-blossom pagodas of Dadu and Shangdu—Beijing, Xanadu.*

But Tengri also governs time. In time, Ashina's children forgot that they belonged to a single pack. The Golden Kin of Genghis Khan parted ways, each adopting the religion and customs of the sheep who served them. Brother fought brother; the Pax Mongolica shattered under the blows of a hundred warring princes. Empires fell away. Khanates split, then splintered. Formerly subject lands flexed their muscles. Resurgent Russia offered a refuge to dethroned Tatar sultans. Kasim of Kazan, among the first to change sides, received for his sustenance the town that later bore his name—Kasimov. Many others followed.

Forgotten, discarded, Tengri and Umai did not desert Ashina's offspring. The ancient legends survive. The World Tree still links heaven and earth with the hunting grounds below. The grandmothers wait and watch. And when the occasion demands it, to those willing to listen, Tengri sends a messenger...

Chapter 1

Kasimov, Sha'ban 940 A.H. / February 1534

THE LYNX FOUND NASAN JUST BEFORE THE AMBUSH. SHE glimpsed its tufted ears through the tangled branches of the birch tree, then lost sight of it when her brother launched his attack. Alerted by his joyous shriek, she jumped sideways and stuck out a foot, sending him somersaulting over the blizzard-kissed ground. She pelted him with snowballs, taunting him. "You forgot again, silly. How can you take me by surprise if you yell like that?"

He lurched to his feet, grumbling, and she laughed. Girei tried, but too often he forgot to save his war cries for battle.

He soon recovered. Most of the snowballs bounced off Nasan's quilted overcoat or hit the birch trees that bounded the clearing they had chosen as their private playground. But a few better-aimed missiles sent icy shivers across her cheeks, reddened by the cold. One smacked her on the forehead, knocking her hat to one side.

She pushed the sheepskin cap into place and aimed another snowball at Girei, who yelped when it broke over his neck. While he scooped ice from inside his coat, she leaped in celebration, bending her legs almost double behind her and shouting, "Hurrah!"

Her moment of exultation cost her. Girei darted toward her, grabbed her round the waist, and tossed her into a drift. The impact jarred loose an entire branch's load, covering her in snow. "Yow," she said. "I'm going to get you for that."

Girei grinned. "You didn't hear me coming, though."

She shook her head, giggling. "No, I didn't. Truce?"

He nodded. Nasan kept a wary eye on him as she wriggled free of her drift. A few months ago, he couldn't have picked her up with such ease. But these days he seemed to grow taller with each passing hour; for him manhood lay just around the corner. Sha'ban led into Ramadan, and the ending of the fast marked his fifteenth birthday. Within weeks, he would ride off to join the army with their father and older brother. He couldn't wait to go.

A pair of fingers snapped before her face. "Are you dreaming?" Girei asked. "Wake up."

She rubbed her gloved fist against his forehead, where the unruly hair refused to accept the confinement of his hat. "A nightmare, more like. You off to the army, and I to supervise the kitchens. Is that justice?"

"Oh, sister," he said, "if only you could join me."

"I wish," she told him, not for the first time. "But I can hear *Ana*'s voice now. 'You must marry, Nasan. Bear children for the clan.' She's told me nothing else since the day I turned fourteen. Two years!"

"A hard life you have, sister." Girei scrunched his nose, as if he could imagine no worse fate for himself. "I'll take Father's shouting any day."

"And no doubt I'll be in trouble again when I go home." She stared gloomily at a tree. "Where are those warrior heroines from my book? They must have vanished with our ancestors." Except in her sleep, when the grandmother spirits whispered their promise: life offered so much more than marriage and children.

As if inspired by the thought, she grabbed snow and bombarded her brother. Girei would leave soon, no matter what. Already a faint mustache showed on his upper lip. Each day his resemblance to their father grew—both short and sturdy, with dark hair and black eyes. Genghis Khan might lie buried in the eastern steppe, his grave marked only by the spirit banners where his soul perched between flights, but his illustrious lineage survived in the rulers of Khankirmän, which the Russians called Kasimov.

"Enough of this." Girei ran for his pony, vaulting into the saddle. "Bet you can't catch me."

Traitor! Set on revenge, Nasan leaped for her horse's back. Girei had a good head start, but she rode better than he did. Her sure-footed steppe pony dashed along the flattened snow that formed the road—the frozen Oka River on one side, unbroken forest on the other. The horses galloped nose to tail by the time a dozen men burst from among the trees and grabbed the Tatars' reins.

Russians.

No doubt about that. Many Tatars had European features, but none looked like the leader of this group. A platinum-haired giant, he towered over his men.

Too late, Nasan remembered her mother's warning that more lurked in the woods than screech owls and lynxes.

A man with brown hair and rotting teeth dragged her off her pony as if she weighed no more than the last snowball she'd tossed at Girei. His grip around her waist forced her to gasp for breath.

But Nasan had spent much of her childhood wrestling her way into boys' games. Small as she was, she had learned a few tricks. She drummed her heels against her captor's shins until, swearing, he released her and grabbed his leg.

As she pulled away, hard fingers clamped down on her shoulder. Another soldier materialized in front of her. Although shorter than his comrade, he made up for it in girth, and the slap he dealt her hurt. The man she'd kicked clenched his fists. She cowered, hoping to prevent a beating.

Her plan worked. The man grabbed her above the elbow. With both arms secured, Nasan faked acquiescence. Nothing to do but pray that the grandmothers would show her an exit. Pray and watch: the more she learned about their captors, the better her chances of saving herself and her brother.

Meanwhile, Girei fought the two men who held him, excoriating them as the offspring of rabid dogs and whores. The soldiers stood, stolid as the trees around them, immune to insults delivered in a foreign tongue. After a while, the leader walked over, tipped back Girei's head, and looked at him. "Bulat's son, I vow. Boy looks just like him."

He said the words in Russian. Nasan puzzled them out, one by one, wishing she had paid more attention to the language. She had learned Arabic, Persian, and Chagatai Turkic, but her Russian came from eavesdropping on her brothers' lessons. Custom required her to marry a Muslim; she didn't need Russian. Everyone said so.

Everyone was wrong. Tomorrow she would insist on learning Russian.

The leader examined Nasan as he had her brother. Determined not to show fear, she stared into his frosty eyes and tugged at the unyielding arms that held her. Branches encased in ice refracted the sun's glare in sparkling patterns and cast shadows that shifted with each passing breeze. Bleached by the effect of sunshine on snow, the Russian resembled an ice man. His brows met in the center, like the tufts of a screech owl. A scar, pale with age, bracketed tight, cruel lips.

"Not sure about this one," he said. "Let's not take chances." He tipped his head, considering. Sunshine danced across his face, highlighting an eyebrow, his hooked nose, the whorls of his ear. The hollows of his cheeks remained in shadow, dark as the empty sockets of a skull.

Why had he captured them? He wore the armor of a nobleman, not the rags of a thief. And he couldn't hope to profit from robbery or murder. Even in these troubled times, the khans of Kasimov protected their own.

The man waved his free hand. "We came to avenge my kinsman. No more, no less."

She gasped. *Kinsman?*

Three months ago, a Russian had killed one of Nasan's cousins in a drunken brawl. The victim's brothers slew the killer and left his companions unscathed—as honor required. Even Russians understood the code of the steppe: a life for a life, and there the matter ended.

Not this Russian, though. The blood drained from her face, leaving her light-headed. This Russian meant death.

They had to get away. On their own, because no one would search for them at this early hour. *Ana* had ordered them not to leave the palace. *Ana* did not expect defiance.

But how could Nasan have guessed Russians were hiding in the woods *today*? She had rubbed the spirit dolls' lips with grease and asked for their blessing, as she did every morning. No hint of regret or warning had crossed her mind.

She must not have listened carefully. Remorse burned her throat.

Ice Man studied her, more monster than man. Nasan shuddered. He liked that, she saw—that he inspired fear. He held her chin a moment longer, then turned back to Girei.

Plans darted through her brain, never settling. Had she not yearned to prove herself in battle? Every heroine, sooner or later, must stand alone against the foe.

The ancestors were testing her. Here, when she least expected it. Spirits often prodded and teased, forcing growth as farmers force a plant. But they helped, too, if asked.

Grandmothers, show me the way!

Her mind cleared, as if an outside force had swept uncertainty from her head. She saw what she must do, laid out before her in miniatures like the ones that adorned her book of epic tales. Princess Chichek drawing her bow, her arrow whistling toward the target. Princess Saljan, wielding her saber against six hundred soldiers.

The two men gripped her arms. Obedient to the images in her head, she went limp. Her collapse caught her captors off-guard.

Using a move she'd learned from her older brother, Nasan kicked the man on her right in the groin and dragged her arm away from him as he doubled over.

The man on her left stumbled. She fell backward, dragging him with her and using his greater weight against him, then twisted away and ran into the forest, shouting, "To me, Girei, to me!" To help him free himself, she dragged a pair of rocks from beneath the snow and hurled one at each of his captors. They staggered.

"The horses!" Girei raced toward her.

Nasan spun on the balls of her feet. Frightened animals surrounded her, bucking and weaving, upset by her shouting. Their hooves trampled the snow. She yelled louder and waved her arms, smacking a few on the rump to increase their frenzy. They spread into an incomplete circle, knocking into one another and their owners.

She hesitated. Horses she understood. Even these horses: the Russians bought theirs from the Tatars. But these beasts had not learned her voice or her smell. Did she have the skills to capture and mount one, let alone keep her seat if she did?

Girei shouted her name in warning. Feet crashing through shrubbery pushed her into a decision. Better to risk a throw from a panicked horse than whatever the Russians planned for her. Amid floundering men and distracted beasts, Nasan vaulted onto the nearest saddle. The animal reared. She clung to its mane with both hands and whispered into its ear.

Mashallah, the horse had spent its babyhood among her people. The familiar sounds of Tatar calmed it. It stopped bucking. She patted its neck in encouragement.

A quick glance over her shoulder revealed Girei heading her way—still on foot, but close enough that she watched him reach for a dangling rein. He raised an arm, and with a wave of acknowledgment she sent the gelding hurtling toward the river road, sure Girei was right behind her. In the pandemonium they'd left behind, she doubted anyone would see which direction they took.

At the edge of the trees, she pulled up. No sounds of pursuit disturbed the wintry scene. Exultant, she punched the air. Success, despite the odds! She had overcome the fears of a frightened animal, then ridden it to safety. A few more yards, and she and Girei would find their ponies. They would free the horses they rode and head for home.

Her horse skittered, its hooves slipping on the packed snow, its ears pricked. Swiftly she leaned over its neck, murmuring soothing words and offering a carrot from her pocket. Silence surrounded her.

Then the truth hit home, and she pulled herself upright in the saddle. Her eyes fixed on the woods, and she held her breath, listening for the smallest noise.

No one had followed her—including Girei.

What happened? He was inches from escaping!

The forest remained silent: no horses, no people. She waited, reluctant to breathe in case the Russians heard her, but Girei did not appear. Closer to the palace stood their ponies, digging grass from beneath the packed snow and chewing it. She nudged the captured Russian gelding with her knees, walking it toward the ponies. Her otherworldly calm vanished, leaving her cramped and lost, horrified that her clever plan had saved herself but not her brother.

What to do? Help waited at home, but by the time she rode there, found someone, and persuaded that person to stop scolding her long enough to hear about Girei's predicament, assistance would arrive too late. She had to stay and free him.

But it would be dangerous to go back into the woods without sending word. Even more reckless than sneaking out in the first place.

The steppe ponies grazed a few feet away. Nasan slid off the Russian horse, tying it to a tree a safe distance from the road. Girei would need it later. She tiptoed through the snow, then darted at her brother's gelding, slapped its flank with one hand, and grabbed her mare's mane with the other.

Girei's horse ran for its stable without looking back. Nasan exhaled and gentled her mare. When the pony arrived riderless, someone would investigate. Meanwhile, Girei depended on her.

She considered the two horses that remained. If she left them in plain sight, the Russians might find them—and her. But if she hid them, her family would not know where to look. And if she chased them off, she and Girei would have no way to reach home before their enemy recaptured them.

She decided to compromise. "Stay, Sorkhokhtani," she whispered in the mare's ear. Then she checked to see that the trees hid the gelding and slipped back into the woods.

Escaping, waiting, sending for help, returning—essential tasks that gobbled time. The sun hovered higher in the sky. Nasan willed the opportunity not lost, again begged the grandmothers for aid.

Her heart smashed against her chest. Every creature in the forest must hear it. But her felt boots glided noiselessly as cat paws across the snow. Fear reined her in, whipped her forward, restrained her once more. She concentrated on her boots: toe, heel, toe, heel, sliding in endless progression across the icy waste. Once her feet found their rhythm, she scoured the woods for Girei, desperate to discover what had kept him from following her. He must be injured, or worse.

No. Across the clearing she glimpsed him tied to a birch tree, thrashing against his bonds. Soldiers surrounded him. The more he fought, the harder they laughed, as if his anger amused them. Nasan's ready temper went from simmer to full boil.

If only she'd brought her bow. *If you must break the rules, go armed.* Her older brother had said that more than once. Her parents, too.

Regrets could wait. She must improvise, and quickly.

But first, reconnoiter. So the men always told her. Stop, Nasan. Think. Take the lay of the land before you rush in.

Her breath sounded loud in the stillness. As she ducked behind a hillock to consider her options, she focused on slowing it. In, hold, out, hold, in, hold, out—another ritual, like the one that pushed her boots across the snow.

She must have spent less time away than she'd thought. The soldiers not guarding Girei were still restoring order. From her perilous refuge, she watched them soothe horses. The two men she had tricked stood in the center of the clearing, staring at the ground while their leader rebuked them. She focused her whole attention on their conversation, picking words like gemstones out of their settings, struggling to find their meaning in the unfamiliar tongue.

"Hunt boy down," the shorter man said—or so much Nasan understood. "Not go far."

Her clothes, borrowed from her brother's attendant, had deceived them. One point in her favor.

The leader shook his head. "Leave him."

"Lord, please. Let me—" The soldier stopped in mid-sentence, cuffed into silence.

"I said no. He took my horse. We finish and go. While we can." The leader pushed the shorter man aside. "Out of my way." The men scurried across the clearing toward Nasan.

To avoid their notice, she sank into the snow. Ice Man shouted, and the men pivoted. Good, they hadn't seen her. She straightened, peering over the hillock for a better view. She had to do something. One brief distraction, and Girei could escape.

Although the two soldiers faced away from her, they stood close enough that she could hear them muttering. "I hate these woods," the taller man told his fellow. "Something's out there, in the trees. A tiger, a bear."

Nasan studied the trees. No bears, and certainly no tigers, although a lynx paw dangled at the far edge of her vision.

Odd. The forest animals kept away from people. Yet she had seen two lynxes today. Or had the first one followed her here?

A spirit messenger, perhaps—the assistance she'd prayed for.

The lynx observed. The two men moved away. Shallow breaths of icy air restored Nasan's sense of suspension in an eternal forest occupied by enemies as schematic as chess pieces on a board. The world turned black and white: snow and branches, ashen sky and leather uniforms, the gray-furred hats of the men, the leader's white-blond hair. Only her brother—ropes biting into his chest, hands pinioned behind him—seemed real, alive, in color.

Potential moves drifted past, presented themselves, withdrew. She had her eating knife, secured by habit to her belt. If she tossed it at the leader…

She would reveal her position. And, hit or miss, she had to incapacitate the other men, too, to free Girei.

A stick or a rock, then? No, same problem.

She surveyed the clearing once more. The tree behind Girei drooped snow-laden branches over his guards. Like the ones that had inundated her when her brother dumped her into the drift.

She searched for rocks small enough to throw but heavy enough to knock the snow off the branches and into the Russians' eyes. Blind the men, dart in with her knife, cut Girei's bonds. Steal a weapon, if possible. Rescue her brother. Even if she died in the attempt, she would live in her parents' hearts. The ancestors would welcome her, the clan honor her sacrifice during their rituals for the dead.

Better to live, though. *Grandmothers, preserve us!*

The area behind the hillock yielded no stones. Nasan had stretched her arm to its fullest extent when the leader snarled at the men who had mumbled about bears, "Get over here and watch." She stopped, transfixed.

He stalked toward Girei and ripped open the boy's jacket. The delicate chasing on the man's scabbard glinted in the sunlight, a terrible beauty reflected in the dull steel of his chain mail. Girei stood on tiptoe, straining against the ropes.

From the sheath at his belt Ice Man pulled a dagger. It glittered—wicked, unrelenting, shooting sun sparks as the light shifted against the blade. Girei shouted his defiance, *"Allahu ak—,"* cut off when the blade slashed across his neck and the cry ended in a gurgle. He slumped in his bonds. His head lolled. Blood sprayed from his throat.

Nasan almost gave herself away then. If she'd had her bow, she would have slammed an arrow into Ice Man's back, whatever the threat of retribution. But she had no weapon worth the name. Shocked beyond thought, she stared at the clearing.

Ice Man's frigid voice focused her attention. "Take that, Bulat." The blond leader kicked snow over Girei's dangling legs while Nasan watched, stunned by the man's disrespect.

Why had the grandmothers not intervened? This Russian had *shed the blood* of a Tatar sultan. Girei's life fluid spilled against the ground. The ultimate taboo, violated.

In response to a gesture from the leader, two of the men untied the ropes that bound Girei. As the boy's body slumped to the ground, the leader did not even glance at his victim. "Leave him," Ice Man said again. "Let's go."

No bolt of lightning sizzled the sky. No pillar of fire descended from above. No lynx raked claws across the villain's shoulders. While the ancestors did nothing to avenge their slain kinsman, Nasan keened silently, her quilted sleeve stuffed in her mouth. Time swirled around her.

Chapter 2

"Now," the Russian leader said. Nasan peered over the hillock. Girei lay face down in the snow amid a crimson circle. A metallic tang filled the air. One of the Russian soldiers coiled a bloody rope and attached it to his saddlebow. His horse shuffled its hooves.

Her head spun, and she gripped the rock to steady herself. *Grandmothers, how could you? He was only fourteen!*

"But the other boy…" That was the man she'd kicked in the groin, still hoping for a chance to pay her back.

"I told you," the leader said. "Forget him. And go, if you want to live." He herded his men from the clearing with blows and shouts.

Nasan, mittened hand pressed to her lips, waited for the ambushers to leave. When only she and Girei remained in the clearing, she scrambled over the hillock and ran to him.

Her brother didn't move. Foolish to imagine he might have survived such an assault. His body dragged on her arms as she struggled to turn him over. When she succeeded, she found a face stilled by death, violated by the deep slash across his neck.

Her vision blurred, and icy particles gathered along her cheeks. She brushed them aside. She couldn't afford to cry. The Russians might return, and she had to get Girei to safety.

Her thoughts came in scattered bursts. Safety. Too late for safety. She had disobeyed her mother, and her brother had died as a result. It wasn't fair!

The tears that fell then hardened her resolve. She didn't want to leave Girei even for a moment, but she had to get him home.

For that, she needed a horse. She pondered how to lift Girei onto her pony as she trudged toward the river.

Her mare waited, cropping bark from a tree. A tall, familiar Tatar patted its mane in a distracted way. He, too, had black hair and eyes. While ten mounted men awaited his orders, he rubbed his gloved finger against his skimpy mustache and addressed her horse. "Where are those imps, Sorkhokhtani? They can't have gone far without you." He sounded annoyed.

Girei's pony had found its stable. The Tatar commander was Nasan's older brother. Relief that she no longer had to bear her burden alone filled her voice. "Ogodai!"

His head snapped round. "There you are. What have you done with Girei?"

Nasan forgot that only she knew what had happened in the woods. In Ogodai's irritation, she heard her own unspoken fear that she had caused Girei's death. Sobbing, she ran to her horse and buried her face in Sorkhokhtani's mane.

"Hell," Ogodai said. She heard him ordering his men. "Something's wrong. Scout around. When you find the sultan, bring him here on the double." Hooves stamped against the snow, harness jingled, silence.

Ogodai pulled her into his arms. "Nasan, where is Girei? Is he hurt?"

The chill seeped into her bones and made them ache. Her whole body trembled, and her throat closed. He shook her— gently. "Nasan, tell me. Where is he?"

Behind her, Sorkhokhtani pawed at the snow. "Nasan?" Ogodai prodded.

"Killed." She could manage only that single word.

He caught her chin, tipping her head back. "*What* did you say?"

Nasan took a deep breath. A warrior does not break down. She must master herself. "Girei is dead," she stammered. "Murdered. A Russian—"

The racket of returning horses and Ogodai's blistering oath cut her off. She only half-heard the headman's report of finding Girei's body. Horror threatened to overwhelm her.

"My sister and I will care for the sultan," Ogodai said when the trooper finished. "Follow the Russians. Bring them to the fortress. My father will want to question them." Nasan turned her head in time to see the mounted Tatars ride away.

Ogodai touched her cheek, his eyes soft. "You're frozen, *sengel*. Show me Girei."

Sengel. Younger sister. The familiar usage held out a shred of comfort. Ogodai would defend her and protect her, as he always had.

Another trek into the woods leading her brother and his horse, her own mare's reins twined around her fingers, ended at the clearing. Snow pitted with hoof prints showed where Ogodai's squad had stopped, then wheeled to return to the path and report. Girei lay, undisturbed, where she had left him. The child part of Nasan that yearned for a miracle—as if somehow, in her brief absence, her brother would have sprung back to life—slid away, abashed.

Ogodai stepped around her and knelt next to Girei, murmuring words she couldn't hear. Perhaps he was praying. She whispered a prayer for Girei's soul, cradled in the grandmothers' loving arms. Why had they let his murderer go free?

The words made his death real. She choked at the thought of Girei anywhere but here.

"Give me your belt," Ogodai said, his voice rough at the edges. "We can put him on my horse. He's war-toughened, whereas yours will spook at the scent of blood."

Indeed, Sorkhokhtani sidled and shivered, her eyes wide with terror. Nasan unwound the belt from her waist and threw it to Ogodai. He caught it, wrapped it around Girei's neck, and closed the jacket over it. With the wound hidden, Girei could have been sleeping, except for that dreadful stillness.

"There are ropes in my saddle bags," Ogodai said.

Nasan searched the bags and pulled out the ropes. Ogodai, powerful at eighteen, lifted Girei without difficulty and arranged his brother's body face down over the horse, tying him in place across the wooden saddle. In silence, they walked the animals back to the river road.

As they passed the Russian horse that Nasan had tethered earlier, it whinnied—from cold and hunger, no doubt. Ogodai left his gelding in her care, tracked down the horse, and returned with it in tow. He retrieved the reins of his own mount from her. "By itself in the woods," he said. "Why?"

"I captured it," Nasan said. "Trying to escape. I thought Girei had followed me."

Ogodai studied her. "That must be quite a story."

"Yes." Shivering, she could hardly form the word.

Perhaps he realized how shocked she felt—at times Ogodai showed true sensitivity—for instead of asking for more details, he led the way back to the road.

"Mount, Nasan," he said when they left the woods. "Before you fall down."

"What about you?"

Ogodai patted the Russian horse. "I'll take this one." He looped the reins of his own gelding, carrying Girei, around his wrist and seated himself on his new mount. "Up. Walk the horses, and we won't dislodge him. When we get near home, you ride for help."

The frozen river shimmered before Nasan's eyes. She blinked. When she could see again, she found herself on the sorrel mare's back. As they headed for the fortress, outlined at the top of the steep hill that rose from the river banks, she tried not to think about the clopping hooves behind and the burden they carried.

Nasan focused on the space between her horse's ears, which flickered each time Ogodai's gelding moved too close. Wind spirits flung snow against her cheeks, mocking her for her failure. Ice spirits tormented her pony, sending the mare's hooves skittering across the path. Or was it the smell of blood that unsettled Sorkhokhtani?

They were almost home. The jutting tops of the fortress watchtowers loomed over her head, menacing gnomes bristling with helmeted soldiers at every casement. Girei's killer could not have stood against them.

Instead he laid his ambush in the woods, the wind spirits sang, waiting for a pair of witless youngsters to fall into his trap. Nasan shuddered.

The soldiers in the watchtowers had seen them. A small troop, equipped with spears and snowshoes, clanked through the gate and slid along the path.

Not long now. The impromptu cortege passed the snakelike hump of the earthen rampart that circled three sides of the town. Ahead, ravines cut long gashes in the earth, revealing the gilt-tipped minaret and the triumphal gates with their Koranic inscriptions, brilliant in turquoise mosaic and gold. Beyond them lay the palace, where Nasan must break the news to her parents. The mockery of the wind spirits seemed less cruel than confession.

The troops from the fortress reached them. Nasan watched the men lift her brother from the saddle and wrap him in a felt rug they had brought. Then Ogodai caught her reins and led her horse as well as his own pony up the steep path that edged the ravine.

She wanted to thank him, but she couldn't remember the words.

Inside the palace, hidden pipes conducted heat from corner stoves, diffusing it beneath the clay benches that lined the walls of each room. The shift from winter to artificial summer made Nasan sleepy. The embroidered silk poppets that housed the grandmothers guarded the entrance.

You took Girei. I can't forgive you for that.

The room hummed with everyday activities. Against beige stucco walls, green and ocher outlined mullioned windows and an ogee-shaped alcove. Elaborate mosaics in matching colors filled one side with geometric patterns. Bright cushions covered sofas that transformed as needed into beds or tables. Bulat and Sumbeka—her parents—sat together, talking in hushed tones. Junior wives, concubines, musicians, and warriors clustered in small groups chatting, tuning their instruments, waiting for orders.

Ogodai stepped in front of her. At first she hung back, tempted to let him take the lead. He had no guilt to hide.

Coward. She pushed past him, dragged the hat from her head, tossed her jacket to the floor. Snow flew from the discarded clothes. "*Ana, Ata,*" she said. "Russians have killed Girei!"

Every head in the room turned in her direction. For one stunned moment, no one spoke. Then *Ana* staggered to her feet and raked her cheeks with long nails painted black. "My baby! Nasan, how could you let this happen?" Nasan wanted to die, right there on the spot.

As if on cue, the soldiers entered and reverently lowered the rug holding Girei's body before his father's feet. Bulat roared, "Who did this?"

From the courtyard outside, cries filled the room. "The khan's son is dead. Our sweet young lord is dead."

Nasan reached for her mother's hands, but *Ana* pulled away, ripped her outer robe from chin to waist, and flung herself on Girei's body. She dragged aside the belt that concealed his death wound. At the sight of bone, Nasan's strength left her. She dropped to her knees, sobbing, "The grandmothers took him. How could Allah permit it?"

Ana fainted. Nasan, too overcome to help, huddled next to her until, unbidden, a servant brought water and patted her mother's brow. Nasan held out her hand for the cloth. If she concentrated solely on her mother, she would not have to see that terrible injury, face her own responsibility for Girei's death.

A child's way of coping. She despised herself for using it, wished she could stop. But she couldn't, not yet.

At the corner of her vision, her father's boots moved into view. She glanced up to find him studying Girei's face. His lips tightened. The muscles in his neck constricted as he swallowed.

"Allah?" he shouted in belated response to her question. "Allah is the Merciful, the Compassionate. Russians took my son. And they will pay. *No one* attacks my family and lives."

He pounded a nearby table with his fist. Small, precious things flew in every direction. A trooper caught one in mid-flight. A concubine snatched another off the table just before it toppled. A porcelain jar shattered against the floor.

"I will tell the imam," Ogodai said in a voice that sounded strangled.

"Yes, do." Bulat knelt beside his dead son, patting the belt into place and brushing Girei's hair away from his forehead.

Ogodai left. Surrounded yet alone, Nasan curled in on herself. Despite the warmth of the room, the stinging taunts of the wind spirits, the ice spirits, swirled around her head, and she wept. Why had she survived, when Girei hunted with the grandmothers?

The service led by the imam ended. Girei had died not long after noon, allowing his family to bury him the same day. As Nasan waited in the town square for the procession to form around her brother's bier, she gazed at the pumpkin sun that hovered over the minaret in its rapid descent toward the horizon. Like the rest of her family, she wore black: high-collared silk tunic and trousers, sable coat with the felt lining facing out, sleeves long and wide enough for her to tuck her hands inside. A pointed headdress of onyx and silver hid her long hair. In summer she would have piled dust on her head to show her sorrow, but in this season snow hid the earth from view. Although servants had swept the log pathways clear, ice filled the chinks. Even in her leather boots she had to step carefully.

Facing the squat mausoleum where her brother would soon lie, she reveled in the sting of sleet against her eyelids. It seemed a fitting tribute to loss.

The mourners' procession extended to the fortress walls, then wound along the palisades to disappear among a tangle of houses and tents—an ant-like stream of Tatars in black robes. Wails rose and fell, interspersed with shouts of "God is great!" and "We will avenge our martyred sultan!" Remembering Girei's cut-off shout, Nasan pushed her hands further into her sleeves, barricading herself against emotions too horrific to bear.

Her brother lay under a pall inscribed with relevant verses from the Koran, embroidery glittering against glossy velvet. Nasan recalled her last sight of him, rigid in white silk, moments before the cloth descended. Still, quiet, neat and clean, his hair untousled—he did not much resemble this morning's companion. She blinked away tears.

Her mother, passing by, pulled her into the procession. They inched toward the mausoleum, keening to honor the dead. Ahead of them, the bier bobbed and weaved as Ogodai and seven selected male relatives fended off frantic women reaching for Girei's body. The cries of faith and vengeance mingled with the songs of professional mourners praising the slain sultan.

Although Nasan shrieked and pleaded as ardently as the rest, she felt numb inside. Her earlier tears evaporated, leaving her wandering amid frigid clouds.

At the cemetery, the procession dispersed among the headstones to let the pall bearers and family pass. The guardians of the dead stepped aside. Nasan and her mother followed her father and brother into the crypt beneath the mausoleum. Lanterns flickered in the gloom, revealing mysterious piles of rocks marking the earthly remains of ancestors. Their souls lived in another realm— riding the steppes of the netherworld, aiming their winged steeds to hunt among the constellations, cooking their captured stars over campfires tended by the grandmothers, nourishing their enduring essence and the silken threads that linked them to their descendants, living and yet unborn. Impossible to imagine that Girei romped among them, tickling the spirit ponies with strands of feather grass.

The bearers lifted the pall, revealing the silent mummy beneath. Bulat bent over his dead son's right ear, whispering the ritual phrases of burial. The mourners' sobbing trapped Nasan in a whirlwind of sound. A hollow crash signaled the breaking of the kettle drum that Girei would never carry into battle. The frigid clouds dissolved, drenching her in tears.

She put an arm around her mother's waist. The two women clung to each other as Bulat said the final prayers. At last, the interment ended.

Ana murmured in her ear, "Each person has his allotted span of time, and when it runs out, he dies. Even if he is fourteen and dearly loved. It is the Will of God."

The Will of God asks too much of us sometimes.

Nasan did not say that. It would be rude. And foolish: a young woman not only should not but could not question the designs of God. Yet the awkward truth nagged at her: suppose Girei had died not because his allotted span had run out and Allah had called him home but because his sister had failed him?

So far, her parents had not asked why she and Girei had defied their mother's order to remain inside the fortress. The horror of the murder precluded such questions. But soon they would demand details, and then what would they say?

What should they say, when she knew herself at fault?

The guards resumed their stations. The procession retreated to the palace courtyard, where it transformed itself into a milling crowd. Standing at the ornate gates that bordered the palace, Nasan smelled the funeral feast in preparation. The odor of cooking meat turned her stomach.

She closed her eyes. It didn't help. Memories assaulted her: her brother's throat bleeding from the Russian's blade, his body face down in the clearing, the terrible realization that she had delayed too long. His final scream echoed in her mind.

She did not protest when her mother steered her away from the crowd. "Come, my child," Sumbeka said. "Time to rest."

Deep in the old-growth forest of the Meshchera, an hour's ride from Bulat's stronghold of Kasimov, Semyon Pavlovich Kolychev held his breath as Tatar soldiers argued. One hand covered his dapple-gray gelding's nose; the other grasped its reins. If a horse so much as whickered or a man gasped for air, the Tatars would fall on his troop and kill without mercy, but the luck that had stayed with Semyon throughout his journey from Moscow held. The Tatars departed. Semyon breathed again.

Hearing the enemy retreat toward the river, he saluted the snow-laden trees. *We fooled them!*

Too bad about the stolen horse. The Tatars would know from its brand that it belonged to a Kolychev. He imagined them communing with the captured animal. Shaking beads over its head, searching its entrails for clues. Banging a drum behind its tail to check which way it ran. Charring its shoulder blades. Whispering in its ears. Magicians with horses, Tatars were sometimes just plain weird.

Even so, it seemed unlikely they could learn more than the clan name, which they might guess anyway. Meanwhile, Semyon would put as much space between his men and the Tatars as possible. His cousin Boris, left behind on the road, could fend for himself. With that goal in mind, Semyon guided the way past massive trees, over musty logs, and through snow-laden brush. As he'd expected, by the time his soldiers pushed aside the last clinging vine to reveal navigable highway, the Tatars had faded from view.

He jerked his head toward Moscow, northwest. "Home," he said, the first word he'd spoken since the ice cloud kicked up by galloping hooves forecast the Tatars' approach.

"Can't, Lord," Timoshka grumbled. "Look at that sky."

Semyon scowled at the darkening heavens. Alas, Timoshka was right. The hours spent dodging Tatars in the woods had soaked up the precious daylight, and the temperature fell with each breath the men took. The horses needed food and rest.

"Time to find shelter." Semyon beckoned to a young soldier, peppier than the others after the long ride, and ordered him to scout out a suitable hamlet.

Settling in for the wait, he swigged brandy from the flask he carried at his belt, relishing the warmth that traveled down his gullet to his belly. Envy shone in his warriors' eyes. "Look lively, men," he said. "You'll be enjoying black bread and cabbage soup before that sun sets."

A trooper's mouth twisted as Semyon retied the flask. Impudent slave!

He smacked the man's ear and relished the yowl his blow provoked. The soldier's reaction again brought Boris to mind. Boris—who, acting for once as if he had some sense, had chosen to accompany his cousin Semyon to Kasimov. Only to… But Boris's idiocy did not bear thinking of. Boris had earned whatever punishment God's chastising hand chose to deal him.

The scout soon returned and led the troops to the hut he had chosen. The shape of the cornice showed that Russians lived there. Semyon heard peasants singing, smelled manure from a cow, watched steam rising from the chimney.

Steam. Heat.

The sound of hooves brought the family tumbling into the yard. Bundled into sheepskin coats over loose shirts and gowns, their toes visible through broken boots, they looked like a set of dolls, arranged from large to small—patriarch in the front, his wife two steps behind, and a bevy of youngsters in their wake.

Semyon tossed the man a Muscovite ruble, pure silver, as much as a family like this earned in a year. That should buy him some loyalty. The setting sun sparked an answering gleam in the patriarch's eyes. He caught the ruble in mid-air and tucked it into his sheepskin sleeve.

"Food," Semyon said. A lordly wave indicated his troops. "Ale, if you have it. A place by the stove for me, a spot in the barn for my men. And fodder for the horses."

The patriarch nodded, bowing till his nose touched his knee. "How should we address you, Lord?"

Semyon blurted out the first name that came into his head. "Boris Nikolaevich."

Damnation! He gripped the reins, lest he make matters worse by slapping himself on the forehead. After brooding over his cousin's misbehavior on and off for hours, he'd implicated Boris without intending to. If the Tatars came out this far…

The patriarch stared, as if wondering what demon assailed his strange guest. What to do? A man can't correct his own name. He'd paid handsomely for silence; he didn't want awkward questions.

The solution came in a flash of brilliance. "Shein," he said in a rush. Boris Nikolaevich Shein had a crippled leg and six great-grandchildren. Even a madman like Bulat wouldn't go after Shein.

The patriarch, satisfied, gestured to two of the youngsters. A lad of about twelve grasped Semyon's reins. Semyon dismounted, grateful to put boot to earth after hours in the saddle. A brown-haired hussy led him into the house. Hot in pursuit, he forgot about Boris.

An hour or so later, he lay atop the family's stove, letting the heat suffuse his bones. Kasha, cabbage soup, and ale filled his belly.

Flames raised specters of light against the walls of the one-room cabin; moonlight cast filigree patterns against the earthen floor. Sounds of breathing ruffled the air—some light, some stertorous. The hussy had resisted, the only flaw in an otherwise pleasant evening, but Semyon nurtured hopes that she might yet climb up and join him.

A wolf howled in the woods. Its pack answered: one, then a dozen, ululating as Tatars did in battle. As the household settled into sleep around him, Semyon clutched the hilt of his dagger. The boy who died today evened the score. Payment for the murder of Semyon's brother, Dmitry, now avenged by his kin. So why did he, Semyon, not feel satisfied?

The answer hit him like a blow from a mailed fist. Because the death could not bring Dmitry back. Dmitry had brought trouble on himself by killing one of Bulat's warriors in a drunken rage. But, three years younger, he had long trailed at Semyon's heels. With both parents dead, a wife who hated him, an uncle who refused support, judgmental cousins, no living children except a worthless daughter—without his brother, Semyon faced the world alone.

An infernal racket roused him. He rolled out of the pile of skins, cursing, and clutched at the edge of the stove to keep himself from tumbling off. The peasant lad reached out an arm, although Semyon's weight would crush that reedy boy.

"It's the rooster, Lord," the boy stammered. "Dawn has come."

The rooster. Semyon glanced around. Dim light pierced the shutters; the peasants rose from their beds and lit lanterns from the stove.

Time to rouse the troops. Have them ready when dawn broke.

He ran fingers through his hair and rubbed his tongue against his teeth. The ale he'd savored the night before left a sour residue in his mouth. The boy handed him a hunk of black bread and a painted cup containing small beer. Semyon nodded his thanks and swilled the beer around his mouth, trying to dislodge the bitter taste of hops. The bread defied human teeth. His jaw ached when he was done.

He straightened his clothes, donned his chain mail and his helmet, nodded to the patriarch and his wife, and sent the lad to the barn where his men had spent the night. Within moments, they clustered in the yard, fully mounted. Timoshka waited with Semyon's horse.

"Let's go," Semyon said as he mounted. "We want to reach Ryazan before dark."

Timoshka's mouth dropped open. "But Lord, the boy who got away. He can identify us."

Semyon cuffed the fool. "Oh, I doubt it. He rode behind, like a servant. Dressed like one, too. What are the odds that some trooper's brat from Kasimov ever sets eyes on any of us again?"

Chapter 3

THE QUESTIONS BEGAN THE MORNING AFTER THE FUNERAL. Later Nasan would think of that interview, even more than the ambush itself, as the day when the spirits twisted the whole direction of her life, recruiting her for a purpose beyond her understanding.

At the time, she saw only her immediate pain. The sun had not cleared the horizon when she received the summons from *Ana* to join Bulat and Ogodai in the room that her father adopted as his own when he first brought them to Kasimov. Custom required forty days of mourning, but the mystery of Girei's murder would not wait.

Nasan settled on a pile of pillows next to her mother. Riches surrounded her. Tiles and silken cushions mingled their hues in the patterned carpets. Iron lanterns decorated with swirls and arabesques struggled to offset the gloom. Bowls of dried rose petals perfumed the air. Yet celadon, gold, and turquoise failed to soothe her troubled mind.

Ana tucked a stray wisp of hair under Nasan's headdress. The loving gesture recalled a thousand like it, but her mother's words shattered the mood. "Speak, my child. I told you and Girei not to leave the palace. What happened? And why, in the name of the Prophet (on whom be peace), did you try to rescue him yourself instead of riding for help?"

Nasan began at the end, where she stood on firmest ground. "If I'd ridden home, the Russians could have done whatever they wanted before we had a chance to stop them. That's why I sent the pony. So you would know we were in trouble."

"They did do what they wanted," Bulat said. "You put yourself in danger, daughter. Did you even take a weapon?"

The very question she had expected from him, and it stung. "I should have," she mumbled.

"You have disappointed me, Nasan," he said. She had seldom heard his voice so harsh. "You had no business in the woods. Confess! Girei left the fortress because you talked him into it. I expect a formal vow, sworn on the Koran and over the hearth fire, that you will not disobey again."

She didn't protest. The memory of Girei, slumped against the tree while his blood spurted onto the snow, required a greater homage than feeble excuses could provide. "Yes, *Ata*," she said through stiff lips. "I'm sorry. It should have been me."

"Don't be ridiculous," Sumbeka snapped. "Would I rather lose a daughter than a son? Or a daughter *and* a son? You both behaved badly."

But only Girei died. Nasan stared at her fingers, tangled in pillow fringe. So many things she could no longer say.

"You stay within the walls from now on," Sumbeka said. "If I have to watch you myself. Whether you like it or not, I *will* keep you safe as I prepare you for marriage."

"Assuming I can get anyone to take such a hoyden," Bulat muttered.

Sumbeka ignored him. "Promise me, Nasan."

"And make the vow," Bulat added. "Pray for guidance. You need many good deeds to offset your bad behavior yesterday."

Too rattled to fight, Nasan promised. Thoughts of Ice Man lurking in the woods frightened her. *What kind of epic heroine am I?*

"Very well," Bulat said. "Tell us what you saw. We must identify this monster."

She took a deep breath. Bringing Ice Man to justice constituted the first of the good deeds she needed to restore the balance of her soul. "A tall man. Huge, with light hair and pale eyes. Inhuman eyes. Soulless. I could see right through them. He hit his soldiers when they displeased him, and when he attacked Girei…" Her voice broke, and she clutched the pillow for support.

"Go on," Bulat said. "When he attacked Girei, what?"

She swallowed. "He told his men to watch him as he killed. Girei meant nothing to him." After the funeral, she would have sworn no tears remained, but here they came, sliding past her closed eyelids, clogging her breath. The image of Ice Man shimmered against her lids.

"How many men? Ten? Fifty?" Her father's voice had softened.

She shook her head. "Not fifty. More than ten. Fifteen, perhaps twenty. They ambushed us from the woods as we rode the river path. Two of them caught the ponies' reins. The rest surrounded us so we couldn't get away." A small voice in her mind pushed her to admit that she'd misjudged the danger, but pride stopped her tongue.

Instead she sought refuge in bravado. "We almost escaped." She flung the words at three skeptical faces. "We did! I created a diversion and spooked the horses, and Girei was reaching for a set of reins. He shouted at me to go. I thought him right behind me. I wouldn't have left him otherwise."

A soft moan escaped her mother's lips. Ogodai studied his clasped hands. "Something went wrong, then, didn't it?" Bulat asked, his voice like satin.

Nasan's defiance evaporated. She dropped her head onto her knees. Again, he was right.

"Enough," Sumbeka said. "She knows what she did."

"Let her go, then," Bulat replied.

Sumbeka pulled Nasan's right hand from the pillow fringe and held it. "No. It's our family, too. You can't shut us out." Bulat growled but didn't argue. The women stayed.

For once, Nasan would have preferred to crawl away and hide. But *Ana*'s determination overpowered her own desire to flee.

Whispering in the wind that whistled past the mica windowpanes, the grandmothers agreed: Nasan must stick it out.

After a while, servants entered, bearing food-laden trays. Nasan had skipped breakfast, as well as dinner the day before. Her stomach growled.

The food brought an air of normalcy into the room. The yeasty smell of fresh *non*—flat bread baked on the sides of a clay oven—mingled with the delicate scent of dried melon and figs, the tang of yogurt cheese. Sumbeka poured tea into porcelain cups and distributed them to her family. Nasan cradled hers between her palms, reveling in its warmth. The blue ducks frolicking on the white clay, the herbal aroma, the clean taste—the familiarity of these things comforted her. When a servant handed her a plate, she reached for a piece of melon. Sweetness filled her mouth.

Sumbeka tapped Nasan's plate. "Eat," she said. "You won't cure what ails you by starving yourself." Lured by the aroma of fresh bread, Nasan picked up the *non*, breaking it into small pieces that she chewed with care.

With every plate filled, the servants left. Bulat, Sumbeka, Ogodai, and Nasan sat in their rough circle, avoiding one another's eyes. For a while, no one spoke. Nasan accepted more tea but refused the cheese and figs. Sumbeka frowned but did not press.

A soldier brought Bulat a scroll, which he skimmed before dismissing the man with a wave of his hand. Nasan studied her father. The scroll's news had invigorated him. He looked the way he did before leaving on campaign, as if force of will could convert the uncertainties of war into an organized battle plan.

"Ogodai's men have returned," Bulat said. He nodded to his right, where Ogodai sat cross-legged on another pile of cushions. "You did well, son, to send them out at once."

Her brother's face glowed at the compliment. Bulat went on, speaking to Ogodai while occasionally glancing at his wife and daughter. "They tracked the Russians for an hour, then lost them in the woods. With evening closing in, though, our headman realized that the Russians would look for a place to stay. He split his force and searched the hamlets, although by the time he found a farmer who'd put up a nobleman, the Russians had gone. But…" He paused for effect. "The leader of that group matched Nasan's description."

Ogodai's eyebrows rose, and Bulat stared at him in a significant way that Nasan could not interpret. She tugged at her mother's sleeve. Sumbeka touched a finger to her lips.

"The guest gave his name," Bulat said, "as Boris Nikolaevich Shein."

Ogodai's face contorted in fury. Nasan couldn't imagine why.

Sumbeka spoke for them both. "I don't understand. We have no quarrel with the Sheins."

"And if we did," Ogodai said, "it would not include Boris Nikolaevich, who's well past sixty. He's missed the last two musters, and rumor predicts he'll take the tonsure any day now— he's that close to the end. Besides, we checked the brand on that gelding you captured, Nasan. We know the killer rode a Kolychev horse."

"Indeed." Bulat again nodded his approval. "A Kolychev horse. And the Kolychevs boast several young men with blond hair and blue eyes."

"But only one with that name. He must think we're idiots." Ogodai clenched his fists.

"Perhaps the whole name is a lie," Bulat said. "Not only the surname."

Ogodai's eyes widened into dark circles. "Oh, no. Boris looks just like that. And would even a Russian implicate his own relative?"

"True," Bulat said. "Then I think we have our man."

Sumbeka waved both hands above her head. "I realize the two of you know what you're talking about, but Nasan and I do not attend your military conclaves. Who murdered my son?"

"Oh," Ogodai said. "That's simple. Boris Nikolaevich Kolychev. His brother is my *qarïndash*."

That caused a sensation. Nasan blurted, "You have a Russian *qarïndash*? And you didn't tell us?" *Qarïndashlar* swore an oath of lifelong friendship and support, a voluntary fraternity in a world where polygamous households produced numerous brothers and half-brothers with plenty of reasons to fight one another. How could a *qarïndash* treat his sworn brother's family so callously?

"Army business." Ogodai shrugged, as if anyone could have sworn brothers and not think to mention them.

If that wasn't typical. "Men!" Nasan said. "You act like war's a state secret."

He gave her his irritating, condescending older-brother smile. Ogodai, like most sultans, had spent years in other regions, learning to rule, returning only when he reached an age to fight at his father's side. Nasan loved him and relied on him, but they were not close as she and Girei had been. She resented his superiority, his self-confidence, and—at this moment—his survival.

Lashed by memories and guilt, she opened her mouth to snap at him, but Sumbeka, with a skill born of long practice, interrupted their squabble in the making. "You will avenge my child?" she asked her husband.

"We will," Bulat said. "We can't stand by while Russians murder my son." He drew his brows together in a frown more thoughtful than angry. "Tell me about the Kolychevs."

That last request had to be directed at Ogodai. "I've seen Boris only from a distance," he said. "Daniil doesn't talk much about his family. He's strange that way."

"But you know where they live."

"Outside the Kremlin, near the marketplace. The usual noble estate. Walls and guards."

"But not inside the fortress," Bulat said. "That helps."

"Yes," Ogodai said. "One set of palisades, and those in need of repair."

"Good. How many men?"

"Boris and his brother, their father most likely. Cousins nearby, but in another house. We have to assume everyone's at home until the muster. Should we wait until the call goes out?"

Bulat chewed his mustache, considering. "Too risky. You and I can handle three nobles. How many troops?"

"Not sure. Judging from Daniil's horse and armor, the family has plenty of money. A healthy number, I'd guess."

"Half a hundred of ours should do it." Bulat studied the ceiling for a brief interval. No one interrupted him. "My duty is clear. A life for a life. I will secure the council's agreement to the raid, but I anticipate no problems. We must retaliate, to defend our honor and proclaim our strength." He gazed at his wife and daughter. "Lest we invite another attack. You would not enjoy an assault by rogue Muscovite warriors."

Rogue Muscovite warriors. A hundred Ice Men. Nasan clutched her elbows and shivered. Would the world ever feel safe again?

The conversation meandered into details of troop strength and planning. Sumbeka rose from the cushions, dragging Nasan up by the hand she held. "We will leave you," she said. Bulat dismissed them with a nod.

"Come, Nasan." She towed her daughter to the door.

Nasan yielded, glad to get away yet pondering how to escape from her mother as well. She needed to move. Time with Sumbeka tended to revolve around housework. Even the thought made her itch.

But Sumbeka surprised her. Dragged into her mother's sitting room, Nasan watched from a bench while *Ana* pounded one fist into her open palm and prowled from window to door, the Crimean khanim who had enchanted Bulat with her fiery beauty never more in evidence. "I hate these Russians," she said. "I dream of slaying the man who murdered my child like the beast he is.

When I wake, I can't believe my own rage. I strive for control, but I can't help myself."

"Nor can I." Could the ambush have done the impossible: turned her mother back into the beloved companion of Nasan's childhood? "*Must* we stay home while the men avenge Girei? It seems so unfair."

Sumbeka stopped pacing and sighed. "Life is unfair, child—for women, especially. You must resign yourself. Allah is compassionate. We must be, too."

And to think that, once upon a time, *Ana* was the one telling tales of warrior heroines, teaching her daughter to revere the grandmothers, encouraging her to master the skills of horse and bow. Before the family moved to Kasimov, Nasan turned fourteen, and her mother became this alien creature, focused on marriage.

Words popped into her mouth. Words better left unsaid, she realized too late. "You don't resign yourself. You ride and shoot as well as Ogodai. Even *Ata*."

She braced for her mother's anger, but Sumbeka surprised her again.

"No, not so well as your father, my sweet." She sank onto the sofa and patted the seat next to her. Nasan inched closer. "Otherwise, you speak truth. You have too much of me in you. Learn to choose your battles, or you can expect a difficult life. You will marry soon."

Marriage again. Sumbeka stilled Nasan's instinctive protest with a finger. "The trick is not always to resist, nor always to surrender, but to fight when it counts and yield when it doesn't."

Nasan frowned. "Girei's death doesn't count?"

"It does."

When Nasan stared at her, puzzled, Sumbeka threw up her hands. "*Ai*, I'm explaining this badly. My husband, Ogodai … they can't express themselves as women do. Chasing this Russian, acting on their anger—it's how men handle problems. Girei's death matters. Punishing the transgressor matters. Protecting the clan matters. But being the ones to strike the blow doesn't matter so much. You and I have other resources."

"I don't think I do," Nasan said. Her grief surfaced without warning, triggered by the kettle drum, a child's shriek of delight, the scent of the honey cakes her brother had loved. The rest of the time, she felt frozen. She yearned for a chance to act out her pain.

Sumbeka tipped back Nasan's chin. Tears glistened in her eyes. "Then you must find them. Read your Koran."

"Yes, *Ana*," Nasan said. Reading wouldn't help, but neither would arguing. Her already heavy burden of guilt increased in the face of Sumbeka's obvious distress.

She should apologize, admit her fault, but her mind could not summon words weighty enough to carry the colossal burden of Girei's death. While she struggled, Tanya, the family's Russian servant, arrived, bringing news of a domestic disaster. Two of the hunting hounds had escaped the kennels and raided the kitchens, disappearing with a haunch of salted mutton intended for the khan's table. The head cook, a Persian not renowned for his patience, was tearing out what remained of his hair and pleading with his ancestors to release him from a household overrun by wild beasts. Would the khatun please come and calm the man before the khan and his son finished their planning session and demanded their dinner?

"What a commotion," Sumbeka said. "Very well. Nasan, we will talk later, yes?"

Nasan nodded and went to her own room. There she changed her clothes, took the sword Girei had outgrown, and found an unused attic room where she could practice her strokes and her footwork. Every sweep of the curved blade strove to undo the ambush and bring her brother back.

Chapter 4

WHITE BIRCHES OPENED ONTO A LEVEL PLAIN THAT STRETCHED to the river. Fields of grass spattered with wildflowers yielded to brown water flecked with dawn light. On the far side, clouds drifted past the fortress that crowned the hill.

Ogodai experienced a certain awe as the forest cleared, revealing Moscow's crenellated fortress, its peach-colored brick set off by a sky as pale as icicles in a cave. Surrounded by water, the Kremlin's massive walls formed a triangle, dotted by towers of various shapes—square bastions along the sides, cylinders at the corners, and multi-part gates monitoring everyone who passed in and out. The citadel drew the eye upward—past one-room cottages, the palisade enclosing the trading quarter, even the clusters of glittering cupolas that floated above the fence—to where it crouched on the hill, emanating controlled power, defying invaders to approach with siege engines or guns.

Only a small part of the population lived year-round within the massive walls. Waiting in the woods at his father's side, with fifty mounted Tatars at their backs, Ogodai remembered hearing that a million people called Moscow home. The estimate seemed impossibly high—inflated, perhaps, by the Russians' extensive use of land. Vegetable plots adjoined even the poorest huts; and the estates included orchards and gardens, stables, chicken coops, ponds, and outbuildings of every imaginable sort from icehouses to breweries.

Kasimov had its share of tangled streets and poorly maintained housing, but the walls kept it compact. The majestic Kremlin could not contain the sprawling town below. Ogodai crinkled his nose, assailed by foul odors wafting across the water from the straggle of one-room huts that covered the rising ground. Mud pathways meandered down to the river. The palisade, falling into disrepair in places, hid the grand households that he knew from previous visits lay close to the Kremlin—collections of brightly trimmed buildings, multistoried and decorated with carvings. Up there, the streets were wider, more imposing, and covered with wood. His father's target lay near the top of the hill—one straight, hard ride away.

On this side of the river, no one heard the Tatar ponies approach. No one lived so far outside the protective walls. Bulat had planned to launch his raid before the spring thaw turned the woodland paths to mud, but the demands of mourning and the holy month of Ramadan had pushed the need for vengeance into April, slowing the raiding party's journey. Yet the thaw had advantages, too: new leaves concealed their arrival, and the mud muffled the sound of hooves.

So far, Bulat's efforts to ensure a successful mission had worked. The wise men who burned the shoulder bones of sheep and examined the cracks had promised good fortune. Together, he and Ogodai had held a libation ceremony to request the grandmothers' assistance, sprinkled the spirit dolls with fermented mare's milk, and fed them with the smoke-tinged fat of spring lambs. Those precautions had kept the warriors safe, but of course, the true danger lay ahead, once they launched their attack on the Kolychev household.

As if the grandmothers had borne his thoughts on the wind, Ogodai heard his father speak. "What troubles you, son?" Bulat asked. "You've said hardly a word since we left Kasimov."

Ogodai bridled at the question. Did *Ata* imagine his son brooding like a girl over a broken friendship? "Nothing troubles me. The Kolychevs attacked us. I don't ask you to spare them."

"No," Bulat said. "Something's bothering you, though. We're heading into battle. If you have doubts, tell me. I need my second-in-command with me, no questions asked."

Ogodai watched his chestnut gelding shake its head, its mane ruffling in the breeze. How to explain? Especially to his father, who seemed so immune to doubt. "I understand why we must avenge Girei. I *want* to avenge Girei. What harm did he do the Kolychevs? It's myself I wonder about. By trusting Daniil when I should not have, did I somehow convince him and his brother to see us as easy prey? Did *I*, in effect, set Girei's death in motion?"

"So that's it." Bulat's eyebrows drew together as he considered the point. "But I know you, son. I doubt you did any such thing. And only a madman would ambush my son, whatever you said." He returned his attention to the awakening city.

Ogodai loosened his grip on the reins. His father spoke the truth. And Daniil was not a madman, whatever his faults. He could predict the penalty for killing a khan's son. Perhaps Boris had deceived his brother.

The thought raised his spirits. In that case, the responsibility for Girei's death lay elsewhere.

Fifty riders sat silent in the woods, awaiting Bulat's orders. Ogodai watched as glorious rose streaked the horizon, then faded as a silver-gilt sun rose above the hill, restoring the sky to icicle blue.

Any moment now.

Nasan watched the oak parapets of the Kasimov fortress emerge as the light strengthened. Already she saw watchmen outlined against the towers. She should get back to her bed before Tanya noticed her absence.

Even so, she lingered. Lit by the rising sun, dew gleamed on every blade of grass, every timid blossom peeking from earth freed of frost.

She hated to leave the serene beauty of the palace garden. In the last six weeks sleep had become her enemy, an arena where spirits taunted her with visions of failure, replaying the ambush in an endless series of images in which she strove and failed to prevent the inevitable outcome. Snow transformed into rivers of blood; knives hung from the trees, tormenting her by bobbing out of reach whenever she stretched up a hand. More often than not, she jerked awake, shaking, her cheeks streaked with the tears she suppressed during the day.

She couldn't talk about the dreams, even to *Ana*, because dreams spoken aloud always came true. And although these appeared to reflect the past, they might prophesy some yet more dreadful future. At first her only recourse was to disappear among the attics, but the arrival of springtime opened the gardens as refuge. Bulat might object—although she had obeyed his dictate to remain within the walls—if her father had not left a week ago to punish the Russians for their attack on his clan.

Taking Ogodai but not his daughter who, being a mere girl, should not desire vengeance.

Nasan fought down her resentment. *Ata* did not understand the pain that drove her.

So far, no one had discovered her nighttime wandering. In her dark jacket and trousers, her hair tied back and covered with a black scarf, she could lose herself among the plants until either exhaustion claimed her or morning arrived.

Last night had brought a particularly horrific nightmare, and Nasan had fled to the farthest corner she could reach. As a result, she couldn't tarry over the sunrise as she usually did. Within the hour, the servants would awaken. The black clothes that provided her camouflage would attract attention in the brilliance of early morning, and that would lead to questions Nasan preferred to avoid. She cast one last, longing glance around the garden and set off for her room.

She had crossed three courtyards when she heard a child crying. She stopped and looked around, but the source of the noise remained hidden. Only after investigating trees, fountains, and benches did she trace the sound to a large stone planter at the far end of the courtyard. Later in the year, it would have been filled with earth and flowers, but the gardeners had not yet reached this section of the palace grounds.

Inside the planter, a small girl crouched. Her one-piece dress and bast shoes marked her as a servant's child.

"But what is this?" Nasan reached down her arms.

The child shrank back.

"I won't hurt you," Nasan said. "Don't you want to get out of there?" The girl shook her head.

"Are you hiding then? Or do I frighten you?"

That provoked a quick nod.

"Which? You are hiding?"

Another head shake.

"Don't be scared. Let me lift you, and you can run home." Nasan looked around and saw no one. Impatience tugged at her. She, too, had to get back to her room.

But she couldn't leave a shivering child stuck in a planter. "Come," she said to the girl. "You can't get out by yourself. The pot is too big. Your *ana* must be worried about you."

The child chewed her thumb and considered this. Nasan slowed her breathing and waited, reminding herself that hauling the girl out by brute force would lead only to screams.

At last the child extended her arms. Nasan pulled her up. Servants' children ran small: this one's gap-toothed smile suggested an age of six, perhaps seven. She looked more like four.

The child wrapped her skinny arms around Nasan's neck. Nasan warmed her as best she could, relishing the feel of the slim, light body pressed against her own.

"Where do you live?" she asked.

The child wriggled, so Nasan set her down. The girl scampered across the courtyard. Just as she reached the colonnade on the opposite side, she stopped and waved. Nasan waved back, and the girl disappeared.

Nasan laughed. So much for her heroic rescue.

But she had helped a child in need. Another small good deed to offset Girei's death.

A shout from the stables ahead of her reminded her of the advancing hour. Pleased with her morning's work, she headed for her room.

The soft thud of oak hitting stucco signaled the approach of a possible supervisor. Semyon was standing guard—if only in principle—at the ornate entrance to the royal reception area, the Faceted Palace in the Moscow Kremlin. Priding himself on his quick reactions, he secreted the dice that had turned dull duty into entertainment for himself and his fellow sentry and faked diligence, his back against the wall and a solemn expression on his face.

His companion didn't react as fast. Slowed by the wine they'd swigged while gambling, the other sentry still sat on the floor when the new arrival turned the corner. With a glare at the inept guardsman, Semyon kicked the wine flask under a nearby footed chest.

He tensed, cursing his bad fortune. Just his luck to draw guard duty with the only man in the Russian army who lacked the wit to cover his tail.

The newcomer wore civilian dress, not military garb. A crimson velvet caftan trimmed in arctic fox brushed leather boots, and a sable hat contrasted with the cream silk of an under-tunic. Not an officer checking on the sentries, then—although the distinction was superficial at best. Russian boyars served in the army from the age of fifteen until death, so any man of the right age was a commander, whatever he wore.

The clothes indicated a member of the royal family's intimate circle. Only the elite noblemen of the capital dressed so richly, but Semyon had already guessed that a visitor must match or exceed him in rank. Even young aristocrats like himself, assigned to guard duty as part of their regular military service, came from the most prestigious clans. He could number on the fingers of both hands those entitled to enter the Faceted Palace for a private audience with the three-year-old grand prince and his triumvirate of guardians or—because power in the palace seemed to shift with each day that passed—the boy's mother, Grand Princess Elena, and her favorite, Prince Ivan Telepnev. Caught in dereliction of duty by one so exalted, Semyon and his colleague could expect a severe reprimand.

Then he recognized the newcomer and relaxed. Short and slender, with dark brown hair and eyes and a barely visible beard, Fyodor Koshkin had married his daughter to Semyon's cousin eight months ago. He wouldn't turn in a family member.

Koshkin frowned, and Semyon's faith wavered. Following Koshkin's gaze, he saw a pool of wine seeping from under the chest. He must have broken or unstoppered the flask in disposing of it. A mess his fellow sentry should have prevented.

Damned if he would suffer for someone else's incompetence. Semyon stared at Koshkin, willing him to pin responsibility where it belonged. The other sentry helped by staggering to his feet, mumbling apologies and excuses as he realized that a member of the grand princess's inner circle had discovered him drinking and dicing during his watch.

Wait. Koshkin hadn't seen the dicing. Semyon elbowed the soldier in the ribs to shut him up before he caused more trouble.

Koshkin's lips twitched. "Walk with me." He placed a hand on Semyon's elbow.

A flattering invitation. Men of Koshkin's standing did not often seek the company of twenty-four-year-old guardsmen.

Semyon hid his eagerness as he stepped away from the wall. At the sound of slithering, he stopped and stared at his fellow sentry in astonishment. The man appeared somewhat lopsided. They hadn't drunk *that* much.

"We won't go far," Koshkin murmured. "We can intercept anyone who thinks to enter the palace."

Semyon nodded. The other guard gave no evidence of having heard. Koshkin grinned at Semyon, then yelled at the inebriated sentry, "Attention!"

The drunk trooper shot upright. The guard's helmet clanked against the wall, emitting a reverberating note like a bell struck off-center. Semyon winced, then dipped his chin in approval. Served the dolt right.

"That's better," Koshkin said. "Semyon will accompany me. Take care of that mess, soldier, and look alert. If you do, I may forget to report this incident."

"Yes, sir!" The sentry's salute looked more like a wave, but his intent was clear.

Semyon followed Koshkin toward the door. When he reached it, he glanced over his shoulder. The guard was on hands and knees, mopping up the spilled wine with his sleeve. How he expected to escape notice with a crimson stain running from elbow to wrist, Semyon could not imagine. But the man's sins lay on his own head. Semyon had succeeded in averting suspicion from himself.

Koshkin paid no further attention to the sentry. Semyon pondered potential reasons for this meeting as he made his way down the main staircase. Despite their family connection, he did not consider Koshkin a friend. At thirty-five, Koshkin had played the power game a decade longer than Semyon—and played it well, by all accounts. As far as Semyon knew, Koshkin had fallen foul of only one fellow noble: Semyon's Uncle Nikolai. But overt hostilities between them ended eight months ago, when Nikolai married his older son, Boris, to Koshkin's daughter. The entire court knew that Kolychev and Koshkin detested each other, but the men in question pretended otherwise. Which raised the question of what Koshkin wanted with Semyon.

The answer exceeded his wildest expectations. "I wish to speak of Prince Yuri," Koshkin said as they entered Cathedral Square. In the clear light of dawn, churches jostled for attention in the deserted space. The great Dormition loomed over the smaller Intercession; the Cathedral of the Archangel Michael stood stalwart in defense of Moscow's rulers, laid in eternal slumber within its walls. The bell tower of Ivan the Great sought to eclipse the tiny, exquisite Annunciation, the grand princes' private chapel, but even a tower could not outshine nine serried cupolas glinting in the sparse sunlight.

"Ivanovich?" Semyon asked. To the discomfort of everyone except, presumably, the royal family, Moscow had at present two princes named Yuri. They had different fathers, which made it possible to tell them apart. Yuri Ivanovich was the current grand prince's uncle, the brother of Vasily III, who had died last December. It seemed unlikely that Koshkin could have anything to say about the grand prince's younger brother, Yuri Vasilyevich, not long past his first birthday, but it didn't hurt to check.

"Ivanovich, naturally." Koshkin waved an impatient hand. "The one your father served as boyar. You *have* heard that Yuri lies in chains, right here in the Kremlin?"

Semyon bridled. Asking an obvious question didn't make him stupid. "My father and you," he said, relishing the wince his reminder provoked. "Grand Prince Vasily assigned you both to Dmitrov at the same time." *You see, I do know things.* "But a decade's gone by, and my father's no more. Nor is Vasily. Meanwhile, Yuri will end his days in that dungeon."

"You think so?" Koshkin looked smug, but then he often did.

"I do think so," Semyon said, still riled by the smugness and the implicit dismissal of his talents. "Why should his sister-in-law risk another conspiracy aimed at replacing her sons with one of their adult uncles?"

"Yuri swore fealty to his nephew," Koshkin commented, his tone mild. "He says he didn't plan any conspiracy."

"So what?" Semyon retorted. "The grand princess doesn't believe him. And the Moscow nobles won't take a chance on Yuri throwing *them* in the dungeon while he takes the throne."

All of which Koshkin undoubtedly knew. Semyon narrowed his eyes, trying to read the other man's mind. Koshkin stared back, unflappable.

When the silence stretched to the point of discomfort, Semyon took the plunge. "What's your game, Fyodor Mikhailovich? My uncle says Yuri's done for. And that his brother Andrei will soon make peace with his sister-in-law."

"Will he?" Koshkin raised both eyebrows. "Your uncle's dreaming. Andrei's too busy sulking at home until those in power grant him a portion of Yuri's lands."

Semyon pondered this statement. Maybe Uncle Nikolai was dreaming, although as a senior noble at the grand prince's court, he was thick as thieves with the three guardians. "No doubt Prince Andrei can figure out that peace is a better fate than joining Yuri in his cell," he said, although in his experience royal princes tended to place the demands of pride above those of common sense.

"So you're your uncle's man, Semyon Pavlovich?" Koshkin shrugged. "I'll let you go, then. I had nothing in particular in mind, so no need to trouble your conscience over this conversation."

But Semyon had already shaken his head, only to regret the gesture as soon as he'd made it. Better to have kept Koshkin guessing.

Indeed, why am I here, listening to this nonsense?

But Koshkin was smiling. "No? Your uncle argued Yuri's imprisonment was necessary to prevent civil war. Do you not agree?"

Semyon snorted, dislike for his uncle overpowering his better instincts. "I don't care about Yuri one way or the other. But like the guardians, Nikolai yearns for power. If Yuri took the throne, he would promote his own servitors over today's leaders."

A prospect that must not bother Koshkin, despite his prestigious position at court. What reward did he expect from Yuri to compensate for his treachery toward Moscow?

Koshkin drew closer. His robes exuded musk mingled with camphor, an effeminate blend that caused Semyon's nostrils to flare. "Hush. Spies flock thicker than pigeons at a feast."

So he did recognize the danger. Semyon decided to let the game play out, taking care not to commit his support until he understood the whole. If he helped Koshkin, Koshkin would owe him. A debt Semyon could call in or repudiate at any time. With skill and luck, he could parlay this offer, whatever it was, into riches and success. His chest swelled at the thought.

Koshkin dropped his voice to a whisper. "Yuri Ivanovich needs friends, or he will not survive. He will reward those who help him. And we must. Because with Yuri under arrest, Russia's security depends on two toddlers and a woman. We can't afford to wait."

His fervor impressed Semyon. This had to be more than a trick designed to incriminate him.

Koshkin pushed on. "The jackals are gathering. Lithuania, Poland. We'll be defending Smolensk before the year's out."

"Ugh." Semyon groaned. "Not Smolensk. I wasted a year there already. Inedible food, insipid women, endless drills, not enough liquor—the place is a regular snake pit."

"Snake pit or not, the Lithuanians want it back."

"They can have it as far as I'm concerned," Semyon grumbled. But as the words left his mouth, he acknowledged them for a lie. Smolensk stood astride the main road to the west. Moscow had seized it in 1514 and sunk a small fortune into upgrading its fortifications. The government wouldn't yield it without a fight. Nor should it, for strategic reasons.

Koshkin ignored this comment. "And that's not all. Sahib-Girei Khan has thrown his horde behind Sigismund's cause. Word has it that his nephews have already left Crimea for the Oka. Defending Smolensk is bad enough, but defending Smolensk *and* Kolomna, Ryazan, Kasimov? The babe and his mother can't lead the armies. The country needs a prince of the blood at its helm. Don't you agree?"

Well, of course. Who wouldn't? Grand Prince Vasily should have appointed his brother Yuri as his successor from the beginning, as people had expected, instead of saddling the country with a hapless child. But alas, Vasily had not.

Semyon radiated truculence, hoping to convey a willingness to listen without admitting too much. "What do you want of me?"

Koshkin smiled, his expression catlike. "Your agreement, for the present. And your silence. We proceed with care." He caressed the hilt of the dagger every nobleman carried. "One word of this conversation, and I'll know where you stand. And what to do about it."

In response to the implicit threat, Semyon summoned his iciest tone. What kind of co-conspirator was this? "Indeed, you speak treason. Why should I trust you with my life?"

Koshkin's eyebrows rose. "Why? Because I'm family."

Semyon's doubts slid away. Family did not let you down. "You can count on me," he said.

Koshkin's smile widened. "Good. I will contact you soon."

Ogodai watched his father's horse shift its weight, impatient for battle. Bulat bent to pat it, fingers gentling the silky neck the same way he might caress a woman. Beneath the roan's shaggy coat, powerful muscles trembled, ready to spring forward at a touch.

"Hush," Bulat told the horse. "You will gallop soon." He might as well have directed his comment to his son, driven by the long wait into fidgets as great as the horse's.

"I've made my decision," Bulat said. "We ford the river at the usual spot, then try the gates. The guards should let us pass. They know our loyalties lie with Moscow. Once we're through, we ride straight for the Kolychevs' estate. We'll be at their throats before they realize we're coming."

"And if the guards don't let us pass?"

Bulat grinned. "We show them why they need to fix that fence." He pointed at an area to his right where the pointed logs that formed the palisade listed sideways. "That area should do fine."

"So it should." Ogodai frowned at the broken palisade. Useful today, without a doubt, but on the whole, he and his father regarded themselves as allies of the grand prince. "Why haven't they fixed it? Are the Russians in that much disarray since the old grand prince died?"

"Infighting," Bulat said, his voice terse. "Among the clans, between the guardians and the grand princess, between the grand princess and her brothers-in-law. They're too busy squabbling to take care of essentials. We'll do them a service if we take that route. It'll wake them up to where the real dangers lie."

Ogodai laughed. "I hope they appreciate it, then."

From the sleeping city, a single bell sounded the call to prime. Others joined it, one by one from each of a thousand churches, until the city reverberated like a great choir. In the woods, a lark sang descant. Ogodai covered his ears to shut out the cacophony and wished himself back in Kasimov, where only the melodious call of the muezzin disturbed the dawn.

Bulat inhaled and raised his arm above his head. *At last.* He swept it down, pointing at the sleeping city. "Charge!"

With whoops of glee, the Tatars raced for the riverbank.

Chapter 5

POUNDING HOOVES AND CLASHING WEAPONS JERKED DANIIL Kolychev awake. He surged to his feet, stark naked, and ran to the window. Behind him, he could hear the slave girl whimpering.

"What's happening, Lord?" the girl asked.

Anufrya? Tanya? Which one caught my eye this time?

Even slaves became impudent if he slept with them and forgot their names.

He spared a moment from wrestling with the window to glance over his shoulder. Light-brown hair, pale blue eyes, well-rounded figure now resuming its tunic: his father owned a dozen such, and Daniil had sampled most of them.

Grusha. How could he have forgotten? She'd warmed his bed often in the last three years. Too often, in truth—enough to take his attention for granted.

He should get rid of her before she convinced herself that she loved him. If he didn't, there would be scenes. Daniil hated scenes.

No time. Deal with it later.

At last the window frame yielded to his hands. He looked onto a courtyard roiling with servants. Four men milled around the entrance. He recognized the herders tasked with taking the animals down to the river. The gates stood open; the men, their work interrupted by the noise, were debating what to do.

The sounds of approaching horses decided them. The four men pushed and shoved, but the heavy gates resisted their uncoordinated efforts. The largest herder grabbed the elbow of a young man racing by, and the youth fetched reinforcements. Slowly—too slowly—the men established a rhythm and the massive gates inched toward closure.

Pigs and sheep added to the commotion, sliding past would-be captors. One hog made a wild dash for freedom, only to dart the other way when a herder yelled and waved his arms. Women wearing thin shifts clutched squawking chickens to their chests; men in coarse linen shirts held loose trousers in one hand as they shepherded children toward the workrooms or animals to their pens. A few, swifter than the others, ran to assist those working to bar the gates.

Daniil's mother and sister-in-law slipped among the crowd, shouting instructions no one seemed to hear. His brother, Boris, chivvied the dozen or so men who traveled with him into forming a phalanx, weaponless but firm. As Daniil watched, his father, stolid and controlled, emerged from a storeroom and stood, frowning at the throng.

The pounding hooves were almost upon them. Daniil grabbed the first shirt and trousers he could find and dragged them on. "Out, Grusha," he said through linen. "Trouble's coming. Find a place to hide."

The girl fled, her unbraided hair floating behind her.

Daniil, searching for his boots, barely noticed. The noise from below snatched up Grusha's footsteps and smothered them. The pounding hooves became deafening. The blast of a hunting horn mingled with a series of mind-splitting howls, as if wolves accompanied the horses.

Recognizing the howls, Daniil flinched. Tatars! Boots in place, he raced back to the window. As he reached it, a troop of armored horsemen crashed through the unbarred gates.

Waterfowl rose shrieking from the courtyard pond. An unwary duck plummeted earthward, an arrow through its breast. One of the invaders caught the duck as it fell, stowing the bird in his saddle bag without checking his horse. The servants became more desperate, tumbling over one another in their haste to escape. Only Boris's impromptu force stood its ground.

The invading troops ignored the frantic servants, formed a wedge, and aimed at Boris's phalanx. Meeting arrows and swords with sticks and stones, Boris and his men didn't stand a chance.

Daniil caught a glimpse of the leader's face. "Hell and damnation," he said aloud. "Bulat."

Fortunately, he had ignored commands to stash his weapons in a storeroom, even if his brother hadn't. Daniil grabbed his bow and an arrow and nocked it, sighting along the shaft. He could expect one clear shot, perhaps two. His place at the window gave him an advantage, but if the Tatars returned fire, they would force him to duck below the sill. He'd have to bluff them into believing he posed a bigger threat than he did.

Hard to remember, at this moment, that the Kolychevs and the rulers of Kasimov fought on the same side. But the Tatars were here—and not as allies.

He considered his options. He could threaten Bulat, but as the horde dashed past, the ponies shifted, revealing a better target: the young man riding at Bulat's right.

Ogodai, Daniil's sworn brother. They'd fought together in last year's campaign—and the two before that. He'd expected their oath of friendship to protect his immediate family from the vendetta simmering between his clan and the Tatars.

Wrong. He and Boris had stayed out of the conflict, only to have Ogodai bring the battle to them.

Daniil pushed resentment aside and focused on the present. He could beat himself up later for trusting a Tatar. First he had to secure his home. And Ogodai had given him the perfect opportunity. Because Bulat, who would shrug off any risk to his own life, might not be so cavalier when danger threatened his son.

He leaned out the window, aiming below Ogodai's jawline, between mail shirt and helmet. "Bulat!" he shouted over the noise. After four years in the army, he knew how to make his voice carry.

The Tatars ignored him. Their front line closed in on Boris's men. The horsemen had the advantage of height and steel, and they made use of it. Blood hung in the sky like a red mist. The screams of dying men and shocked spectators formed an eerie accompaniment to nomadic howls.

Daniil saw one Tatar raise his curved sword and realized, as his heart jerked in his chest, that Boris stood in the arc of the blade's downward stroke. He shifted his aim and released the bowstring. The arrow skimmed past Bulat's nose and hit the Tatar soldier threatening Boris.

The Tatar fell, Daniil's arrow through his back. The saber flew from the man's hand. The curved tip slashed Boris's throat, and he, too, dropped to the ground. A servant grabbed Boris and dragged him into a corner.

Daniil slammed his fist into the windowsill. *So close!* A fraction left or right...

Had he saved Boris?

No time to find out. No one else on the Kolychev side had a weapon. Suppressing a huge lump in his throat, Daniil grabbed a second arrow and aimed at Ogodai's neck.

Bulat raised an arm. In the silence that followed, Daniil's voice rang clear.

"One wrong move," he said, "and Ogodai dies."

To his astonishment, Bulat laughed. The Tatar archers swiveled, directing their weapons at Daniil. One man, less disciplined than the others, released his bowstring.

Daniil threw himself sideways as the arrow shot past his head, so close he heard it whistle by his right ear.

The move saved his life but disrupted his aim. Against a troop of armed opponents, he had no hope of threatening Ogodai now. He needed another plan.

Bow and quiver in hand, he ran from the room.

Daniil charged through the house, collecting military equipment as he went. Some of it belonged to him; he didn't stop to check. Broadsword, pointed steel helmet, leather armor, wrist guards— good enough.

As he reached the door leading into the courtyard, his father slammed him against the wall. "Get out the back. Semyon has guard duty; he can't help us. Head for Sheremetev's. Ask him for aid. When he gives it, station his men around the periphery of the estate. Don't shoot unless I signal, but whatever you do, don't let Bulat leave."

Daniil nodded. "Boris?" The word choked in his throat.

"Dead," his father said. "He and his men." For an instant, Daniil saw the stoic face crumple. Everyone in the household loved Boris, a gentle soul who rarely said an unkind word. Daniil, five years younger than Boris's twenty-four, had tagged at his brother's heels for years. Unlike most brothers, Boris never shooed him away.

Women wailing outside marked his brother's passing. Daniil flinched at the sound.

"No time," his father said. "Go, before others die."

Daniil went.

Sheremetev lived next door. The noise of the raid must have alerted him, for he had forty men armed and standing by when Daniil arrived. When told of Boris's murder, he announced his readiness to lead his troops into the fray.

With difficulty, Daniil controlled his tongue. He should have anticipated this renewal of what was, after all, an old conflict between them. No matter how often he proved himself capable, Sheremetev continued to regard his junior officer as a hothead— as if four years of intensive training had not turned Daniil into a competent officer capable of directing a dozen small operations like this one. That was the trouble with serving under someone who had known you from birth.

Still, he had great respect—and considerable affection—for Sheremetev, and the same four years of army service had taught him the value of leaving some thoughts unspoken.

But pandering to the whims of a fifty-year-old commander with a limp would not help either. "My father wishes us to prevent Bulat from leaving. He urged haste, Sir. I think he has a plan." He waited for Sheremetev to draw the obvious conclusion.

"And I will slow you down." The older man glared at him. "Is that what you're implying, you young pup? I still command."

Daniil bit the inside of his cheek. Sheremetev scowled, rubbed his thigh, gazed at the courtyard—his eyes avoiding Daniil's. Daniil observed how the soldiers stared straight ahead, their faces impassive under the steel helmets, bows and swords at their sides. Their leather armor and trousers robbed them of individuality. He wondered whom they preferred to follow: a healthy lieutenant or an experienced, familiar, but frail general. The former, he guessed. That would be his choice.

Sheremetev bowed to the inevitable with a sigh. "No, such claims are vanity. This cursed leg. Take the men and go. I will follow at my own pace."

"Thank you, Sir." Daniil ran for the gates, soldiers at his heels. He soon had them deployed according to his father's orders and an arrow aimed at Bulat's head. His fingers itched to let it fly. Only his father's order stopped him. "Don't shoot unless I signal," Nikolai had said.

Another old man who thought he knew best. Yet Papa seldom made pointless demands. Daniil decided to wait and see. He could defy the order later, if necessary.

Sheremetev, wielding a cane, hobbled along the street toward the Kolychevs' house. Daniil silently thanked the Virgin Mother that Sheremetev had not delayed them further. Indeed, the soldiers had almost arrived too late. Open hostilities had ended, and the Tatars looked ready to depart. "Load your weapons," Daniil told the archers, "but don't fire unless I give the word."

The Tatars sat motionless on their stolid ponies. Servants cowered whenever a horse ruffled its mane or stamped a hoof. A group of women clustered in one corner, huddled over a pile of booted legs.

Boris and his men. Daniil swallowed, hard.

Papa stood in the middle of the courtyard, facing Bulat, still mounted. Daniil marveled at his father's calm. How could he bear to confront the man responsible for his son's murder?

Daniil braced himself against the parapet. To either side bowmen stood, armed and ready, arrows pointed at the Tatars. The distance from palisade to courtyard corresponded to one story of the main house; the troops could hear and see everything that went on below. One hint of renewed aggression, and the soldiers would retaliate.

And Papa would die. But Nikolai showed no awareness of his danger. Head thrown back, he stared at Bulat. "Why Boris?" he said. "He did you no harm."

Ogodai snorted. So did Bulat. "He killed my son. A boy too young to serve!"

"*Boris?* Kill a boy? Are you mad?"

"We have proof." Bulat's face was implacable. "An eyewitness."

Nikolai shook his head. "Your eyewitness is wrong. Boris has not left Moscow for weeks. And what had your son to do with the quarrel between my nephew and yours?"

"Nothing!" Bulat slammed his hand against the hilt of his sword, causing his horse to shy. "And this *happened* weeks ago. Six, to be precise."

That was bad. Boris had left for the Holy Trinity Monastery in early February and returned only in mid-March. Daniil knew that his adored older brother abhorred revenge killing, but his belief would not convince Bulat. And if an eyewitness swore to Boris's presence in Kasimov...

Except that the only Tatar likely to recognize Boris by sight was Ogodai, and if Ogodai witnessed a murder, he would retaliate on the spot, not wait six weeks. Something didn't add up.

"Enough, Bulat," Nikolai said. "Whoever started this feud, we need to end it. Or do you want to head back to Kasimov with my army on your tail?"

The Tatar laughed, an unpleasant sound. "Army? I saw one cub at a window." Daniil's fingers tensed on the bowstring.

Nikolai gestured at Daniil and his archers. "He's an excellent shot, though, my cub. And no longer alone. You won't get past the gate."

Bulat glanced over his shoulder. His eyebrows lifted. "Not bad, Russian."

His eyes swept over his troop. Shocked, Daniil realized the raiding party contained half a hundred-unit, no more than fifty men. Such arrogance!

But justified. Boris and his soldiers would not see tomorrow's dawn.

Daniil closed his eyes in agony. A blood-red haze filled his vision, and against his shut lids Boris tumbled like a straw puppet at a fair.

With a deep breath, he forced away the sickness and focused on the confrontation below.

Chapter 6

OGODAI FIXED HIS EYES ON NIKOLAI KOLYCHEV, WHOM HE had not met before. A swift glance at Bulat had revealed an impassive face yielding nothing to the enemy, and Ogodai sought to imitate his father's style. He did not look for his sworn brother; their friendship had ended the day Boris took a knife to Girei's throat. Daniil's actions today commanded a certain respect, but Ogodai's mission required unwavering support for his father. He communicated that support through his upright stance and steady gaze.

Tall and broad-shouldered, Nikolai displayed an air of serenity even under these trying circumstances. Beneath the shock of white hair and arched brows, keen blue eyes assessed Bulat for weaknesses. The trimmed beard framed a craggy face, a mouth strong but not inflexible. Ogodai decided Kolychev was a worthwhile opponent.

"What do you propose?" Bulat asked. "I have lost a nephew and a son."

"I too," Kolychev said, "have lost a nephew and a son. And a dozen competent soldiers. But I have another son who lacks a wife. Since I cannot replace the boy you killed, I must have grandchildren to continue my line. Send me a maiden of your house, and I will wed her to my Daniil. Then we can end the feud."

"Any maiden?"

Ogodai abandoned his straight-ahead pose long enough to stare at his father. The tone of the question suggested Bulat was taking the suggestion seriously.

Well, his father's harem contained plenty of girls, some still virgins. A small price to pay for peace.

"Any maiden of your lineage—reasonably well favored, nubile, and healthy." Kolychev paused. "She must convert to Orthodoxy."

Bulat hesitated, then shrugged. "Of course. The mullahs will complain, but I can handle them. It's customary, after all." He paused again before adding, "I think we can reach an agreement. The daughter of my chief wife should meet your needs."

Ogodai's jaw dropped. *Nasan?* His father had offered *Nasan?* A concubine was one thing, even a kind of secret joke: most of them would shock a Russian noble family into hysteria, although Daniil might enjoy that marriage. But hand over his spirited little sister to his former sworn brother, now an enemy? Bulat had lost his mind.

With an effort, Ogodai shut his mouth, controlled his expression, and turned his stony gaze frontward once more. There Nikolai bowed and murmured agreement. And while the demons of Hell rejoiced, the deed was done.

Daniil glared at the parapet. Wed Bulat's daughter? He recalled legends Ogodai told around the campfire—Tatar women who slaughtered six hundred knights to save the men they loved, wives who dressed unwanted husbands in venom-soaked shirts or dropped hemlock in their koumiss. No shrinking violets there.

Although a woman warrior *did* have a certain appeal...

No doubt Ogodai exaggerated, and Tatar women had no more gumption than their Russian counterparts. Images of Anastasia danced before Daniil's eyes. Three years ago, his first wife had been a delicate fourteen-year-old with rose-petal skin, trusting brown eyes, trembling lips, and hair that floated, wispy and faint, around her heart-shaped face.

Anastasia—a stranger who died in childbirth ten months after their wedding. Recalling how she shrank from him when he touched her still made him squirm.

Since her death he'd restricted himself to girls who enjoyed a quick tumble—Grusha and those like her. He hadn't intended to disappoint Anastasia, but it happened. Best not to repeat his mistakes.

Now, like it or not, he was again heading for the altar. Watching the two fathers negotiate his future in the courtyard, Daniil groaned. His life suited him fine. He didn't need another wife. *Especially* not a daughter of Bulat's.

A hand touched his shoulder. Sheremetev had reached the walls in time to hear Bulat accept Papa's offer. "Your father has no choice, boy," Sheremetev said. "Too bad. I wanted you for my Darya."

One point of light amid the fog. Daniil had no desire to marry Darya, either. The negotiations had dragged on so long he had forgotten the phantom betrothal's existence.

He had enough sense not to say that to Darya's father. And given a choice, he would pick the child bride next door over the exotic tsarevna with murder in her veins. Sheremetev was right, though. No one else could make this match. And, as Sheremetev had not said, a match must be made. Even if Boris's Maria had conceived a child—and so far the family had seen no evidence of that—one infant would not secure the lineage. With Boris gone…

Daniil abandoned that train of thought. The resolution of the vendetta lay on his shoulders. A parting gift for Boris, killed by his younger brother's poor judgment. He retreated to the shadows of the wall, where he could grieve in peace.

"Why Nasan?" Ogodai asked as soon as the Tatar forces left the Kolychev compound. The red wine Nikolai had served, in blissful ignorance of Muslim custom, to seal the marriage contract still left traces of fruity richness on the tongue. Since his father had accepted the cup without comment, Ogodai had seen no reason to refuse. In truth, he rather enjoyed the taste.

"She needs a husband," Bulat said, as if this statement explained everything.

"Of course she does. But why this husband? She'll be in a strange land with a language she doesn't speak, and now they want her to change her religion as well. Aren't there any Tatar khans she could wed?"

"No," Bulat said. "Our family already holds Kazan and Astrakhan. You'll marry Firuza and take over my sworn brother's horde on the steppe, and the Crimeans hate our guts since the Russians gave Kasimov to my father. They won't take Nasan. I'm not sending her off to Samarkand or Bokhara; we'd see even less of her than if she lives in Moscow, and the rulers there are too distant to help us."

"But Daniil is nowhere near her in rank," Ogodai protested. Not something he cared about in general, but important in terms of his sister's happiness.

"A good warrior, though," Bulat said. "The Kolychevs will value her for the prestige she brings to their lineage. And she can speak on our behalf in the grand princes' court, as well as ending this feud. That seems like a good beginning to me. What are wives and daughters for, when all's said and done, if not to knit families together and make peace?"

Ogodai sighed. He was wasting his time. *Ata* had made one of his typical lightning decisions and would brook no opposition. Why bother to point out that Nasan wouldn't appreciate being handed over to the brother of Girei's murderer, despite her future husband's proven ability to seduce women—itself an attribute that ought to give a caring father pause?

"It'll do us all good," Bulat added. "A wedding will brighten everyone up. And Kolychev's young lion will be a good match for Nasan. She needs a man she can respect."

Ogodai made one last effort, although the opportunity to undo the decision had already passed. "And will her new husband and his family welcome a bride who aspires to imitate the heroines of old?"

Bulat roared with laughter. "Fortunately, Kolychev didn't ask for a submissive bride, just a pretty one. And our Nasan's a beauty—no mistake about that." He slapped Ogodai's arm. "Come on, son, let's ride. This is the time of year when raiders come up from the south, and now that we've done what we came for, I want to make the best possible speed back to Kasimov."

Ogodai couldn't argue with that. He'd never been more eager to put Moscow behind him.

The servants had laid Boris out in the icehouse. Daniil stared at a face that bore little resemblance to his brother's and tried to avoid comparisons with the slabs of meat stacked nearby.

Boris looked serene in his open coffin. The servants had restored neatness to his pale hair and trimmed the beard that church and custom required of Russian men. The high collar of his best brocade robe concealed the wound that had drained his life force so quickly. His booted feet pointed to the icehouse door and his head toward a triptych of icons that someone—probably his mother—had brought in. Those who washed and dressed him for burial had already placed the small scroll between the fingers of his right hand identifying him to St. Peter as a good Russian who had died in the Orthodox Christian faith. The scroll would ease his pathway into Heaven, especially important given his brutal death.

The candles before the icons flickered, casting shadows that set the slaves muttering about unclean spirits. Unless appeased, the ghosts of those who died by violence roamed the earth, wreaking havoc on those unlucky enough to encounter them.

Daniil could not imagine his gentle brother wreaking havoc on anyone. He raised a hand to rebuke one chattering servant, then lowered it when he recognized the woman as Grusha, arranging the ritual offering of grain and beer before the icons. Had he really lain with her a few hours ago?

"Get out of here, Grusha," he said, "and stop talking rubbish."

The words sounded harsher than he'd intended. She ran from the icehouse before he could apologize. He'd make it up to her later.

Later. Time lost its meaning, speeding up and slowing down in a whirligig of emotion. Last night, this morning, now: the usual orderly progression fractured into shards, disconnected images of a lost and broken life. Boris's life, mostly, but his family's too. Their square had become a triangle—its severed sides not yet closed, leaving a void as empty as the place that would remain vacant at the dinner table throughout the forty days of mourning.

As if anyone wanted to eat at such a juncture.

Off to one side, Daniil could hear his father talking with Father Job, the priest who served their household. The servants must have dragged Job away from his vegetable garden: a narrow strip of leather confined the priest's long hair, and mud streaked his white cassock.

"Of course, Lord," Job said in soothing tones. "We will bury him as soon as the clan assembles. But your son died by violence, unshriven and unanointed and at the hands of infidels. Some will argue that he must not lie in hallowed ground. You heard your servants just now, spreading tales of unclean spirits."

"The devil take such nonsense." Nikolai loomed over the priest, a towering presence of power and pain. "If he had died in battle, you would bury him in a churchyard."

"I know, Lord," Job repeated. "Such is not *my* view. God's law prevails. But I warn you to expect dissent."

Daniil glanced their way in time to see his father relax his tense stance. "Very well," Nikolai said. "Refer the dissenters to me. I will deal with them as they deserve."

"Yes, Lord." Job bowed and withdrew.

Daniil waited until the priest had left before he spoke. "He's right, you know. I encountered one group of mischief makers the moment I walked in the door. There are sure to be others." When his father nodded agreement, Daniil bit his lip. A hideous question tormented him, and no one offered better counsel than Nikolai. "It's terrible, Papa. I can't help wondering. If I had stopped to calculate the impact of my arrow, could I have caused that man's sword to miss Boris?"

Nikolai took three steps forward, enfolding Daniil in a bear hug. "It was God's will, son. You did your best."

Daniil nodded. People said the same after every battle, and he accepted the statement as truth. His brother had practiced a piety sufficient to gain early entrance to Heaven. God could have chosen to push the Tatar's sword aside.

So why do I still feel guilty?

Natalya Kolycheva poured claret into a goblet and handed it to her husband, relishing this small relief from the horrors of the day. Numerous miscarriages, stillbirths, and even the deaths of two toddlers had not prepared her for the agony of losing her adult son.

Usually she and Nikolai reveled in their evenings together, meeting whenever he could spare time from his duties at court or with the army. Today the sitting room seemed more like a sanctuary. Here she could be herself, not the lady of the house.

She glanced at her husband, elbows on his knees, staring at his clasped hands. As ever, her pulses leaped at the sight of him. Nikolai Kolychev in middle age was an imposing man, but Natalya saw him still as the handsome giant of their youth. Daniil had inherited that leonine strength, those classic features, his father's intelligence—combined with an insouciance entirely his own. As the eldest son of a prodigal clan, Nikolai, even at seventeen, had demonstrated a gravity unmatched by his relatives. She had seen that quality again today.

"You were magnificent this morning, Kolya." When they were alone, she used his nickname. He called her Natasha.

Kolya shook his head. "Bulat took me by surprise. Sheremetev had his troops to hand, but where were ours? Sleeping in their huts. Except for Boris's dozen, and they lacked both weapons and armor. If I had planned better, our son would be here, not laid out in the icehouse."

The grief in his voice tore at her heart. Kolya seldom revealed his emotions or even acknowledged their existence, but she knew, as none other did, the depth of his feelings.

She reached for his hand. "How could you have predicted Bulat would kill your son, and in such a fashion? To raid Moscow with fifty men? Insane."

His fingers, warm and steady, clasped her own, as they had on that long-ago day when they met and married within the hour. "That's why he did it, because no one expected it."

"Then how could you have guessed? Anyway, what brought him here? I don't believe Boris murdered his son, do you?"

"No, despite the eyewitness." He squinted at the goblet. "But whoever killed Bulat's boy expanded the fight. The Tatars balanced the scales by slaying Dmitry, but the boy's death set off another round. And once Bulat linked the murder to a Kolychev, he *would* hit back. That's Tatar justice. Russian justice, too, more often than not."

"But not yours. You chose to settle."

Kolya twirled the stem of the goblet and studied the small whirlpool this created in the wine. "Because we would fight until we ran out of kinsmen. Bulat can imagine no alternative."

He closed his eyes. Natalya clasped the hand she held in both her own, seeking comfort as well as offering it. Images of her dead son laughing, playing—his first tooth, his first steps—pounced on each word as it struggled to leave her mouth.

"Can you enforce the settlement?" she asked when speech became possible again. "Semyon can be headstrong. Daniil too, at times."

"I'll have to, won't I?" He sounded weary. "Daniil agreed to the match. He won't fight me. I'll visit Semyon in the morning."

"And invite him to the wedding?"

"He's family, Natasha. He has a right to attend."

A horrible thought occurred to her. "You don't think Semyon killed Bulat's son, do you? He looks much like Boris, and Dmitry was his brother."

Nikolai stroked his beard. "No. Semyon has his flaws, but he does listen to reason. I warned him not to seek vengeance, because attacking Bulat endangered our whole clan. He swore on the cross that he would leave the Tatars alone."

"I suppose you're right." A vow on the cross would deter most potential oath breakers. How accurate was the eyewitness, anyway? To a Tatar, she suspected, many Russian men resembled Boris.

She changed the subject. "And the girl? Her father is single-minded to a fault. Are we to welcome the child of such a man into our household? A Muslim?" *Wed her to my charming, scapegrace Daniil, still smarting from the death of his beloved Anastasia?*

No point in saying that. Anastasia's virtue had won her an early release from this sinful world. The clan needed heirs, and only Daniil could provide them. Daniil married to a virgin of ancient and illustrious lineage, not Daniil amusing himself with a strumpet from the kitchens.

The new bride might fall in love with her husband, but that happy outcome seemed unlikely. Although Daniil could lure a wild doe from the woods if he chose, the chances of him cooperating seemed slim. They were young. The young did not readily resign themselves to fate.

Nikolai shifted in his seat. The movement fixed Natalya's wandering attention on her husband. She shouldn't lose heart. If maturity could temper Nikolai's seriousness and turn her from a bashful bride into a woman capable of wielding authority over two hundred servants and as many peasants, it would also work its magic on Daniil and his wife.

"Father Job will baptize her when she arrives," Kolya said, answering her question about the bride's religion.

She tried another tack. "This girl will have her own ways, her own customs. Suppose she doesn't conform?"

His eyes crinkled at the corners. "Personally, I hope she's a hellcat."

"Kolya!"

"Sorry, my dear." He lifted his glass to her in an impromptu toast. "I realize our new bride will be your responsibility. I wish for you a meek and biddable daughter-in-law."

"Like Darya Sheremeteva. You've dashed her father's hopes."

"Sheremetev understands. Did you not see him? Daniil arrived first with the troops, but Sheremetev followed. I went to thank him when Bulat left."

She had not seen Sheremetev. She had been gathering her women to bathe and dress the corpses.

Kolya squeezed her hand. "Think, my love. Could Darya keep that young scamp of ours away from the maidservants? Do you think I dragged my feet on the negotiations for no reason? The chit's a perfect choice—for anyone but Daniil. I'd give the two of them a week. How many girls have you sent to the villages since Anastasia died?"

Natalya performed a quick mental calculation, stopping when the numbers became alarming. "A dozen at least, and several of them with child. I do wish he would find another way to cope with his grief. The housekeeper complains about him every day he's home."

"But not the girls, I'll wager. He doesn't force them, you know. They line up outside his door hoping he'll notice them."

Detecting a hint of pride in his son's sexual prowess, Natalya frowned. She'd heard the maids gossiping: Daniil—tall and strong, with tawny hair, liquid brown eyes, and a reputation for an elusive heart—set off flutters in far too many female breasts. "It's not funny, Kolya. Sometimes I despair. If only Anastasia had lived."

He regarded her, his face impenetrable. "Perhaps."

"I am sure of it." Who could doubt the power of a virtuous wife? The Lord Himself defined how women should behave by selecting Mary as His handmaiden and chasing Eve out of Eden.

"Then we ought to have found the boy another wife years ago."

"And if this one can't reform him? What then?"

Kolya pounded the arm of his chair as laughter briefly subsumed his grief. "A daughter of Bulat's? She'll take off his ears—or worse—if he strays!"

Daniil saw Grusha waiting at the doorway to his room. When he reached her, she clasped her hands, her face intent, then spoke before he could apologize for his earlier harshness. "May you have life, Lord." The standard expression of condolence to someone in mourning.

She hurried on, not waiting for a response. "I offended you with my careless chatter. Pray forgive me."

Daniil swallowed. "It's nothing. I reacted too strongly."

He studied her—the pretty face, the blue eyes misty with emotion. He didn't love her, but at that moment he needed the comfort offered by her full, responsive body—even if she took him for granted, even if it meant future trouble. In the aftermath of Boris's death, tomorrow seemed at best a fuzzy concept. Grusha was here, warm and willing and alive.

He pulled her into his arms. She yielded with a groan of pleasure. Without another thought, he picked her up and carried her to the bed, kicking the door shut behind him.

Chapter 7

NASAN LEANED HER ELBOWS ON THE WHITE STONE WALL OF the khan's palace. Beyond the fortress, beneath the ravines, the Oka flowed. Usually it rolled with magisterial calm toward the Volga, but today the water rippled in the afternoon sun, as if the river, reminded of its long-lost youth by the changing season, raced in joy toward its destination.

One of the Oka's tributaries circled Moscow, where Ogodai and Bulat pursued their drive for retaliation against the Kolychevs. At first, riders had appeared at regular intervals with messages for Sumbeka, reassuring her of the raiders' safety. No courier had reached Kasimov in almost a week. The atmosphere at home had become tense.

Nasan, too, yearned for news that her father's campaign had ended in victory and without injury to those she loved. The fear that she might lose more family members darkened the beauty around her. She said a quick prayer for the men's safe return.

Such extremes of emotion had become her life. Yet three months after Girei's death, the family was learning that life went on. Fewer dreams troubled Nasan, and she spent more nights in her own chamber. When she did roam, her search for people in need often led her outside the gardens. As time passed, her courage revived. She lost patience with her parents' restrictions, but the vow of obedience, sworn on the Koran and over the hearth fire, constrained her. Bulat had ordered her to remain within the fortress unless she traveled with an escort, and she must comply.

Staying within the walls did not limit her much. The town offered plenty of opportunities for atonement. Did *Ata* and *Ana* know how many townspeople needed help? Nasan had not known until her ventures into the streets revealed an underground Kasimov filled with wives hiding from abusive husbands, lost children, servants kept from their beds by illness or fear, a kitten trapped in a tree. Accustomed to life in a nomadic horde, where no one's good or bad fortune remained secret for long, Nasan had not guessed how much misery the night could conceal.

The streets of Kasimov drew her with the promise of what she had loved about the nomadic camp: the freedom and the challenge of pitting her wits against another's. Some of her rescues involved fighting; most did not. The law operated with speed and efficiency in Kasimov, and Nasan had no qualms about reporting violators to the relevant authorities. She didn't need to overpower a miscreant to feel justified; the knowledge that she had righted a wrong made her happy. The credit side of her soul's ledger grew with each good deed.

To conceal her identity, she tied a scarf over her head and another across her face, revealing only her eyes. Tales of the mysterious black-clad savior swirled about the town, but the gossips did not guess that their latest hero was a woman. Rumor favored a ghost sent by the grandmothers. Nasan had seen the shock in people's faces when she emerged from a dark alley, watched them clutch amulets to their chests in superstitious awe, heard them muttering prayers even as they tried to catch their breath to thank her.

As the nights passed, she lingered longer in the shadows, attacking from behind at the last moment. To placate the town's guard dogs, she left home with a stash of dried meat stolen from the palace kitchens. Soon they learned her scent and stopped barking when she appeared, slinking into the night in pursuit of thrown treats. Their failure to announce her presence added to her legend and further protected her from exposure. The more people thought her a magical creature of the night, the less they could imagine any connection with the khan's daughter.

This morning, just before dawn, the grandmothers had sent a message she could not mistake. A dream in which the blond Russian from the forest strode toward Girei with the dagger in his hands, but as he drew close, a bow and arrow materialized on the hillock before her. Nasan grabbed the weapon and shot. The monster's huge body thudded against the snow, his last breath escaping with a whoosh. The troops swarmed toward her, but like the heroines of old, she dispatched them one by one, not missing a single target. In the end, the survivors fled screaming into the woods and left her brother unharmed.

Her father had told her to pray for guidance, and at last it had come. The ancestors had tested her resolve. They wanted her not to give up but to work harder for victory. That meant honing her skills, so that when they called her into service, she would be ready. So today she would travel *outside* the walls. Taking an escort as ordered, but returning—for the first time since her brother's death—to the clearing where she and Girei had spent their last hours before the ambush.

Snow no longer lined the river road, and leaves the bright green of early spring softened the oak and birch trees. But Nasan, imagining the clearing on that winter day, missed Girei. The other members of her family loved her when she met their expectations. Only he had shared her vision of a world that would value her for her flaws.

She wiped away her tears. Useless to weep or to rail against fate. She must find a way to control her own destiny. Nasan left the playful river and went to fetch her dead brother's helmet, filled with his scent and his essence.

As she crossed the entryway, the dolls housing the grandmothers' spirits caught her eye. Small silk bodies about the length of her hand, embroidered in detail from their enormous eyes to their tiny toes and fingers, elaborately dressed in robes like those Nasan herself wore on ceremonial occasions, beads and feathers adorning the headdresses that covered their horsehair coiffures, they sat in the place of honor to the northwest of the hearth. She stopped in front of them, brushed her fingers across their lips, and bowed her head. She had not fed them since the day they took Girei. Yet they had continued to support her, to guide her through dreams. She pleaded for their forgiveness and asked them to look after her brother's soul, to guard Bulat and Ogodai in Moscow, and to watch over her as she moved forward on the trail they had laid for her.

The wind ruffled her hair. The grandmothers had answered. Nasan took a deep breath of contentment and headed for her room, making sure to avoid her mother as she went.

With the arrival of spring, the soldiers had set up a straw man in the clearing to use for target practice. Nasan had timed her visit with care: the troops not pursuing vengeance in Moscow had duties that kept them in the fortress, and she and her escort had full use of the space. She stationed her men at opposite sides of the clearing, then walked toward the open ground, swinging her bow. Her quiver hung from her left shoulder, within easy reach. She had twisted her hip-length black hair into a tight knot to keep it from getting in her way, so the cool winds blew against her neck. Despite the breeze, Girei's armor and helmet on top of her jacket, trousers, and tight male sash caused her to perspire. She paid no attention. A warrior does not complain of minor discomforts.

Approaching the edge of the ground, she strung her bow, steadied her stance, and shot. The string hummed past her ear as she released the arrow. The bone plate that strengthened the natural suppleness of the wood warmed her hand. She pulled another arrow from her quiver, drew her right arm as far behind her shoulder as she could, turning her body sideways to the target, and loosed another shot.

She felt a twinge in her shoulder and realized the cost of weeks without practice. Her arm and back would ache by tomorrow morning. Even so, she had not lost her skill. Both arrows, she noted with satisfaction, struck home.

Her pony whinnied. Sorkhokhtani, too, had missed their daily exercise. Nasan pulled a treat from the pouch at her belt. The mare's ears flickered as she ate. Nasan petted her, then whispered to her and went to stand in front of the target.

About three horse lengths separated Nasan from the mare. Tucking her bow into its case and attaching it at her left hip, she took a deep breath and raced toward Sorkhokhtani, leaping onto the saddle and tucking her feet into the stirrups. The mare went from standing to full gallop in the flick of an eye, circling the target, sweeping by the place where Nasan had begun her run. One of the escorts laughed, saluting her as she dashed past his post.

The wind whipped Nasan's face, and a whoop of joy broke from her mouth. As she approached the far side of the circle, she pulled her bow from its case, stood in her stirrups, and shot at the target. Dropping back onto her seat, she drew the pony to a halt and examined the results.

A miss. She had to train harder. Ogodai would have hit it. So would Girei.

"Timing, Khanim," the second man said. "You need to shoot from where the horse will be, not where it is. And stand sooner, so that your aim is steady before you release the arrow."

She winced. Girei used to say the same. So short a time into her training, the knot had reappeared in her throat.

Had she come to practice or to mourn? No amount of weeping would retrieve Girei from the hunting grounds of the dead. She swallowed her tears, thanked the man for his advice, and tried again. And again. Each time she drew closer. After a dozen tries, the rhythm worked its way into her muscles. No arrow hit the center, but more landed on the target than not.

Her mare blew air through her nostrils. Nasan patted the glossy neck, where a pulse beat rapidly under her fingers. "Good girl, Sorkhokhtani." She pulled a carrot from her saddle bag and leaned forward to feed it to the horse.

"I'll keep working," she told the men. "Sorkhokhtani and I have had enough for today." As she kneed her pony toward the main road that ran along the embankment, she heard her escort fall into line behind her.

At the river, she stopped. In her mind the water turned to ice, sunshine bleached the sky, and packed snow covered the earthen road. "Bet you can't catch me," Girei's remembered voice shouted. Nasan slipped from her horse and buried her face against the silky mane. Memories inundated her: the tricks she and Girei had played on each other, the thrill of beating him in a race, the warning shriek he gave as he launched one of his surprise attacks.

Her shoulders shook, and her hands tightened in her patient companion's mane. Here, by the water, no one paid attention to her; the people were locals, focused on their vessels or their crafts. When she could, she raised her head, gazing at the horizon. The men waited in respectful silence.

The flat plain extended along the river, then blended into woodlands. Kasimov lay north of the grasslands that had given the Mongols their start, yet the Eternal Blue Sky her ancestors had worshipped loomed over the whole like an upside-down bowl. She breathed deeply, inhaling flowers and fresh grass. Her booted toe touched the pony's hoof. Time to go home. She mounted and cast a lingering glance at the road bordering the Oka.

A troop of soldiers had come into view. As she watched, uncertain whether to sound the alarm, she recognized her father's nine-horsetail standard.

"*Ata!*" she yelled at the top of her voice. Forgetting everything but joy at her family's safe return, Nasan set her pony flying toward the advancing troops. The hooves of her escort's horses thundered behind her.

An hour later, Nasan stood in her room. After a furious tirade about her leaving the fortress even with an escort—and how, pray, could she have known that Crimean raiders were camped south of Ryazan?—*Ata* had ordered her to change her clothes and report to him at once. Ogodai refused to explain why. Refused to say anything, in fact, except when she asked about Boris Kolychev. Her enemy was dead. The soldier who killed him had given his life in the raid. *Mashallah*, the Tatars had suffered no other casualties.

She felt only relief at Ice Man's death. The small part of her that had crouched in a corner of her mind, worried that he might return to ambush her again, crept toward the sun. The news of invading forces from the south was troubling, for sure, but she trusted her father to let no harm come to her and her mother. She would obey his every command until the raiders left.

But why did *Ata* want to see her? He'd scolded her already. It wasn't like him to rant at her twice.

Ana had already gone downstairs, leaving Nasan in Tanya's care. Tanya—once a rival khan's concubine, a Slavic beauty stolen and enslaved in Crimea—tugged the helmet from Nasan's head, then removed the borrowed clothing, grumbling as she worked. "And why you can't act like the young lady you are, I'll never know," she finished.

Nasan sighed. No one understood. But the muttering would continue if she protested, so she kept quiet and washed herself with jasmine-scented soap. The tight knot at her nape released, and hair uncurled along her back. Tanya ran a carved ivory comb through the strands, then braided them while Nasan donned silk under-tunic and trousers and topped them with her favorite pink brocade robe.

"What Father want?" Nasan asked as Tanya looped the finished braid over one shoulder. She spoke in Russian. Despite some resistance from Tanya, who claimed she had almost forgotten her native tongue, Nasan had kept her promise to herself, made on the day of the ambush. But Russian took time to master, even for someone who spoke four languages already, and she could manage halting phrases at best.

Tanya, a virtuoso in the art of gossip, did not disappoint her mistress. The Russian leaned forward and murmured, "Man."

Man? Nasan frowned, then remembered the word also meant "husband." "Who?" she asked as Tanya wrapped a broad sash around her waist.

Tanya shook her head. "You won't learn the answer from me, Khanim. Your mother would skin me alive. But you don't want to stay here forever as your brother's dependent, do you? Better to run your own household."

The maid had fallen into Tatar again from the moment she used Nasan's title, "khan's daughter." "Speak Russian, Tanya," Nasan reminded her.

"Yes, Khanim." Tanya made a face but complied.

"I miss the steppe," Nasan said. "I want to go home." Images danced in her head: the vast grasslands dotted with round tents of white felt, herds of sheep and goats as far as the eye could see, spirit banners waving, clouds the shape of winged steeds racing across endless blue sky on their way from Hungary to China. There, while winds soughed in the feather grass, horses would call to one another outside a south-facing tent that belonged only to her. There she could ride from dawn to dusk if she liked and no one would complain…

"It won't happen," practical Tanya said. "Marriage is politics, Khanim. And whom would you wed? Most of the nomads have no khan, only beys. Beneath your station."

"Kazan, then?" she asked. But no, her father wouldn't give her there. His younger half-brother already ruled in Kazan. "Astrakhan?" The khan there was a relative too, but more distant.

Tanya laughed and shook her head. "Your father will tell you."

Nasan grimaced at the brass mirror, watching nimble Russian fingers arrange strings of pearls around her neck.

Tanya picked up a sleeveless silk coat of forest green, embroidered with flowers and leaves in shades ranging from the palest pink to the rose of Nasan's sash, and eased Nasan's arms into it. She smiled and spoke in Tatar. "Remember, Khanim, if your husband proves unpleasant, you will not have to endure him alone. Junior wives and concubines will share the burden. There are advantages to being Muslim."

Nasan groaned. Another harem. "Please, Tanya. I can't stand the suspense. What have you heard?"

"Off with you, Khanim," Tanya said. "Your parents don't like to wait."

Nasan slipped her feet into embroidered slippers and turned. "Am I presentable?"

Tanya's fingers grazed her cheek. "Lovely. Now go."

Running down to her father's receiving room, Nasan tingled with apprehension. Life was changing before her eyes, and she had no reason to think she would like the result.

As she crossed the threshold, Nasan bowed to her parents. Bulat gestured, and in response she sank onto a pile of cushions. The same pile she had occupied the day Bulat and Ogodai had decided to raid the Russians' house—one more fading echo of Girei's murder.

Nervous, she rubbed tassels between her fingers. No Ogodai today, only herself and her parents. Something serious was afoot.

Bulat still wore his riding clothes: loose trousers tucked inside embroidered leather boots, layered tunics with long narrow sleeves. Sumbeka sat next to him, her robes similar to Nasan's except that her caftan lacked the defined waist of a maiden's dress. As always when Nasan saw them together, it struck her how similar they seemed, as though their personalities had merged over their decades of marriage. Sumbeka's colors were brighter, her fabrics softer, her features more delicate, her hair more elaborately arranged, but these differences were superficial compared to the identical expressions on her face and Bulat's.

Usually that expression meant someone was in trouble. Herself, in this case. Nasan shivered. Could they have learned of her activities in the town? Sooner or later, the news would reach their ears. And they might consider her behavior a violation of her oath, even though she had taken care not to disobey any direct command.

Tanya had not mentioned it, though. The maid heard everything that went on. Tanya had not chided Nasan or warned her. Instead, she'd talked of marriage.

"Ogodai says he told you," Bulat began, "that we killed Boris Kolychev."

Sumbeka's lips tightened, but she did not speak.

"We have defended our honor," Bulat went on. "Both families have suffered. But if we leave matters there, we cannot guarantee that the Kolychevs will refrain from another attack."

Nasan felt a sinking sensation in the pit of her stomach. Blood feud, potential solution, private conference with her parents: these things did not bode well. What did *Ata* have in mind?

He told her. "Kolychev has proposed a marriage between you, Nasan, and his son Daniil, and I have agreed."

"I won't!" Nasan jumped to her feet, hands clenched. "Marry the brother of my enemy? I will run away. I will kill myself first."

Bulat rose from the bench and roared. "Yes, you will. I am your father, and I have given my word. We signed the contract. We accepted the betrothal gifts. We set a date for the wedding."

You sold me? Nasan bit her tongue, lest the unforgivable words break free. She knew what *Ata* meant: he had agreed to the match, and he would accept no defiance from her.

"You will not disgrace me," Bulat said in biting tones, as if he could read her mind. "You have had too much freedom for too long, and look at you. You run about, more hoyden than khanim. And you dare to contradict your father. I will not have it. This time you do what I tell you. Without question, Nasan."

"I hate you!"

She would have run from the room, but Sumbeka clamped onto her wrist. "Behave yourself. Will you shame me before my husband, before our kin, before the ancestors?" Nasan sat.

Sumbeka released her and held up a hand to quiet Bulat. She narrowed her eyes at Nasan, who did not dare look away. "Listen to me, Nasan. Your father arranged this match for the good of the clan. That is his right—and his duty. You will marry this Russian boy, and you will represent us in his house."

I will not!

Her rebellion must have shown on her face, because Bulat's forehead creased in a scowl guaranteed to set any hardened warrior quivering in his boots, and Sumbeka's eyebrows compressed into a single line.

"If you cooperate," Sumbeka said, "you will save lives. You will atone for your prior disobedience and your part in Girei's death. You will do what a woman *should* do—make peace for her family. And if your husband dies—although not before, Nasan—you may come home."

"But if you do not," Bulat interjected, his voice harsh, "I will cast you out as I did your older brother Tulpar. The grandmothers will reject you. You can never come home: not in this lifetime, not in the next. Is that what you want? To live without kin? To kill others as you did Girei?"

Nasan studied the tassels, determined not to cry. She remembered her brother Tulpar—not well, because he had left the family before she turned six, but well enough to get her father's point. *Ata* had banished Tulpar, who had died in exile. If she refused to cooperate, she would face the same fate.

Even *Ana* and *Ata* regarded her as a pawn. They watched her, the tormentors who hid behind her parents' eyes. Only this morning she had received her vision from the grandmothers. And now this?

The spirits were testing her again. Bulat laid out a stark choice: obey or spend eternity alone, abandoned not only by the living but by the dead and the unborn.

I can live alone. Dress as a boy and join some Tatar army where no one knows me.

Girei reproached her. "Your love is worthless, sister, if you place yourself above our clan." She heard the words as clearly as if he had wafted into the room to speak them.

Indeed, she could not live without her family. A person belonged to a community, or she was prey to every vicious force—animal, human, and spirit.

Very well. She would wed the Russian. She could not watch her relatives die when she had the means to save them. And she would not make the mistake Tulpar had made.

Her father's face softened. "I'm sorry, Nasan, but you have to marry someday. And Kolychev and I must settle this before we lose more kinsmen."

Nasan studied the patterns on the rug at her feet, unwilling to surrender her anger. "Yes, *Ata*."

Her father gently tugged her braid. "Thank you, my child."

Nasan looked up, startled by the warmth in his voice. Next to him, her mother was smiling.

"You'll see, Nasan. It won't be so bad," Bulat said. "The boy is Ogodai's *qarïndash*. Go and talk to your brother. And you, wife, please ask Tanya to pack. You leave in three days."

Nasan's knees shook as she stood and bowed. As she left the room, she heard Sumbeka speak. "Three days? She's not ready. And what do you mean, *we* leave? Will you not attend her wedding?"

"If I can. But I told you what we learned in Ryazan. That villain in Crimea has forty thousand men camped south of the

Oka, Safa-Girei and Islam-Girei in joint command. I must defend Kasimov, but I want you and Nasan out of here. Ogodai will protect you, and you can stay at Shah-Ali's estate near the Kremlin." Bulat sounded weary. "As for the preparations, do your best. I'll find her a tutor. But ready or not, you set off on Thursday."

Sumbeka contemplated her husband, fidgeting in his seat as if he couldn't wait for her to leave. No point in asking him what Daniil Kolychev was like. In Bulat's mind, a boy who took orders and performed well in battle made the perfect husband.

But he would expect Sumbeka to convince their daughter. And *that* was going to be difficult. Sumbeka would have spared the girl this marriage if she could, but she had not tried to dissuade Bulat, who had already signed the papers.

"Which of our people will you send with her?" she asked. A khan's daughter did not travel alone to the lands of her husband. She brought her dowry, which remained under her control and would one day support her daughters. She also brought servants— many servants. Just so had Tanya come with Sumbeka from Crimea. The custom ensured that the bride's new clan could not isolate and demean her. Yet the families selected would also need to prepare for the move.

Bulat's tanned skin darkened. Even before he spoke, Sumbeka guessed from the way he twisted his hands what he would say. "None. There is no time to gather them before you leave. Besides, the Kolychevs cannot accommodate Muslim servants, and I will not require my people to convert. Bad enough that Nasan must do so."

"Husband, no!"

"Wife, yes," he said, his voice flat. "While the marriage lasts. Longer, if she bears sons. As for the servants, I have agreed to increase her dowry by an equivalent amount."

"That will raise her prestige, but she needs people of her own. A dowry cannot speak on her behalf." With an effort, Sumbeka kept her seat, hands resting in her lap. Open opposition made Bulat more stubborn, but she had not ruled his harem for two decades without learning how to govern him. Nothing would induce her to deprive her child of every link with home. Sumbeka recalled her own first days of marriage, the difficulty of the adjustment. Intimacy with a stranger strained the capacity of any bride.

She offered the simplest solution first. "What about Tanya? She's Russian."

"And Muslim by choice," he said. "No. Nikolai Kolychev is a decent man. He will not mistreat our daughter."

Perhaps not, but he had family. And who could guess what Nikolai Kolychev would do when he had Nasan in his power? Sumbeka waited, allowing her displeasure to show on her face.

"I'll send a courier every week," Bulat growled after a while.

"I will tell her to write often." Sumbeka crossed her arms and looked straight at him. "And between letters?"

He refused to meet her eyes. She sat and watched him, neither moving nor speaking.

At last he rose and strode about the room, kicking pillows ahead of him. "Oh, very well. I swear that when this year's campaign ends, I will hire a household for her. Russians, Christians, but they will answer to us, not to the Kolychevs. Will that satisfy you?"

"Yes. Thank you, husband." She would ensure he kept his promise—and impress on Nasan the need to write long and truthful letters.

"I should talk to her," she added, now that they had settled that question, "before she takes out her anger on Ogodai."

"I had no alternative." Bulat sounded defensive.

"I understand. *She* understands. But we don't have to live with your decision; she does. Even a submissive girl would balk at such a match."

This simple observation had an unanticipated effect. His shoulders slumped. "It's my fault," he said. "You tried to prepare her, but I let her think she could evade her destiny. I saw it when she dashed toward me on that mare of hers. Forty thousand Crimean warriors on the way, eager to grab any woman they see, and she hadn't a thought of danger. I like having a daughter who rides and shoots better than the boys. But she believes she can make her own rules, and I have no one but myself to blame."

How to respond, when he spoke the truth? Sumbeka said nothing, and after a while Bulat waved her away. "Talk to her, then."

Hating the necessity, she left to search for their daughter.

She hadn't far to go. Tanya had cornered Nasan in the main corridor and was remonstrating with her. "Khanim, you cannot," she said as Sumbeka joined them. "Ogodai Sultan is in the stables. You will ruin your fine slippers and gown if you go there."

At the sight of her mother, Nasan pulled her arm out of Tanya's grasp.

"Come with me, child. We have matters to discuss." Sumbeka dismissed Tanya with a nod. "I won't let her visit the stables in these clothes."

She led Nasan to the family area and pushed her onto the nearest bench. A plate of pastries stood on an ebony table inlaid with lighter woods. Next to the tray Sumbeka saw a brass pot with a long, elegant spout. Steam perfumed the air with the distinctive grassy scent of green tea.

She poured a cup and offered it to Nasan, who shook her head. Sumbeka sipped the drink herself. It calmed her nerves. "Pastry?" She indicated the platter with one hand.

"I'm not hungry." Nasan hesitated, then blurted out, "*Ana*, how could *Ata* marry me to a Russian? To *that* Russian, whose brother killed Girei?"

"You know the answer as well as I," she said. "I will help you as much as I can. Everyone marries a stranger."

Her daughter's mouth compressed in a stubborn line.

"Ogodai liked him, Nasan. That must count for something."

"I don't care. I won't submit to a Russian barbarian, whoever he is."

Sumbeka, tempted to laugh at that militant declaration, stopped. Despite her surface defiance, Nasan was close to tears. With intense nostalgia, she recalled the plucky five-year-old who had fought her way into the boys' games and bested them. Her heart ached for that indomitable spirit.

And for herself. She would miss these exchanges. "I told you before, my sweet, marriage is not about submission. Cooperate with your husband, and he will want to cooperate with you."

"I won't cooperate with any Russian whose family killed my brother."

Sumbeka sighed. Nasan would learn. Life teaches us, whether we like its lessons or not.

"Go and find Ogodai, then." She placed her empty cup on the table and smoothed her daughter's hair. "But first, change your clothes."

"You knew, and you didn't tell me." Nasan hurled the words at her brother. Dressed in her oldest robes, she swung on the door of an empty stall, her arms hooked over the top.

"*Ata* asked me not to." He cracked his whip against the post. "And I could guess you'd have a fit. Not that I blame you." He untied a black velvet pouch from his belt and held it up. "Look, I bought you a present."

She didn't want to be distracted like a child. Her anger warmed her, and she clung to it. But Ogodai, oblivious, pulled his gifts from the pouch and dangled them before her face. Two matching golden chains, each with a stylized lynx hanging from it. "They reminded me of you. The trader in Ryazan claimed they come from an ancient steppe people, although I don't know that I believe him.

Russian merchants will say anything to clinch a sale. Still, aren't they gorgeous?"

Gorgeous, yes. Almost alive. The lynxes drew her with their beauty. Ogodai spoke truth: the unknown artist had captured, in the unlikely medium of metal, the elegant lines and contained power one saw in forest animals.

A spirit lynx had appeared on the day of Girei's death. She had not mentioned that to anyone. Only the grandmothers knew. And Girei himself, now that he hunted with them. A thrill shot through her. A message, perhaps, that she had taken the right path. She stepped away from the gate and extended a hand.

Ogodai dropped the chains and their enclosing pouch into her palm. "A wedding gift," he said. "One for you, one for Daniil—if you choose to share it with him."

Nasan tucked the pouch into her belt and ran the chains through her fingers, caressing the lynxes in the same way she stroked her pony. She hated Daniil because of Girei. Because of Ice Man. But for some reason Ogodai didn't. She needed to understand why. "You and Daniil are sworn brothers."

He kicked a tuft of hay. "Were. Not since Girei's death."

"If I marry him, you will be brothers again."

"I had a brother. The Kolychevs killed him. I don't forget that." He shrugged. "I don't think Daniil forgets it either. Last time I saw him, he had an arrow aimed at my throat."

"He threatened to shoot you? And you're not angry? Men are so strange."

"I was raiding his house, *sengel*. He fought back." He studied the tip of his crop as it snapped against the wood.

"So you're friends again?"

"No. Brothers can be enemies. Look at our uncles: they'd kill each other for Kazan."

She tried again. "Tell me about him. What kind of man is he?"

"Like that." Ogodai tapped the lynx dangling from her fingers. "Light brown hair, brown eyes. Tall, strong, quick, fun to be around.

Easygoing. He should have been wed by now. I heard something about the sweet young thing next door. Daniil didn't act like he wanted to settle down, though."

Nasan dropped both chains into the velvet pouch and tied it to her sash. She shouldn't have asked. Now her brother imagined her trying to please his obnoxious no-longer-*qarïndash*. "I don't care what he wants. He means nothing to me."

Ogodai laughed. "He has women by the score. Watch out, *sengel*. You could lose your heart."

Worse and worse. An obnoxious, womanizing no-longer-*qarïndash*. "I am not like other girls." She used her loftiest tone.

That only made her horrible brother laugh harder. No wonder he and Daniil were friends. Nasan went to talk to her mare. For sure, no one else understood a thing.

Chapter 8

Moscow, Dhu l'Hijja 940 A.H. / June 1534

THE WEDDING PARTY DID NOT LEAVE KASIMOV THAT THURSDAY. Bulat had not spent more than a full day at home before messengers arrived from Ryazan with orders to move out and meet the enemy on the other side of the river. Bulat deployed one portion of his men around the fortress, charged Ogodai with the defense of Kasimov, and departed with the rest of his forces across the Oka. From atop the walls, Nasan watched troops pouring in from Moscow and points west. She heard the roar of cannon, the howls of the invaders and the screams of those invaded, but although couriers arrived regularly with news of devastation in the lands beyond the river—many of them occupied by people in service to Kasimov—the raiders did not reach the citadel.

As May turned to June, her father and his men returned, flush with victory. Three days later, Sumbeka declared the whole family ready to set off. Even then, the journey proceeded slowly. A bride could not arrive without her trousseau, so every afternoon, long before sunset, the riders halted and set up their tents, waiting for the wagons to catch up. Nasan's father and brother grumbled at every meal about how they could have reached Moscow in half the time.

Sumbeka ignored their complaints. Nasan treasured each moment of delay. She had accepted the necessity of marriage, not the unknown husband. A woman chaser, Ice Man's brother. She couldn't decide which was worse. Throughout the long ride, *Ana* deluged her with anecdotes, explanations, advice. Nasan half-listened. What use to know that marriage to a kinsman took effort when she faced a union with someone she hated? Why learn arts to allure a man she didn't want? She would live with him as agreed, but no one could force her to *like* him.

Yet she couldn't shake the memory of Ogodai describing his sworn brother. A lynx, golden and deadly—the perfect image for an intimate enemy. Her rebellious heart wove the pictures into her dreams. Or was that the grandmothers, working their magic? Nasan rejected the idea, as she rejected Daniil, but the question tugged at her mind.

And so it went, push and pull, for two and a half weeks, until the time finally came for Nasan to emerge from her palanquin. The noonday sun beat down on her head as she pulled her gauze veil into place and straightened her scarlet robe. From her pearl-strewn headdress to the curled toes of her velvet slippers, her finery proclaimed her clan's honor to the world.

Ahead of her stood the most bizarre house she had ever seen. A decorated tree in which she would be expected to nest—denied the soothing gurgle of water pouring from a hundred fountains, the intricate patterns of sunshine reflected through grille work, the fragrance of sandalwood and spices. In her most fevered imaginings, she had not considered the prospect of life in a wooden box. The grandmothers whispered, "Daughter of Ashina, remember your heritage."

Her heritage. But who was she, when even her name had changed?

And hadn't *that* turned out to be a disgusting experience? After purifying herself as was proper, she had realized within moments of entering the unfamiliar building that the people around her smelled as if they hadn't bathed in a week. Standing half-naked in front of a crowd of witnesses, dunked in chilly water, daubed with oil by a bearded stranger who muttered one incomprehensible phrase after another and kissed her on both cheeks as if her inundation married her to *him*, Nasan reeled from one shock to the next. Another old man whose name she didn't catch during their hasty introduction stood at her side. He kissed her, too, when the priest pronounced her "Irina"—explaining that the name meant "peace," in honor of the truce her marriage brought. For the first time since she had crossed the threshold, he spoke clearly enough for her to follow.

Worse was to come. After stripping her of her name and her dignity, the priest launched into another round of prayers that ended when he placed a small square of bread on her tongue and told her not to chew it because it was the Body of Christ. She had to stand there, trying not to gag, while he prayed some more. As she felt the last crumb dissolve in her mouth, he handed her a cup of wine and told her it was blood. Her brother and father drank wine once in a while, but women never did—and *blood*? Were these Christians insane? She almost spat the dreadful stuff out on the priest's embroidered shoes.

In retrospect, she wished she had. *That* would have put paid to this wedding. But Girei's soul had crouched on her shoulder, urging her to persevere.

The spirits could find her in Moscow, at least. And they might like the tree house, with its echoes of the forest. When she had a chance, she would ask the grandmother her father's man had carved from the fallen limb of a birch tree. The doll lay tucked inside her favorite chest, atop her sword and Girei's smuggled clothes, ready to bless her new home.

Bulat and Ogodai dismounted. Sumbeka climbed out of the palanquin. Nasan turned from her contemplation of the house to find her family gathered around her.

"Time to go in," Sumbeka said.

The house boasted an outside staircase, roofed to ward off inclement weather. No rain today: the June sun chased every cloud from the sky, and the heat was stifling. Nasan's white veil blocked the slightest breeze. She fought the urge to tear it from her head and trample it against the planks that lined the courtyard.

Bulat prodded her in the ribs. Skirts tangled her feet as she inched toward the stairway. At the top waited a gray-haired man in robes of gold silk; a woman with a broad, friendly face; and a pouty redheaded girl. No lynx-like young man. Nasan relaxed, then tensed again, unable to decide whether she preferred to end the suspense or not.

Behind her, Ogodai argued with Bulat. "Go," *Ata* said. "With all the troublemakers here, we don't need you nursing a grudge. It's your sister's wedding, and I will have order."

Whatever Ogodai snarled under his breath provoked a roar from *Ata*. Ogodai stood his ground, but not for long. Whispering "Good luck" to Nasan as he passed, he ran to greet the three Russians before returning to street level and disappearing through a side entrance. Nasan resumed her climb.

At last she reached the top. The tall man introduced himself as Nikolai Kolychev and the women as his wife, Natalya, and his daughter-in-law, Maria.

Nasan searched Nikolai's face, looking for signs of Ice Man. The same blue eyes, but not so pale, and the crinkles at their corners suggested kindness. Natalya hugged her, pressing cheek to cheek against the veil. Nasan relaxed. Perhaps this would not be so bad.

Then Maria said, "Welcome, sister," hissing "sister" as if it were a synonym for "snake." She kissed Nasan's veiled forehead and stepped away, ostentatiously wiping her lips against her sleeve. Nasan stared, shocked by such blatant hostility.

Then she realized Maria must be Ice Man's widow. She had not pictured him with a family, let alone married to this girl her own age, still living in his parents' house. Angry, as if she mourned him. Wanting revenge against his killers, with only Nasan nearby. Her heart beat faster again.

Sumbeka greeted the Kolychevs and ushered Nasan through the door. Inside, a crowd of faces converged on her. Her head spun as one stranger after another grabbed her and kissed her on both cheeks. What kind of savages didn't know that kissing was for husbands and wives, not for any stranger who walked into your house?

A sobbing breath escaped her. *Ana* slipped an arm around her waist, murmuring soothing phrases in Tatar. Nasan whispered her thanks, only to blush when Sumbeka squeezed her hand. She had to remember: a bride should remain silent, except to take her vows. At least the Russians understood that.

"Stay here." Sumbeka slipped into the crowd. Nasan managed not to clutch her mother's sleeve. Nikolai Kolychev passed her, leading Bulat to join the boyars. *Ata* ignored the pleading glance she sent his way.

Chattering women surrounded her. They spoke at top speed, sentences spilling over one another until they sounded like a flock of starlings. Nasan made no attempt to follow the thread. *Ata* had kept his promise to supply a Russian tutor, and her grasp of the language had improved a good deal since that day in the forest, but this inundation of sound overwhelmed her.

Freed from the need to converse, glad that guests had stopped mauling her for a while, she surveyed the room. Tension hung in the air like a pall of smoke. Nikolai, Natalya, Bulat, and Sumbeka exuded hospitality as they moved among the guests, but the room divided into clusters of Tatars here, tight groups of Russians there, with no intermingling. The clan leaders had declared a truce and banned weapons from the ceremony, but more than one hand rested on the hilt of the eating knife every person carried. Troublemakers, Bulat called them. He was right.

Nasan shivered, wondering if her sacrifice would, in the end, bring peace. A nearby group of women drew her gaze. The Russian guests blended together—brown eyes, brown hair, beige skin. But this group contained a striking blonde, dramatic in sunshine yellow, her hand on the arm of a slender girl in sky blue. They were talking to Ice Man's widow.

Maria, too, stood out from the crowd. Pleasant or not, she was beautiful, with coppery hair, dark eyes, and creamy skin. She did not wear black, like a Tatar in mourning, but a robe the color of flame over an ivory tunic. Her loose caftan sported a rounded collar and ankle-length false sleeves.

"Daniil," the girl in blue said. "Barbarian. Not *Christian.*"

She spoke in full sentences, of course, but Nasan grasped only those four words. She could guess whom the girl considered a barbarian. Not Daniil, for sure.

Barbarian, indeed. Russians did not read the Koran in Arabic or quote Persian love poems. *They* did not live in exquisite palaces adorned with patterned rugs and silken cushions. Did their tree houses have running water? Unlikely!

Maria scowled. "Absurd, Darya. How Daniil marry not Christian?"

"Friend her, then?"

Nasan frowned. What difference did it make to Darya? Yet she felt a flicker of hope. In this alien household, she would miss not only her mother but her aunts and cousins—yes, even the concubines, with their endless gossip about how to attract a man. If Maria could overcome her resentment enough to befriend...

"When I die!" Maria said.

Nasan understood *that.* She leaned forward to say, "Same here."

Her mother appeared from nowhere, grabbed her shoulder, and hissed in Tatar, "Silence. Silly chicks squawk loudly. Let them fluff their feathers and preen."

Nasan clamped her mouth shut. Despite her brave front, she was shaking. She had agreed to go through with the wedding, and she would. But if life proved intolerable, she knew what to do. Her hands clenched, touching the knife hidden in her brocade sleeve.

Grusha must have been lurking nearby for a while, waiting for Daniil's male relatives to leave. She darted in the moment the last boyar heaved his bulk through the door and flung both arms around Daniil's neck.

He fended her off, but she clung with surprising determination. Hadn't they said their goodbyes this morning? Yet here she was, weeping and carrying on as if his wedding actually meant something. Beyond an opportunity to leave the house without wondering whether Tatars would kill everyone inside before he returned, that is.

He did his best to calm her without letting her stain his wedding robe. Although it was flattering to have such an impact on any woman, he wasn't a complete fool. At any moment, the uncles would return to collect him. And Grusha's sobs lacked conviction. The two of them hadn't exchanged anything but pleasure, had never spoken of fidelity (which he didn't want and felt pretty certain she couldn't offer). As for love, if such a thing existed, it had nothing to do with them. So whatever had her weeping as if a thunder cloud had unloaded its stored water over his head didn't involve genuine emotion. Pique, maybe.

The sound of a fist smacking wood preceded by an instant a familiar voice. "What the… You're contracted to marry my sister. *Today.*"

"Ogodai." Daniil looked up. "You have a nerve, showing your face." But his sworn brother's arrival solved one problem. He patted Grusha on the rump. "Off with you, love. And cheer up. It's a wedding, not a funeral."

Ogodai lounged against the jamb, forcing the girl to brush past him as she left. Annoyed, definitely.

He had a point. People don't expect to find their sister's bridegroom embracing a weeping servant. But what brought him here? Sworn brothers or not, they had nothing to say to each other.

"A lot is riding on this truce, you know," Ogodai said. "You don't have to like it, but you agreed to it. You could make an effort."

"Sorry," Daniil said, meaning nothing of the sort. "We've been lovers for years."

"Years? That's not like you." Ogodai cursed under his breath, and six months of war evaporated in a flash. Their time in Sheremetev's camp had gone just like this: Daniil caught in some scrape; Ogodai securing the moral high ground, only to undercut his own efforts and act human after all.

They'd known this day would come. Might as well make the best of it. The wretched wedding would take place no matter what. "On and off," Daniil admitted. "I won't humiliate your sister. I can't promise fidelity, but I do play by the rules."

Ogodai nodded. "Fair enough. I regret your loss."

The one you caused? "And I yours. But I don't believe Boris killed a boy."

"He didn't tell you, then? I wondered about that."

Was it worth going into this? Yes. Essential, in fact. "He saw vengeance as futile. He was a priest in armor, Boris. How could you suspect him?"

Ogodai bristled. "We didn't pull the name out of thin air. An eyewitness described him. We captured a Kolychev horse. And a peasant identified him as the man who stayed at his hut."

"I still don't believe it."

"Neither did I, at first. But if not Boris, then who?"

Now that was a good question. For all Daniil knew, the Tatars had a dozen enemies, but enemies who masqueraded as Kolychevs? "I'd have guessed my cousin. But we talked to him. He swore he didn't leave home."

"And Boris? Did he swear?"

"No." Boris had not sworn. Could not have, in fact. "He went on a pilgrimage. To the Trinity Monastery. The monks would have vouched for him. Too late now, though, isn't it?"

Ogodai said nothing. He didn't have to. His face showed his thoughts. He didn't believe a word of it.

Daniil waited. Ogodai stayed in the doorway, arms forming a barrier across his chest.

This was pointless. Like it or not, their families would be joined by the end of the day. Daniil waved his future brother-in-law in. "Enough. Take a seat. You and I had better observe this cursed truce. No one else wants to."

After a long, considering pause, Ogodai joined him at the window. "True."

Daniil switched topics. "If I had a sister, you could have found yourself in my shoes. Why aren't you married, anyway? You're older than I was when I wed Anastasia."

"Betrothed since I was twelve." A surprise. Ogodai had never mentioned a betrothal. "Haven't seen her since. I'm to collect her after the fall campaign. Maybe then I'll know more than her name."

His problem in a nutshell. "I don't even know that. Irina, they say, but that can't be how she thinks of herself. Tell me about her."

"Nasan?" Now Ogodai sounded surprised. But after the scene he'd witnessed when he walked in, he probably thought Daniil had no interest in his new bride.

"Nasan?" Daniil echoed. "That's her name?"

"Yes. It means 'life.' Suits her better than 'peace,' as you'll discover. I love her dearly, but she has to be the least peaceful person on earth."

"A firebrand? Well, that will be different." He meant different from Anastasia, so terrified of breaking the rules that she would not offer an opinion on the weather. He didn't bother to explain, and Ogodai didn't ask.

The Tatar leaned forward, his face intense. "Be gentle with her. She is beautiful and passionate and young, and she knows nothing of your customs. But she has the heart of a lion."

As if it mattered. Daniil shrugged. "I don't intend to beat her. I'm sure we'll rub along well enough."

A yell from above saved him from further conversation.

A hand Nasan could not see pushed her toward a pillow placed at the far end of the hall. Her father tapped the shoulder of her youngest cousin, and the ten-year-old came to sit beside her. In the short time since the Tatars' arrival, he had tousled his hair and acquired dirt on his left cheek. Hoping no one would notice, she licked a corner of her veil and dabbed at his face. He edged away, muttering, "Stop it, Nasan."

Boot heels and men's voices sounded at the door. Nasan's nerves tightened until she had to remind herself to breathe. Ice Man's brother. Could she go through with this?

Two large men entered, arm in arm. Her fears hurtled the opposite way. Not one of these!

On closer inspection, she decided not. They had huge beards and paunches the loose caftans could not conceal. They were much older than nineteen.

One of them shouted down the stairs. "Daniil, hurry up!"

A rich baritone spoke words she couldn't understand. Then a young man stood on the threshold, Ogodai at his side. Behind the veil, Nasan felt her jaw drop.

Ice Man's brother. Another giant, taller even than Ogodai, with Ice Man's powerful shoulders. Light-haired, too, but golden— tawny, not platinum. And, *mashallah*, he had real eyes. Brown like his mother's, not inhuman blue. A pleasing appearance, in truth: slender silhouette, flat stomach, long-fingered hands with clipped nails. A young man's beard, trimmed close, adorned his chin. His cream robe, edged with pearls and embroidered in gold and green, set off skin tanned by campaigning. He looked every inch the golden lynx of her brother's description. And, o grandmothers, that smile.

Will he think me beautiful?

The long wait had addled her brain. What Ice Man's brother thought of her didn't matter a whit. Nasan, glad that her veil defied a casual glance, hastily shut her mouth.

Ogodai and Daniil, appearing amicable but wary, strolled toward the wedding pillows. The man who had summoned Daniil extended a purse to Nasan's cousin. "There's a horse for you in the Horde," he said. "The golden ones are at the Ugra."

He meant, "Go away." The boyars guffawed and slapped their knees. Nasan got the joke because Sumbeka had explained it in advance: the purse, although customary at Russian weddings, seldom went to a true "golden one"—a descendant of Genghis Khan.

Her cousin accepted the gift and vacated his seat. Nasan studied her groom from under her veil. He did not look cruel, like his brother. Instead he resembled his father. If she didn't hate him, she would admire the clean, strong lines of his face.

He sat beside her. Her cheeks grew hot, and an odd trembling attacked her stomach, right where her scarlet jacket met her skirt. She dropped her gaze to her hands. Her internal pendulum swung from fear to anticipation and back. He would not talk to her; he must know she couldn't reply. Yet she felt desperate for reassurance.

High-ranking guests gathered at the tables; others lined up against the walls. Indigo and lilac, vermilion and emerald, crimson and bittersweet added their hues to the rainbow of colors. The chatter in the room stilled as a priest stepped through the door. His gold brocade cape and white miter stood out even amid the brilliance surrounding him. He looked familiar. The man who had baptized her? Nasan couldn't tell.

A long service followed. Song swirled around her head, blending with the scent of beeswax and incense, drawing her into another world. Daniil's silent cues became her lifeline.

The priest handed her a lighted candle, and she worried about wax dripping on her brocade sleeves. The four parents appeared behind her, as did the elderly man who had stood by her at her baptism. Hearing a hum from the crowd, Nasan recited a prayer to Allah in her mind.

The words settled her. Giving up on the archaic church language, she imagined the room as it would have looked in Kasimov—decorated to resemble a felt tent, the benevolent gaze of the spirit dolls blessing the clan. She added a plea to the ancestors for happiness, fertility, life, and health. Girei perched on her shoulder, supporting her through her ordeal.

The priest's rich bass rang through the hall as the crowd settled into a silence charged with anticipation. Nasan opened her eyes to see the man's arms above his head, his palms facing outward. "Daniil … Irina," he intoned, "the Lord."

"Lord, have mercy," the crowd responded in harmony.

Nasan, remembering *she* was Irina, wriggled her shoulders as a puppy shakes off the rain. Daniil glanced at her, that attractive curve to his lips. Blushing, she looked away.

"Children," the priest said.

Another word she recognized. The Christians, too, prayed for fertility—for her and this Daniil, with his many lovers. Who looked only a bit like Ice Man. Would she enjoy having him touch her? Lines of incomprehensible prayer went by as she considered the question.

The priest picked up a pair of rings: one gold, one silver. He gestured and murmured—lifting, signing, lowering. Sumbeka plucked the candle from her daughter's hand. Nasan let it go with relief. Daniil gave his candle to his mother, took the silver ring from the priest, and pressed it onto Nasan's finger. Her hands trembled as she pushed the gold ring onto his.

A long sigh ran around the hall, ebbing and flowing like a wave. Natalya ran behind Nasan to kiss Sumbeka on both cheeks, and the fathers hugged. The priest's venerable face creased in an almost boyish smile.

More touching, more kissing. What *was* it with these Christians? Nasan glanced at Daniil and found him gazing at her. Her concealing veil gave her an advantage, and she used it to search his face. Without success: he hid his thoughts too well.

Their parents rejoiced because the exchange of rings secured the peace. But she and Daniil had to make the truce stick. If Daniil faced the prospect with grim determination, well, so did she.

Only she didn't, not completely. Nasan looked at her fingers, cradled in his. How perverse of her to feel safe in the hands of this courteous stranger. Why trust him, her enemy, of all those whose embraces she had endured today?

"Amen," the crowd sang, ending the betrothal. The wedding would follow, but nothing could break the bond already created.

Priest and parents hugged her. "Welcome, daughter," Natalya and Nikolai said.

"Well done, my child," her own parents murmured in Tatar.

The guests retreated to their clusters, and the noise returned to its previous level. The priest led Daniil and Nasan to the pillows, where he urged them to sit before launching into a long lecture, even more incomprehensible than the betrothal rite. Nasan caught one word in five and could make no sense of those. Russians had sex with chickens? No, surely she had misunderstood again.

Her thoughts drifted. Heat and lack of fresh air blurred the room around her until she feared she would doze off. Then the crowds cleared for an instant, and in her half-dreaming state, she saw a tall man—blue-eyed, hair silvery pale. Cold, coarse, cruel. Ice Man, in the flesh.

Everything inside her contracted. How could her brother's killer be *here*, at her wedding? Ogodai swore he died in the raid!

Daniil closed his hand around her wrist, startling her anew. The priest was rising. She tripped over her robe as she scrambled to her feet. Daniil, swift as a cat, caught her around the waist, steadying her as he thanked the priest. When she surveyed the crowd again, Ice Man had vanished.

She pushed the gauze far enough from her face to draw breath. A fantasy. Girei's killer was dead. The grandmothers wanted to remind her of what they required of her and why.

The priest left to mingle with the crowd. Daniil bowed and went to talk to a group of men who looked about his own age. Cousins, she guessed. The six of them resembled one another. He didn't offer to introduce her. Just as well. They would kiss her, and she would have to stand there like a dummy, listening to men's idea of talk, uninteresting in any language.

The blonde in yellow rushed over and—of course—hugged her, immersing Nasan in a cloud of sandalwood. The scent transported her to the courtyards of home. She inhaled, an unsteady breath. "Natalya's busy," the woman said. "Let's not wait till she has time to spare. I'm Solomonida. Daniil's cousin by marriage. I saw you watching us earlier."

"Hello," Nasan said, forgetting the rule again.

Solomonida giggled. "Horrid, isn't it? Standing here, the center of attention, and expected to behave like a stuffed bear? I thought I would die of boredom."

"Bear?" Nasan asked. "Attention? *Ai*, I do not understand."

When Solomonida explained, slowly, Nasan giggled, too. A friendly person, at last. "It is horrid," she admitted.

"So you do speak Russian," Solomonida said. "We wondered."

"Yes. Badly. Must learn."

Solomonida dragged her toward a group of young Russian women. "Come with me, then, Irina. Maybe you can't talk, but you can listen. It will help."

Nasan did not resist. So what if she didn't understand most of what Solomonida's friends had to say? At least she would have something to do.

Chapter 9

DANIIL ACCEPTED HIS COUSINS' FELICITATIONS. WHEN THEY jeered at him for refusing to empty his goblet of wine with every round, he laughed and saluted them. The last thing he needed was to get roaring drunk at his wedding. Assuming he could avoid it: from here to the end of the banquet, the toasts would continue nonstop.

In truth, he missed Boris, who had filled the role of dutiful son to perfection, leaving Daniil to amuse himself in his own way. With his older brother gone, his parents expected him to step into Boris's shoes. A hopeless task, when he had none of his brother's virtue. He accepted the need for peace; he recognized that his family had no one to offer in his place. Yet, standing among his cousins, he couldn't control his resentment at the turn his life had taken.

But resentment paled beside his conversation with Ogodai, so certain that Boris had planned and executed the ambush against the Tatars. Daniil believed in his brother's innocence, but the evidence troubled him. A description, an identification, a horse bearing the Kolychev brand. *Could* Boris have killed a boy—in cold blood, to avenge a cousin he'd never respected or liked? Then lied about what he'd done and left his family in the dark, despite the danger of retaliation? Boris knew the workings of a blood feud as well as any of them. He could have predicted Bulat's reaction. Whatever Ogodai said, the brother Daniil loved would not have acted that way.

Perhaps the Kolychevs had an enemy. Daniil decided, then and there, to find out. He had at least a month before he had to report for military duty. As soon as this interminable ceremony ended and the guests departed, he would gather his horses and gear and set out. If nothing else, he would interview the eyewitness.

A flash of red caught his eye as two cousins shifted places. His bride. Nasan's Tatar robe with its full skirts and tight bodice revealed a superb figure. The veil gave her an air of mystery, permitting glimpses of flashing eyes and reddened lips through the translucent gauze. Daniil's aversion to marriage did not inure him to the allure of a maiden hidden and therefore intriguing. One described by her brother as beautiful and passionate. A firebrand. Life, not peace. Admittedly, he had yet to see any evidence that Nasan had a tempestuous side, but perhaps he should give her a chance.

The long ceremony continued: the hair combing; the blessing with coins and hops for fertility; the sharing of bread and cheese to symbolize the new couple's joining; endless toasts in red wine; Father Job, who had performed the betrothal, praising the Lord. Nasan and Daniil met and parted again, their hands bound and released. But the ritual allowed them no opportunity to speak, revealed no hint of personality that might lessen the distance between them. He could not even catch a clear view of her face. She remained the bride—*nevesta*, unknown. They might as well have been ceremonial objects, carried from pillar to post.

He became frustrated. When his cousins converged on him and dragged him off for another round of toasts, he welcomed the diversion. Darya crossed his line of sight, and he smiled at her. She stopped dead in her tracks, then blushed to the tips of her ears and scurried off. Solomonida, the hussy, winked at him. Daniil considered joining her. Twenty-two, a beauty—the woman had a gift for repartee and the wit to discount his compliments. He enjoyed flirting with her. But she was chatting with Maria. He decided to stay where he was for a while.

His cousin Roman proposed another toast. As Daniil swirled the wine against his tongue, a sinuous voice caught his attention. "A shame Kolychev took the coward's way out," it said. "A *man* would have stood his ground and let the Tatars do their worst." Fyodor Koshkin, Maria's father, who had arrived earlier with Solomonida's husband, Semyon.

Daniil clenched his fists. He disliked Koshkin even more than he distrusted Koshkin's daughter. And the man had the nerve to insult his host. If this were not a wedding…

Semyon, a well-meaning ox, found his voice first. "You're harsh, Fyodor Mikhailovich. We defended our honor."

Someone else cut into the conversation. "Honor? Your *honor* requires you to cut the throat of an unarmed boy as if he were one of your thrice-accursed swine? Your Boris had no honor!"

Daniil's unhealed grief exploded in rage. He spun on his heel. In a blur of action, he saw a face. His fist connected with the chin beneath the Tatar mustache. Wine rained on the bystanders as the Tatar's goblet headed for the ceiling in a long, lazy arc. Only then did Daniil recognize the offender as Ogodai. His sworn brother. With whom, not an hour ago, he had promised to support the truce.

He had no time to appreciate the irony. Before he could do more than extend a hand, five Tatars standing nearby hauled Ogodai to his feet and leaped for Daniil and the Russians next to him. The Kolychev cousins did not hesitate. A free-for-all broke out.

Daniil, knocked backward, surged to his feet. One of the Tatars shoved him in the chest. He retaliated, and the man staggered. As Daniil stepped forward to push his advantage, a cane cracked against his ribs. Yelling, he twisted to confront his attacker.

It was Sheremetev. Cheeks scarlet, hair flying, eyes blazing, his former commander looked as if someone had held him up by the heels and dipped him in boiling water. He poked Daniil in the stomach with the hilt of the cane. "Devil take you, you young roustabout! Why aren't you looking after your bride?"

Daniil peered over the mob, shoving the occasional combatant aside. An unidentified arm slugged him in the rib cage, and he kicked, sending a Tatar flying. Not Ogodai, he noted. One mercy, at least. Or had he knocked his brother-in-law out?

"The mothers have her," Sheremetev said. "No thanks to you."

Daniil identified a knot of women at the far end of the hall: his mother, Sumbeka, and Solomonida clustered around a floating veil. Gratitude flickered, but the need to defend Boris's honor against her brother's slurs consumed him.

Sheremetev prodded him again. "Help your father stop this nonsense before someone gets killed." He piled into the fray, whacking any body part within range.

"Maniac," Daniil muttered. "Someone's going to knock the old brute into a fur hat, if he doesn't suffer heart failure first." But the pause had settled his temper, and he couldn't let a former commander fall in battle, even a misplaced tavern brawl like this one. He took a deep breath, ignored his bruised ribs, and dove after Sheremetev.

Bulat and Nikolai charged in from opposite directions, swearing in two languages. Daniil caught up with Sheremetev and grabbed the old man by the elbow, wresting the cane away. He was about to offer assistance to the forces of order when he noticed Koshkin at the edges of the crowd. The man who had started the trouble stood by, a serpentine smile on his face, neither restraining nor participating. Daniil felt the cane twitch in his hand. He was aiming it at Koshkin's head when his father caught it in mid-swing.

"Drop it," Nikolai said. Daniil wrestled with his instincts, then chose the wiser course. Nikolai handed the cane to Sheremetev, who doddered off to stand near Koshkin.

Bulat grabbed Ogodai, in the thick of the fight, and hauled him over to stand next to Daniil. A dozen senior nobles walked among the combatants, asserting their authority with blows and harsh words until they created a rough circle with Daniil, Ogodai, Semyon, and the two fathers in the center.

Blood streaked numerous faces. Daniil saw clutched wrists and obvious limps, reddened eyes that would soon turn many shades of purple, torn clothing, mussed hair. He probably looked no better: he could feel the bruises from Sheremetev's cane and a certain tenderness along his jawline from a hit he hadn't even realized he'd taken. Still, Nikolai and Bulat—aided by the indomitable Sheremetev—had acted quickly enough to prevent serious injury.

"What happened?" Nikolai demanded. "Who threw the first punch?"

Ogodai rubbed his jaw and didn't answer.

"I did," Daniil said through stiff lips. "He insulted Boris."

"*Mat´ tvoiu*." Ogodai snarled. "Murderous dog. And after I went out of my way to apologize!"

Nikolai's roar drowned Daniil's attempt to explain. Bulat boxed his son's ear and, spewing threatening sounds in Tatar, shoved him to the other side of the room. When they reached the wall, he beckoned to his men. The Tatars shuffled off, and the circle tightened.

Nikolai turned on Semyon. "What's your part in this?"

Semyon widened his eyes. His soulful expression didn't fool Daniil, but in this case he couldn't argue. Semyon bore no guilt for this mêlée.

"None, Uncle," Semyon said. "A guest impugned your honor. I defended it. The Tatar insulted us, and Daniil attacked him." He spoke loudly enough to be heard halfway across the room.

Height had its advantages. Across the circle of men, Daniil caught a glimpse of Nasan. She had moved a few feet from the other women and was standing on tiptoe, straining to discover the source of the noise. She lifted her veil, but he had no chance to see her face before her mother descended on her and dropped the gauze back into place.

Someone smacked his shoulder. "You. Pay attention."

His father, angrier than Daniil could recall hearing him in years. He looked Nikolai in the eye. "Sorry, Papa." He offered no excuses.

He should not have hit Ogodai, but the Tatar had asked for it. Too bad everyone else had piled in, but that was not Daniil's fault.

Nikolai scowled. "I'd send you upstairs, if you weren't the bridegroom. *And* the man you punched—if he were not the bride's best man. Have you forgotten that I am personally responsible to the grand prince for what happens in my house?"

The reminder shocked Daniil into genuine contrition. It hadn't occurred to him that his father would pay the price for any violence that resulted. "I'm sorry," he repeated. "I behaved badly."

"Demon-inspired troublemakers, the pair of you," Nikolai grumbled. "And here I thought I could trust you two to behave yourselves, even if no one else did."

A low blow. Daniil kept his mouth shut. After what felt like forever, his father shifted his focus to Semyon. "You, out." He jerked a thumb toward the door and surveyed the former combatants, hemmed in by senior nobles. "The rest of you, too. No argument."

The senior nobles created a small opening and urged the miscreants through it. Nikolai grabbed one of them as he passed. "Not you, Roman. You're the groom's best man."

Roman sidled into place while Nikolai berated him. "And you couldn't keep your nose clean either? God save me from hotheaded youth."

Semyon waved his goblet. "But, Uncle, why should I go? I didn't do anything."

"You took part." Nikolai raised his hand. "I said no argument. Out."

Koshkin whispered in Semyon's ear. Grumbling, Semyon shook the man off and left.

Daniil lost track of him then. His father shoved him in the other direction. "Get back to your bride and stay there. No more trouble. Understood?"

Daniil turned over replies in his head and decided none would satisfy him enough to justify another explosion. Avoiding his mother, who was heading in his direction with a determined expression on her face, he did as he was told.

When he reached Nasan, he noticed that even through the gauzy veil her cheeks looked pale. He wasn't anticipating a greeting, so it startled him when she said, in halting Russian, "Who shouted?"

He looked down at her, for the first time perceiving her as more than an object, "the bride." The crown of her head reached the level of his collar bones. Surrounded by burly Russian noblemen, she probably had only the vaguest idea of what had happened. He patted her hand. "Ogodai lost his temper. He insulted my family, and—I'm sorry, I swear I didn't know who was speaking—I punched him. That was my father you heard shouting. He's angry with me."

"You hit Ogodai?"

"I did. He's not hurt, though."

"You *hit* Ogodai?" She mimicked a punch, as if to ensure she'd understood. "So?"

He caught her fist inches from his chin. It looked like quite a serviceable jab, but he assumed that was an accident. "Yes. He said something rude. But I shouldn't have done it."

She shook her head, as if the vagaries of male behavior—or the intricacies of Russian—were beyond her, then returned to her original question. "No other shouted? Ogodai, your father only?"

"It turned into a fight. Lots of people were shouting. Does it matter?"

She hesitated for so long that he wondered if he should explain again, but eventually she spoke. "Not matter. I thought … no, mistake. Must be. *Ai*, I forget again."

Despite her Tatar accent, she had a lovely voice, a rich contralto with a husky edge. Her obvious dismay in the last sentence made him laugh. He touched her cheek through the veil. "Forget what? Not to speak?"

She nodded vigorously.

"Don't worry," he said. "I don't believe it means bad luck.
Except for you, poor thing, stuck keeping silent for hours. Come.
I see my parents beckoning. It must be time to go to the church."

Nasan accepted Daniil's help as they left the banquet room. Ham-
pered by skirts and blinded by the veil, she hadn't much choice.
As she descended the precipitous wooden staircase, as she set off
in a beribboned closed carriage to wed this handsome, charming
stranger who had attacked her older brother, she tried to convince
herself that anxiety was natural. So much simpler to ignore the
hand that caught her when she stumbled, the reassuring baritone,
the finger that caressed her cheek. Yet this groom of hers was these
things, too. Ice Man and not Ice Man, in one confusing package.

She wished she knew what had caused the fight. Bulat had kept
Ogodai in his corner, so she couldn't question her brother, and her
Russian didn't stretch to wringing more details from Daniil. He'd
said Ogodai insulted him, but that didn't sound right. Her brother
seldom lost control, and what could he say that would merit a
punch from a bridegroom? Perhaps Daniil saw insults everywhere.

Outside, she heard horses, Daniil and his groomsmen riding
escort. People on the street cheered as they went by. She tried not
to imagine what lay ahead.

Before long, the carriage stopped. The door opened on Daniil,
ready to help her out. Behind him, four sapphire domes, speckled
with golden stars, surrounded a fifth of pure gold. They couldn't
have traveled more than three or four streets. *Ana* had pointed out
the cupolas that morning. The Church of St. Nicholas stood, its
doors ajar. Daniil escorted her toward them.

Nasan gasped as she entered the building. She had seen
exquisite mosques, filled with turquoise faience, mosaics, and
gold lettering. But nothing in her experience prepared her for
the inside of St. Nicholas's. Even the church where she'd been
baptized seemed austere in comparison. Here the stucco walls

glowed crimson, emerald, celestial blue. Painted saints stretched up the walls and extended over the ceilings. An enormous face surrounded by points of the cross hovered from the dome above her head, spooking her whenever she looked up.

The ones with wings must represent angels. She knew about angels: the archangels Jibrail, Mikal, Izrail, Isfahil, and the junior messengers who served them. But she had never seen them. Holy figures should not appear in art. Their presence in a church seemed blasphemous.

Ahead of her towered a wall of ancient images encased in gold. The reflected flames of hundreds of wax candles glittered in the gem-encrusted icon frames, imparting expression to the saints' olive faces and elongated dark eyes.

Perhaps those were ancestors, not holy people, arranged in their niche as her own people arranged the grandmothers. She found it comforting to believe that Daniil might have brought her here to introduce her to his clan spirits. It made her feel less disloyal to Allah.

In front of the wall of images, a table stood. The heady smell of incense swirled about the sanctuary as more priests than Nasan had ever seen in one place made their entrance, each in finery more magnificent than the last. The effect overwhelmed her: massed satin and velvet mixed with cloth of gold, jeweled crosiers, mushroom-shaped miters adorned with gemstones. Sonorous bass voices intoned the opening notes of the service.

A priest passed by, waving his censer. Its brass chain clinked as he swung it over the heads of the congregation. Nasan's senses reeled with the musky fragrance. Desperate for air, she tipped her head back. In the distorted shadows cast by the candles, for one agonizing moment she saw Ice Man in the contours of her bridegroom's face. A sob broke from her throat. Instinctively, she pulled away from him. Oblivious to her unspoken terror, he caught her around the waist and pressed her face against his shoulder.

"Are you all right?" he whispered.

Not Ice Man's voice. She tried to catch her breath. How could she spend the rest of her life like this, beset by images of her brother's murderer—seeing him, hearing him, wherever she went?

Daniil's arm tightened. She let him hold her, but the experience had shaken her.

Her doubts returned. Suppose she had misread the grandmothers' intentions after all? Were these flashes of insight designed to warn her of what would happen if she married, or if she didn't?

The ancestors sought peace and the continuation of the lineage. She had to move forward, trusting them to guide her through the thicket, because without them she would be lost.

She raised her head and stepped back. Daniil took her hand. Together they walked toward the covered table where another priest, the most magnificent yet, waited. The archpriest of the Annunciation Cathedral in the Kremlin, *Ata* had told her, had himself agreed to bless this truce between noble clans. And to think she had considered, even for a moment, that the fight might put a stop to the marriage.

A phalanx of assistants backed the archpriest. The old man from her baptism gave Nasan, then Daniil, a lit candle, placing it in their left hands. As she and Daniil stood before the table, the archpriest raised his arms and intoned the opening prayer. Again Nasan understood barely a word.

Daniil tried to concentrate on the prayers, but memories of his last few hours kept intruding. He had agreed to marry for the sake of peace, then almost scuttled the truce through an ill-considered blow. He'd consoled Grusha, expecting to feel nothing for his bride, only to fall under the sway of dark eyes and a gorgeous figure—then forgotten them both in his haste to defend Boris's honor. He had to get a grip on himself. Tomorrow—or the next day—he would set out to discover the truth about his brother.

That done, he could return to the life he loved. To Grusha, if he wanted her. Today belonged to his family. To his bride.

His attention returned to the young woman standing beside him, her right hand clasped in his. For a moment there in the narthex, he'd thought she would faint.

She couldn't be ill. The grip on his fingers suggested strength. And Ogodai would have warned him. "Beautiful and passionate," he'd said. Not ill.

Forget custom. He'd wring a response out of her somehow.

The archpriest moved from one prayer to another. In response to his gesture, Daniil removed his wife's veil, handing it to an attendant. A chance to see her, at last. As he reached to retake her hand, her fingers jerked in his hold, and she looked up at him.

Daniil gazed into a face exquisite as porcelain—great black eyes, ivory skin smoothed with rice powder, a delicate flush at the cheekbones, reddened lips that begged for a kiss.

By the heavenly powers. "Beautiful" doesn't begin to describe her.

And passionate, Ogodai had said, although as the girl's brother he presumably had something else in mind than the lust drying Daniil's mouth to sand.

Sheremetev hobbled to stand behind the bride and groom. Daniil's cousin Roman approached with his younger brother—substituting for Ogodai, since Muslims were barred from the church—each holding a crown. A white satin ribbon joined the crowns together. More prayers and the triple sign of the cross, and the attendants removed the candles and held the crowns above the bridal couple's heads. Sheremetev took the ribbon in his right hand, symbolizing his support of their union.

"The servant of God Daniil is crowned unto the handmaid of God Irina," the archpriest chanted. "In the name of the Father, and of the Son, and of the Holy Spirit, now and forever and unto the ages of ages."

"Amen," the assembled priests sang. They repeated the statement and response, reversing the names to crown Nasan. The archpriest launched into yet another series of prayers, followed by a sermon on the importance of peace and harmony in marriage and in society. Daniil, transfixed by his wife's loveliness, let the words wash over him.

The Lord's Prayer brought a flash of memory, a fleeting image of Anastasia. Daniil realized that the ceremony was reaching its high point. In the flickering, candle-lit dark, drowning in a sea of sensation, intensely aware of Nasan's hand in his and those cherry lips and the fast-approaching moment when he would taste them, he struggled to stay aware of his surroundings.

The priest held out a fragile clay cup that contained red wine. Daniil sipped from it and handed it to Nasan, who did the same. They repeated this twice more. When she gave the cup back to him the third time, he drained it, placed it on the floor, and stepped on it. It broke into several pieces and a shower of dust.

Someone had instructed his Tatar bride well, for she stepped around the shards and bowed at his feet. He raised her, accepting her implicit vow of obedience, fighting an odd taste in his mouth that could not be nausea. Another submissive bride he could not hope to please. Another Anastasia.

Hardly. Anastasia had not broken tradition and spoken at her wedding. Anastasia did not have lips that would torment a saint.

The archpriest wrapped an embroidered velvet cloth several times around the young couple's joined right hands. Singing, he led them three times around the makeshift altar, stopping to pray each time he turned a corner. Bound together, Daniil and Nasan took their first steps as husband and wife while their attendants carried the wedding crowns above their heads.

When they returned to their places, backs toward the silent congregation, the archpriest freed their hands. The attendants took the crowns away, and Daniil faced his wife. She trembled as he took her into his arms. Gently, so as not to alarm her, he touched his mouth to hers. Her lips parted, and her body relaxed in his hold. Instinctively he deepened the kiss, forgetting where they were until another clinking chain presaged the arrival of a frankincense cloud. Daniil drew back. Wide black eyes stared into his.

What just happened?

The archpriest intoned the benediction. Daniil pulled Nasan close as boyars and clergy surrounded them, slapping him on the back and kissing them, congratulations tumbling over one another until he could no longer separate the voices.

Nasan quivered in his hold like a nervous hound. He could feel her cringing from the onslaught of strangers. For a horrible moment, he thought intimacy repelled her, as it had Anastasia. But the kiss suggested otherwise, and her withdrawal from those around her pressed her against his side. He could almost believe she found contact with him reassuring.

He was an arrogant fool, imagining the impossible.

The recessional sounded. It was time to return to the house.

Semyon waited in the icehouse doorway for the wedding procession to pass. Resentment left a sour taste in his mouth—unless that came from Uncle Nikolai's claret.

Thrown out of his own cousin's wedding—and for what? Had *he* started the fight? He had not!

So the barbarian's brother carried a grudge. And Daniil, chafing at his remarriage, lost his temper and took a swing at his brother-in-law. How did that lead to *Semyon* getting tossed out on his ear? What a family!

Tough that Daniil got the short stick, of course. Semyon rather liked his younger cousin, the only family member who understood the value of a good brew and a saucy wench. But Daniil was bound to remarry someday, and this girl beat the pack in terms of connections. A tsarevna, no less. Not many noble clans could claim a khan's daughter for their lineage! A chance she had looks, too, judging by the mother—a tasty piece, not a dumpling like Aunt Natasha—if you liked them dark and exotic. If Daniil didn't

… well, it wasn't as if marriage hemmed a man in. If the Tatar expected fidelity, she'd be disappointed.

But she wouldn't, would she? The girl must have no concept of monogamy. Her father ran a harem overflowing with wives and concubines. A good argument there for marrying a Tatar!

Enough. He had more important topics to consider. After almost two months of silence, Fyodor Koshkin had appeared on Semyon's doorstep this morning and offered to accompany him to the wedding. On the way, Koshkin had asked for Semyon's help. When he dodged, Koshkin insisted, pressing for a commitment before the feast reached its midpoint. Semyon was tempted to agree, especially after the wine kicked in, but he refrained. His father, now reposing in Heaven, had always insisted his sons wait twenty-four hours before accepting an offer. "No man," Papa used to say, "respects another who leaps at tidbits like a puppy."

Still, the task Koshkin proposed lay well within Semyon's abilities: scout out the situation in Dmitrov—the former principality of Yuri Ivanovich, now incarcerated in the Kremlin—to discover whether any supporters of the prince remained there, then report back to Moscow. Tomorrow Semyon would accept the offer, but today he wanted to savor his triumph.

The sound of sobbing penetrated his self-absorption. Semyon frowned at the icehouse, the source of the noise.

Another problem not his to resolve. But as he rounded the far side of the building, he discovered a brown-haired maidservant huddled against the wall. She looked up as he passed, gazing at him with tearstained eyes. She was pretty, despite her woeful expression, and rounded in all the right places. Not an aristocrat like Daniil's bride. Available. Semyon much preferred available.

He could spend the night with her. Why not? His wife would be busy for hours. The bitch had no loyalty. Six years of marriage, and she chose to stick around and enjoy herself at the banquet after Uncle Nikolai threw her husband out. It would serve her right if he played her false.

"Now then," he said. "What's to cry about? Didn't they tell you it's a celebration?"

Her lower lip trembled.

"What's your name?" he asked quickly, to fend off another deluge.

She hiccuped. "Grusha."

Semi-inebriation sharpened his mind. Weeping servant, handsome cousin known for his tendency to break hearts, cousin on his way to the altar, servant not on his arm. Semyon leaped to the obvious conclusion without difficulty. "Daniil's latest. No wonder you're sad."

"He's mentioned me?" She hiccuped again, drying her cheeks on her sleeve and sniffling.

"Often."

Silly chit. Like all Daniil's women, she refused to believe he forgot her the moment she left his bed. No doubt he'd be looking for her again tomorrow—virgin brides were overrated, in Semyon's experience. Meanwhile, no harm in profiting from Daniil's inattention.

He chucked Grusha under the chin to jolly her into a receptive frame of mind. "Don't think twice about it, my dear. He's doing his duty. A girl as pretty as you can get him back, I'm sure, especially if you make him jealous."

Her eyes narrowed. Semyon blinked. She caught his hand, and the calculating expression yielded to a smile. Semyon shook his head. He must be more drunk than he'd thought.

But then, it didn't matter what the wench had planned. He wanted a night with her, not a lifetime. He pulled her to her feet. When he left his uncle's compound, she trotted at his side.

Altogether, a most promising afternoon.

Chapter 10

THE FEASTING HAD ALREADY BEGUN WHEN DANIIL, NASAN AT his side, reached the Kolychev estate. The courtyard was awash with people standing around rough wooden tables quaffing kvass and eating pancakes, fresh from the pan, slathered with sour cream or butter and filled with mushrooms. A huge joint of meat sat on the central table, and more turned on spits at the side of the yard. Every dog in the neighborhood had come to visit; in the parade of guests they managed to gather more than a few handouts. With visitors and horses and distracted servants chasing hungry canines away from the fires, the noise level was astonishing.

A quartet of psaltery players with accompanying drummers entered the yard and stopped to grab a quick bite before tuning up. At the moment, Daniil saw no free space where they might play or guests dance, but he felt sure one would appear.

Eight straining servants staggered into view, carrying an enormous litter hung with amber velvet and decorated with carved gryphons trimmed in gold. The servants lowered this equipage to the ground right inside the gates. The curtains parted to reveal a richly dressed man as mammoth as his conveyance. Lounging against piles of pillows, wearing layered silk caftans of various colors, a ruby the size of a pigeon's egg topped by sprays of diamonds holding his white satin turban in place, jeweled scimitar belted at his waist—he looked like a creature of legend.

Nasan jumped six inches in the air, an impressive feat given her floor-length robes. She exclaimed in Tatar, of which Daniil caught only "Shah-Ali" and "*Ata.*" Then she remembered her surroundings and switched to her odd, halting Russian. "My uncle. Father say he not come."

"The grand princess must have given him permission to attend," Daniil said. "She has him under arrest for interfering with her dead husband's plans for Kazan." Which suggested that Elena, too, backed the truce.

His wife acted as if she hadn't heard him. His image of her underwent a rapid shift as she tugged him with her and ran to greet her father's half-brother. Shah-Ali accepted the assistance of two panting bearers and rose with unexpected stateliness.

Nasan's enthusiastic hug knocked her uncle's turban to one side. Shah-Ali lifted his niece off her feet with one arm and rescued the descending turban with the other.

A brief exchange in Tatar followed. Fast and fluent and expressive, the incomprehensible words tumbled over Daniil, hinting at yet another facet of his mysterious bride.

Shah-Ali set his niece on her feet and held out a hand to Daniil. "You're the husband, I'm guessing. Pleased to meet you, young man."

"The honor is mine, Khan." Daniil bowed over the proffered hand. "Our profound gratitude for gracing our ceremony."

"Can't resist a wedding." Shah-Ali pushed Nasan toward her husband. "She's a handful, this one. No Tatar khan is up to her weight, including me." He guffawed at his own pun.

Another flood of Tatar. From the hiss emitted by Nasan, Daniil guessed her uncle had supplied a translation. Her reaction provoked more laughter. Obviously, he enjoyed teasing her.

"Thank you," Daniil said, for lack of a better response. "Won't you go up? My parents will be eager to greet you."

His mother appeared at the top of the stairs. Daniil held Nasan back as the bearers assisted Shah-Ali's progress. By the time he'd reached the tenth step, shrieks of delight were floating down from above.

Daniil squeezed his wife's fingers. "I was worried about you," he said, "there in the church, before the priests arrived. I thought you would faint. Are you ill?"

"Not ill." With the return to Russian, her voice had lost its animation. She sounded strained. "Forgive. Nothing."

"You're sure?"

She hesitated, although it seemed a simple enough question, then said, "Too much. Sounds. Candles." She swung her arm, as if waving a censer.

She must mean that the cloying scent had overwhelmed her. Daniil took her hand. "I remember. Everything felt unreal."

Her fingers curled around his. "Yes. Unreal."

Natalya called to them. Daniil looked up. Shah-Ali and his attendants had reached the banquet hall. He helped Nasan ascend the steps. As they came through the door, his mother and Sumbeka swept Nasan into a hug. Until the end of the banquet, he could watch her but not converse with her. To his own surprise, he regretted that.

Nasan stopped on the threshold, disoriented. The big room where they had gathered before church had been cleared and reset for the wedding banquet, and the crowd seemed to have doubled in size. The dishes here were richer and more varied than those in the courtyard: smoked salmon and sturgeon, pickled herring, baskets of nuts and cheese straws, roast duck and goose redolent of garlic, chicken glistening from the spit. Tureens suitable for a giant held borscht and cabbage soup; herb-scented fish broth leaked wisps of savory steam. No swans, her mother had promised, in deference to the Tatars' respect for those sacred birds. And no pig—or none that she could see. Even so, the food seemed strange.

One sideboard held a bowl of lemons, vivid against a backdrop of great joints of beef and mutton. Her family had brought the lemons—a gift from her cousin, the khan of Astrakhan, near the Caspian Sea. The fruit baffled the Russians, who picked up cut slices and sniffed them, then put them down. Their perfume mingled with the sharp scent of ginger, the tang of pickled cucumbers, and the aroma of cracked pepper blended with oil.

The guests were already seated at long tables running down the hall—men on one side of the room, women on the other, arranged by rank. Nasan followed Daniil to the center of the high table.

Shah-Ali's arrival and Nikolai's decision to expel two dozen of the rowdier guests had necessitated changes in the seating plan. The tables in the hall looked lopsided, the women's side longer than the men's. The new arrangement at the high table maximized the distance between Daniil and Ogodai. Shah-Ali held the cherished spot next to the bridegroom, with Nikolai, Bulat, Sheremetev, and Daniil's best man pushing Ogodai to the far end of the benches. Natalya occupied the place next to Nasan. Sumbeka, Nasan's pouty new sister-in-law, aunts from both sides of the family, and Solomonida of the primrose silk filled out the women's side.

Nasan's plan to quiz her brother about the fight would have to wait.

The moment she reached her seat, her elephantine uncle raised his goblet and offered a toast suggestive enough to set her cheeks afire after he repeated it in Tatar for her benefit. An intense wish for the return of her veil gave way to a rush of gratitude. Yes, she had married an enemy, but a young and handsome one (who kissed … but better not to recall the kiss yet).

Natalya touched her arm. Nasan tipped her head, a silent question. To her right, men were competing to top Shah-Ali's toast. She focused on Natalya. From talking to Solomonida and then Daniil, from listening to the girls, her confidence in her Russian was growing. If she concentrated on one person at a time, she could understand him or her, especially if the person spoke slowly and used simple words.

"Good," Natalya murmured. "No, child, do not speak. I saw you break tradition. Several times. I think it only right to warn you. You have a high standard to meet. Daniil was married before, to a young woman of great virtue. And we almost wed him to Darya there..."

She pointed to the girl in blue silk. Something clicked in Nasan's head. She remembered Darya challenging Maria, asking if she would befriend the new arrival. And Ogodai, talking of "the sweet young thing next door." No wonder Darya sought assurances of Maria's loyalty and tossed accusations of barbarism into the air. She must feel displaced. More hostility: it pressed in from every corner.

The grandmothers supported the marriage. Girei, too. Nasan must not forget them. But it would be nice to feel that *one* person in this alien household welcomed her. So far, only Solomonida had.

And Daniil, when he wasn't punching her brother. But suppose Daniil wanted Darya—or his first wife? That was a shock: he seemed too young for a second marriage. What happened to her? Nasan's throat ached with unasked questions.

"Good," Natalya said again. "You have self-control. Use it. To attract Daniil, you must match his first wife in propriety. Be gentle, obedient, and womanly, and he will love you."

Nasan bit her tongue until she tasted blood. She could manage gentle, but only this stranger could imagine her capable of obedient or womanly. If Daniil favored propriety, she might as well give up. The advice sounded harder to follow than the endless lectures from her father's concubines.

Kasimov. The harem. She had years of experience dealing with women: she could handle Natalya and Maria. And Daniil...

Why can't I get that kiss out of my head?

The kiss. Her first. Unexpected, delightful, confusing. An experience she longed to repeat.

As if he could read her unruly thoughts, Daniil slipped an arm around her waist and nuzzled the edge of her jawline. Her barriers crumpled as he kissed her, urged on by the company. He whispered in her ear, then laughed when the throaty edge to his voice made her shiver.

Briefly she recalled her boast to Ogodai—*I am not like other girls*. Yet amid this whirling panorama centered on her and Daniil, reality had no more substance than her missing veil. Her resistance to him melted.

Moments passed, it seemed, before Sumbeka left the table and returned with the gold-embroidered veil. Bulat walked to an open space in front of the high table and, looking endearingly uncomfortable, beckoned to his daughter. He blessed the new couple, and Daniil's parents followed suit. "Remember what I told you," Natalya whispered as they hugged.

Nasan nodded. Fear fled. Anticipation triumphed.

Again, she let Daniil guide her down the stairs. On the ground floor his mother, her coat turned inside out for some reason, led them hand in hand around a capacious bedroom decorated in a style too strange not to carry a meaning, although Nasan couldn't imagine what that was. In each corner, a pair of sables lay on crossed arrows, a small white roll atop the furs. On one of three tables, next to a platter of bread, two young men placed candles. A second dish was empty; a third held goblets.

The great bed in the center drew her eye. Above the bed hung an icon: a moon-faced woman with penetrating eyes. A man-shaped child pressed his cheek against hers, his tiny hand clutching her robe. The tenderness between Madonna and infant gave depth to the flat image. Nasan frowned. Bad enough that the Christians displayed holy figures in their churches. To hang one in a bedroom seemed completely inappropriate. Bizarre people, these Russians.

Relatives crowded into the room. As the last Tatar cousin squeezed his way in, Nikolai stepped forward and pulled Nasan's veil from her head. "The bride!"

Daniil smiled—responsive, appealing, delightful. Hers. They would soon be alone. The future, pearl-strewn with possibility, drew her as Natalya led her behind the screen that stood in one corner. The women accompanied them, while the men remained outside.

Behind the screen, confusion reigned. As Nasan stood mute, female family members crowded around her, removing her clothes. The women chattered endlessly as she strove to understand them. Every so often, she caught Daniil's name.

She raised both eyebrows at her mother, who smiled. "Nothing to worry about, my love," Sumbeka said in Tatar. "Shall I tell them to hush?"

"But what are they saying, *Ana*?"

"Nothing worthwhile."

Nasan listened harder. If her mother refused to tell her, it must be bad.

With pinpoint timing, Maria struck, dashing Nasan's half-formed hopes in a few devastating sentences. "Oh, my dear," she drawled to Solomonida, who had removed Nasan's headdress and placed it on the empty platter, "did you notice that Daniil's favorite maidservant missed the wedding? Sulking, I bet."

"No," Solomonida said. "I don't gossip." A patent lie, but Nasan appreciated the thought behind it.

"You?" Maria retorted. "Don't be absurd. I'm sure you noticed. And why wouldn't Grusha be upset? Not that she's the only one who lies with him, by any means: the man must have bedded every woman in Moscow. And now here's our little bride, quite besotted." She gestured at Nasan, who had stopped pretending not to listen and stared at her, openmouthed.

"Maria! Have you no shame?" Solomonida asked.

"Can you deny it?" Maria said hotly.

A slap interrupted her. "Stop that at once," Natalya ordered, "and help me with Irina's hair."

Solomonida patted her arm. "Don't listen to her, Irina."

Nasan shrugged her off. *Besotted? With a man who has bedded every woman in Moscow? I am not like other girls!*

Too angry to speak, she forgot that *she* was Irina until the sensation of hands releasing her braids reminded her that the Christians had changed her name.

Daniil had duped her. He was a liar and a cheat, an enemy of her clan. He had picked a fight with Ogodai. He cared nothing about the truce. She should leave while she still could.

She turned to her mother, ready to plead, but Sumbeka's fingers dug into her arm, urging restraint. In her rage, Nasan barely noticed as the two mothers stripped her robes from her, leaving only her linen shift.

Ogodai had warned her. Daniil had women by the score, he'd said. You could lose your heart, he'd said. And she almost had. But no more.

The look in Sumbeka's eyes would shatter glass. "Come," she said in Tatar. She tugged Nasan toward a table that held a wash basin, a towel, and a jug.

Natalya approached, eyebrows raised in a question. "A moment," Sumbeka said. "I need to speak to my daughter."

Natalya nodded and withdrew. Nasan heard her chivvying female relatives into gathering discarded clothing and folding it for storage. Sumbeka poured water into the bowl and waited while Nasan rinsed lipstick and powder from her face, then handed her a towel.

"Listen to me, Nasan," she said. "Men stray. It is their nature. Look at your father's household. Do you imagine I like knowing that my husband spends time with other wives and concubines?"

Nasan shook her head. Sumbeka had often said that she hated sharing Bulat with others. But Nasan had had trouble, then, seeing herself doing with Daniil the things her mother had described. The idea that Bulat, so much older even than Uncle Shah-Ali, might do them with many wives left her hovering between incredulity and disgust.

"But I make sure," Sumbeka said, "that whatever pleasure he gets from them cannot equal what I give him. And I remain his chief wife, the head of his household. We have a bond no concubine can match. Profit from my example, child."

"But, *Ana*, my husband is Christian. He is not supposed to have more than one woman."

"Silly girl. Christian, Muslim—it makes no difference. Take my advice. Don't reproach your husband when he strays, and he will always return. And remember, you make this marriage in the cause of peace, to protect your clan. Nothing can alter that."

Yes, peace. The truce Daniil had not kept. An argument that might convince even *Ana*. "He doesn't care about peace," she said. "He hit Ogodai. Will you not take me home?"

Sumbeka sighed. "Young men are like wolves, always at one another's throats. Ogodai hit him too. No, Nasan. Your father cares, and so do I. You must do your part."

"Yes, *Ana*," she said, but rebellion roiled in her heart. She could not go home. She could not change her husband's nature. She must keep the peace even if he did not. Very well. But she would not let Daniil hoodwink her. She must remember. He was Ice Man's brother, and even more dangerous, because less obvious in his cruelty.

"Good girl." Sumbeka patted her cheek and retrieved the towel, urging Nasan to join the waiting women.

But the women were no longer waiting. They had returned to the main room for the next part of the ceremony. The pile of folded clothes drew Nasan's eye. Her knife.

She had thought to use it on herself, but now she saw another option. What better way to show Daniil Kolychev that he could not play with her heart, whatever sway he had over other women?

Sumbeka left Nasan alone and went to join the others. Seeing her chance, Nasan extracted the knife from its hiding place and slid it under a pillow.

⚘

The wedding party left. Daniil ran a hand through his hair, releasing a long, relieved breath. The banquet had ended—not for the guests, who would still be celebrating when dawn arrived, but for him. He needed only to focus on the task at hand.

Task? Making love to that beautiful girl? Daniil laughed. He was losing perspective.

Anastasia's tears haunted him, and he pushed away his discomfort. He'd learned a lot in three years. He could initiate a new bride.

Fortunately, Nasan didn't know (yet) that two of his more disreputable cousins mounted guard in the hallway and would not hesitate to embarrass him by demanding a progress report. And given that Roman and Pavel had probably spent the last week concocting plans to unsettle him—it was a game Daniil himself had played more than once—he had to stop waffling and act. He stripped off the tunic and nightshirt his uncles had wrapped him in and turned around. His jaw dropped.

His demure pillar of gauze had disappeared. In her place a fury crouched on the bed. Unbound black hair tumbled to her knees. Her linen chemise, pulled up to mid-thigh, revealed long legs as slim and graceful as the white birches across the river. She was breathing fast and hard, and each inhalation pushed her breasts above the band of the sheer fabric. In the somewhat fuzzy state caused by too many toasts, Daniil found himself unable to focus on anything but the rise and fall of those ivory mounds.

"Stop staring," Nasan hissed. From behind a pillow, she pulled an embossed knife and held it to her right shoulder, ready to strike. "Stay!"

"By the saints." He'd married a lunatic. "What are you doing? Put that down."

Instead she hunched into herself, her eyes narrowing. He spread his hands, showing he meant no harm. "What happened? We were getting along fine upstairs."

For some reason, that simple comment increased her rage—or so he judged from the sound she produced, more snarl than speech. "Wrong."

"Weren't we?" He took a few steps toward her, softening his voice to a soothing purr, suitable for coaxing madwomen and terrified virgins alike. "Relax. I'm not planning to rape you. Give me the knife and we can talk."

Most women melted at that tone, but this one tightened her grip. "No talk," Nasan said. "And *you* … stay."

She pulled the weapon against her shoulder, as if she might throw it. His plans for coaxing her into a more reasonable frame of mind fled. Daniil hurled himself forward and wrested the knife from her grasp. He pinned her to the bed, holding her wrists above her head while she thrashed under him. She had a wiry strength that he had not expected in a woman, and soon the pair of them gasped like warriors in hand-to-hand combat.

Once she stopped struggling, he transferred both her wrists to his left hand, wondering what kind of wildcat he had married. Beautiful and passionate, indeed. With gallows humor, he remembered wishing for a woman who would push back. Perhaps he should have left well enough alone. Tempestuous bedmates had their disadvantages.

At the same time, he found the idea of winning her exhilarating. The heart of a lion, Ogodai had said. The claws of one too, it seemed.

With his right hand he grasped her chin and turned her face toward him. "Don't ever use a weapon against me. If you have a problem, say so. I'm not a barbarian you have to fight off."

"*Not* a barbarian."

"Dammit. I didn't call you a barbarian." He released her chin, noting with satisfaction that she did not look away. "Let's get something straight, wife. I didn't ask for this marriage any more than you did. After today we can go our separate ways. And if you insist, I will get up from this bed, tell everyone that you refused me, and let you go home in disgrace. End of arrangement. More kinsmen die. Is that what you want? Because I do not force myself on women, and I don't intend to start with you."

"Let me go!"

Her anger still made no sense, but she didn't sound deranged. Restraining her would only convince her that she was right to fear him. And now that he'd taken her knife, she couldn't do much damage. He rolled away from her and propped himself on one elbow. She pulled her chemise over her legs and sat up, curling her feet under her.

He realized she probably hadn't understood most of his last speech. He repeated it, slowly, using the simplest words he could find. "Let's start again, shall we?" he finished. "What went wrong?"

More chest heaving ensued, but he refused to look away, just as he refused to cover himself with the sheet. After a moment, she reached out and ran a finger over his ribs, where Sheremetev had whacked him. When he winced, she said, "Hit Ogodai. Fight."

Was that the problem: because he had punched her brother, she felt threatened by him?

"That's nothing," he said. "A bruise. That old brute Sheremetev's too free with his cane. I told you: hitting Ogodai was a mistake. We're friends, sort of."

"Friends." She sounded incredulous. "You hit friend. She hit you."

"He. He hit me."

Hair slapped his cheek as she shook her head. "He, she. Unimportant. What matters, we marry for peace, and you don't care."

"I do," he said. "It was an accident. I wouldn't have agreed to the marriage unless I cared. No more deaths, right? Your father, Ogodai. We keep them safe."

The curtain of hair covered her face as she lowered her eyes. He thought he heard a frightened sob, quickly suppressed. The sound touched his heart. Facing this lovely, half-naked girl, Daniil felt the ceremony slip away. With it went his awareness of the cousins waiting outside the door.

He pulled her close, murmuring in her ear, "Trust me. I won't hurt you, I promise."

Chapter 11

"HOW GOES IT IN THERE?" A MAN'S VOICE BELLOWED.

Nasan's whole body tensed. She couldn't prevent it. She had been reveling in the sensation of Daniil's arms encircling her, his skin pressed against her cheek. This demonic shout hauled her back into the unwelcome present, a world of enemies and alien customs, in which she could not and should not trust the man at her side.

He had been gentle with her, at least. She had enjoyed his touch until the crucial moment that made her a woman. Now the region between her legs felt scraped raw. But they had fulfilled the contract. And it would not hurt the next time, *Ana* had promised.

She opened her eyes to find Daniil scowling at the door, although he continued to caress her cheek with his thumb. "Go away, Roman," he called. "We're fine."

While she stared at him, puzzled, he rolled onto his back and brushed her hair behind one ear. "Relax, love. It's my cousin."

"But he heard…" Nasan, at a loss for words, added the rudest phrase she could think of—in Tatar, to relieve her feelings.

Daniil's arm tightened around her. "No, he didn't. That door is solid oak. Ignore him."

She studied his face. He seemed to mean what he said. It had been a long day, after a restless night. Nasan let herself snuggle once more into his hold. "Tired," she whispered. "Didn't sleep."

He didn't answer. She was drifting off when he startled her awake. "May I use your birth name? Nasan? When we're alone."

"Yes, please." She yawned. "*Not* Irina."

He laughed. "Ogodai told me. That he loves you, but you are life, not peace. I didn't think he meant you would stab me."

She touched her nose to his chest, memorizing his scent. "Mistake. Sorry. Scared." Should she mention the women and their chatter? But she couldn't bear to repeat Maria's gossip.

"I won't frighten you anymore, then. Could be bad for my health."

Nasan was still forming a reply when the pounding on the door resumed. "*Gospodi*," Daniil said. "Excuse me while I murder Roman."

Her sense of the room as a sanctuary snapped. She pulled away from him and hugged her knees to her chest, wrapping her chemise around her. The room faded to black and white, and Daniil's face again took on the contours of his dead brother's, looming over her in the forest. Shaking, she lowered her forehead to block him from view.

He clasped her hand. "What did I say?"

Her faulty Russian drained from her head. Even in her native tongue, she had no idea how to explain.

He took her in his arms. "Tell me."

"Can't." She pressed her face into his shoulder, weeping. "No words."

He patted her cheeks with the edge of the sheet. "You'll feel better soon."

He didn't sound as if he believed it himself, but he was trying. Nasan took big gulps of air until the tears stopped.

When she could, she raised her head. The colors of the room had returned, and Daniil no longer looked like Girei's murderer. Yet the horror lingered, ready to leap out at the next thoughtless phrase. Of course, Daniil wouldn't kill his cousin. His brother's crime lay between them like an unhealed wound. Perhaps it always would. Her father had not considered *that* when he sacrificed her happiness for the truce.

A chasm of distrust yawned before her, uncrossable by will alone. She'd done her best to put the ambush behind her, yet the memory of Girei's death refused to fade. Meanwhile, she had to find a way to live in this house where everything reminded her of a violent past. Her moment of joyful communion dissipated like smoke.

"Roman, go away," Daniil shouted, but the knocking continued.

Nasan took a deep breath. "What she want?" Her throat ached with unshed tears.

"It's custom. I have to tell him we're done, so the mothers can inspect the sheets. Let's get it over with, shall we? Then they'll leave us alone, and we can sleep."

When she managed a desolate nod, he bent and picked up the nightshirt he'd tossed on the floor, rubbed it over his body, and threw it on the bed. He pulled on the tunic he'd worn over the nightshirt and kissed the tip of her nose. "Button that chemise, wife of mine."

Nasan hurriedly complied. Her cheeks burned. She had let this womanizing stranger touch her in the most intimate way possible, and she had enjoyed it. Could any greater humiliation exist?

She sensed Daniil watching her. Her confusion grew, and she focused on each button as she fumbled it into place.

As she finished, she heard Daniil walk to the door and open it. "Tell my parents the bedding ended as it should," he said. A yell of triumph sounded from outside.

Nasan, unable to bear any more, fled behind the screen.

"Sumbeka, yes." Natalya Kolycheva fixed the assembled women with a stern eye. "The rest of you, no. Have you girls no shame? A flock of magpies, chirping about matters that don't concern you."

Nasan's mother—no, Irina's mother since this morning—heartily endorsed this sentiment. She had come within a hair's breadth of rebuking the girls earlier. Lucky for them they were not *her* daughters!

Natalya beckoned to her, and with a parting frown at the chattering women, Sumbeka joined her hostess at the top of the stairs.

"Dreadful lot," Natalya said as she led the way to the storeroom converted for the use of Nasan—no, Irina—and Daniil. "I can't wait for them to leave."

They were the first honest words to pass her lips since the Tatars arrived. After hours of punctilious politeness, Sumbeka heaved a sigh of relief at hearing something human from her straitlaced hostess. In the same spirit she offered, "At least they only talk. Our young men concern me more. Can they keep this peace we have worked so hard to make?"

Natalya's broad face creased in worry. "I don't know. Your son and mine. We call them brothers, but in their minds they are enemies still. What will solve that, I wonder?"

"They are sworn brothers. They can become friends again. But it will take time."

"Which we may not have. Even in the women's quarters, I hear rumors. The land seethes with plots." Natalya gestured at the staircase. "But we can discuss that later. Come, I want to find out how our children are faring."

A few moments, and they had traversed the short distance, packed with rowdy boyars of various ages. Natalya's generous form cleared the way, and Sumbeka soon found herself in the large room where she had left her daughter an hour before.

She saw only Daniil, his eyebrows drawn together, and one blood-stained nightshirt on the bed. The turned-back sheets showed more streaks of red.

"Nasan?" she asked him, again forgetting her daughter's change of name.

He had caught his mother's elbow and was whispering to her, but when Sumbeka spoke, he gestured at the screen. "She won't talk to me. I hurt her. I didn't mean to."

His bewildered expression reminded her of her own boys. "Don't worry. I'll take care of it." She patted his arm, then left him in Natalya's capable hands while she searched for her child.

On the other side of the screen she stopped, stunned. Her daughter sat on a heap of pillows, tears streaming down her face, her hair a silk curtain around her, and blood on her shift.

Sumbeka went to her and pushed the curtain of silk behind one ear. "My darling, what is it?"

"*Ana.*" Nasan tumbled into her mother's arms. "Don't leave me here. I will go mad!"

Soothing murmurs and her mother's embrace worked their magic. "Tell me," Sumbeka said. "What happened? Did Daniil force you?"

Nasan shook her head. Her mother's face relaxed.

"Then what?" Sumbeka stroked more loose hair away from Nasan's cheek. "This is not like you, my brave girl."

The urge to confide was overwhelming. Two years of discord had not obliterated the lost closeness of childhood. And Nasan and her mother no longer had marriage to fight about. Soon *Ana* would go, leaving Nasan in this house where nobody loved her.

"It's me," she choked out. "Among these Russians, I see Girei's killer everywhere. At the wedding." Her voice dropped to a whisper. "In my husband. During the ceremony. A few moments ago. How will I stand it, *Ana?* The moment I feel happy, that man comes back to haunt me. The grandmothers have cursed me because I didn't protect Girei."

Sumbeka drew her daughter's head onto her shoulder, rocking her. "Ah, baby girl. It will fade. You'll see. Once you get to know them, they will no longer look alike. Especially Daniil. And what nonsense is this about the grandmothers? They wouldn't curse you for obeying your father. You helped our clan today. Girei is proud of you, I'm sure."

Nasan could hardly speak through her sobs. "I wanted to save him, *Ana*. I wanted it so badly."

"I know, sweeting, I know."

Somewhere behind her head Natalya sounded like a cooing dove, murmuring a rush of vowels and sibilants that Nasan's brain refused to interpret.

"I must tell her something," Sumbeka said. "I don't want to mention her son's crime. She must find it difficult enough to entertain us, whom he wronged."

Before Nasan could answer, she heard her mother speak in Russian. "There, there, love," Sumbeka said. "Such silly girls. I don't believe they upset you. Tell us the rest. Natalya and I will understand."

Nasan pulled back. A hand reached over her shoulder, dangling a square of linen. "Daniil went to the bathhouse," Natalya said. "You may speak freely."

Sumbeka took the offered cloth and wiped her daughter's cheeks. Nasan stumbled along the trail laid by her mother. "Girls. Maria say my husband—"

"Daniil," Natalya interjected. "He has a name."

Nasan stopped, confused. She should dishonor her husband?

"It's not our way," Sumbeka said smoothly. "A wife does not speak her husband's name. A mark of respect. My daughter, continue."

"Maria say husband have many women. Too many. I . . ." Nasan's Russian deserted her again, and she switched to Tatar. "Bad enough that I marry a man who strays, *Ana*. But to have Maria tell the world I am besotted with him and make fun of me—I can't bear it. You heard her. She said he had bedded every woman in Moscow."

Sumbeka repeated this in Russian for Natalya's benefit. "That was dreadful, to be sure. But not every woman, surely. There must be a few he's left unscathed."

Natalya muttered something under her breath. It sounded like "Not in this house." Sumbeka laughed and did not translate.

Nasan, gathering her confidence, essayed Russian once more. "Not you too, *Ana*."

Natalya intervened. "Anastasia was good but not strong. Daniil didn't like to trouble her, especially after she became pregnant." She made a face Nasan could not interpret. "She died in childbirth. And after her death, well, he became accustomed to amusing himself with servants. But you can reform him if you behave with propriety. I told you that before."

Nasan sent her mother a pleading glance. Sumbeka translated, and Nasan couldn't suppress a groan. Surely *Ana* understood the unlikelihood of her daughter meeting Natalya's demands.

But probably *Ana* agreed. The last two years had witnessed many such arguments between them. Nasan shifted her gaze to her clenched hands, expecting another scolding.

Instead Sumbeka clasped her fingers and said in Tatar, "Keep the propriety for your mother-in-law, my child. Whatever she believes, most men prefer a little spice. Especially if you must fight off servants and camp followers. Remember what I taught you."

Nasan's jaw dropped. *Ana* held up her daughter's chin with one finger and added in Russian, as if in translation, "My sweet, when we arrived, you were distraught. Because of one wretched girl? I don't believe it."

"Indeed," Natalya said, accepting the bait. "Maria can hurt you only if you let her. No one takes her seriously."

Caught in her mother's well-intentioned lie, Nasan gulped for air. What else could she say without mentioning the murder? She settled on a partial truth, delivered with as much aplomb as she could manage. "Cousin. Roman. She knock, knock on the door. Husband say, go away, but no. Knock, knock…"

Her Russian vocabulary had reached its limit. She switched mid-sentence to her native tongue. How would she manage without her mother to translate? "I felt safe, *Ana*, and that made it worse.

My husband said he would murder his cousin. He didn't mean it, I know. But when he said it, I saw that man. I thought I could cope, but I can't. It makes me crazy. And then, when he told me to button my chemise because you would be here soon, I realized he had seen me naked and touched me in *such* an intimate way, and I don't even know him."

Sumbeka patted her back. "Breathe, love, breathe. We understand."

She switched her attention to Natalya. "It is nothing. Your son did his best, but you remember what that first time is like. No one can remain indifferent to being deflowered by a stranger." She glanced at her daughter. "Even one who has practiced on every woman in Moscow."

"*Ana!*" Nasan could not hold back a giggle at the mischief in Sumbeka's face.

Natalya laughed too. "We'll have to work on her Russian, I see. As for the rest, well, it is ever thus. The men arrange life to suit themselves, and we women must adjust."

"Indeed," Sumbeka said. "We live in different places, but some things don't change."

Natalya picked up an ivory comb and applied it to Nasan's head in long, soothing strokes. She braided the hair and tied the ends. "He's a good boy, my Daniil, even if he does drive Father Job to distraction. And kinder than Maria, as you will soon discover. So let's get you cleaned up and find you something to eat. You must be starving, poor child."

When Daniil returned from the bathhouse, he found a scene quite different from the one he'd left. The bed had been remade and order restored. The gold knife lay on the sideboard. His wife— clad in a fresh nightdress, her hair neatly braided—sat at the table, demurely eating chicken and kasha with a mother at each elbow.

He studied her. Despite his best efforts, he'd hurt her. A girl didn't weep like that without cause. So much for his hopes of not replicating the experience with Anastasia.

Although Nasan had not withdrawn from him. Once she decided to yield, she had yielded with great sweetness. And later he had coaxed her to relax in his arms. If that idiot Roman hadn't interfered, she would be cuddling with him now.

As he came in, she looked up and smiled. A strained smile, but a real one. He was moving toward her when his mother caught his arm.

"Careful, my lamb," she murmured. "She's exhausted. And fragile. Comfort her."

Daniil groaned. As if he hadn't the wit to handle his own affairs.

If he said that, he'd only enrage her. Instead he used his pet name for her, an acknowledgment of her skill in managing the household. "Yes, General."

She smacked his forearm. "Do as I tell you, bad boy. It will work."

"Very well, Mama." He headed for the table, where Nasan was picking at the dish in front of her and conversing quietly with her mother. Exhausted? Yes, her eyes looked propped open; her mouth drooped. But fragile? The firebrand with the knife did not lack strength. Or passion.

Perhaps Mama meant emotionally fragile. That he could see. Roman's prank had unleashed a deluge, as if Nasan feared for her life.

And why not? Marriage threatened his freedom, but it stripped her of everything she valued. No wonder she wept. She must feel abandoned, betrayed. And he had no idea how to help her.

For the first time in years, Daniil wished he knew more about girls than how to get them into bed. His sisters had died in infancy. Maria irritated him beyond belief. Anastasia had entered his life only to leave it, and he had never understood her either. But he did hate repeating his mistakes.

As he sat next to Nasan, she offered him a piece of chicken. Her slim fingers pressed against his lips as he took it. He leaned forward, touching his hand to her waist. A delicate floral scent brushed his nostrils. He wanted nothing more than to be alone with her, to sleep.

He swallowed the chicken and shook his head when she held up a second piece. "It's for you. I didn't fast most of the day."

Her eyes were dark pools rimmed with shadows. "I'm finished." She pushed the food away and thanked his mother.

Natalya picked up the bowl and kissed Nasan, then Daniil. "Until morning, then, my doves."

Sumbeka rose in one graceful movement. She rubbed her nose against Nasan's and touched Daniil's cheek. "Sleep well."

Daniil latched the door behind them, determined to prevent any more interruptions tonight. He sat on the bed and held out his hand. "Come here, Nasan. You look ready to drop."

When her fingers clasped his, he pulled her onto his lap. "I hurt you," he said. "I'm sorry."

"Necessary. No need sorry."

"But I made you cry. I don't want to make you cry."

She flushed, then blurted out, "You say, 'kill Roman.' Silly, yes. But you hit friend, brother kill mine, I feel not safe."

So that was it. This he could handle. He asked softly, "Will you let me take care of you, then?"

She murmured an incomprehensible reply. Her eyes closed. He stood up with her in his arms, placed her on the mattress, moved the bedcovers aside, and slid her into position. She curled up against the pillows. As his arms withdrew, she whispered, "Don't go."

The most promising thing she'd said yet. Daniil pulled the nightshirt over his head. "I can't sleep in this tent," he told her.

She blushed again, which amused him. He joined her in bed and enfolded her once more. She snuggled against him.

He had decided she was asleep when she said in a drowsy voice, "Must say. I dream. Wake you, maybe."

Dreams. Nightmares, more like. He kissed her forehead. "You won't. I'm here to protect you, so no bad dreams tonight." She exhaled against his shoulder—a soft, contented sigh. Very pleasant.

Too bad he had to leave the day after tomorrow. But the truth about Boris could not wait.

Grusha sat up as the reverberations from the slamming door died away. Hair tumbled down her back, and her cheek smarted where Semyon had struck her yesterday. She experimented with moving her jaw: it ached, but if she rubbed it, the pain lessened. He'd chafed her wrists, too—restraining her even after she forced herself to lie still. She didn't scream for help. No one would hear her except his soldiers and servants, and they would not interfere. Instead she'd let him do what he wanted, then rolled away from him and pretended to sleep. Now she felt dirty and used.

The harsh light of morning forced her into an honest appraisal, and candor made her heart sting worse than her cheek. As badly as Semyon had treated her—and Grusha knew he had broken the law, even though she couldn't imagine lodging a complaint against a lord—she had brought this predicament on herself. She'd blamed Daniil for agreeing to a marriage he couldn't avoid—as if a virgin bride had any chance of holding his interest. And in her anger she'd accepted Semyon as an alternative to Daniil—someone who would guarantee her financial security in a world where women like her depended on their own scarce resources to survive.

Grusha had always considered herself a realist. Youth and prettiness don't last. Without money and a powerful protector, she could expect to remain a slave her entire life. But why should she?

What did Daniil's Tatar bride have that Grusha lacked, except the good fortune to be born a tsarevna instead of a peasant?

Then Semyon touched her, and her cool calculations went out the window. When she tried to convince herself that Daniil was the one caressing her, her mind rejected the lie, distracting her with unwanted images: the laughter that seldom left Daniil's eyes; the arms that lifted her as if she weighed no more than the Tatar's gauze veil; the consideration he'd shown for her pleasure even on the night of his brother's death. When her eyelids fluttered open despite her best efforts to keep them shut and she saw the cruel twist to Semyon's mouth, she had pushed him away, announcing she'd made a mistake, she wanted to leave.

Daniil would have listened. Even if he said something cutting, he would have let her go, probably with a shrug to show that her loss of interest meant nothing to him. Of course, when Daniil wanted her, she had never said anything but yes.

That was when the truth she'd worked so hard to ignore seeped in. Semyon forced it on her by *not* listening. While he pinned her hands behind her back, Grusha struggled with the unwelcome realization that Daniil had stolen her heart, causing her to forget the simple goals she'd set for herself when she first grew old enough to understand what it meant that her parents had sold her into slavery to feed her brothers and themselves.

Her stomach lurched. How could she love Daniil, who had just married another?

She couldn't, but she did. A vow formed in her head. *He chose me, not her. I will get him back.*

Her decision made, Grusha scrambled into her clothes and ran for the outside staircase, not stopping to braid her hair.

Chapter 12

NASAN'S FAMILY LEFT ON THE THIRD DAY AFTER HER WEDDING. Blinking, she watched from the window of the bedroom she would share with Daniil from now on, hoping for a last glimpse of her father's horsetail standard as it turned onto a cross street. Her parents, Ogodai—gone. How fervently she had sought solitude when she lived in Kasimov, not recognizing that her pleasure depended on having a family to escape. Here she had no one, except her husband and a gaggle of women who had judged her and found her wanting even before she arrived.

The women gave her no peace. Daniil she saw only in passing. Nonstop ceremonies kept them apart. He seemed pleasant enough, patient and undemanding. He had not touched her again, saying he would wait until they knew each other better. A nagging voice in her head insisted she must have displeased him: what could an inarticulate virgin offer a man of experience? The memory of her initiation left her wondering how it would feel without the pain.

His bow stood propped against the wall, not far from her right thigh. Nasan picked it up. For a moment, she cradled it, treasuring the familiar heft of the weapon in her hand, running her fingers along the polished wood. With practiced ease she snapped the bowstring into place and pulled it, aiming at a window on the far side of the room and imagining the flight of the nonexistent arrow. On a good day, she could hit the compound gates from here.

Oh, if she had her mare! She could practice shooting from horseback. Intense nostalgia—for Kasimov, for Girei, for her unfettered childhood—tugged at her chest.

She took an arrow from the quiver arranged next to the bow and repositioned herself to draw the bowstring to its full extent, only to discover that she lacked sufficient strength. No wonder Daniil picked her up without a second thought. Shorter than he by at least a head, she could not pull her elbow back far enough to make effective use of the weapon. She needed a smaller bow.

"Irina!" Natalya's cry ripped Nasan's reverie to shreds. "Put that down at once."

Startled, Nasan released the bowstring. The arrow shot through the window and landed mid-courtyard, narrowly missing a servant. She grabbed for the bow as Natalya dragged it from her hands. "You have to unstring it first." The words came out in Tatar. Ignoring her mother-in-law's basilisk glare, she freed the bowstring, holding the weapon well clear as it snapped back to its natural curve, and dropped it into its case. To her chagrin, Maria sniggered in the doorway. Daniil, standing behind Maria, raised both eyebrows, but his mouth curved and glints of amusement lit his tawny eyes.

"Don't give me that defiant look, young lady," Natalya said. "Weapons are not for women. I can't imagine why your mother allowed it. My dearest Anastasia—"

"Did not shoot," Nasan said through gritted teeth. As if she could not guess that spineless, precious Anastasia would shrivel up and die before she did anything worthwhile. "I do. Did."

Natalya muttered an automatic correction. Nasan had forgotten (again) to give the verb its feminine form. Tatar words had no gender; she doubted she would ever remember that Russian ones did—even chairs and tables, silly as that sounded.

She was plotting how to distract Natalya with grammar when Daniil interrupted his mother's scolding. "Enough, Mama. She drew a bow—and did it well." He grinned at Nasan, who felt heat suffuse her cheeks. "I'll swear her feminine attributes can survive the strain."

Maria muttered something; Nasan heard only the disgust in her voice. Natalya thrust her jaw forward and stood her ground. "Her job is to bear children and care for your household, not to act like a wild nomad."

Daniil pushed his mother toward the door. "I suspect she knows that, Mama. Take Maria away, please. I'd like to say goodbye."

"Goodbye?" Nasan had been astonished to hear Daniil defend her against his formidable mother, but this news unsettled her more. "Gone? But we..." She stopped before the words "just married" could slip out. Daniil could count the days as well as she.

Count—and discount. With a sickening thud, her heart registered what Maria had tried to tell her at the wedding. That Daniil wanted only one thing from women and, when he got it, moved on. Even if the woman in question was his wife.

Or perhaps she *had* displeased him, and he didn't like to hurt her feelings by telling her. It shouldn't matter—they had married to secure the truce, and the truce would stand. If she had a lick of sense, she'd rejoice that this womanizing stranger planned to go about his business.

Obviously, she had no sense whatsoever.

"I know," he said. "I'm sorry, but I have to leave right away."

The lump in her throat further impeded her Russian. "Where?"

"Don't worry about that." He wrapped his arm around her waist and tugged her to him. "Come here so I can kiss you."

For a moment, Nasan took heart from that statement. He wouldn't want to kiss her if she had displeased him. But why leave her before they spent even one whole day together? She pressed her palms against his chest, resisting. "How long?"

"Not one day longer than necessary, I promise." Then he did kiss her, with the same devastating competence as before. Nasan forgot her questions, her surroundings, the blessed Anastasia, everything but the pressure of his mouth.

They were still kissing when a low moan interrupted them. Daniil released her and nodded at a maid who stood in the doorway, a stricken expression on her face. The maid dropped her eyes and apologized.

"It's nothing, Grusha," Daniil said.

Nothing?

Nasan scowled at the maid. Except for a bruise that disfigured one cheek, the girl looked no different from the others: brown hair, blue eyes, pretty except for the pasty complexion. Then Nasan looked at her husband. The softness in Daniil's face shocked her.

Grusha. The servant Maria had mentioned. The one who had missed the wedding, his lover. Who still meant something to him, she saw. More than his wife did, no doubt. How could it be otherwise, given the circumstances of their marriage?

She made a mental note: Grusha = trouble.

The girl lingered in the doorway, tears misting her pale eyes. "You, work," Nasan snapped.

The maid scurried from the room, and Nasan hissed. To think that mere moments ago she had melted into her husband's arms.

Her reprobate husband, who showed no evidence of remorse. Quite the contrary. No sooner had Grusha made her escape than Daniil brushed past Nasan to collect his bow and arrows. He pecked her cheek as he went by. "Don't fret, sweetheart," he said. "Only you from now on."

As if she had learned nothing growing up in a world of multiple wives. *Me and how many others?* Nasan, fuming, watched her husband walk out the door.

Semyon shifted his feet and stared at the "beautiful corner," its triangular table holding an icon triptych and candles, their feeble flames no match for the sunshine that transformed the mica windows of Fyodor Koshkin's estate near the Kremlin into glowing panels. He wished he had the nerve to sit in one of those winged armchairs with the velvet upholstery. He'd left the inn before dawn and ridden at a speed appropriate to news of a military invasion— all to complete his mission in three days. As a result, he was tired, irritated, hungry, and thirsty. If he'd guessed Koshkin intended to keep him dragging his heels, he could have spent another half-hour in the arms of the innkeeper's daughter instead of riding hell-for-leather for Moscow. Or stopped on the road for borscht and a beer.

Boys played at war in the courtyard, their calls drowning the sound of the opening door until the yeasty aroma of mead wafted past Semyon's nose. A servant. How long did Koshkin plan to keep him waiting?

Could he at least get a drink?

"Be seated," Koshkin said, his snakelike hiss well in evidence. "Refresh yourself."

Semyon jerked his head. Koshkin and his steward must have entered together. The nobleman stood, his head level with Semyon's shoulder and amusement in his eyes. Behind him, a middle-aged man in simple shirt and trousers held a tray with tankards.

Sneaking up on people. Really. As if they were no older than the boys in the courtyard?

Well, let Koshkin have his fun. At least he'd deigned to make an appearance. Semyon could present his report and go home.

Where Solomonida would jump for joy at his return. *Right.*

Urged by his host, he took a seat in one of the armchairs, accepted a tankard of mead, and prepared to summarize his trip to Dmitrov. Judiciously edited, of course. The innkeeper's daughter concerned no one but Semyon himself.

"How is support for our prince?" Koshkin took the opposite chair, placing his tankard on a side table.

Semyon debated whether he, too, should not drink. But the long ride and the hour's wait had left him parched, and what was a swig of mead between friends? He swallowed before answering Koshkin's question. Semyon had prepared his answers in advance, out of a desire to prove himself the right choice for this mission.

But he saw no harm in a few moments' delay after Koshkin had made *him* wait.

He took another swig, savoring the frothy brew. The steward handed him a cloth napkin and left the room. A sensible precaution. Missions to discover the level of support for Prince Yuri could prove hazardous if Grand Princess Elena—a touchy broad if Semyon had ever seen one, worse than Solomonida—got wind of them. Elena saw Yuri as a threat to her son, after all.

He glanced at his host, who said, "Did you fulfill your mission or not?" Against the crimson velvet of the armchair, Koshkin's sapphire caftan gleamed, its hue picked up in the swirling patterns that decorated the cream paint on the walls.

He would gain nothing from further delay. "I did, Fyodor Mikhailovich. The court at Dmitrov is a skeleton of its former self, with most of its servitors recalled to Moscow. The residents remember Prince Yuri with kindness. Dmitrov flourished under his rule, and his departure has orphaned it. If you can spirit him out of his cell and convey him there, I think they will rally to his cause. Otherwise, I doubt they will risk their necks. They are traders, not warriors."

Koshkin nodded. "We must move swiftly in any event. Elena grows more powerful by the day, and she and her brother-in-law Andrei have come to terms, as your uncle predicted. Are you prepared to assist me?"

Semyon hesitated. His father would say, "Wait twenty-four hours, son. Don't leap at every offer." But his father's caution had not saved him from the attack of dysentery that killed him on campaign years ago. It had not kept him around to assist Semyon's career.

He had forced Koshkin to wait for one answer; that should be sufficient. Time to act on his own behalf to secure the advancement he sought. Even young Daniil landed assignments that gave him an opportunity to distinguish himself in battle. Semyon refused to rot in place while a cousin five years his junior forged past him.

"I am," he said. "What would you have me do?"

Koshkin's lips curved in his serpent smile. "You will find out in good time. For the moment, I think it's time you got off guard duty, don't you?"

When Semyon nodded, Koshkin's grin widened. "Good. You just became my personal assistant."

Daniil caught Grusha by the arm as she passed by with a load of shirts and pulled her into the nearest room. It happened to be an unoccupied bedroom, but that didn't matter. He would leave the door open. He needed only a moment; then he'd let her go.

He didn't love Grusha, but he cared enough to take an interest in her welfare. He'd seen the mark on her cheek. And here, standing closer, he could not miss the chafing on her wrists.

"Who gave you those bruises?" he asked.

She faced him, her face wooden, the shirts forming a barrier between them. "No one, Lord. Don't trouble yourself."

Her obvious unhappiness sparked his ready compassion. He brushed her cheek with one finger. "Tell me. You're part of the family. We don't leave our servants to the mercy of strangers."

Shirts scattered around his feet as Grusha, sobbing, launched herself at him. Daniil staggered, righted himself with an effort, and, not knowing how else to respond, put one arm around her waist and patted her back with the other. The soft scent of herbs rose from her hair, and he breathed it in, remembering their nights together. Many nights—too many, in retrospect. He shouldn't have lowered his guard when Boris died. But he couldn't push her away. The bruises told their own tale. What had she been up to?

Pottery smashed against the floor. He turned his head to find Nasan and Maria gaping at him. Shards of painted clay littered the floor; cherry juice from the jug Nasan had dropped spattered her robes and stained the rug at her feet. The smell of ripe fruit overwhelmed Grusha's herbs.

Too late, he let go. Grusha shoved past the other women and fled down the corridor. Maria laughed, a piercing yowl that made him want to throttle her.

"I didn't mean," he began, but Nasan raced toward him. While he stumbled between apology and explanation, she slammed both palms into his chest and yelled something in Tatar. He doubled over, gasping.

He saw her spin on one crimson velvet toe. A cloud of jasmine swirled around him as her robes swept past his face. The swift clack-clack of heels against the wooden floor signaled her departure. Maria's mocking laughter assailed his ears. By the time Daniil recovered his breath, his wife had vanished.

Nasan fled down the outside staircase, too angry to think, never mind speak. "Only you from now on"—the words pounded in her brain, interspersed with images of Grusha wrapped in Daniil's arms. How dare he humiliate her that way? She was a descendant of Genghis, not some third-class concubine he could woo and cast aside.

Halfway down the second flight, she tripped over her hem. Her skirts tangled around her legs, and she pitched forward. Pure terror squeezed her heart as she catapulted into space. Unbidden, words imprinted themselves on her brain. *Daniil will have Grusha if I die!*

Her body hit the banister, and she clung to it. Her head reeled. When she could, she dropped onto the stairs and, shaking, pressed her face against her knees. She'd almost killed herself over a husband who had never wanted her and whom she, if she had the wits of an unfledged duckling, would not have trusted for an instant. Let Daniil have his servants and his whores. He would not also have his wife.

But her torment had not ended. Footsteps sounded above her. Nasan leaped to her feet, but too late. Natalya stood three steps up.

"Why, child, what possessed you to sit on the stairs?" Natalya descended, majestic as always, and pressed a hand against Nasan's back. "And your gown! To the courtyard, my dear, and quickly, before your husband takes his leave."

Nasan, cornered, gave in. No doubt the blessed Anastasia would have done no less.

The moments that followed were among the most hideous of her life. It took every bit of Sumbeka's training to keep her standing in the Kolychev courtyard, flanked by Maria on one side and her in-laws on the other, mouthing pleasantries she did not mean to a husband she could not wait to see the back of.

"Goodbye," she said. Her voice sounded flat even to her own ears, but she could do nothing about that. If the grandmothers cared one bit for her, they would take him to their hunting grounds and let her go home.

"Journey well," she added. *Until a forest spirit eats you.*

Daniil's hands closed about her upper arms. He bent to murmur in her ear, "That scene with Grusha, it was not what you thought—"

She shook her head, breaking the contact, blocking whatever lies he meant to tell. She had seen him with her own eyes. How could he explain it away?

"Not important," she said. Anger and shame wrestled with her mother's warning that no husband is faithful. Could he not have waited until he left the house?

Tears choked her, but she would not cry in front of these Russians. "Goodbye."

Daniil tightened his grip on her arms. She stared straight ahead and hardened her heart against his sigh. He held her for a moment, then kissed her forehead. "All right, love. We'll work it out when I get back."

Not if I have anything to say about it. But she nodded, desperate to get him out of her sight.

She could sense him studying her, but her resolute refusal to engage him at last bore fruit. "Till later, then," he said, and withdrew his hands.

Through a watery prism, Nasan watched him mount his horse and ride away. The moment the gate closed behind him, she ran. Natalya called after her, but for once Nasan paid her no heed.

Maria's voice, clear and shrill, floated after her. "Don't worry, Mama-in-law. There's nothing wrong with her. She found out what her husband's really like, that's all."

Nasan did not stop to hear Natalya's reply.

Voices drove her from one storeroom to another until she found a refuge in the icehouse, blessedly cool on this hot June day. She broke the seal on a jar of apple cider and took it with her as she wedged herself into a corner behind a barrel the height of a full-grown man. No one would see her there even if they did come in for supplies.

The cider, sweet and tart together, smelled of autumn and home. The home barred to her by the very husband who had so shattered and confused her—as if his kisses had provoked some caring in her despite their short time together, impossible as that seemed. And she had only herself to blame, putting her faith in a man whom everyone insisted should not be trusted with women. The memory of him with Grusha made her cringe.

If her family had stayed, if his mother did not scold so often, if Maria had decided to befriend her—then Nasan would not care that her husband had left. He was a stranger, an enemy. But to live in a house where everyone hated her and even the slaves could laugh in their sleeves as she passed because they knew Daniil better than she, that was intolerable.

Where had he gone, anyway? Had he told Grusha? The thought added to her sense of mortification. To Russians, a wife might mean less than a slave.

When he returned, she would spurn him. *That* would teach him not to embarrass her with servants.

She considered running away, but her parents had minced no words: the truce depended on her presence in this house. Break it, and even the grandmothers would cast her out, leaving her without protection wherever she went.

But if she stayed, what then? A life of housework and embroidery with women who thought her a barbarian would destroy her. She might as well kill herself now.

Images of Girei, their last snowball fight, their years in the nomad camp beset her. She imagined him sitting cross-legged on the barrel that sheltered her, urging her not to give up or give in, to find her own path to womanhood. By staying in the Kolychev house, she protected her clan. And since Daniil had chosen his old allegiances over her, she owed him nothing. Since childhood, she had sought a life like the one she had created in Kasimov, masked and dressed in Girei's discarded clothes. What better time than now to revive that dream?

Of course, it would be more difficult here than at home. There she had known where to go, what to do, where to find help. Anyone who discovered her masquerade would have reported to *Ata*, guaranteed to scold but usually amenable to persuasion. Moscow was a huge town filled with unfamiliar streets, a barely intelligible language, strange customs—a place where she had no clear understanding of the law and no loving family to support her. But if the ancestors stood with her, she did not need human aid. She could go it alone.

She considered this point for some time, choosing one option, then the other, while Girei's spirit teased her with images of needles and laundry soap and pictures of the princesses in her book of epic tales. Eventually she realized she could test the idea, find out if she liked it, then decide. And in preparation, she would master the language and customs as fast as possible. Natalya wanted to teach her, and she would learn.

The act of decision calmed her, and her mind turned to practicalities. She had brought her boys' clothes and her sword, but she needed a bow, quiver, and arrows. A raid on the storerooms would supply what she lacked.

More important was a plan. The servants barred the gates at nightfall. Her exit and reentry would require thought. Secrecy was paramount. Just as in Kasimov, women remained within the family compound most of the time. Discovery would put an end to her scheme.

There would be dogs. She had learned in Kasimov how to handle them. No doubt Moscow dogs liked dried meat, too. No one would notice small amounts disappearing from the pantry.

At this point in her deliberations the bell rang for supper. Nasan left the icehouse and, practicing for a future exit, reached the house without attracting attention.

Natalya pounced on her the moment she came through the door. "Where have you been? How could you run off like that, a dozen tasks left unfulfilled? Why, you haven't even changed your clothes. My dear Anastasia—"

Nasan mumbled apologies and slid onto the bench. Natalya signaled to the nearest servant, and a bowl of fish soup appeared.

"You must eat," Natalya said. "Look at you, skinny as a bird. How will we get a babe from a child with no flesh on her bones?"

Nasan studied the soup. Its herbal aroma was pleasant enough, and the chunks of white fish looked appetizing. But among the fish and carrots and diced onion floated slivers of cabbage. Russians seemed to eat it at every meal; its smell pervaded the kitchens and dining areas and crept into her clothes. If someone cut her open, they would soon find her green and curly inside.

At least it was a fast day, and Maria could not amuse herself by slipping chunks of pig into the food as she had yesterday. Grateful for that shred of comfort, Nasan picked up her lacquered spoon and sipped broth.

When the meal ended, she fled to her room. In the chest where she'd stowed her black outfit, she uncovered the spirit doll, wrapped in a prayer rug. She touched the grandmother's lips and murmured the traditional greeting before propping it on her dressing table. With Daniil gone, she could display it. She tucked the rug under the bed. Whenever possible, she would say her prayers to Allah, as a good Muslim should. Starting tonight.

Moving the doll revealed her sword. She lifted it from the chest, ran her fingers over the chased scabbard, then replaced it. No need for weapons yet.

She rummaged in the chest again until she identified the right bundle. As she pulled the clothes out, a small object clanked against the floor. She picked it up.

Ogodai's golden lynx glistened in the sun. She swung it on its chain, remembering the day he'd given it to her. She unwrapped the cloth, searching for the black velvet pouch where she'd stashed the chains that day. Yes, there it was. The second pendant lay inside.

Daniil's lynx. Which she would not give him, because he loved another. Grusha or Anastasia or Darya. The name did not matter. She threw his pendant onto a pile of veils and clasped her own around her neck. Tears pricked her lids, and she scolded herself.

Forget Daniil. His indifference sets me free.

She had done her bit for others, sacrificed her interests to theirs. Now the time had come to pursue her own destiny. From now on, she refused to be a pawn on the political chessboard.

Amid the upper branches of the World Tree, leaves shiver in the mists. The grandmothers smile. Tengri rejoices to see his messenger acknowledged. At last, Ashina's daughter has belted on her sword.

Chapter 13

"BUT WHY MUST I STAY, PAPA?" MARIA LEANED FORWARD, HER hands clasped together and a coaxing expression on her face. "Mama says Lyuba wears her out. She wants my help. I can't bear Boris a child now that he's dead. And everyone's so mean to me there."

Koshkin smiled at his daughter, the one person he regarded as a kindred soul. They were seated in the winged armchairs of the room where, a week ago, he had received Semyon Kolychev's report. Kolychev had been on duty again until Maria arrived and had had the nerve to grumble when dispatched to cool his heels outside. For that piece of bad attitude, Koshkin intended to make him wait twice as long. If Semyon didn't understand that assistants spend most of their time twiddling their thumbs while their masters make policy, it was high time he learned.

But for now he focused on Maria. "That's the problem, kitten," he said. "Not bearing a child lets you come home and try again, but who's going to take you if you're barren? And you can be of use to me there."

"I'm not barren."

Maria's deviousness was part of her charm, but her naïveté made her malleable. He raised an eyebrow to goad her further.

"I'm not," she insisted. "Boris consummated the marriage, then left me to sleep alone. You might as well have married me to a monk."

He shrugged. That statement had the ring of truth. Rumor said Boris Kolychev would have preferred the church to soldiering. No chance of that, though. The aristocratic clans wanted heirs and a direct say in policy, neither of which went with monastic vows. Even the metropolitan, who had the grand prince's ear, could only intercede and exhort.

How Boris, a milksop from a family of milksops, had attracted the ire of the Kasimov Tatars remained a mystery. But with Boris dead, Koshkin had another opportunity to dispose of his beautiful daughter in the manner that would best benefit them both.

A rare miscalculation, that match with Boris. At the time, he'd sought an alliance with Kolychev to strengthen his own position at court. He'd picked the elder son so Maria could one day take over the household. She'd like that. But these days the younger son looked like the better bet. Daniil had the temperament to manage her, a gift his brother had conspicuously lacked.

Worse, it had all been for naught. Within days of the wedding, the grand prince whom Koshkin had been courting contracted what proved to be a fatal illness; and not much more than a week after the ruler's death Nikolai Kolychev stabbed his new connection by marriage in the back—supporting the incarceration of Prince Yuri, the grand prince's younger brother, just as Koshkin was gathering his forces to put Yuri on the throne.

Kolychev would pay for that. Koshkin took great satisfaction in having lured Kolychev's lame-brained nephew into supporting his scheme. With Maria's help, he would bring Kolychev down.

Once he secured her cooperation. "Yes, I see," he said. "Not much of a man, our Boris. We'll find you someone better next time."

"So I can come home, Papa? Please. I'm miserable there. Natalya bosses me from morning to night, and I can't move without tripping over the Tatar."

He chucked her on the chin. "I know, kitten. I understand. Soon, I promise. I have high hopes for you."

The walnut eyes that provided such a striking contrast to her alabaster skin and copper hair narrowed. "Who, Papa? Tell me, and I swear I will do whatever you ask."

Should he tell? Absolutely not. They would both be safer if he kept quiet. Yet the temptation to share his plans with someone overwhelmed his natural caution. The news would horrify his wife; his other children would bore him with stupid questions and probably divulge the whole to the first person they met; and his subordinates, even if he trusted them not to betray him, could not appreciate the subtle brilliance of his mind. But Maria had a brain as twisty as his own. Give her a sense of how the system worked, and she'd go after the goal like a bird dog scenting squab.

"Well, love," he asked, "what would you say to becoming grand princess?"

Her mouth opened, but no sound came out. He laughed. When had he last left his daughter speechless? "I'm trying to free Prince Yuri. The old grand prince's brother. Our grandfathers would have named Yuri next in line for the throne. They wouldn't have considered giving the crown to a child. We need to bring the old ways back. Even the Tatars know that."

"But, Papa, how will freeing Prince Yuri lead to me becoming grand princess?" Maria's eyes widened until he could see himself reflected in their depths. He had her full attention.

He patted her hand, which lay on the arm of his chair. "That's why it's vital that you're not barren, kitten. Freeing Prince Yuri is the first step. We free him and put him on the throne to win his gratitude. When he's seeking a suitable reward, that's where you come in."

Her brows drew together as she tried to follow his reasoning. Koshkin relished the telling, the information withheld followed by the moment of revelation. A few more facts, and Maria would grasp the whole. "The most powerful figure at court," he said, "is the father-in-law or brother-in-law of the reigning grand prince. Under normal circumstances, Prince Yuri would have married years ago. He's fifty-four."

Maria's face contracted in a moue of distaste. "As old as that."

"A few years with that old man, my pet, and you're set for life."

She nodded, and he went on. "Old Grand Prince Vasily was no fool. Those twenty years when he hoped for an heir and couldn't get one, he kept his brother from having legitimate children. And even after Vasily divorced his first wife and got sons on his second, his brother Yuri remained a threat, because many of us boyars would back an adult ruler over a baby. So Vasily refused his brother permission to marry, and unmarried he remains to this day." He waited for her to weave the stray pieces of information together.

"But once you put Yuri on the throne," she mused, "he will seek a bride, to have heirs of his own and keep his brother's children out of the line of succession." She clapped her hands, her face alight with the satisfaction of discovery. "And if *you* put him on the throne, you can persuade him to marry me, and you will be the most powerful man in Russia. Papa, that's brilliant."

"Exactly, my clever girl. Will that make it easier to endure another few months with the Kolychevs?"

"If you promise I can come home at the end, no matter what." She clasped his hand. "You will promise, won't you, Papa?"

He had nothing to lose by agreeing. If his plans fell short, he would find another use for her. "Of course, my child. And while you remain there, you can perform a small service for me." She would love this, his duplicitous darling.

"Anything, Papa. How may I help you?"

Definitely the best of his offspring. "Watch Nikolai Kolychev. Report anything odd that happens inside his household." He patted her cheek once more when she nodded agreement. "I trust no one more than you, kitten. I will visit you soon."

Maria could take a hint. She stood at once, kissed him on both cheeks, and arranged her veil to cover the upper half of her body. "Yes, Papa," she said as he led her out of the room.

Daniil halted in front of the gatehouse that marked the entry to the Trinity Monastery, one of Russia's most prestigious religious institutions. These days, the monastery seemed a far cry from the shack that Sergius of Radonezh had built with his own hands in a wilderness so uninhabited that the saint shared his meals with a bear. Bread and honey, and if fate didn't supply enough for two, the saint went hungry rather than disappoint the bear.

Boris had loved that story. Studying the massive palisades that ringed the stucco cathedrals, their cross-tipped onion domes glittering against the clear June sky, hearing the voices of a hundred monastery servants, Daniil wondered what his gentle brother had made of Sergius's legacy. The dedicated monk at home with the creatures of the woods seemed so much closer in spirit to the Boris Daniil had loved than this massive enterprise, which diverged only in scale from the noble estates their mother managed with such skill.

Had the brother Daniil loved ever existed? That nagging question had propelled Daniil onto this journey, which he prayed would not turn out to be a fool's errand. He needed to find out whether he had been mistaken in his brother's character before he could stride with confidence into the future. Because if he could sustain for years a false image of his brother, how could he trust his instincts with anyone else? His new wife, his family, his men?

His new wife, probably still spitting at the sound of his name. Daniil's self-image as a suave manager of women had suffered a severe blow from the incident with Grusha. But he didn't see what else he could have done. Someone had hurt her. What kind of master—never mind former lover—would not ask what happened? He hadn't expected her to throw herself at him. Nasan should have listened to his explanation.

To be fair, Nasan had also seemed upset. They hadn't had time to build trust between them. After he learned the answers to his questions, he would go home and reassure her.

One of the monastery's peasant servitors, to judge from his clothing—linen shirt and linsey-woolsey trousers, birchbark shoes and hair that looked as if his wife had dropped a bowl upside down on his head and cut around it—had come out to greet Daniil and his party. No one traveled the roads alone; a man could expect to have his purse if not his throat slit within a few miles of the city walls. Daniil had brought a dozen of his father's soldiers, those most capable of riding long hours and defending themselves if necessary. Like him, they wore chain mail and pointed steel helmets, a clear signal to bandits to seek their prey elsewhere.

"We need food," Daniil said. "A bed for the night. And someone who can confirm whether my brother stayed here between the Presentation and Annunciation Day. Can you help us?"

The peasant bowed and stood aside. "Of course, Lord. You are welcome. But you will not go armed into the abbot's presence?"

He sounded horrified. Daniil, embarrassed by his own discourtesy, unbelted his sword and handed it, with his bow case and quiver, to the peasant. One of his men swung down from the saddle, collected a pile of weaponry from his fellows, and helped the monastery servant carry it into the gatehouse for storage.

The servant called, and a small army of peasants gathered around the horses. Daniil and the rest of his men dismounted, surrendered their beasts to the peasants' care, and followed the gatekeeper into the monastery compound.

Koshkin waved goodbye to his daughter—who, closed in by veil and box on wheels, could not see him. His four sons dashed from one corner of the house to the fence, shoving and pushing one another despite the shouts of the stablehand assigned to watch them. At one side of the courtyard a tall guardsman with pale blond hair kicked a large pebble from one side of the square to the other. Semyon Kolychev. Koshkin walked over and tapped Kolychev on the shoulder.

The great lunk turned. Forced to look up, Koshkin experienced a surge of self-directed irritation. Surely he could have arranged this meeting in such a way that he didn't have to endure Semyon towering over him.

But he'd wanted to hold the discussion here, in the open air, where he could see in every direction and need not worry about eavesdroppers. He shouted his sons into silence and, when he got it, told the groom to take all four to the stables. Only when they ran off did he turn back to Semyon. "Matters are coming to a head," he said. "Next month, while the boyars worry about whether Lithuania or the Tatars will attack first—that's when we make our move."

"I'm ready."

"You're not," Koshkin said, underlining who was in charge. "But you will be. Soon, if you know what's good for you. You need a woman. And a storeroom, comfortably appointed but out of the way. With a padlock. A few trusted men to guard it."

He had Semyon's attention now. "But who will stay there, Fyodor Mikhailovich? And what kind of woman?"

"A nursemaid." Koshkin kept his voice curt. Kolychev had a hard time remembering that his job was to take orders, not ask questions.

"A nursemaid? For Prince Yuri? Is he that bad off?"

Koshkin cuffed him. "Idiot. Not for Yuri!"

"Then what's going on? I agreed to help you free Prince Yuri."

This was the trouble with depending on well-born mutts. Koshkin had no intention of taking Semyon into his confidence, but he'd have to supply enough information to keep Semyon from balking.

"We are freeing Yuri," Koshkin said. "We can't walk in there and haul his manacles out of the wall, though, can we? We have to make it worth Grand Princess Elena's while to let him go. And there are only two things that would persuade that woman to release Yuri in exchange. That's why you need the nursemaid and the secure location."

Semyon's jaw dropped, and his shoulders slumped to the point where Koshkin no longer felt as if he were staring into the eyes of a giant. "You're going to abduct the baby princes and hold them to ransom. Have you lost your wits? If you can get them out of the Kremlin, why not Yuri?"

"Because Yuri's locked up," Koshkin said, exasperated by such simplemindedness. "The princes have a nurse and servants, but the palace guards know you. You can get past them. Now follow my orders and report when you're finished. Dismissed."

"Yes, Fyodor Mikhailovich." Semyon saluted and left. Koshkin could almost see wheels spinning in that silver-gilt head.

Hmm. Had he placed too much stock in Semyon's gullibility and his own ability to ensure the man's continued loyalty?

He thought not. So far, Kolychev gave every evidence of remaining committed to their joint enterprise. Wouldn't hurt to keep an eye on him, though. Koshkin beckoned to one of his own men, a youth named Stenka, a soldier from some backwoods village who'd sold himself into service in the wake of a famine—not an uncommon tale. A little thick but reliable, with the sturdy common sense that peasants often exhibited. The combination should equip him well for the task Koshkin had in mind.

"Shadow the blond man who just left," Koshkin said. "Kolychev, Semyon Pavlovich: that's his name. If he talks to anyone, try to hear what he says. And if he gives you an opportunity, offer to enter his service. Whatever happens, watch him and report to me. Do you understand?"

Stenka saluted and trotted out of the courtyard. Koshkin inhaled several lungfuls of summer air before going back into the house to ponder the day's events.

Semyon left Koshkin's estate in a thoughtful mood. What an interesting day it had turned out to be. Who'd have thought Old Ramrod-Spine Koshkin would melt like the mother of a newborn over that hussy of a daughter? Then Koshkin dropped his bombshell: it wasn't enough to attack Grand Princess Elena indirectly by freeing her brother-in-law and putting him on the throne. No, Koshkin had decided the only way to secure Prince Yuri's release was to attack Elena directly by abducting her sons, ensuring that if the whole plot failed to run as smoothly as an Italian cannon, someone would pay for it with his life. Leaving Semyon wondering whether to tell Koshkin what to do with his master plan.

With so much on his mind, he headed for the marketplace instead of home. It was Wednesday, so the stalls were open. Bread and sausage, plucked birds and haunches of beef, a panoply of vegetables and fruits dangled from kiosks or lay spread on tables to lure passing customers. Grandmothers in smocks and headscarves held headless chickens by the feet, assessing their age and quality for the stewpot. Stewards bargained on behalf of their masters. Other merchants traded in silks and cottons, velvets and brocades, jewelry and art. Colorful lacquer ware, ivory combs, incense and perfume, icons, medallions, candlesticks, kvass—this was the Moscow market. You could buy anything here. The noise of storeowners hawking their wares and purchasers' haggling, the smell of food raw and cooked, the colors and textures, the satisfaction of cinnamon-splashed donuts against the tongue drew Semyon like an angler's lure.

He washed down the donuts with watery beer and settled in one corner of a makeshift tavern to consider his options. Forward or back?

Forward meant advancement and risk. But not necessarily risk to Semyon. Koshkin had opened himself to charges of treason. A word in the right ear would bring him down.

Back meant trusting Uncle Nikolai, the only relative with the clout not only to circumvent Koshkin's schemes but to do so in a way that hid Semyon's involvement in them.

Uncle Nikolai, who had chucked Semyon out of a family wedding because Daniil started a fight. Who like as not would raise those bushy eyebrows and suggest that Semyon should have thought twice about placing the entire clan in jeopardy of guilt by association.

No, Semyon wanted no favors from his uncle. Better to play the game to its end. If Koshkin's plans succeeded, Semyon would prosper. If they failed, too bad for Koshkin. Semyon had done nothing wrong.

For the moment, then, he needed a woman and a storeroom. How to provide those in a way that ensured no one could blame him if Koshkin's plans went awry?

A brown-haired strumpet approached the booth opposite, swinging a wicker basket against ample hips. She reminded him of that slave of Uncle Nikolai's, the one he'd seduced after his relatives kicked him out of their fancy wedding. He'd planned to look her up when he returned from Dmitrov, then forgotten about her. She'd do fine as the nursemaid. He had a hold on her, too: the slut wouldn't want Daniil finding out how she behaved behind his back.

Solomonida would cause trouble, if only by forcing him to work around her, so it was time she and her sister set off on their pilgrimage. He'd have them both packing before supper. A word in her escort's ear would guarantee that the abbess kept the women for a good long stay.

With any luck, Solomonida would decide he was banishing her to the convent, as old Grand Prince Vasily had done with his barren wife, and would return suitably chastened when Semyon deigned to receive her.

Not that Solomonida *was* barren: she'd lost two fine boys before they opened their eyes and wept over each one until Semyon wanted to smack her. Then she bore a living daughter, whom she coddled as if the worthless brat equaled a son. A pretty thing, golden like her mother. Semyon avoided the girl as much as possible.

He would allow Solomonida to take their daughter with her. That should reconcile her to the journey—and get the brat out of the way, to boot.

That left the estate. His own wouldn't do. Servants' chatter spread like wildfire. Semyon wanted no clear link between himself and this wild scheme of Koshkin's.

Uncle Nikolai owned a small property near the palisade that ringed this portion of the city. It lay near the river, close to the broken-down hut where that old witch dispensed herbal remedies for toothache and broken hearts. The family no longer used it: it held moldy furniture and the like. Too far from the center of town for anything else.

Secure. Unguarded. Perfect for holding a couple of kidnapping victims in a place where no one would look for them. And it gave him a hold on his uncle, if he needed one. Nikolai would rage, but he'd have to cooperate. Teach him to raise his eyebrows.

Semyon considered the next stage in Koshkin's scheme. How would he get the children out of the Kremlin, if it were up to him? He couldn't corrupt the boy's nurse. He knew her, too well for comfort: Agrafena Cheliadnina, a middle-aged noblewoman with the mind of a ferret. She'd whacked him once when she caught him dicing on duty. Bitch.

Dicing. Koshkin had caught him dicing that first day. And spared him, even as he'd threatened to report Semyon's companion. Semyon had seen that man, still on guard duty, earlier today.

That's how he would do it, if it were up to him. He'd threaten that guard, set a couple of henchmen to watch him, and when Agrafena fell asleep, they could smuggle the princes out of the palace. If Koshkin asked for suggestions, that's what Semyon would recommend.

A nondescript soldier in battered leather armor—brown hair, gray eyes, brown clothes, with a broad face and snub nose—stopped in front of Semyon's chair. "Do I know you?" he snapped, lest the man take him for an equal.

"No, Lord." The soldier bowed, removing his helmet to reveal a bald spot on his crown.

"Then what's your business here?"

The soldier turned his helmet in his hands and shifted his feet. "I wondered, Lord…"

"Speak up. What do you want?"

"If you could use another man." The words came out in a rush. "My last master died in battle, and his sons had no use for me. I need a position."

Semyon drew his sword. The soldier leaped aside, pulling his saber from his sheath in time to divert Semyon's thrust. The ringing of the weapons as they clashed drew the attention of everyone in the tavern. The soldier crouched, shifting his gait, ready for Semyon's next move.

Semyon laughed. He shoved his blade into its sheath and held out his hand. "You're hired. What's your name?"

"Stenka."

"Well, Stenka, report to me tomorrow morning." He gave his address. As he watched the peasant walk away, Semyon continued to chuckle.

God must smile on their enterprise to send such a man right when Semyon needed someone to prepare Nikolai's warehouse for its new purpose. Stenka could begin in the morning, as soon as Semyon had his wife and sister-in-law on the road. He would send the men who had accompanied him and Boris to Kasimov, otherwise a useless bunch. They should be able to handle a few decrepit chairs without assistance. Furniture doesn't fight back.

His plans made, Semyon drained the last of the watery beer and went home.

Chapter 14

NASAN, POISED ON THE OUTSIDE STAIRCASE, SAW THE courtyard gates open to admit Maria's carriage. As the conveyance drew to a halt, Nasan turned on her heel, determined to postpone an encounter with her sister-in-law as long as possible.

Two steps up, and her shoulders slumped. Natalya sailed down, pushing Nasan before her. "Mushrooms, Irina," Natalya said.

Mushrooms. Of course. And if not mushrooms, wheat. Or oats. Rye, fruit, drying meat, beets, cabbage, beer. Natalya's list of chores appeared endless.

Nasan did not protest. Mushrooms carried no appeal whatsoever, but little more than a week had passed since the wedding, and already her mother-in-law had produced worse tasks than drying fungi. No point in complaining. Better to use the opportunity to practice her Russian.

Maria emerged from her carriage, slinky as a coursing hound. Her supercilious smile vanished as Natalya grabbed her arm, shepherding both girls ahead of her. "Come along, daughters. Irina, don't dawdle. And Maria, take that smirk off your face. It's unbecoming. If Boris could see you…"

A servant distracted her, and she broke off in mid-sentence to listen. Maria clutched Nasan's wrist and muttered, "Well, he can't, can he? Thanks to you and your wild-beast relatives."

"He wild beast." Nasan dragged her arm free. "Leave me alone."

"Gladly," Maria said. "Just stay out of my way."

Natalya arrived in time to hear this last comment. "Girls, girls, stop this bickering. Have you no shame, wicked ones? Women speak softly and behave decorously, like my dear Anastasia. Do not forget."

The girls hung their heads, but under cover of her robe, Maria kicked Nasan's ankle. Nasan stepped on her sister-in-law's hem. It made a delightful ripping sound as Maria, prodded by Natalya, moved forward.

"Sorry." Nasan removed her foot. "Mistake." She widened her eyes at the glowering Maria.

Natalya surveyed them, scowling, then marched them to the far side of the courtyard, where a small group of servants waited. Several slatted wooden racks stood there. Each one held a flat rectangular sieve filled to the brim with mushrooms. Half a dozen servants, male and female, stood waiting. As Natalya approached, they bowed their heads.

"That one." She pointed to the nearest sieve. When two of the servants presented it to her, she selected a mushroom and dangled it in front of Maria's face. "What type is this?"

Maria shuffled her feet and looked pained. "I don't know, Mama-in-law. Does it matter?"

Natalya glanced over her shoulder at the servants holding the sieve. "Does it *matter?*" She returned her gaze to Maria. "It will matter if you pick the wrong one and poison your household, don't you think?"

When Maria did not answer, Natalya held the mushroom out to Nasan. "What is it, Irina?"

"*Narat gömbisi,*" Nasan said. Her Russian tutor, lacking Natalya's direction, had failed to cover the many varieties of edible mushrooms. Nasan envied him.

"Saffron milk-cap," Natalya said. "Pronounce it, Irina."

Nasan pronounced it—over and over, until her mother-in-law indicated satisfaction. Natalya signaled for more mushrooms, and the whole process repeated: Maria claiming ignorance, Nasan supplying the mushroom's Tatar name, Natalya correcting her.

After eons of this, Natalya launched into a discussion of the mushrooms' preferred environments and the proper methods of storing and cooking them. She had moved onto pickling recipes when Maria's patience snapped. "Who needs this? My father says the country will be at war any day, and you can spend hours talking about mushrooms? Let the servants deal with them."

Nasan's jaw dropped. Maria losing control, challenging the formidable Natalya?

Who at this moment looked formidable indeed. "Maria, go to your room. Women do not meddle in politics. The Lord in His infinite wisdom made us the handmaidens of men."

For one stunning instant Maria stood her ground. "He'll take me back, my Papa will. That's what I went to him to ask. We'll see then what women can and can't do."

Nasan watched her sister-in-law run up the stairs. Maria wanted to go home as much as Nasan herself did? While Natalya resumed her lecture, Nasan pondered the significance of that.

The monk who showed Daniil to the hut set aside for guests mumbled apologies for the sparse accommodations. Short and narrow, the monk hunched his shoulders and bent his shaggy head as he held the door for Daniil to enter, mentioned supper in the refectory in an hour, and vanished. Back to his devotions, Daniil guessed. The monastery showed its wealth in numbers of servants and lavish churches, but the priests and monks who lived here did not seem to profit from the community's good fortune. Boris might have felt comfortable here after all.

Pashka, the servant who had accompanied him from home, as he did whenever Daniil went on campaign, grinned as he came in with Daniil's bags. "Not so bad, is it, Lord? We've seen worse, you and I."

"Not bad, indeed," Daniil agreed. The hut looked watertight and boasted pallets of clean straw. The stove in the corner—no doubt a concession to noble guests—was unlit, but in June he much preferred it that way. Compared to the often damp and dirty tents inflicted on the army, this hut looked like a palace. It would suit him and his men very well.

Leaving Pashka to unpack and make the beds, Daniil strolled around the courtyard, admiring the exquisite lines of the cathedral, said to hold Russia's most beautiful icon, Andrei Rublev's rendition of the Old Testament Trinity. He made a mental vow to see it before he left. Boris, who loved to paint, had raved about its composition: the delicate colors and exquisite faces of the three angels gathered around a table that contained only a chalice filled with wine.

Boris had visited the monastery, then. He must have, to describe the icon in such detail. He had first mentioned it this spring, between his return and the Tatar raid that killed him. Several times, in fact, as if he had encountered something wondrous. Surely he hadn't faked excitement to cover up his involvement in Girei's murder?

After a light supper of bread and vegetables, Daniil had a chance to question the monk who maintained the monastery guestbook. An old man with a round, cheery face and none of the humility appropriate to his station, the elder Artemy greeted Daniil as if they were teacher and pupil, separated for years but miraculously reunited.

"Come in, come in, young lord." While Daniil found a seat, Artemy reached for a large book, pulled it onto his lap, and rustled through the pages, stopping from time to time to peer at one. "Your brother, the gatekeeper said. In February or early March, between Christ's Presentation and the glorious Annunciation to His Most Pure Mother?"

"Yes." Daniil suppressed a smile. Artemy—so round, so brisk and competent—reminded him of the legendary house elf, the *domovoi*.

"And what is his name?" Artemy asked.

"Was." Daniil heard the ache of loss in his own voice and steadied it. "He died a few weeks after leaving here, in a Tatar raid. His name was Boris Nikolaevich Kolychev."

"Ah." Artemy winced. "May his memory be eternal. He impressed me as a pious youth."

"You remember him then. Good."

The monk nodded, and Daniil went on. "The Tatars believe he killed one of their own, a boy of fourteen. I don't think Boris would have done such a thing, but now I wonder if I ever understood him."

"It sounds most unlike him."

The monk's lively brown eyes glowed warm with compassion. Daniil found himself confessing to this receptive stranger things he could not share with his parents, still less his new wife. "I left my bride of three days to find the answers to my questions. I didn't tell her where I was going, because her brother and her father were the ones who organized the raid."

"So your parents married you to end the feud? And you agreed? That was well done, my son."

Daniil touched the monk's hand in thanks, but his thoughts were elsewhere—in a tangle of half-healed grief and repressed resentment, yes, but also in that state of unexpected passion and surprising possibility that had attended his wedding ceremony.

The elder said, "Forgive me, my son, but from what I know of the Tatars, they might have killed your brother even if they suspected his innocence. Or were certain of it."

Daniil, called back to the present, looked up. "Yes, they might. They had evidence of my family's involvement in the murder; they could justify an attack without settling on Boris as the killer. But that's the odd part. They did settle on him. My wife's brother..." He stopped, swallowed. He was still avoiding the connection forced on him by circumstances.

Determined to behave like an adult, he resumed his tale. "My brother-in-law told me at the wedding. They had an eyewitness, and the eyewitness identified Boris. My brother, who told us he came here. That's why I started with you. And why I didn't tell my wife that I had set out to prove her family wrong."

"Understood. Let me see what I can find out." Artemy studied the book, turning pages one by one. Daniil couldn't see the writing, and it would have done him no good if he had, since he had never learned to read. Boyars kept clerks to do their paperwork.

He wondered if he should learn. Artemy seemed reliable enough, but was it wise to depend on others, with no way to verify whether they told the truth?

Artemy closed the book, and Daniil forgot the unaccustomed thought at the sight of the monk's glowing face.

"You found the record?" Relief threatened to choke him.

"I did," Artemy said. "Your brother arrived in mid-February and stayed for a week."

Which left an entire month unaccounted for. Daniil groaned.

Maria did not appear for dinner. Except on special occasions, the women ate apart from the men, so it would have been a silent meal with only Natalya and Nasan had Daniil's cousin by marriage Solomonida not arrived unannounced. She brought the news that she and her younger sister, Darya, were leaving the next day on a long journey to Suzdal.

"A nunnery," she said with a laugh that sounded forced.

Natalya said, "Oh, my dear!" in anguished tones. She embraced Solomonida. "It's good that your sister accompanies you. And what of your little one?"

"She travels with me, of course. I won't leave her with Semyon."

Natalya nodded. "Yes. Better to take her with you. She and Darya will keep up your spirits."

Hearing undertones she did not comprehend, Nasan frowned as she hugged Solomonida in turn. Nasan's one potential friend, and she was leaving.

"Six months away from Semyon will restore my spirits admirably," Solomonida said, her voice tart. "But I don't want to take the veil merely to get away from the man." She waved a sleeve the color of spring leaves. "I enjoy life too much to spend the rest of it in a habit."

Natalya patted her hand. "The priests won't give him a divorce."

"They gave one to the grand prince," Solomonida said.

Nasan remembered that. The scandal had reached the steppe, where she and her family lived then. Old Grand Prince Vasily had forced his first wife into a convent—oh, in Suzdal, where Solomonida was heading. No wonder she was worried.

"Come. Eat." Natalya ushered Solomonida onto the bench and beckoned to a servant. "And stop your nonsense. Semyon is not grand prince. The priests will make no concessions for him. Sooner or later, he will summon you home."

"You're right, Auntie." Solomonida slid onto her seat. Her face had lost its taut expression. "And until he does, wretched man, I intend to enjoy my time away."

Natalya tut-tutted. "My dear girl. Show some respect for your husband."

"Why?" Solomonida ladled stew into the lacquered bowl a servant placed before her. "He shows none for me. You should hear the way he carries on among the maidservants. He thinks I don't hear him frolicking with the girls, but I do. I'd leave him if I could, but I won't join a convent to make his life more convenient. Cheating husbands are the devil."

A comment with which Nasan wholeheartedly agreed.

After Solomonida left, Nasan washed her face and hands, spread her rug on the floor, and whispered the required sunset prayers. She spread fat taken from the kitchens earlier in the day across the grandmother's lips and asked for her blessing. Eyes closed, she reached into the other world, seeking a hint of Girei's spirit. There? No, there, surely!

Or was it? The presence didn't feel like her fun-loving brother. More like the energy that had entered her the day of Girei's death, clarifying what she should do and when. This must be how a shaman felt when the clan spirits entered her. Uplifted, resolute, outside herself. Transcendent. The ancestors had chosen Nasan, as they had once chosen each warrior heroine in the sagas. She had dreamed of this day. The mystical presence validated her decision to resume the life she had known in Kasimov, to free herself and help others. The grandmothers would guide her.

She opened her eyes, and the presence vanished. Nasan addressed the spirit doll in Tatar. "Did I interpret your wishes correctly, Grandmother?"

The doll offered no response. Nasan waited, then shrugged and pulled out her black trousers and shirt, the scarves she'd worn in Kasimov, her best felt boots. There was no accounting for spirits. They replied when and where they willed.

She had plenty of time. So near the summer solstice the sun did not sleep for more than five hours. It took self-discipline to wait for the skies to darken enough for her to leave the Kolychev estate unchallenged.

At last, twilight came. She disrobed and bound her breasts, then donned the trousers. Her fingers picked up the rhythm she had established for them in Kasimov as she wound her braids in a coronet around her head, pinning them in place. The shirt and boots went on next. She tied one scarf around her head, concealing every lock of hair, and the other round her face, leaving only her eyes visible. No one would realize that she lacked a beard. If they noticed her at all, they would believe her a man.

Had she forgotten something vital? Beef jerky for the dogs, dagger, sword—no, she had everything.

Except her lynx pendant, for luck. She clasped it around her neck and stuffed chain and emblem under her shirt. No one need see it; its presence would remind her of her mission. An animal guardian to walk with her, as in the ancient legends.

Nasan blew out the candle, went to the window, and pushed back the shutter. With one knee on the sill, she stopped. Servants had interrupted her ransacking of the storeroom where the Kolychevs stored their weapons before she could select a bow and quiver of the right size and weight. Should she make another attempt?

She decided not. The search would delay her, and she had yet to confirm that she could climb down the walls and reach the street unobserved. Tonight she had no grand plans: a reconnaissance of the area, a test of her ability to leave and to return, the identification of a safe place to stash a bow and arrows when she obtained them. Then she would come home and figure out what to do next. She had bait for the dogs and steel to protect herself from bandits: the rest could wait.

The courtyard appeared deserted, but a flash of movement from one of the kitchens stopped her cold. With growing impatience, she delayed until the combination of darkness and silence convinced her the flash resulted from nothing more than a trick of the light. She could begin.

Before the moon rose, she clambered down the side of the house. The walls of the Kolychev estate offered few impediments to an experienced climber, and the watchmen focused whatever attention they could spare from their chatter on prospective invaders, not on the household within.

The house stood near the marketplace that adjoined the moat protecting the Kremlin. Not long after leaving the compound, Nasan had put enough distance between herself and her home not to fear discovery. She slipped among the houses, one shadow among many. Heads turned as she passed, shook in disbelief, turned back. Dogs slid away, as if blown by a breeze. The heads were few, the streets quiet, the dogs more numerous but easily diverted.

Another dozen or so streets, and she decided she'd seen enough for one night. On her way back she came across an old man, incapacitated by drink and about to lose his purse to a pair of thugs. The victim looked pathetic, lying by the side of the street, and the would-be thieves reminded her of the soldiers who had captured her and Girei on that fateful day in the woods. Two of them and one of her—could she defeat them?

If she had stopped to find a bow, she'd have no trouble. Two shots, and she'd incapacitate them both. But she hadn't planned to rescue anyone. Her besetting fault: failure to anticipate every possibility. And here she was, alone against two villains.

But not weaponless, as before. And she couldn't leave the old man to suffer. It would be like failing Girei a second time. Nasan crouched under an overhang and considered what damage she could inflict with a sword and a dagger.

Two men. The smaller one stood about a hand's breadth taller than she, and lack of food had left him scrawny. If he weren't victimizing an old man, she might let him steal. She couldn't see him well enough to identify features, but she had an impression of wispy, sticking-out hair and tattered clothes on bony limbs.

His companion towered over him by a head and sported beefy shoulders. Defeating him would require skill. And luck. Her hand rubbed the lynx pendant concealed by her shirt.

Who led, and who followed, or did that matter?

She decided not. If Brute led, and she defeated him, the other man would run away. And if Brute followed, then his leader would have to fight alone after she dispatched his henchman, and that would give Nasan the advantage.

If she incapacitated the bigger man first, before they learned of her presence, she would improve her odds of success. But the smaller one stood closer to her. She'd have to pass him to reach his companion. Better to remove him quickly, then fight one on one.

Decision made, she drew her sword from its scabbard. Feet silent on the wooden pavement, eyes fixed on the two assailants, she crept forward. She clouted the smaller man on the head with her sword before either realized they had anything to fear. He fell, unconscious. She raced for the shadows.

The larger man pivoted in a slow arc. Moonlight's gleam alerted Nasan to his dagger. She circled him, saber at the ready, then darted in and slashed the hand that held the knife. The brute yowled and dropped his weapon, but he was not ready to admit defeat. As she danced away, he lunged, grabbing her around the knees with his undamaged arm.

As she hit the pavement, the breath left her body with a whoosh. The man's face loomed over hers, distorted by moonlight, a mass of broken teeth and scars mixed with dirt and scraggly beard. She smelled the garlic and onions of his evening meal. And something else, sweet and sickly.

Pig. I'm going to vomit.

The thug reached for her neck. His hand closed around her collar and the gold chain of the pendant beneath. He twisted fabric and chain together, and she gasped for air. The world went black and white around her.

Her senses reeled, spinning her back to her wedding night. Again her husband's body pinned her to the mattress as she struggled to free herself. Then the ancestor spirit flooded her. Spurred by its strength, she kneed her attacker in the groin, bit his hand, and rolled free. He convulsed in pain. Before he could recover, she knocked him, too, out with the flat of her blade. Taking no chances, she ripped strips of fabric from his tattered shirt and bound him, then his smaller companion. After immobilizing them, she grabbed the purse and went to return it.

She found its owner propped against a wall. He stared at her through bleary eyes, brow furrowed with the owlish gaze of the very drunk. She held out his purse and, when he did not take it, pressed it into his hand.

"Here, Uncle," she said, deepening her voice as much as possible. "Let's get you home. Did they hurt you?"

When he didn't answer, she repeated her question. He pointed at her. "Lynx. Golden lynx."

Oh, dear, had she risked her life for a man too befuddled to remember whether he had a purse? Bruised and sore, tempted to leave him there and go home to bed, she sighed. It would defeat the purpose of saving him. Someone else would rob him.

"Come, Uncle." She put a hand under his elbow, urging him to his feet. "Tell me where you live." Staggering, he took a few steps forward, then stopped and touched the slender chain around her neck. Only then did she realize that the thug had pulled her pendant free, revealing the lynx. With one hand she tucked it beneath her shirt.

"You don't want to give your name," the old man slurred. "I understand. Your secret is safe with me."

What was he talking about? But her questions brought no rational response. After a while, she gave up and asked him again for directions to his house.

He pointed across the square, heading down the hill away from the Kolychev estate. She should have guessed: if Moscow bore any resemblance to Kasimov, social status rose as one went up the hill, and his clothes suggested he didn't belong to a noble clan. The purse weighed heavy in her hand. A well-off merchant, maybe.

In fact, after she helped him to his gate and delivered him to the servant there, she discovered he belonged to the gentry. His estate was small but tidy, clean, and in good repair. The servant hovered over him in a way that suggested long acquaintanceship. She prepared to leave.

The old man caught her arm, saying, "How can I thank you?"

He tugged at the knot that fastened the purse, as if he intended to offer a reward.

"No, please. Nothing." Gentry or not, the idea of him rewarding a khan's daughter was ludicrous.

"You were wounded. Aiding me. You must let me give you something."

Nasan touched her throat, drenched in the big thief's blood. "Not mine. The robber's."

"Still—"

She cut him off. When he persisted, she held up her palms. "No more."

"Very well," he said. "Accept my gratitude, in that case. And if you need help, come here."

Nasan laughed and wished him well. Of course, she would not need his help, but it felt good to have one friend in Moscow, however intoxicated. As she reached the opposite side of the square, she glanced over her shoulder. He must have watched her go, for he gazed in her direction—although it seemed unlikely he could see her, black on black in the shadows.

"A good night, Grandmothers," she whispered. "Thank you for preserving him—and me. Always you care for me when I need you most."

A kiss of wind brushed her cheek, and Nasan ran for home. None of the sleepy watchmen noticed the specter scaling the walls.

Daniil left the Trinity Monastery the next morning, heading east. He had spent the preceding evening interviewing one resident of the monastery after another until he found a young man of fifteen who remembered that Boris left with another lord. They could have been twins, the young man opined, alike as they were. They had combined their forces and left, together, traveling toward the sunrise.

Kasimov lay to the southeast, a good week's journey on horseback. Leading his men along the Ryazan road—the first leg of the journey—Daniil frowned at the surrounding fields, filled with industrious peasants. Had he placed too much weight on the testimony of an army-mad youth struck by Boris's weaponry, envious of an opportunity denied to bondsmen like himself, and unaware that Boris felt every bit as constrained by his heritage as those who served the monastery? Boris had longed to lay down his sword and don a monk's black robe, to paint icons like the glorious Trinity, at which Daniil had glanced before his quest drew him away.

To himself, Daniil admitted he didn't share his brother's admiration for the icon. Three outsized angels looming over an empty table that reached no higher than their knees, a hint of minuscule building and tree behind their haloes, flat expressionless faces—it took someone as unworldly as Boris to see the beauty.

But Daniil didn't aspire to be more than a soldier. He concentrated on his journey. In truth, he saw few alternatives to following the trail set by that army-mad youth. The Tatars had killed the men who accompanied Boris to the monastery and beyond. The monks had no other information. Boris himself had concealed some part of the truth—Daniil had yet to determine how much.

In short, Boris had lied. Daniil, used to regarding his older brother as one step away from sainthood, found that idea shocking. For as long as he could remember, he had been the family mischief maker, sentenced to one penance after another for drinking, fighting, whoring, gambling, and general misconduct. If either of Nikolai Kolychev's sons had chosen to link up with their cousin Semyon—Daniil had no trouble guessing the identity of the lord who looked like Boris's twin—to cause trouble in the Tatar lands to the east, the odds against that son being Boris would have been too high to calculate. Or so Daniil would have said until today.

Semyon bore a grudge for the murder of his brother, Dmitry. Understandable. But Boris had scorned Dmitry and argued against retaliation. Why accompany a cousin bent on revenge?

Unless Boris had always had this capacity for deceit, and Daniil—idolizing his older, wiser brother—had failed to see the truth.

It was a puzzle, and not a pleasant one. And yet, as the fields gave way to woods and the distance between Daniil's small troop and the monastery grew, he found himself almost heartened by the realization that his brother might not, in the end, have been so much more virtuous than he. If Boris could lie and mislead but still qualify as future head of the family, perhaps Daniil could fill his brother's shoes after all.

Chapter 15

SEMYON GRABBED GRUSHA AS SHE PASSED BY ON HER WAY TO the marketplace. After a week of successfully avoiding him, she'd thought herself safe. Shock held her immobile long enough for him to haul her through the gates of his estate.

"You're going to help me," he said. The cruel set of his lips made her shiver.

"I don't want to help you." She tugged her wrists away, but he held her fast.

"Who cares what you want? You'll do what I want, or I'll tell your darling Daniil where you spent his wedding night."

Grusha cringed. Daniil had comforted her before he left. He still cared for her. She could win him back.

Unless Semyon followed through on his threat. Daniil did not demand fidelity—or offer it, either—but he had his pride. Better he not discover that she had slept with his cousin.

"What do you expect me to do?" She infused her voice with loathing, but he only laughed, the beast.

"I need a nursemaid," he said.

Grusha stared at him, astonished. "A nursemaid?" Didn't he have one, for his baby girl?

"You heard me. Be here tomorrow evening." And with that he let her go. "Don't fail me. I won't think twice about telling my cousin what you get up to behind his back."

Grusha scuttled through the gate, cursing him under her breath. What new trouble had she brought on herself by her stupid jealousy?

A week after leaving the Trinity Monastery, right on schedule, Daniil led his men out of the wooden citadel of Ryazan. Soon they would enter the Tatar principality of Kasimov. Extensive questioning confirmed that Boris and Semyon had passed that way but not much more.

That did not surprise Daniil. Only the striking resemblance between his brother and his cousin made them memorable. Ryazan was large enough to swallow more than a few travelers, and it had passed into the possession of the grand prince of Moscow during Daniil's own lifetime. A certain resentment lingered among the local populace against visitors who spoke in the accents of the capital city. But a pair of noblemen from Moscow, alike as two chessmen, stuck in the minds of certain residents. No need to protect such outsiders, either.

What did disturb Daniil was his informants' insistence that Boris and Semyon got along famously. Without exception, the reports portrayed them as laughing, joking, in perfect accord. A description so unlikely that Daniil wondered at times if Semyon had somehow enthralled Boris with sorcery. Impossible, he would have said, until he found himself in this situation where no explanation made sense.

He decided to press on, keep asking questions, and hope for satisfactory answers. The closer he came to Kasimov, the more difficult it would be, because of the language difference. Still, Russians lived scattered throughout the region, which had once belonged to the prince of Ryazan. He just had to find them. And persuade them to talk.

Daniil sighed. If he had brought his bride, she could translate. However faulty her Russian, it was better than his nonexistent Tatar.

Had he made a mistake in leaving her? At best, they would have had a few weeks to become acquainted before the muster; now he would be lucky to reach home before the call went out. One big error of judgment in the war, and he might die without ever learning more about her. But how could he bring a sheltered young girl on such a journey?

He saw her standing at the bedroom window, bow aimed at the courtyard. In his haste to calm his mother, he had neglected to ask Nasan where she learned to shoot. She'd looked competent, though. And she was a Tatar, if not the wild nomad Mama called her. She probably rode better than he.

The thought made him laugh. His spirits restored, he waved to summon his men and dispatched them among the hamlets dimly visible through the trees.

Boris and Semyon must have traveled this road, for they had no alternative if their destination was Kasimov. If fortune favored Daniil, he would trace them within the week. Then he could return to Nasan with his questions answered.

And if he discovered that his brother had assisted Semyon's scheme for revenge? The two Borises—gentle and saintly versus deceitful and vindictive—warred in Daniil's mind, one familiar if daunting, the other repellent.

More than anything, he wanted to know which was the real Boris. Until he found out, he could not go home.

Nasan sat in front of her dressing table, her head in her hands. Last time she'd glanced in the mirror, she'd looked like a mountain spirit ready to waylay an unwary traveler, her hair sticking up in tufts from where she'd tugged at it. Precious paper dotted with thick ebony ink lay in crumpled piles around her feet, mute evidence of her struggle. Here and there, ink/saltwater blotches stained her shell-pink sleeves. She might never wear the robe again—and it had always been a favorite—but right then, bigger problems warred for her attention.

She had promised to write to Sumbeka. *Ana* insisted: regular letters, especially at first. The courier from Kasimov waited below for her reply. If she sent him back without a letter, *Ana* would panic. No excuse would serve. But if she told the truth, she could expect no sympathy. At best, Sumbeka would respond with platitudes. At worst, she would descend on the Kolychev household in a flurry of rosewater—not to sweep her darling daughter home, spitting her contempt at the uncaring Russians who stopped at nothing to make Nasan miserable, but to tell that daughter to pull herself together, win her husband back, and abandon any hope of escaping the prison to which her parents had consigned her. If that happened, Nasan would have no choice but to take her dagger to either her mother or herself—probably both—dooming them to wander eternity as hungry ghosts due to her own lack of self-control.

The desire to avoid that ugly fate explained the pieces of crumpled paper. But the chasm between Nasan's reality and what she could tell her mother loomed wide, and the right words eluded her.

With a groan, she pulled yet another square of paper toward her, scrunched her nose like the clay lion dogs who guarded the Kasimov gates, gritted her teeth, and began anew.

Dearest Ana,

Everything is fine here.

So far, so good. She had written these two lines a dozen times. But no sooner did she pen them than difficulties swarmed in on her like bees. Because in fact, very little was fine here. Could she tell *Ana* that a servant or a dead woman held Daniil's heart? Confess her hurt at the sight of Grusha in his arms, when moments before he had sworn loyalty to her, Nasan? Should she share the fury that filled her at the memory, the unwomanly way she had smacked him and shouted at him, her refusal to listen to apologies that she could predict would be as false as his kisses?

A big tear ran down her cheek and plopped onto the paper. She blotted it with her sleeve, glad it hadn't smeared the ink. Tears already accounted for two of the crumpled balls at her feet.

No. She would say nothing about Daniil except that he had gone. Write a few sentences, and her unhappiness poured onto the page. Then she had to rip it up and try again.

Daniil left the same day as you, she wrote, *and we have not heard from him.*

That sounded odd. Why had they not heard, besides the obvious explanation that Daniil hadn't wasted one moment wondering if she missed him? Another tear traced its pathway to the floor. She swiveled in her chair long enough to divert it from the letter and patted her face with the much-abused sleeve.

The Russians do not send letters as we do, she added to allay Sumbeka's doubts. *His parents assure me that a messenger would bring news if he suffered an accident.*

His parents. On more solid ground now, Nasan decided she could expand a bit.

Natalya Vasilyevna treats me kindly. I have learned all the Russian names for mushrooms, and in general much about how to manage a household.

Which, most of the time, made her want to scream with boredom. But Nasan could not imagine telling her mother what did give her pleasure: the surge of power when she defeated the two thugs and restored the old man's purse; the gratitude of those she had helped since; the sense that the streets, unlike the rest of this alien city, welcomed her.

Instead she wrote, *Natalya Vasilyevna says I am too thin. Every time I turn around, I find her offering food. She tells me I will never bring a child to term, skinny creature that I am.*

Oops. A third tear signaled another mistake. Another blotch on the pink brocade. Have Daniil's child, after the way he'd behaved? Not if she could help it.

But suppose he had impregnated her before he left? They had made love once. That was enough, wasn't it? Only two weeks had passed since that night, and even she knew that you couldn't tell for sure in two weeks. Also that she did *not* want a child. A child would tie her to the Kolychevs for the rest of her life. To live in this tree, her felt tent forever barred to her—the prospect didn't bear thinking of.

Her mother would want a full report on any potential grandchild, but Nasan could not bear to confide her fears. Naming them might make them real. She changed the subject.

Only I cannot eat, Ana. All the food tastes the same—onions and garlic, beets and mushrooms. Everything smells of cabbage. And Maria keeps trying to trick me into eating pig. She is such a strange girl. Sometimes I think she's lonely, but she refuses any offer of friendship.

Another area to avoid. Nasan's loneliness crushed her; and *Ana*, miles away in Kasimov, could not help. Fighting desolation, Nasan returned to her task.

We pray a great deal, as often as at home. So I can think my prayers in Arabic while the priest says his aloud. I hope Allah will forgive me if I do not make all the gestures. I do what I can. And I honor the grandmothers every day.

That was true. Nasan had never behaved so piously in her life. But she needed divine protection as, masked and dressed in black, she swung down from a wall or darted from the shadows. The thug who attacked her during her rescue of the old man had revealed her own vulnerability. As she became a creature of the night, a secret avenger, she had to face the fact that a pulled-off mask, a ripped shirt that exposed her as a woman, even a wound she could not conceal would end her imposture. The risk thrilled her, exhilarated her, a reward for the hours spent appeasing Natalya.

Ana would be shocked.

The sound of shuffling feet at the door alerted her to the courier's return. She hadn't finished. She called to him to wait and frowned at the paper before her.

The letter was too short. But what could she say, when everything important was off-limits? Something that would convince *Ana* that indeed, Nasan had adjusted to wifehood and had no need of maternal intervention.

An idea came to her, and she scribbled it down.

My Russian has improved a lot. Soon I will be able to converse with others in the household. If only the words did not have so many forms! I fear mine are always wrong. But people do make an effort to understand me. I will manage.

Please hug Ata *and Ogodai for me when you see them. And give Sorkhokhtani extra apples and carrots. I miss you all.*

Love,

Your Nasan

She read the letter through and sighed. It was still too short, but it would reassure *Ana*. She could take comfort in that. Even a certain pride.

She melted wax and sealed the letter, then handed it to the courier.

Ogodai raised an eyebrow at the courier reining in his mount. The air in the courtyard of the khan's palace in Kasimov thrummed with the sounds of men at archery drill: arrows whistling to their targets, thudding into the straw; teasing comments mixed with cheers, jeers, and laughter. The late morning sun beat down on armored bodies and helmeted heads, but the men accepted the discomfort—or knew better than to complain.

The courier—squat, dark, and bowlegged, like most of his kind—pulled a tied scroll from his saddlebags and bent over the horse's steaming flanks to hand it to Ogodai. "From Moscow, Sultan," he said. "The khanim your sister sends greetings to your honored family. And I have an intelligence report for the khan."

"News?" Ogodai flicked the red ribbon that protected the privacy of the scroll's contents. As his father's second-in-command Ogodai had the right, even the duty, to open reports from the scouts who patrolled the outlying areas of Kasimov.

And a letter from his sister! His fingers itched to rip off the ribbon. But Bulat would expect his son to question the courier first. Plus Sumbeka would complain if he forestalled her with the letter. He had to curtail his impatience.

The courier dismounted. When he stood at attention, the pointed tip of his helmet reached Ogodai's chin. In other respects they looked much alike: fringes of black hair brushed their foreheads, black eyes gleamed above olive cheeks, and black mustaches lined the edges of their mouths. Their clothes were similar in style if not in richness: loose trousers tucked into boots; layers of tunics in different colors, topped with a belted vest and armaments. Ogodai's boots were worked leather, his shirt of silk, whereas the courier had to settle for felt and linen. But their sabers were fashioned of Turkish steel, and their bows and arrows would prove equally deadly, regardless of the level of decoration on their cases. Bulat would not let any soldier of his—and couriers were far from unimportant—enter into battle without the means to defend himself.

Ogodai conducted this mental survey in less time than the rider needed to steady his winded horse. With his beast stilled, the courier answered Ogodai's question. "News, yes, Sultan. A young man, a Russian, with a small troop has been traveling throughout the hamlets for the last eight days, asking questions about Girei Sultan's murder."

A surprise. Ogodai had thought his brother's death no longer concerned anyone outside the immediate family. Without further ado, he stripped the ribbon from the scroll, revealing two pieces of thick paper, rough to the touch, covered with swirls of exquisite Arabic calligraphy in black ink. He glanced at the sheet from his sister, frowned, then moved it to the back and skimmed the report.

Halfway through, he stopped. His hand stroked his mustache. He would have sworn he had convinced Daniil of Boris's guilt. But unless the Kasimov woods teemed with tall, blond Russian boyars in their late teens or early twenties, Daniil was here, asking questions. Bulat needed to hear the news right away.

"I will speak to the khan," Ogodai told the courier. "Go, rest yourself and your horse. You have done well this day." He nodded at the man and left the courtyard.

A short search uncovered Bulat with Sumbeka in the family sitting room. Ogodai handed Nasan's letter to his mother. "From Moscow," he said.

She exclaimed. Her painted nails scratched his fingers as she grabbed the letter from his hand, and she muttered an apology even as her eyes scanned the ornate script. Nasan tended to write in haste, and Ogodai had already noted that this missive appeared even more blotched and blotted than usual, although his cursory glance had revealed the main points. Leaving his mother to puzzle it out, he handed the intelligence report to his father.

Sumbeka emitted a sound halfway between a wail and a sigh. Ogodai swiveled to see his mother dangling the letter between thumb and forefinger.

"But this is terrible," she said. "What are those Russians doing to my poor child?" She glared at his father. "She needs her own household."

Tears glimmered in her eyes. Ogodai opened his mouth to ask what had upset her.

"Doing to her?" Bulat looked uncharacteristically sheepish— in response to the household comment, Ogodai guessed. Bulat's violation of custom had puzzled him, but it wasn't his place to reproach his father. "If they're mistreating her, they'll hear from me. What does she say?"

Sumbeka twisted the letter between her hands. "It's not what she says," she announced after a pause. "It's what she doesn't say. She speaks nonsense. About how Natalya presses food on her—

well, that I can believe. That her Russian has improved and she prays a lot. Privately, in Arabic."

"Nasan?" Ogodai tried, in respect for his mother's distress, to keep the laughter from his voice, but the idea of a devout Nasan made it difficult.

"Yes," Sumbeka said in tones of gloom. "Everything tastes of cabbage, and she misses us."

"That doesn't sound so bad," Bulat said in a bracing voice. "You're reacting too strongly, my dear. I'm sure Nasan is perfectly happy."

Sumbeka's dark eyes widened. Ogodai could have sworn he saw her bite her tongue. Then she said, in a voice that brooked no argument, "She is not. In fact, she tells us only one thing of substance: that her husband left Moscow the same day we did." She flicked the top of the letter. "Since she doesn't say where he went, I suspect he didn't tell her. And since she doesn't mention how she feels about that, I can guarantee you that he has made her extremely *un*happy."

Bulat hissed. Ogodai regarded his mother with awe. How she had deduced so much from a single sentence escaped him.

"I know where Daniil is," he said. "Right here in Kasimov."

His parents turned their stare on him. He pointed to the sheet of paper Bulat held. "He's looking for the eyewitness to Girei's murder. To clear his brother, I'd guess."

"But Nasan is the eyewitness," Sumbeka said.

"Exactly," Bulat confirmed. "She must not have told him."

"*I* didn't tell him," Ogodai said. "When I saw him at the wedding." Anticipating disapproval, he spread his hands. "He was about to marry her, whether he liked it or not. Should I have told him she was the one whose testimony led to his brother's death?"

"No, of course not," Bulat muttered. "But it's a problem. He has to find out someday. Meanwhile, what are we going to do with him?"

Ogodai grinned as a plan sprang, full blown, into his head. "I think I should help him with his inquiries, don't you?"

"Help him?" Bulat and Sumbeka spoke in unison. Ogodai, watching Nasan's letter slip from his mother's lap, concluded he could not have startled them more if he'd tried.

"To find the eyewitness?" Bulat added.

"Your sister, whom he already despises?" Sumbeka reached for the letter and cradled it next to her heart, as if by doing so she could comfort its sender. "Your father's right. He must find out sometime, but I want her to decide how and when."

"Agreed," Ogodai said. "But I know Daniil. Whatever set him off, he won't stop until he finds his answers. I'll intercept him and show him where to look."

"But Nasan…" Sumbeka clenched the letter until her knuckles showed white. "I must go to her, Bulat. She's suffering."

"Not yet," Bulat said absently. "Better if they work it out for themselves."

Sumbeka opened her mouth as if to argue, but he stopped her with a wave of his hand. "We'll discuss it later."

"Let me talk to Daniil first," Ogodai suggested. "He may not have intended to reject Nasan. Suppose he just didn't take her into his confidence? He doesn't know her."

Sumbeka nodded, although worry still creased her brow. "And the eyewitness?"

Ogodai shrugged. "Daniil only thinks he needs the eyewitness. Nasan can't swear that his brother killed Girei. When Daniil hears the evidence, he'll accept the truth. And if he insists, I'll say we sent the boy away. Nasan can tell him what she saw, if she likes. He'll blame me, not her."

"It might work," Bulat said. "Give it a try. But make it quick. I expect the order to muster any day. It should have come already, but no doubt the powers that be are still gathering intelligence so they can deploy the troops properly."

Ogodai nodded. "You can make my excuses for a week or ten days, can't you? It won't take longer than that. Daniil has to muster, too."

"I can," Bulat said. "You're on an urgent mission." He smacked Ogodai on the shoulder. "Make it convincing, son. Your sister's happiness depends on it."

"Yes, sir." Ogodai snapped to attention like any soldier. But as he bowed in farewell, hopes for his sister's happiness were already blending with plans for steering Daniil in the direction that best served the Tatars. And while he waited for the first groom he saw to fetch his horse and the ten members of his immediate entourage, he laughed.

The next few days were going to be fun.

As the weeks passed and Daniil did not return, Nasan stopped thinking of herself as a wife. That brief period of intense emotion had no more substance than the spirit messages that robbed her of sleep. She didn't know what caused them, only that whatever she did or said while awake, images of Daniil plagued her the moment she closed her eyes. Daniil lost and hurt. Daniil dead.

To elude them, she sought refuge in the streets. Her rescues became bolder. Her confidence grew as she fought men half again her size, swung off parapets, ran as far as she could before the approach of dawn forced her return. Physical exhaustion smothered the dreams.

The townspeople rejoiced when they saw her. Before long, people greeted her by name. "The Golden Lynx is here," she heard them cry.

Their enthusiasm amused her, but it touched her, too. For the first time since her arrival, Moscow no longer felt like foreign ground.

Chapter 16

LATE IN THE AFTERNOON, THREE WEEKS AFTER LEAVING HIS bride to fend for herself, Daniil dismounted in yet another unfamiliar clearing and regarded the river with a jaundiced eye. Three days to travel to the Trinity Monastery, two there, six to Ryazan, and ten scouring what appeared to him in retrospect to be every hut within a hundred miles of Kasimov had turned up next to no useful information about his brother or his cousin. A dozen or so bystanders admitted to having noticed the matched pair of Russian noblemen ride by. Several commented on their resemblance to Daniil, so he knew he was traveling in the right direction. Then the trail fizzled. For all the trace Boris, Semyon, and their combined troops had left, they might as well have flown out of the Kasimov woods in Baba Yaga's magic mortar.

Daniil had learned nothing, either, of the boy Girei, still less the mysterious eyewitness. Unless people were refusing to talk, which became increasingly likely as Daniil and his soldiers narrowed the distance between themselves and the Kasimov fortress. Every unproductive day raised his doubts as to whether he had chosen the right course—and not only because of Nasan. As little as Daniil liked the knowledge that he had abandoned his new wife without explanation, he would have (God willing) time to make it up to her. The grand prince's messengers would slap him in jail without a moment's compunction if he ignored their summons to join the army. His father's courier might already be chasing him through every Kasimov hamlet, desperate to deliver the message. And by the time he returned to these woods, the trail would have gone cold. Colder.

If anything could get colder than this. Daniil made a silent vow that he would give himself a few more days, then go home—or, if the muster had begun by then, to wherever the government chose to send him on the young grand prince's behalf. Lord alone knew when he'd have a chance to make his peace with Nasan in that case.

Weary after hours in the saddle, the men stopped with alacrity at Daniil's signal and began setting up camp. The peasants who slashed and burned this corner of the woods had abandoned their plot long ago: only the grown-over stumps and the occasional patch of wild oats indicated that anyone had cultivated here. The men broke into groups—one gathering wood and water, another tending to the horses, a third unpacking pots and pans or unloading blankets from the half-dozen packhorses that trailed their small force. The silence of the forest must weigh on them, for they spoke in low tones, without their usual raucous teasing.

Daniil monitored the whispers with one ear while keeping the other alert for indications of trouble. Although his father-in-law held dominion over this region, Daniil could not shake the sense that he rode through foreign territory. Lands nominally loyal to Moscow, but also lands that did not welcome Russians in general or Kolychevs in particular. Where a dozen horsemen could vanish in the boggy woods and no one would care.

Face it, the place gave him the creeps. To stop his imagination from running riot, Daniil leaned against a mossy stump, focusing on the evidence supplied by his senses. He savored the aroma of roasting venison, brought down by his own arrow while the troop was still on the road, hastily cleaned and butchered for the men to share. As the commander, he didn't need to involve himself in the daily chores of the camp. His job required him to think, to plan, and to order.

A rumble of thunder sounded in the distance. The air, hot and muggy, enveloped him. Woodland scents—bark, matted leaves, grass baking in sunlight—mingled with the hint of fish that rose from the water. Bees buzzed overhead, pollen-laden bodies zooming toward a hollow in an ancient oak, their lazy circles belying the intensity of their labor. June had graced the travelers with unusually fine weather, but Daniil guessed that rain would seep into their tents tonight.

The venison, although it made his mouth water, would take another hour on the spit, if not more, before it became ready to eat. Surrounded by the soothing bustle of soldiers performing this task or that, Daniil could relax. Remember. Imagine.

His eyes closed as visions swirled through his head. Grusha—bruised, sobbing, distraught—flinging shirts to the floor and her arms around his neck. What had she done that she couldn't admit?

He should have alerted his mother. If Grusha had tumbled into trouble, the family must help her. But Mama would notice. She was good at that.

Better to concentrate on Nasan. Another mystery. So demure at her wedding, and after it anything but. "Life," not "peace." Nasan releasing his arrow, crashing pottery, slamming her hands into his chest, standing stolid and unyielding as he said his goodbyes. Nasan yielding to his touch with a warmth that astonished him.

A pleasure he had walked out on, to repair his family's honor. This responsibility game had its costs, and the benefits seemed far from clear. Being the bad boy had been much more fun.

A rustle from behind brought him from his semi-doze into a warrior's crouch. "Footfall," an inner voice said, but he was already lunging for the intruder's throat. His hands closed around his opponent's neck and he squeezed, using his weight and the power of his leap to bear the other man down. As they hit the ground, the intruder kneed him in the stomach and shoved both arms upward, forcing Daniil to break his grip. The man rolled away, then onto his feet while Daniil gasped amid last year's fallen leaves.

"Curse you, Daniil," Ogodai said. "What's wrong with 'hello'?"

Semyon regarded his uncle's warehouse with unalloyed satisfaction. The newest guardsman, Stenka, had exceeded expectations. On the outside, Nikolai Kolychev's unused estate looked as decrepit as ever, except for the shiny new padlock that hung from the warehouse door. But inside! Under Stenka's supervision a crew of soldiers had swept and soaped and rinsed until every surface gleamed. Soft rugs hid the dirt floor, and tattered hassocks and broken bureaus had given way to a cradle and a small bed, lace-ruffled sheets against emerald velvet, a rocking chair and a table, its linen cloth piled with empty bowls. Candles lay stacked next to the bowls. For the moment, Stenka held high a torch to illuminate the scene. The warehouse had no windows.

"Excellent." Semyon felt his chest expand in anticipation of victory. He deserved to bask in Stenka's reflected glory. Had he not seen the potential in that stolid face and chosen the right man to perform this delicate task? Without Semyon, Stenka would be nothing.

I will promote him, and he will serve me loyally. At last, a man I can trust.

Koshkin would be impressed. More impressed. As Semyon had hoped but not really expected, Koshkin had asked how Semyon would remove the children and had nodded sagely when told. He had ordered Semyon to implement the plan, but Semyon had held off until Stenka proved he could prepare the estate properly. The man would have his orders before Semyon left.

Stenka stood at attention, except for the raised arm holding the torch, his face impassive except when Semyon praised his work. At the word "excellent," Semyon saw a small smile crease the soldier's face. Even then, he didn't relax. Sturdy as an oak, he seemed prepared to wait forever for Semyon to elaborate.

"We have our orders from the Kremlin," Semyon said, implying a legitimacy sure to throttle questions unborn. "Soon I will send you two children and a woman. She may come and go as she pleases, so long as she remains throughout the night, but you must not mistreat the children or leave them unattended. If she does not appear one evening, send for me at once."

Stenka nodded. "How will I recognize the cart?"

"I will accompany you. Be ready. It should arrive in a few days."

Daniil lay on his back and groaned as he fought to catch his breath. A hand dangled in front of his eyes. "Did I hurt you?" Ogodai asked. "Sorry. I reacted on instinct."

"Me too." Daniil hauled himself to his feet and shook his sworn brother's hand before collapsing onto the mossy stump. Soldiers formed a circle—no, two circles, Tatar and Russian—about them. He drew a deep breath, glad that his lungs retained the power to inhale. "They're friends," he told his men. "Go back to setting up camp. We'll be sharing that deer."

The troop dispersed. He intercepted numerous suspicious glances before the two sides fell into a routine. Convinced that he could prevent trouble if it arose, he turned his attention to his brother-in-law, last seen glowering at him from the far end of a banquet table. Ogodai sat on a neighboring stump, hands clasped. Lingering hostility hung like a curtain between them.

Not knowing what else to say, Daniil answered Ogodai's last question. "I'm not hurt. You?"

Ogodai glanced his way then. "No."

Silence.

When it became daunting, Daniil tried again. "That's the second time I've punched you. Apologies. I'd have said so at the feast, but with one thing and another, I couldn't get near you."

"That wasn't an accident, I think." Ogodai stared at the river, where men were filling buckets and watering horses. Daniil assessed the amount of jostling between Tatars and Russians and decided he didn't need to intervene—yet.

"It was, actually," he said. "Sort of. I heard someone impugn my brother's honor and reacted. I realized it was you only after I'd downed you."

"I meant that the families kept us apart afterward," Ogodai said. "And the fight wasn't all your fault. I lost my temper, too. With—your cousin, was it?"

"My cousin, yes. What brings you here?"

"You," Ogodai said. "I hear you want information about Girei. Can I help?"

Typical of Ogodai to get straight to the point. But why the brusque tone?

Daniil swept his arm in a circle, indicating the men milling around the clearing. "We've been searching for your eyewitness. I'd like to meet him."

Ogodai winced. "Not possible. I'll show you what we found."

"Not possible," Daniil repeated, staring at a fist that had clenched without conscious direction from his brain. So much for Ogodai's help. "Why not?"

"He's gone," Ogodai said. "My father sent him away, for his own safety." His eyes didn't meet Daniil's.

"I don't want to attack him," Daniil said, annoyed. "I need to talk to him. Hear what he saw. If Boris could do this, he's not the man I knew. That matters to me—and to your sister."

As the words left his mouth, Daniil recognized their truth. Clearing Boris would help them both. Because while her family considered the matter over and done, for Daniil and Nasan the killer's name made a difference.

Ogodai did not respond. Rather than plead, Daniil stared at the fire glowing at the center of the clearing, the venison on its spit dripping juices and fat into the embers. High in a tree at the far side of the clearing a lynx, drawn by the cooking meat, perched, golden paws dangling, nose twitching. From a distance, it resembled a large house cat. Concentrated patience in a tense, agile frame.

Daniil watched it. Lynxes were shy creatures. He had never seen one so close. Kasimov lynxes must be different.

Ogodai paid it no heed. He chewed the tip of his mustache until a chittering squirrel broke his concentration by dropping an acorn on his head. It bounced off his helmet with a metallic ping.

He swore, laughed, and held out a hand to Daniil. "I suppose it does. Matter to you, that is. I wish I could provide the eyewitness, but I can't. I'll show you the evidence, though. You won't like it, but it will answer your questions."

Daniil hesitated. Ogodai's evidence had convinced the Tatars of Boris's guilt. What good was that? Charging in opposite directions, he and his brother-in-law would trip over each other.

But he didn't have much to lose. With the muster looming and his investigations at a standstill, he might as well accept Ogodai's dubious assistance. They could argue about the results later.

He shook Ogodai's hand, sealing the deal. "Let's. You've traveled this road once. Where do we start?"

Rumors of Nasan's activities reached the marketplace. From that hub of commerce, tales of her exploits spread, accompanying merchants on their way home. Russia under minority rule had plenty of problems: a royal family in conflict; quarrelsome noble clans; invaders poised at every border. Peasants worried about war and unrest, trampled fields, homes burned over their heads, injury and death, rape and plunder, then higher taxes to pay for the rebuilding. How delicious to imagine a new hero—the Golden Lynx—a man of unusual height and strength, wielding broadsword and battle ax, riding a mighty steed like the warriors of old. Although some dissenters insisted this one blended into the night, attacked without warning, and retreated unnoticed, leaving a whiff of jasmine on the air.

Jasmine? The peasants shook their heads and confiscated the ale barrels when those befuddled souls joined their gatherings.

⚘

For several weeks after her first excursion into the streets, Nasan enjoyed her masquerade to the hilt. Until the night of July 10, when it ceased to be a game.

At supper, the evening gave no sign of what it had in store. Natalya caught Nasan by the arm as she tried to leave the dining room. "I am concerned about you, daughter. Are you sure you're not with child? You seem so distracted lately."

"I don't know, Mama-in-law," Nasan said. "Too soon to tell."

Natalya sighed. "You are so thin. You must eat more. We need a babe. My dear Anastasia was a tiny thing like you, and look what happened to her."

Nasan patted her hand, unwilling to argue. "Soon, Mama-in-law. Please excuse. I sleep."

She tugged at her arm to free it, but Natalya held on. "You retire early every evening. Why then are you so tired?"

Nasan juggled explanations before settling on a partial truth. "Bad dreams."

Natalya hugged her. "There, child. You miss Daniil. But have no fear. He'll return soon, astonished that we could feel the least anxiety. Men always assume we need no reassurance."

Nasan stood still until she could, without being rude, wriggle free and say good night. Once through the door, she held her breath and listened to the click of Natalya's shoes receding down the corridor. Then, confident that no one would disturb her, she pushed a small chest against the door and began her evening ritual.

About to leave, she extinguished the candles and dangled her pendant before the spirit doll's face. "Is this not amusing, Grandmother? If these Russians only knew my brother bought this necklace in the Ryazan marketplace. What would they say then, I wonder? How shocked Mama-in-law would be to learn the real reason I am tired."

She touched the carved nose at the center of the doll's face. A breeze blew through the window, and she shivered. "I wish you would not send me nightmares, though. Even though I can go home if my husband dies, even though he loves Grusha, I can't help worrying. I am every sort of fool, losing sleep over him."

She glanced at the bed. Closed her eyes, let her head drop back. Licked her lips, remembering Daniil's kiss before he left. Twenty-one days that seemed like a year, ten years. "Sweet, though. I never imagined a man's body would feel so good."

Her head snapped up, and she stared straight into the brass mirror that hung above the ancestor doll. "As Grusha knows better than I," Nasan told her reflection. "Forget him. Moscow is waiting for its Golden Lynx."

From the chest that barred the door, she pulled a crude dummy, little more than a pillow with fake black wool hair, and slipped it between the sheets. It had taken all her sewing skills to create it over several evenings. She studied the effect, rearranged the hair for a more natural look, then headed for the window.

A cloaked figure was leaving the estate. Nasan leaned over the sill, watching it, until it swiveled its head and she drew back.

The figure returned its attention to what lay in front of it. Something about it reminded her of her own surreptitious entrances and exits. It skulked from one dark corner to the next and darted out of sight at the slightest noise.

There could not be another Golden Lynx in Moscow. Nevertheless, someone else in the Kolychev household had a secret. Intrigued, Nasan climbed down the wall and trailed the mysterious person in the cloak.

Her impromptu journey ended no more than two blocks away, on a street so like the one bordering the Kolychev estate that she would have had a hard time telling the difference. Wooden logs paved the road, and tall fences punctuated with watchtowers circled noble houses, visible only by their roofs. She lurked under the jutting eave of the farthest tower, watching the figure she was trailing scuttle along, hood pulled over its face. By the time it stopped in front of a gate about halfway down, Nasan still had no idea who hid beneath the cloak.

The figure pounded on the gate, and after a while a man opened it. He said something Nasan could not hear. She crept closer, hoping to identify a voice, anything. At last, she had discovered a bow in the storeroom that she could handle. When she got as close as she dared, she strung the weapon, then balanced it against the wall of the building next to her. Unless she had to fire in self-defense, she would avoid using it. It would call attention to her presence, and an estate like this one probably held more warriors than the Golden Lynx could handle.

The man at the gate spoke again. "You're late."

Harsh tones, blunt and inflexible. Nasan felt uncomfortable for no reason she could identify. She bit her lip and crouched deeper into her hiding place, waiting for understanding to dawn.

The cloaked figure pushed back its hood, and Nasan shifted position to see the face of the other Kolychev who carried secrets into the night. Instead her movement revealed, in the glow from the lantern hanging next to the gate, the face of the gatekeeper.

She almost cried out. A few inches taller than she, stolid, almost square, brown-haired, with a flat, coarse face: it was the man she had escaped in Kasimov, the man who had argued with Daniil's brother for the right to hunt her down.

Boris Kolychev's servitor, and someone from the Kolychev household. She had wasted her evening trailing a person who had no secrets to hide.

Except ... she had not imagined the cloaked figure's furtiveness. It made sense that Boris Kolychev's man would find a new master after the first one's death. Even a thug might have friends from his former place of service. But in that case, why sneak out to meet him?

The cloaked figure moved into the light, and Nasan had her answer. An all-too-familiar buxom figure, light-brown hair and pale blue eyes, unmistakable to someone with burning memories of seeing that same figure clasped in Daniil's arms.

Nasan staggered, reached out a hand to steady herself. "Grusha," she muttered. "Always Grusha. Why?"

"Let me through, Timoshka," Grusha said. "And stop your fussing. Your master won't like it if I tell him you were the one who delayed me."

He stepped aside with an extravagant flourish. Nasan watched her husband's lover sail past, ignoring him. Another male hand reached out and pulled her inside.

"Grusha," she murmured, "and Boris Kolychev's man. In the Name of the Prophet (on whom be peace), what have I stumbled onto?"

"You're late," Stenka said by way of greeting. "He's been expecting you for an hour. Get upstairs, if you know what's good for you. That room he calls his office."

Grusha kicked the wall. Every conversation with Semyon and his servants started the same way, with complaints about her tardiness. Did they expect her to keep a timepiece in her head, like that tick-tock the Venetian ambassador had given Nikolai Kolychev in return for arranging a royal audience? How did they even know she was late? She listened to the church bells, like everyone else. They must want to keep her off-balance. Semyon would love that.

Although Stenka sometimes sent her sympathetic glances when he thought she wasn't looking. He was sending one now. And every so often he tried to shield her from Semyon's wrath. It didn't seem to bother Stenka that Semyon could dismiss him on a whim.

She studied him. A pleasant face, with its snub nose and square features. Gray eyes with a twinkle. If she had not tumbled into love with Daniil, she could do worse than Stenka.

He gave her a gentle push toward the stairs. "Off you go, then. Don't stand there gawping. His high-and-mighty lordship will take it out on you."

She hurried up the stairs, considering what story to tell as she headed for Semyon's office. He lounged, scowling, in a chair while she manufactured a tale of urgent tasks imposed on her way out of the house. Apparently the lie served, for Semyon refrained from beating her.

"Come on time tomorrow," he said. "I have a job for you. But don't meet me here. Stenka will show you where to go."

When she stared at him, frowning—what did he want from her now?—he laughed. "And remember, my dear," he said, "you obey without question. Force me to talk, and your precious Daniil will get quite an earful. I won't hesitate to exaggerate the truth. We both know you don't want that, so off you go and tell Stenka to show you the way."

Glad to have escaped so lightly, Grusha left, puzzling over what Semyon had up his sleeve now and how she could thwart his plans without risking exposure.

Chapter 17

AMID THE HUSH OF A SUMMER MORNING, NOT MORE THAN AN hour after sunrise, every sound pierced the air with unnatural force. Birdsong stilled as two dozen caparisoned horses proceeded along the woodland path. Murmuring voices mingled with the soughing of a light breeze among the birches—graceful maidens shaking their jade locks against a pastel-streaked sky. Last night's rain seemed a distant memory except when the breeze shook moisture from the birches, sprinkling the riders as they passed under the trees. Ogodai rode, stern and self-contained, at Daniil's side. He had promised answers within the hour.

The dense canopy opened, revealing a ragged circle of earth and crops amid the trees. Daniil signaled his men to halt. His own horse responded to the pressure of Daniil's knees against his flanks, shifted his hooves as another gelding jostled him, stilled again under Daniil's hand.

The clearing contained a hamlet. Like so many that Daniil and his men had visited over the last week, it consisted of three huts— one large and well built, two little more than lean-to shacks— clustered around the opening created by slashed and burned birch trees. Spring wheat and oats fought for light with the weeds, rising around hewn stumps that must threaten the blade even of the light, horse-drawn plows that were all a small settlement like this would own. A single family, Daniil guessed, spread among the three huts to make incessant proximity tolerable.

Or perhaps the lean-tos housed animals. The peasants often shared their huts with pigs or fowl, but the horse that pulled the plow would need its own accommodation.

He would soon find out. Ogodai insisted that this unprepossessing hamlet had hosted a visitor who identified himself as Boris. On the evening of the day when someone matching that visitor's description had killed Ogodai's brother. Which made Boris the murderer, the Tatars believed.

But the Tatar intelligence net clearly had some gaping holes in it. Ogodai had mentioned one visitor, not two. And since it seemed too much to expect that the otherwise striking pair formed by Boris and Semyon had escaped the notice even of a harried peasant, Daniil suspected this visitor was someone else altogether. The unknown enemy, perhaps.

He did not reveal that Boris had traveled with their cousin. Irritated at Ogodai's refusal to produce the eyewitness, Daniil clung to his one solid piece of information. If his brother-in-law shared, he would too. If not, then not. But the more he chewed at the problem, the more likely it seemed to him that the Tatars had rushed to judgment. If their scouts could ignore an extra suspect, what else had they failed to notice?

A yawn stretched Daniil's mouth. His stomach rumbled, reminding him that he had left camp at dawn. No doubt the farmer's wife, if rewarded, would provide a bowl of porridge. Or the omnipresent cabbage soup. "*Shchi da kasha—pishcha nasha*," the peasants said. "Cabbage soup and porridge are our food."

"Why aren't they working?" he asked Ogodai. By this time of day, the hamlet's residents should be visible, hoes thwacking the light, acidic soil.

"Someone's around." Ogodai tipped his head. "Listen. Children in the woods. Berrying, probably. And a cow."

Daniil heard it then: the unmistakable sound of lowing. Families this poor usually didn't own cows. Cows needed proper pasturage, not this excuse for a field.

"Go and talk to them," Ogodai added. "They're Russians. They'll respond better to you, especially if you take off that helmet. I'll stay here with the men."

Daniil dismounted, handing Ogodai his reins. He stuffed his helmet into his saddle bag, checked that his tunic covered the mail shirt beneath, unbelted his sword. "I won't be long." He headed for the largest hut. As he crossed the open space, he kept his distance from the young crops. He would make no friends by crushing his hosts' livelihood.

As Daniil approached the hut, the door opened. The man in the doorway had, from the looks of him, seen middle age somewhere around the year of Daniil's birth. He was small and thin, with a leathery, faded countenance that spoke of long hours working in the sun. Wispy hair peeked from beneath a sheepskin cap worn with the wool side out. His linen shirt and homespun trousers, belted with a length of rope, showed more evidence of repeated darning than of contact with soap. When he smiled, the reek of raw onion made Daniil's nostrils flare. To offset any offense caused by his instinctive recoil, he pulled a kopeck piece from the pouch at his belt and handed it to the old man.

"For your health, Grandfather," he said. "And in anticipation of whatever food your good woman can spare a hungry stranger."

"Come in, come in." The man stepped back, gesturing with one hand while using the other to keep the plank portal from swinging shut on his visitor. "Wife, the young lord here needs to break his fast. What have you to offer him?"

"Much obliged," Daniil said. "Is it too much to ask for a moment of your time? I didn't happen on this clearing by accident.

I am searching for news of my brother, who stayed in one of these villages, I am told, late last winter."

The old man frowned. "A boyar, like yourself? Yes, we did entertain a nobleman and his troop. Well before Annunciation Sunday, it was. He stayed right here, on our stove, and his men in our barn. A cold night for them, no doubt, but we gave them plenty of straw."

Daniil frowned. Boris had treated other men as his equals, including his own soldiers. Another way in which he stood out from his comrades-in-arms. Daniil had argued with him to no avail: be kind, yes, but someday you will have to order them into battle; don't let them think they have the right to order you. But Boris didn't listen. He was the older brother, convinced he knew best. Whatever anyone said, he would have stayed with his men and let the family sleep in peace.

Odd that he had not recognized Boris's stubbornness before. He'd written off his brother's behavior as misplaced humility. More evidence of Boris's virtue and his own failure to measure up. Wasn't it, in truth, another imperfection?

Semyon, though, drove his men too hard. He would sleep in comfort while his soldiers shivered.

Daniil entered a large, well-lit room. Benches lined the walls, and a rough-hewn table filled the center. The far corner housed a large clay stove—the same one, no doubt, that had warmed the visiting nobleman. Over the rim of the stove, Daniil could see a pair of bright gray eyes and a tousled red-gold head: a boy of twelve or thirteen, he guessed. He wondered what kept the boy in bed and the family inside on a workday. Bad enough that he had led his troops on this chase. He should not also expose them to pestilence.

But the apple-cheeked woman who stood at the table, kneading dough, looked healthy. So did the much younger woman—probably the first one's daughter, because she wore her hair uncovered, in the single braid of an unmarried girl—who wielded a broom with considerable ferocity if little effect on the dirt floor. From the irritated glances the sweeper cast at the baker, Daniil concluded that the ferocity expressed an argument interrupted by his arrival.

Women's fusses. Noble estate or peasant hut, the issues did not vary. A man didn't concern himself with mundane household chores.

Daniil's thoughts strayed to his mother, at this moment ordering the life of his bride. He wondered how Nasan was coping with that, given her limited Russian. Whether she felt homesick, lost—or simply resentful, as this girl seemed to. If he'd stayed, he could have shepherded her through the transition.

The older woman used a cloth lying next to the dough to rub at the flour that covered her to the elbows. She seemed younger than the man who had ushered Daniil into the room: a strong, solid female of the type favored by peasants; a hard worker, no doubt, with vestiges of prettiness in her round face. In her forties, Daniil guessed, about his mother's age. Although the common people worked so hard and lived so poorly that one could not always tell: they aged faster than the nobles. Once upon a time, this woman had probably resembled the young sweeper, a sylph with light brown hair and honeyed eyes that lost their ferocity as she gazed at Daniil.

Out of habit, Daniil smiled at the hussy, who blushed. Under different circumstances, he'd have been tempted to pursue the opportunity she offered. But he had a new bride and a mission that left no time for girls, however attractive. He would ask his questions, eat the food they provided, and go.

As if prompted by his thoughts, the older woman said, "Sveta, kasha and kvass for the boyar."

The broom wielder propped her implement against the wall and moved to obey. Daniil watched her hips sway as she crossed the floor, heard the older woman tsk-tsk under her breath, and dragged his eyes above Sveta's waist. She reached the stove and turned, giving him an excellent view of her ample bosom as she picked up cloths to protect her hands, opened the oven door, and lifted out a covered clay pot. This she carried to the table, where she ladled buckwheat porridge into a wooden bowl and held it out to Daniil. The smile she bestowed on him conveyed a hint of mischief, a sense that the two of them stood alone amid the trio of relatives. His resistance wavered, until the appetizing steam rising from the bowl reminded him of a more basic hunger.

With a nod, he thanked her. The older woman handed him a spoon shaped like a wide-bottomed boat, its hull smooth, its carved prow forming the handle. He thanked her, too, and sat on the bench that edged three sides of the room. The kasha had the nutty, buttery taste that spoke of skilled cooks and long hours on low heat. He chewed each morsel with pleasure, stopping every so often to quench his thirst from the cup that Sveta handed him— filled with kvass, the dark beer made from fermented rye bread that peasants drank most often.

This one had more kick to it than usual. Daniil timed his sips accordingly. He needed to keep his wits about him.

The old man, who had followed Daniil into the room, addressed the bread maker. "Sonya, he asks about that boyar who stopped here last winter. His brother, he says. Do you remember?"

Sonya's blue eyes grew bleary as she studied Daniil. "Indeed, he looked not unlike you. Another big blond, traveling with fifteen men. I put the soldiers in the stable, but the lord slept here, on the stove. Ate up half our stores, they did, but they paid well. My man here had to take the cart to Kasimov for supplies when they left."

He looked not unlike you. Ogodai had some right on his side, then. Boris *had* resembled him. So did Semyon. "A big blond," he said. "That sounds like my brother. Did you notice anything unusual about the man? Marks, scars?"

Sonya considered, then shook her head. "No. He looked angry— not with us, but in general. As if he'd had a hard day. But no scars."

"Not true, Mama," Sveta said. "An old one running down his cheek."

Not Boris, then. Semyon did have a healed scar from a saber cut, acquired in some long-ago battle. "Here?" Feeling lighter already, he drew his finger down the left side of his face, ending at his mouth.

"Yes." She duplicated his gesture.

"What name did he give you?" Daniil asked. Ogodai had told him, the day of the wedding, but that couldn't be true. He had no idea why the Tatars had made the story up, but they must have.

Sonya tapped flour-covered fingers against the dough, her gaze fixed on the room's one window as if it contained an answer. Daniil bit his tongue to keep himself from shouting at her.

"I don't think I remember," she said at last. "Do you, Sveta?"

Sveta came forward. "No." Her honeyed eyes darkened. "I kept my distance. Didn't like the way he looked at me. As if I were a tasty dish he wanted to sample."

Who wouldn't? I bet you flirted with him, too.

Yet the comment heartened him. Boris did not chase women. Maria used to insist Boris neglected her (although Daniil believed that Maria would turn anyone into a eunuch). He couldn't imagine Boris lusting after Sveta. Unless this was one more indication that Boris had hidden his true face from his family.

The three peasants were still debating the name of their visitor.

"Let me see," Sonya said. "What was it? Nikolai? No. Foma? No, not that either."

"Pyotr?" Sveta offered. "Mikhail? Lots of grandees named Mikhail."

The old man smacked her. "Silly wench. We're not trying to make up a name. Stop throwing out every idea that enters that hair-filled head of yours."

Sveta wailed. "Go back to your sweeping, girl," Sonya ordered. Sveta, sniffing, complied. Every so often, she cast a sulky glance over her shoulder.

"The boy," Sonya announced. "He spoke to the lord once or twice, and his memory is better than ours." She twisted her head toward the stove. "Andryusha, get down here."

"So he did." The old man, too, spoke to the stove, where the tousled head and gray eyes were acquiring cheeks, a mouth and chin, a neck. "Your mother called you, boy. Don't dally. Answer the boyar if you can, then go do your chores, like your brothers and sisters. What's got you malingering, anyway? That cow will low down the barn before you get to her."

The neck attached itself to a body, which scrambled down the side of the stove and landed a few feet from Daniil's bench. A scrawny youth. Like his father, the boy wore a loose shirt over homespun trousers and shoes woven from the bark of the birches that lined the clearing. The eyes, large in his thin face, sparkled with intelligence, like the drummer boy in Daniil's regiment.

Daniil extended a hand to the boy. Andryusha, his mother had called him. Named for Andrei, the adventurous apostle who had visited the Dnieper River and predicted the emergence of Kiev, centuries later. A good name for this lively boy.

"Andryusha," Daniil said. "You heard us talking. The nobleman who stayed here last winter may have been my brother. For family reasons, I need to find out. But no one else recalls the man's name. Can you help me?"

The boy scratched his chin and crinkled his nose. His eyes crossed in an intensity of concentration.

"He forgot," Sveta said from the door, where her sweeping had taken her. Envy distorted her pretty face.

"Did not," Andryusha said. "Boris. Papa asked him, remember? Boris Nikolaevich."

"That's right." Sonya patted the boy's head. "Boris Nikolaevich. That Tatar came here looking for him. It's the same man, right?"

"Yes." Daniil couldn't suppress a groan. The Tatars hadn't invented the story after all.

The young woman spoke. "I think he lied."

The old man hissed. "Drat that girl." He bestowed a gap-toothed grin on Daniil. "Pay her no heed, Lord. Can't bear seeing Andryusha the center of attention, she can't. You know how it is."

Jealousy? Perhaps. But someone had lied. Not Ogodai. Boris or Semyon, perhaps both. Or an unknown adversary, bent on concealing his own hatred. Daniil turned to face the girl. She stood in the doorway, broom upright at her side and a combative expression on her face.

"Why?" he asked. "What made you think the man lied?"

The girl's broom slumped at an angle. "Because it was strange," she said. "Papa asked how to address him, and he said, 'Boris Nikolaevich.' Then he stopped and glanced at his men. They were staring at him, blank like. The way you would if someone said something you didn't expect and weren't sure how to take. His head whipped round, and he said, 'Shein'—in a hurry, as though he'd just thought of it."

"Shein?" Daniil made no attempt to keep the astonishment out of his voice. "Are you sure?"

"Absolutely," Sveta said. "He stopped looking uncomfortable then and repeated it, 'Boris Nikolaevich Shein.' Seemed almost proud of himself."

Her father, so recently full of advice to ignore her, confirmed it. "Correct," he said. "Good work, my girl. I'd forgotten that."

"Boris Nikolaevich Shein," Daniil echoed. His head, spun this way and that by the rapidly shifting news, felt as if it might snap off. "And this was a young man, you said?"

"Oh yes," Sonya put in. "Definitely a young man. A few years older than you."

"Does it matter?" the old man asked.

Daniil fished another coin from his pouch, then made it two. He pressed them into the eager hands of his host. "Very much."

Striding to the door, he caught Sveta round the waist and kissed her full on the mouth. She sighed when he loosened his grip.

Amused, he chucked her under the chin and addressed the old man. "Your daughter was right. The nobleman lied to you. To what extent, I can't tell. But I do know one thing. That was not Boris Nikolaevich Shein. He died last month at the age of sixty-four."

The next day, Nasan kept a watch on Grusha. Subdued, with dark circles under her eyes, the maid did the jobs assigned to her without joining the other servants in their chatter. From time to time, she stared into space until called to attention by Natalya.

Nasan felt an unexpected sympathy for her rival. Grusha looked miserable. Whatever had taken her away from the Kolychev estate last night did not seem to have brought her joy.

But what had taken her away? As Nasan worked through the day's chores and parried advice from a mother-in-law determined to turn her into a wife perfect enough to conceive the longed-for heir as soon as Daniil returned, she pondered what had led Grusha to contact Boris Kolychev's former soldier. She considered and, with some regret, dismissed the obvious explanation: that another man had supplanted Daniil in Grusha's fickle heart. The maid's downcast eyes and strained face did not suggest that she had found a new lover.

Nasan's curiosity was piqued. Whether she liked the Kolychevs or not, marriage had tied her fate to theirs. If Grusha's sneaking around affected them, it affected Nasan, too.

And if scotching Grusha's plans upset the maid or Daniil, Nasan would not mind one bit.

Daniil's elation carried him a third of the way across the clearing before a glimpse of Ogodai, waiting under the trees for confirmation of his convictions, stripped his relief from him and dumped it amid the weeds. What had he learned that would exonerate his brother?

Only that a man who from his coloring, age, and social station could have been Boris had lied about his last name and—if Sveta's memory of the scar was accurate—had deliberately misstated his first name and patronymic as well.

Promising, but nothing the Tatars couldn't have figured out on their own. Bulat and Ogodai, too, knew the age of Boris Nikolaevich Shein. Obviously, they had not concluded that the misstated family name took Boris out of contention as a suspect.

He had too many unanswered questions. The role of his cousin Semyon, for example. Most likely, he, not Boris, had stayed at the hamlet that night. But which of them had murdered Nasan's brother? Why lie to their own clan, when telling the truth would have protected everyone better? And had Semyon meant to implicate Boris?

Whatever Ogodai said, Daniil needed to talk to the eyewitness. The man—Daniil assumed it was a man, because the Tatars secluded their women just as the Russians did—must have a key that would unlock this mystery. Some subtle detail that, although it meant nothing to Ogodai, would reveal to Daniil whether the killer had been his brother, his cousin, or that unknown enemy. The eyewitness had information that no one had thought to ask him. Like the scar.

The sun had risen in the sky. By the time Daniil reached the soldiers, they had repacked their rations and remounted their horses. Ogodai watched, unspeaking, arms crossed over his chest. Daniil ordered the men toward Kasimov, donned his helmet, and retrieved his animal's reins from his brother-in-law. Staying in the rear, he and Ogodai walked their horses so they could argue without being overheard.

Daniil wasted no time. "I want to interview the eyewitness," he said. "And stop pretending you don't know where he is. You told me yourself, before the wedding, that you 'had an eyewitness.' You must know."

Ogodai said something in Tatar that sounded like swearing. "Yes, I do. But the eyewitness can't tell you anything you haven't heard."

"Rot. Boris was my brother. I can ask questions you wouldn't think of." Daniil's horse shook its head as his hands tightened on the reins. By the saints, Ogodai was stubborn.

"My father sent the witness away," Ogodai said. "I'd have to check with him before I could tell you where." He pointed his whip behind them. "You're wasting your time, Daniil. We didn't settle on your brother at random. We already conducted an investigation."

"Hah!" It felt good to say what he felt. "Some investigation. I talked to those peasants. A big, light-haired Russian boyar—not a rare type—gave a false name. Unless you think Boris Nikolaevich Shein exchanged bodies with his own grandson three months before he died."

"Of course not. But that wasn't the only information we had. Our clan wasn't fighting with anyone else. Girei didn't hold power, so no one wanted to assassinate him. And I told you we captured a Kolychev horse."

"A Kolychev horse," Daniil scoffed. "Anyone can steal a horse."

"Except that anyone didn't. We took the horse from a troop led by a tall man with light hair—not like yours, almost white—and blue eyes. Then we tracked the group here, where the leader gave his name as Boris Nikolaevich."

"Shein," Daniil reminded him.

"Shein," Ogodai said. "Who was not young, blond, or blue-eyed."

"No," Daniil admitted. He and Ogodai rode in silence for a while, side by side, knees almost touching on the narrow path, miles apart in outlook.

As they rode, Daniil wondered what to do next. He could insist they split forces, but he didn't have enough time left before the muster to fight both Ogodai and his own ignorance of Tatar language and customs. Yet he refused to abandon his search. If nothing else, he wanted—no, needed—to find out what had brought Boris to Kasimov, what role his brother had played in Girei's death. What relationship between Boris and the eyewitness made identification possible.

His horse shied as it passed under a tree. A striped cat paw, claws extended, dangled from a branch inches from his face.

Through the verdant summer foliage, a pair of golden eyes gazed into his, then the lynx sprang from the branch and disappeared.

A different lynx? In the primeval forest, he could almost believe the animal was following him, mirroring his mood. Intense and focused last night, today jumpy as Daniil himself.

Again Ogodai said nothing. But the lynx had crouched right above their heads. Ogodai should have noticed. Daniil opened his mouth to ask, then shut it. Why waste his time?

Somewhere in Kasimov lay the answers to his questions. What would convince Ogodai to renew the search?

"All right," he said. "Let's forget the eyewitness for the moment and trace Boris instead. Don't you want to find out what brought him here?"

Ogodai frowned. "Isn't it obvious? He came seeking vengeance."

"He didn't believe in vengeance. What changed him?"

"What difference does it make? He came, he killed, he died."

"It makes a difference to me," Daniil said. "If Boris did that…" His throat closed up, and he couldn't finish the sentence.

Ogodai's scowling face softened. "Yes, I see it means a lot to you to prove that Boris did not. Why, Daniil?"

But Daniil couldn't explain. "Let's go." He wheeled his horse and spoke to his men. "Back toward Ryazan, boys. Until we pick up my brother's trail."

That evening, as soon as supper ended, Nasan again withdrew to her room. After asking the grandmother for guidance, she blew out the candles and crouched by the window. From there she could see most of the estate. Clouds had blown across the sky a dozen times and more before she spied a shadow slip across the courtyard.

She didn't wait. It might not be Grusha, but from this distance she couldn't tell. Better to take the risk of following the wrong person. If she failed, she could try again the next night. She climbed out the window and down the wall, blessing the logs that made ascent and descent so much easier than the stone architecture of Kasimov had.

By the time she reached the street, the shadow was vanishing around a corner. Nasan ran, soundless in her felt boots, keeping to the sides of the street near the houses where she could easily slide behind a barrel or a planter if her quarry looked around.

But Grusha—if it was Grusha—gave no evidence of hearing her pursuer. She walked slowly, head down in her hooded cape, staring at her feet. Nasan soon caught up to her. There were no street lamps, but every so often they passed a noble estate with a lantern at the gate. Nasan recognized the cape from the night before when Grusha passed under one of these. Satisfied, she drew back, staying close enough to follow any twists and turns. The night was cloudy and cool, with a light breeze, but the moon cast sufficient glow for eyes accustomed to the dark.

Streets she patrolled every night gave way to less familiar pathways, ending in a part of town that Nasan had not visited before. Grusha headed down the hill, as far as the palisade that ringed the merchants' quarter of the city, then circled to her left. Eventually she stopped before the gates of a small, rundown estate. Here too a man waited, larger than the one before.

Not the same man, yet his shape seemed familiar. Nasan's mouth went dry with fear.

He grabbed the maid by the arm. "Curse you and your lateness," he hissed. "Get inside at once. They should be here any moment."

Nasan froze. *That voice...*

This part of town, hard against the city walls, had few estates prosperous enough to merit lanterns. Clouds obscured the moonlight, revealing shapes but not details. The man pushed Grusha through the gate and stood, a silent shadow. Nasan crept closer, careful to maintain her cover, toward the man's silhouette outlined against the wall. When she reached the palisade, she pressed against it, fighting the terror that gripped her.

The present ebbed, dragging her in its undertow and tossing her ashore amid the ambush that killed Girei. The world drained of color. Through her fear she sensed, lurking at the edges of her consciousness, the ancestral spirit that had guided her on that fateful day.

A breeze sent clouds scudding across the face of the moon, illuminating silvery hair and pale skin. Cold, hateful blue eyes. A cruel face. The kind of face one would expect on a man who could kill a boy in cold blood. As on that day in the Kasimov woods, Nasan shoved her sleeve in her mouth so she would not give herself away to her enemy.

The soldier she had escaped in Kasimov had not, it appeared, changed masters after all. Girei's murderer lived. He had Grusha's cooperation, willing or otherwise. And in some way Nasan had yet to discover, the Tatars had made a horrendous mistake.

Boris Kolychev had survived.

Chapter 18

NASAN, STUNNED BY THE REALIZATION THAT GIREI'S KILLER lived, watched the small estate for as long as she dared, but no one else arrived. Kolychev abandoned his vigil and went inside. Grusha emerged not long before dawn. Nasan hurried home, not waiting for the maid to precede her.

Back in her room, she drew the shutters, stripped off her disguise, and donned a simple wool robe. She unpinned her braids and let them fall. By feel she located the spirit doll, picked it up, and rubbed a smear of grease across its lips. A small box that masqueraded as a rouge pot held the hardened fat. "Grusha," she murmured to the ancestor. "And that man. The two people I hate most, together. What binds her to him? How did he escape the raid? I don't understand, Grandmother."

She stopped, considering. *Ata* swore he had avenged Girei. Ogodai, too, and her brother knew Boris Kolychev by sight. So the man she had seen tonight could not be Boris, miraculously escaped, as she'd first thought.

Someone else, then. Who? Most likely, a relative. That would explain the resemblance. Someone close enough to be invited to her wedding, in any case. Those moments written off as a waking nightmare, when she saw or heard Girei's killer and thought she was imagining things—they'd been nothing of the sort. If she'd seen the man clearly, she would have realized that.

But she hadn't. She'd believed her father and her brother when they assured her he was dead. She'd thought him a ghost, a message from the ancestors. Instead, he was right there, where she could have identified him, and…

And what? Her family wouldn't have taken her back to Kasimov. For the sake of peace, they had wed her to a man whose brother had died at their hands. A man whose brother had died for no reason, a mistake. Based on *her* faulty description of the killer. Leaving her with two lives to avenge, Boris's as well as Girei's.

Because no one else knew, except for the killer and his men. No one else could identify him. She was the only eyewitness.

She should confess, of course. Whatever Daniil had done, she owed him that much. But she had no way to reach him. He had walked out on her the day after the wedding.

Then what should she do? Seek a life for a life, as the steppe code required? In the safety of Kasimov, she had prayed for the opportunity to exact vengeance. Her enemy didn't deserve pity. It would be like killing a mad dog. A public service, in truth.

But the murderer's death wouldn't solve anything. On the contrary, it would reignite the feud. Nasan had married an enemy to protect her family. She couldn't put her relatives at risk. Not to mention Nikolai and Natalya, Daniil, Maria, even Grusha— she knew them now. Yes, she liked some and disliked others, but she couldn't toss them to the flames or she would become as depraved as the man she hated, ready to sacrifice the first innocent who came to hand. She rubbed the grandmother's wooden belly between her palms, searching for guidance.

This killer frightened her, but she would conquer her fear. Warriors do not run for help like children facing monsters in the night. She could handle him, with the grandmothers' assistance.

"Justice takes many forms," the spirit said in her mind. "Exile, isolation, imprisonment, exposure. That man—that maid—they're doing something they shouldn't. Stop them."

Something they shouldn't. Yes, the spirit had it right. Whatever tied Grusha to Girei's killer, they wanted the association kept secret. If they were involved in a love affair, Nasan would not interfere, but Grusha's unhappiness made that unlikely.

And last night they had met at a tumbledown estate, waiting for a delivery important enough for the killer to supervise it in person, rather than sending one of his men.

"They should be here any moment," he'd said. But "they" had not arrived.

A secret, possibly a crime. In that case, stopping them might be vengeance enough.

"Thank you, Grandmother," she said. "I have a place to begin."

Content, she positioned the doll on her dressing table, pulled the dummy from between the sheets and returned it to storage, dragged the chest from the door, and slipped into bed. For once, no nightmares forced her awake.

Less than a day's ride back toward Ryazan, Daniil watched his brother-in-law in urgent and incomprehensible dialogue with a fisherman. Daniil dismounted and handed his horse to Pashka, who led the beast toward the river. To either side, Tatar and Russian troops were doing the same.

The men had time to down dried meat and hunks of bread from their saddlebags before Ogodai said, "*Sau bul,*" left the fisherman on the bank, and came to join the rest of the group.

"*Sau bul,* Sultan," the fisherman said to his back. Even Daniil knew enough Tatar to recognize that phrase: Farewell, Sultan.

Daniil retrieved his horse and swung onto the saddle. He pushed his way through the throng of soldiers, eager to catch up with Ogodai, already racing down the Ryazan road. His brother-in-law maintained his lead without effort but stopped on his own before long. To his right, a trail headed into the woods. He waited there, his horse's nose pointing toward the new path, until the others reached him.

"What's going on?" Daniil said, miffed. This was his expedition. It hadn't become Ogodai's merely because Daniil had trouble with Tatar.

Ogodai's mustache bristled. "That fisherman saw your brother. Or someone who looked just like him. *And* someone who looked just like him, in fact. Your cousin?"

"Yes, I think so." With an effort, Daniil kept his voice even.

"So you did know. What game are you playing, Daniil? You accept my help, then withhold information?"

Daniil's frustration boiled over in response to that combative tone. "It's not my fault that you and your clan can't see past the end of your noses. What kind of feeble investigation did you mount that you didn't find out that Boris and Semyon traveled together?"

"We didn't come out this far," Ogodai said. "Why should we, when we'd already learned the truth? And by the Prophet (on whom be peace), Daniil, listen to yourself. You've proved that your brother *was* in Kasimov. He didn't come here to pick daisies."

"Well, he didn't come to murder a boy. I don't know what brought him here. I'm trying to find out. And if you would produce the damned eyewitness instead of blocking me at every turn, maybe I would."

"I told you. The eyewitness can't answer your questions. We got a full report from her the day after the murder."

Daniil's jaw dropped. "Her?" Was that why Ogodai was shielding the witness? To protect her honor?

Boris, with a Tatar woman? Then again, maybe she wasn't a Tatar. Sveta couldn't be the only willing Russian in Kasimov. Out of character for Boris, but more plausible than vengeance.

Ogodai waved a dismissive hand. "Her, him. You know I have trouble remembering those Russian pronouns."

Daniil stared at him. Tatars did often mix up masculine and feminine. Nasan had done it a dozen times in their three days together. But Ogodai spoke Russian like a native. Daniil didn't recall him ever making that particular mistake.

He couldn't shake the sense that he'd heard something important. "I still want to talk to him," he said after a while. "Or her. I told you. A description of the killer would mean more to me than it did to you. I knew Boris better than you did. I know Semyon."

Ogodai interrupted him. "Then why don't you ask your cousin?"

"We did, months ago. He swore he'd come nowhere near Kasimov."

"He lied, in other words. Which suggests a guilty conscience, don't you think?"

"Yes," Daniil said. "I'll ask him again, in Moscow. In the meantime, I'm here. Where you promised to help me. So hand over the eyewitness. Preferably before the government orders us off in different directions and I never find out what happened."

Ogodai growled. There was no other word for it. "Honestly, Daniil, I could wring your neck. When you get stuck on an idea…" He let the sentence hang, unfinished, then added, "Follow me, and based on what the fisherman said, we will make the acquaintance of *one* eyewitness."

One eyewitness. So they had more than one. More suspicious than ever of his brother-in-law's motives, Daniil grudgingly accepted the distraction. "Why, what's down this road?"

The soldiers had joined them. Horses jostled and whinnied and crowded the path. Ogodai pointed down the trail with his whip. "A tavern," he said. "We don't allow many, because this is Muslim land. But we let the Russians keep a few. The fisherman saw our two noblemen, your brother"—he produced a satirical bow—"and your cousin, there not long before Girei died."

Daniil stared at him in astonishment. "Boris joined Semyon in a tavern? To do what?"

Ogodai lifted one sable eyebrow. "Get drunk, of course."

⚘

The next morning, Nasan made a complete mull of her embroidery, a much hated and seldom successful pastime that she practiced only because her mother-in-law would accept no excuses. Maria laughed until she almost fell from the bench.

"Oh, Mama-in-law, look what she's done." Maria held her own exquisitely smocked baby's robe in one hand and pointed at Nasan's monstrosity with the other. The green leaf in the center looked more like a stagnant lake, and the red rose resembled a bloodstain.

Like the one that surrounded Girei on the snow. Nasan dropped the handkerchief and strove to control her breathing as her senses swam around her. She would have sworn she had put such episodes behind her. Recognizing Girei's killer had revived the past.

"Enough, Maria," Natalya said. "Your meanness of spirit does you no credit. Can you not sympathize with your sister's distress?"

"Not important," Nasan said, so softly no one heard.

Maria stopped laughing. "Meanness," she muttered. "We'll see who's mean."

"*What* did you say?" Natalya's voice would chill soup.

"Nothing."

"You did," Natalya snapped. "I heard half of it, so don't bother pretending. You need to mend your ways, my girl, if you want to remarry someday. A word from me, and you'll be lucky to find yourself wife to the lowest type of gentry servitor."

"You just wait." Maria sprang to her feet. "You'll be bowing at my feet one day, and I'll be glad, glad, *glad* to see it. Because I'll be living somewhere else, away from you horrible people. I hate it here." She stormed out the door, slamming it behind her.

Nasan barely registered Maria's departure. Daniil, Grusha, Girei, Girei's murderer, a disillusioning marriage that Bulat would never have contracted for her if not for her own fatal error, too many nights wandering the streets without adequate sleep, her wrenching separation from the customs and religion and even the food and drink and language of home—the image of the blood-red rose draped over these many other causes of distress like a hideous shroud. She clutched the cushion to her face and sobbed.

Arms circled her, and she smelled the lavender that scented her mother-in-law's robes. "Daughter, what is it?" Natalya said. "Maria would try the patience of a saint, but she has no power unless you give it to her."

Nasan shook her head violently. "Not Maria." The words tumbled out before she heard them in her mind. "Brother. On the snow. Blood. Like that flower."

Oh, no. Last night she had vowed not to confide in her in-laws yet. She must stop, right away.

Natalya held her at arm's length. "Brother on the snow? Brother's blood on the snow? *You* witnessed his murder?"

Nasan gulped, nodded, wiped tears away with one finger. Unnoticed, the cushion fell from her arms. She need not fear unwanted confidences. A bear had grabbed her throat, and no words could escape.

"Oh, my poor child," Natalya said. "Why did no one mention it?" She shook Nasan gently. "If you saw the boy murdered, then you saw his murderer. Was it my Boris?"

Nasan bit her lip. The bear squeezed her throat. Tears flowed. How could she explain without revealing the whole? She closed her eyes.

Natalya answered her own question. "No, you can't tell me. Boris died before you came to us. If he'd lived, you could have testified to his innocence. But he didn't live."

Her grief was audible, but instead of dwelling on the injury Nasan's family had done her, she pulled Nasan close again and rocked her. "Ah, daughter-in-law," she murmured. "What a pair we are. I watched my son die, and you your brother, and now we must live together in harmony, like it or not."

Nasan, for the first time since she had entered the Kolychev house as a bride, put her arms around Natalya and returned her hug. The older woman's sympathy, her willingness to forgive, touched Nasan's heart. She wanted to tell Natalya that Boris had not committed the dreadful deed attributed to him, to confess her family's fatal error, but too much hung on her silence.

Natalya would learn the truth very soon. A few more days should make no difference.

If she succeeded. She had to. If she failed, no one else could exonerate Boris.

"Get drunk, of course." Daniil puzzled over that one as he trailed Ogodai's horse through the woods. Beech trees in full leaf cast emerald shadows as they passed. He half-expected to see a lynx paw dangling from one of them, but none appeared. Sunlight glinted off harness ornaments, turning them into necklaces worthy of the grand prince's treasury. The path wasn't wide enough to ride abreast, and Daniil told himself it made sense to let the person who knew the way take the lead. It still rankled. His mission, not Ogodai's.

Resentment paled next to the image of Boris, rollicking drunk in Semyon's company. Boris drank, yes. Everyone knew water would kill you. A tankard of ale with dinner, a glass of French or Rhenish wine at a family celebration. But Boris did not *get drunk*. Such a thing had never happened in Daniil's experience. And as an army man, Daniil rather prided himself on the breadth of his experience—except today, when he felt as baffled as any raw recruit.

He had idolized Boris. He saw that now. Yet admiration had not left much room for conversation; he'd felt more comfortable with Ogodai, before their clans went to war, than with Boris. The thought brought a flood of relief. Good or bad, he was himself, not a myth. Better that than a vision of sainthood that only lies could sustain.

Ogodai reined in his gelding. Ahead of them, the trees cleared once more. A pond, slick with lichen and bordered with reeds, glowed dark against sandy soil. On the far side stood a hut not unlike the one that Sveta and Andryusha's family called home but twice its size. Its open door, wisp of smoke curling past the jamb, beckoned with the aroma of roasting chicken. Shutters flung wide revealed a couple, presumably the tavern keeper and his wife, caught in the midst of an argument. The man—short, bald, and sturdy—waved a clay cup in emphasis, mouth spread in a shout, cheeks red. Daniil couldn't make out the words. The woman, undaunted—perhaps because she surpassed him in both height and weight—flapped her dust cloth at him and shouted back.

On a bench outside the hut, two peasants—one young and muscled, the other wizened and bent—traded jokes and occasionally raised their mugs toward the couple, saluting (Daniil assumed) a particularly fine riposte.

He dismounted and tied his horse to the nearest elm. "Let's go in," he said to Ogodai.

The Tatar nodded, dismounted, then fell into place beside him as Daniil strode past. Behind them two dozen pairs of Tatar and Russian boots hit the forest floor, and two dozen bits jingled as horses lowered their necks to graze.

Daniil kept walking, wondering what new facet of his brother this interview would reveal.

The argument, Daniil soon learned, revolved around the bird perfuming the air as it turned on the spit. The woman insisted the hen had met a premature end; the man disagreed. Daniil and Ogodai's arrival in a clank of armor and weaponry brought the discussion to an immediate halt.

"Who owns this house?" Daniil asked, before the debate could reignite.

"I do," the man said. The woman hissed, and he amended his answer. "And my wife, Yulia here."

Daniil opened his mouth to ask the man's name, but Ogodai spoke first. "I've seen you about the town. Kasimov. Volodka, isn't it?"

Impressive. Daniil recognized his own men, his parents' servants, any soldier he'd served with, most of the court. He did not store the name of every citizen who crossed his path. But then, identifying people was Ogodai's job, in a sense. Tatar khans and sultans faced constant assassination attempts from others of their kind. And the heir to a throne needed to monitor everything that went on in his future principality. The health, the happiness, even the lives of himself and his supporters could one day depend on his remembering the name and the occupation of a Russian tavern keeper.

"Yes, Sultan," the tavern keeper said. "Volodka. I came here to live when I married Yulia. The tavern belonged to her father, and to his father before him." That explained the wife's hiss. Her property, not his, even if she did let him manage it with her.

During the brief silence that followed, the tavern keeper returned the cup to its shelf and dismissed Yulia with a curt, "Be gone, wife." She shuffled off. Daniil soon heard her whisking her dust rag across the timbers. He suspected she had circled the hut and stationed herself outside the nearest window. He didn't mention it. He planned to talk to her before leaving, and it would save time if she'd already overheard him questioning her husband.

The peasants came into the hut. They positioned themselves on the bench nearest the fire, inhaling the succulent aroma. Volodka turned the handle, spinning the hen on its axis.

"Good you didn't listen, Volodka," the old man opined. "Women. More hair than wit. That hen's better off where she is."

The tavern keeper grunted an assent. The whisking from outside speeded up.

"Better for us than the hen, Granddad." The young man upended his tankard over the bench. "My belly's as empty as this mug." He held the tankard out to Volodka, who left the spit and headed for a barrel suspended at the back of the tavern.

Daniil pulled the conversation back to the present. "Beer, if you please," he told the tavern keeper. While the man turned to his cask, Daniil raised an eyebrow at Ogodai, standing shoulder to shoulder. "You?"

"Yes," Ogodai said. Volodka reached for a second cup, filled them both, then handed one to Daniil, the other to Ogodai.

"A big hut, for two," Daniil remarked, keeping his tone casual while he sought an opening for his real questions.

Volodka stared at him with surprising hostility. "No offense, Lord, but who might you be? I'm an honest man. Your kind caused me enough trouble a few months back. I've no desire for another go-round."

Daniil hooked the closest stool with his foot and settled himself next to the bar. "Well, that's what I came to talk to you about," he said. "I suspect that I, for my sins, am the brother of your unruly customers. What trouble did they cause?"

He gestured to Ogodai with his free hand. Ogodai took the stool next to him. Volodka leaned his elbows on the bar, eyes fixed on Daniil's face.

The two peasants crowded closer, muttering disconnected phrases—"drunk," "rowdy," "cups flying," among them. Volodka waved them away, and they went, feet dragging across the dirt floor.

"We'll make sure you don't lose by it," Ogodai said.

Daniil caught his eye and grinned. It was like the old days— the two of them, working together. The first time he'd felt such camaraderie in months.

He spoke to Volodka. "Right. So tell me. What did they do?"

Yulia answered. Eavesdropping while dusting must not have satisfied her, for she returned to the fray. "Shameful, it was," she said. "You look like an honorable man, young lord, and we know our sultan by sight, of course." She saluted first Daniil, then Ogodai, with the dust rag and went on without giving either of them a chance to interrupt. "But those two who came here—begging your pardon, Lord—right thugs they were, for all that they paid my good man for their revelry. Drank themselves senseless, tossed my best cups in the fire before falling off the benches, brought in half the local sluts, then tired of them and picked a fight with Mishka here." She pointed to the old man who had spoken first.

Daniil blinked. *Boris?* Amusing himself with loose women? Punching a graybeard? Impossible!

"And muttering the whole time about vengeance." Hands clasped over her heart, she bowed to Ogodai. "They did not name Girei Sultan, Lord. If they had, we would have reported them right away."

Daniil had his doubts, but what else could the woman say, with the victim's brother sitting right there? His mind reeled with images of Boris carousing, fighting, whoring, planning a coldblooded murder. However much he'd idolized his older brother, he couldn't have misjudged him as badly as this.

Perhaps Semyon had done these things, and Boris made no effort to prevent them. But if so, what kept Boris here? In the past, he'd always walked away from Semyon's shenanigans.

Daniil twisted on his stool, placed a hand on Yulia's arm, and drew her forward to sit on his other side. "Tell me everything you remember."

Middle age didn't inure her to his smile. He saw her reaction and used it; his need for information outweighed other scruples, and it wasn't as if he could hurt her feelings. On the contrary, she bloomed under his approving gaze.

The lingering hostility in Volodka's eyes acquired a spark of jealousy. Good. He might spill a secret he would otherwise have held back. Daniil asked him to serve his wife and himself and to join them. Volodka dawdled, but he complied. Not to be left out, the two peasants pushed forward. Daniil authorized them with a nod.

"Now." He gestured to Yulia, in the center of the rough oval. "The two noblemen arrived, with their soldiers. You put them up. Did they identify themselves?"

She shook her head. "Boris and Semyon, they called each other. More than that, they didn't say. The soldiers stayed in the barn, and Volodka took them ale and food."

"And they seemed on good terms?" Ogodai's casual tone stung more than the question. Daniil felt himself bridling, then forced his distaste down. He would have asked if Ogodai had not. And since he no longer knew what to believe, why resent the implication that Boris had shared Semyon's vices?

The elderly man, Mishka, slapped his knee and guffawed. "Like two ducks on a pond, they were. Each egging the other on." He rubbed his jaw, as if in recollection. "Mind you, that Boris was worse than the other. I'd have been looking at my eighth grandchild four months from now if I hadn't hauled my Annenka off his lap and sent her home with a smack. That's when he hit me. Claimed he was defending her."

Probably true. Defending a woman *did* sound like Boris, although dandling her on his knee—not so much.

Yulia nodded, her head bobbing like the wooden puppets the wandering minstrels carried. "He led the way," she agreed. "Urged that other one to drink up, asked what he planned to do, laughed when Lord Semyon took his sword to my furniture."

Daniil glanced at Ogodai, who avoided his gaze. Something didn't add up: if he could just find the right question to ask, the whole muddle would untangle itself, and his world would become recognizable again. But he couldn't think what that question should be. "Are you certain," he said, "that Lord Boris urged Lord Semyon to vengeance and not the reverse?"

She frowned. "No, I wouldn't say that, Lord. Not exactly. Looked uncomfortable then, so he did."

"Not with my Annenka he didn't," the elderly man interjected with a coarse laugh.

Yulia whacked him with her dish rag. "Get your head out of the ditch, you old fool. A girl's a girl. The lord asked about vengeance. Lord Boris didn't encourage that. Asked a lot of questions, rather."

Daniil exchanged glances with Ogodai, who said, "Questions? About Lord Semyon's plans?"

As if Boris wanted to interfere in those plans. Feeling his way, Daniil said, "And did Lord Semyon answer the questions?"

Yulia and her husband responded in chorus, "Not a word."

Yet Boris had covered up for his cousin. The more Daniil learned, the less sense it made. "But they left here together?"

"Together," Volodka affirmed. "And forgive me, Lord, but I was glad to see them go. A real pair of troublemakers, from beginning to end."

They left together, but only one man arrived at Sveta's hut. Which meant—what? Daniil still didn't know. He should be getting closer, yet he felt more confused than before.

But he had nothing left to ask Yulia and Volodka. "Thank you," he told them. "You've been most helpful. Let me pay my brother's debts. What do I owe you?"

A short time later, Daniil led his troop back toward the river. Riding through the woods, looking neither left nor right, he could not remember a time when he had felt more depressed. Not only depressed but shamed—before Ogodai, who to his credit had said nothing triumphal, and before Ogodai's absent sister, abandoned so that her husband could chase a savage, uncatchable goose masquerading as a nice fluffy duckling.

As their horses trudged single file through the forest—Daniil brooding, Ogodai silent behind him—a furry paw brushed Daniil's cheek. His gelding reared as Daniil's grip dragged on the bit. "By all the saints," he said. "What kind of animals do you keep in these woods?"

"Animals? What animals? Ours are the same as yours."

Daniil forced his horse down and turned it, blocking the path. "They are not. Three times I've seen a lynx, this one close enough to touch. Have you noticed nothing?"

Ogodai raised one shoulder. "A wood spirit, perhaps."

"Wood spirit?"

"The bards tell us that Mother Earth sends them. Or Father Sky. As messengers." Ogodai snapped his reins against his horse's neck. "You know old folks. They love a good tale."

Daniil resumed his ride. He didn't believe in spirit messengers. The dense, ancient woods fed on his inner turmoil, and his imagination ran riot. No more than that.

The path widened, rejoining the main road. The river glittered on the horizon, amber highlights floating like dragon flies atop rippling green water.

Ogodai urged his horse forward to ride at Daniil's side. "Where now? Kasimov? We can offer you more comfortable housing and a better meal than that stringy bird."

Daniil hesitated. Kasimov meant his in-laws, a daunting prospect at the best of times, worse in the face of his own mistreatment of his bride and Yulia's testimony. But Kasimov also meant—maybe—the eyewitness whom the Tatars were protecting. The person he'd sworn to find.

Who might simply confirm that Boris had killed the boy. Or had stood by while Semyon committed murder. Did he, in the end, want an answer that would strip his parents of their last illusions regarding the son they had lost?

Yet some stubborn core of Daniil refused to give up. Before he followed his brother-in-law's advice to tackle Semyon, he might as well make one last effort to wring the truth from Kasimov. He raised his whip to Ogodai. "Kasimov, then," he said. "You can introduce me to the eyewitness. The real eyewitness."

Ogodai groaned. "Daniil, you're impossible. The eyewitness is not in Kasimov. I've told you that a dozen times."

"So you have. You've told me lots of things, most of which I don't believe."

"You're more shortsighted than a boar. The peasants say it. The tavern keepers say it. I say it, and you still deny what you don't want to hear. Tell me, Daniil, what brought your saintly Boris to Kasimov and forced him to drink and whore with your bestial cousin if he did not come for revenge?"

"I don't know." Daniil spat out each word. "That's the whole point. *I don't know.* The Boris who lived in my parents' household, who hated war, who prayed six times a day and spouted poetry over the Trinity icon—that Boris would not have done any of those things. I need to find out what happened to him, and you are no help. All you care about is proving that your clan didn't make a mistake."

"Excuse me." Ogodai's mustache quivered with fury. His clenched fist hovered inches from Daniil's nose. "Your despicable brother killed a fourteen-year-old in cold blood, and I'm supposed to apologize because I don't lay myself flat on the road like a rug and let you ride over me? Go to hell, Daniil. Or to Moscow. Or follow me to Kasimov, if you like. You have the right. In case you've forgotten, we're relatives now." He rammed both heels into his horse's sides, and the beast went from standing to full gallop in the flick of a tail.

Daniil watched him go. At one level, he understood Ogodai's anger. For someone who had only a passing acquaintance with Boris, Daniil's intransigence must indeed seem pigheaded, the unnecessary probing of unhealed wounds. But he was angry, too. Boris had died because the Tatars took the first answer that made sense to them, oblivious to whether they picked the right person so long as they had someone to kill. And Boris's death had forced Daniil to undertake this uncomfortable quest, to face up to the reality of a brother he'd been content quietly to admire. Which made Ogodai and his people in some sense responsible, too, for Daniil's disillusionment, Daniil's questions.

Leave? Pursue? The gap between him and Ogodai was widening; and the Tatar troops, startled when their sultan dashed off, were hot on his trail. Wait much longer, and he'd have no decision to make.

His last hope for information about the location of the eyewitness was heading at top speed for Kasimov. Daniil signaled to his men and kicked his horse's flanks. Ogodai was already no more than an outline on the horizon.

Daniil had cut the gap by two-thirds by the time the Kasimov fortress loomed atop its hill. Turquoise minarets, gold inscriptions, white stone palace—he had not visited the town before, but no one could mistake it for a Russian citadel, despite its palisades and earthen ramparts. It proudly proclaimed its alien lines.

Nasan had lived here. What might he learn about her? He thought of her, exhilarating and tempestuous, as unlike the passive women he knew—his mother and sister-in-law no less than Grusha—as Kasimov was unlike Moscow. Outward trappings the same, wholly different in essence.

The gleam of pointed steel helmets distracted him. His stomach clenched, and his horse shied as his hands tightened on the reins. Then he recognized the standard. St. George spearing the serpent. Not a Tatar force (should that concern him? wouldn't Kasimov send an honor guard for its sultan?) but a Russian one.

A Russian one. Daniil sighed. He should have hoped for Tatars. The moment he feared had arrived. These were the grand prince's soldiers, bearing the call to muster. Only swift talking would win him enough time to complete his quest.

A dozen horse lengths down the river road, Ogodai drew up beside the captain of the approaching force. Daniil could see his brother-in-law gesticulating.

Good. Ogodai was arguing with them. Two pleading together had a better chance than one of being heard. He wasn't asking for much, after all. A few days would do it.

The captain nodded to Ogodai and rode forward. The Tatars had long since joined their leader. Daniil watched in astonishment as the Russian force surrounded him and his men.

"Daniil Nikolaevich?" the captain asked.

Daniil imagined his father responding to the present situation. He favored the lowborn captain with his most aristocratic glare. "Indeed. And you?"

The captain jerked his head. Two men came forward and, before Daniil could protest, clapped manacles around his wrists. The captain bowed, with the same ironic air that Ogodai had used before leading Daniil to the tavern. "My name need not concern you. By order of the grand prince and his mother, Daniil Nikolaevich, I am arresting you. You will accompany me to Moscow, where you will answer for your failure to respond to the muster."

Ogodai had reported him. Knowing that Daniil had not received orders to muster, Ogodai had reported him as refusing to serve. When Daniil thought his brother-in-law had been arguing with the Russian troops on his behalf.

That betrayal lit the fuse of Daniil's emotions. "Bastard!" he yelled to Ogodai's distant person. He wasn't sure his brother-in-law heard him until Ogodai threw his head back and yowled in triumph, saluted Daniil with a flourish of his sword, then wheeled and sent his horse galloping toward the fortress, his men forming a solid pack behind him.

Unfortunately, the arresting captain heard Daniil as well. He scowled and raised a fist, then dropped it. Subordinates did not assault boyars, whatever the provocation.

"Not you," Daniil told him, but the captain had already turned away.

Furious at this ignominious end to his inconclusive mission, Daniil snarled at the soldier who wrested the reins from his grasp and led his horse, surrounded by troops as if he were a common criminal, away from Kasimov and the eyewitness Daniil had risked so much to find.

His resistance did him no good. As soon as they could, the troop bundled him into a wagon and bound his feet as well as his hands. They piled his men in next to him, until Daniil struggled to breathe.

Like it or not, he was heading home.

From the base of the ramparts, Ogodai watched the Russian troop retreat, Daniil a bound captive in their midst. His ploy seemed dishonorable—the betrayal of his *qarïndash*.

But the move had protected his sister and fulfilled his parents' wishes. His clan, as ever, came first. And Daniil had brought this outcome on himself with his obstinacy. What more proof could he need?

The Russians trudged along the packed dirt road. Ogodai smiled as a thought occurred to him. The perfect solution. He beckoned to his best courier. "Get a fresh horse and head for Moscow. Take the gold pass. Tell anyone who objects that you travel on my orders. And when you get there, alert Nikolai Kolychev that his son needs help."

He kept a tight rein on his steed until the man was well away, then followed him up the hill. No reason to wait. He'd done all he could for his family. Including Daniil.

Chapter 19

A SERIES OF MID-JULY THUNDERSTORMS KEPT BOTH THE Golden Lynx and Grusha indoors until Nasan felt that even the weather conspired against her. The grandmothers wanted her to stop and think, not to dash off without considering consequences, as she had on the day Girei died. Sensible, if less than helpful in terms of specifics. What, exactly, should she do?

Confess that Boris had not killed her brother, for starters. So far, Natalya had asked no more questions about Girei's death. Perhaps she saw no point, if the answers could not clear her son. Perhaps she found the whole topic too painful. Nasan, at once grateful and guilt-ridden, turned over options in her mind. But every potential solution required her to admit where she had seen Girei's real killer, threatening her plans to avenge her brother by disrupting the killer's latest scheme.

She wrote a note for Daniil, laying out the whole story so that, if the grandmothers called her to join them, his family would learn the truth. For an entire day, she faced the possibility of eternal life with a clear conscience. Her husband wouldn't miss her. He had Grusha.

Then she realized that Natalya and Daniil could not read Russian, never mind Arabic. She tore up the note. If the grandmothers let her live, she would tell them in person. Ice Man had defeated her the first time because she tackled him without sufficient resources.

She would gather as much information as she could, then trust the ancestors to bring her home. If they failed to save her, no one could.

As if in approval of her decision, the skies cleared. Late on the evening of July 14, Nasan watched from her window as Grusha set off once more. Their second journey through the silent streets ended at the palisade with Girei's killer beckoning. "Tonight, for sure," he told the maid. "Why must you always be late?" He dragged her inside, and Nasan settled herself on a hitching post in the shadows to wait.

And wait, and wait some more. The life of the solitary warrior became less appealing with each moment that passed. An unending flow of moments, each trudging past like a turtle. What she wouldn't give for a companion!

The night watchman went by on his rounds, waving his lantern and calling. A cat slunk past Nasan's post, accepting a stroke along its spine as it headed out in search of mice. Stars rose and twinkled, slid behind clouds and reemerged, bright and sparkling as if new-washed. Nasan thought of Daniil and wondered if the stars saw him, too—where he was, what he was doing, whether he entertained similar questions about her. Her head drooped, then her shoulders, and she had to fight to keep drowsiness from toppling her from her perch.

The rumble of cartwheels against the pavement snapped her awake. She shrank farther into the shadows as the cart drew to a halt before the small estate. Four men leaped down. Two of them went to the back of the cart and lifted a pair of bundles from the wagon. The other two headed straight for the gate. It opened on her enemy, standing fists on hips.

His voice carried in the clear night air. "Success?"

"Achieved, Semyon Pavlovich." The speaker was the man she had seen with Grusha when she still thought he served Boris Kolychev. The man who had grabbed her off her horse that day by the river, whose groin she had kicked. Timoshka, Grusha had called him.

Nasan's flash of fear mingled with satisfaction. She had learned her enemy's name: Semyon Pavlovich. Not a full identification, but given the probability that her in-laws knew this man, it should be enough. Indeed, was not Solomonida's husband named Semyon?

"Then bring them in," Semyon Pavlovich said. "And for the love of God, don't use names. Have you no sense?"

"Sorry, Lord." Timoshka waved at the two men with the bundles. "Hurry up, lads."

One bundle mewled as the man holding it took his first step. Timoshka raised a hand as if to strike, only to receive a blow across the ear from Semyon.

"Idiot!" Semyon said. "Treat them as the blessed babes they are, or you answer to me."

Timoshka cringed and swore obedience. Nasan's pleasure at the sight lasted no more than the few moments it took for Semyon's words to sink in.

Blessed babes. This wicked man had kidnapped children. But how was she to free them?

Grandmothers, aid me. I can't do this alone.

After the men retreated within the compound and the cart departed on its journey, Nasan padded, silent as her lynx namesake, across the street. Scaling the nearest tree, she peered over the fence, but the only sight that met her eyes was a collection of living quarters, storerooms, and kitchens. The blessed babes, whoever they were, had disappeared into the gloom.

Daniil spent four rain-drenched days on the road. The morning after his arrest, he persuaded the captain to return the Kolychev horses. Riding—even in manacles, with the captain holding Daniil's reins as if he were a child in disgrace—marked an improvement over jolting in a wagon from dawn to dusk.

Alas, his achievements stopped there. The most rational arguments failed to convince the captain to release him. The government had commanded that shirkers be brought to Moscow in chains, and bring them in chains the captain would. Daniil could explain himself to the authorities in due course. Such officious single-mindedness raised Daniil's hackles. Knowing he had no other options until he reached Moscow made matters worse. After four days of jaw clenching, his teeth hurt.

Riding shackled in silence, he had nothing to do but think. He spent the first day fuming at Ogodai—his pretense of assistance, his refusal to produce the eyewitness, his insistence on Boris's guilt, that final betrayal.

A second day of rain doused his anger, freeing him to consider what he'd learned. The Tatar raid should have taught him that Ogodai, like everyone else, put his own clan first. And unless Ogodai had paid the woman Yulia to lie—which seemed so unlike Daniil's straitlaced brother-in-law that he couldn't entertain the idea for longer than it took for the words to form—the evidence did point to Boris. He had been present in Kasimov, had appeared to support Semyon, and had failed to prevent the ambush. And he had concealed his journey. Why?

But he had not, from what Yulia said, urged Semyon to vengeance. The drinking, the pursuit of girls—those things seemed unlike Boris, but one could explain them. A moment's weakness, fueled by opportunity. A desire to trick Semyon into revealing secrets that he would share with a comrade but not his virtuous cousin.

No way to know, with Boris gone. But whatever he intended, it hadn't worked. The boy Girei died, and before or after the fact, Boris and Semyon separated. One of them had killed. Probably Semyon, but without the eyewitness's testimony Daniil could not be sure.

And he had nothing firm to tell Nasan. He looked forward to seeing his wife, although she had every right to be upset with him. He hadn't confided in her before he left, he was returning empty-handed, and she had last seen him consoling Grusha. Yes, he had work to do there.

Grusha, at least, he could handle. She had given him pleasure in the past, so he would let her down gently, but peace was more important than casual passion. He'd learned that much in his month away.

Assuming, that is, he could get out of jail.

Maria's love of gossip proved useful for once. By admitting to ignorance and refusing to react to insults, Nasan determined not only that Solomonida's husband indeed bore the name Semyon Pavlovich but that Semyon had a known resemblance to Boris. Understanding what lay behind her family's error lessened her guilt.

"But why do you ask?" Maria said.

Nasan glanced over her shoulder, as if fearing Natalya's approach. "Because," she whispered, "yesterday Grusha say he see Semyon Pavlovich. Nobleman, must be. And Solomonida's husband make Solomonida go away. So—"

"Oh!" Maria cut her off, which suited Nasan just fine. "So Grusha is fooling around with Solomonida's husband. And he sent Solomonida to the convent to keep her from interfering. What a delicious tale." She glanced at Nasan, her expression sly. "And you, of course, would like Grusha to develop other interests."

Nasan felt her cheeks flush. "To leave Daniil alone, yes." Remembered anger almost choked her. "Thank you for help." With a nod, she left the room, embarrassed by her own duplicity but on the whole pleased with the results of a conversation that had produced the information she sought and might—once Maria started chattering, as she doubtless would—create friction between Daniil and his lover. Perhaps Nasan had learned something useful from Bulat's harem after all.

Her escape didn't last long. Natalya caught her on her way upstairs and hauled her off to supervise the laundry, a massive enterprise that required lots of oversight but minor personal involvement. For once, Nasan didn't mind. She needed time to plan the Golden Lynx's next move.

She decided that sneaking into Semyon Kolychev's estate was her only viable option. She could not expect to make any more discoveries, never mind stop him, by watching the street. She must pick her moment, find out what she could, and leave as quickly as possible.

If he discovered her… But fear would not deter her. A heroine trusted the grandmothers to protect her. A heroine did *not* let thoughts of the blade slashing her brother's throat frighten her off. The lives of two children hung in the balance, and only she could save them. She must be strong.

The weather had cleared, and tonight offered a perfect opportunity to test her plan. Nasan hid her boy's clothes in a vacant storeroom so she could leave as soon as the sun showed signs of setting. Less than an hour later, she scaled the fence surrounding the small estate and dropped into a bank of shrubs.

The stone walls of the Kremlin guardhouse smelled damp, although Daniil could tell at a glance that the captain had brought him to a room intended for those of noble birth. The furniture consisted of no more than a straw pallet, but it sat on a crude bed frame, not the floor, and the sheet and blanket looked clean. The sun was sinking in the sky when two soldiers pushed him into the cell and swung the oak door shut behind him. Scarlet-gold shadows streaked the dirt floor. A hole ringed with stones marked a makeshift privy in the corner. Anticipating an uncomfortable night, Daniil thanked his patron saint that his arrest had not taken place in winter. The rain had soaked him to the skin, and his clothes clung to him: add freezing temperatures, and he could kiss life goodbye.

Still, the sheets suggested that the guards trusted him not to hang himself. He guessed that he'd been placed in a holding cell, where he would stay until the secretary in charge had time to interrogate him.

As the door closed, he heard his own soldiers being released. Good. His servants had traveled to Kasimov on his orders; they shouldn't suffer because of his misdeeds, real or imagined. He hoped Pashka would remember to warn Mama and Papa before he went home.

Scraping alerted him to an opening near the bottom of the door. The faint smell of cabbage indicated the arrival of dinner, the first meal he'd eaten today. He walked over and picked up the wooden bowl. Shredded carrot and minced onion drifted in chicken broth amid the ever-present cabbage. A slab of dark rye bread, sliced almost to the crust, straddled the bowl upside-down. Daniil sat on the floor and ate, trying to ignore the rustling that hinted of mice in the straw.

The soup had faded to a watery memory and his clothes dried against his skin before the sound of boot heels against the flagstones announced the approach of a visitor. Daniil rose to his feet, readying himself to face the officious captain or an even more officious and touchy bureaucrat, but the opening door revealed his father's craggy features. Nikolai Kolychev greeted him with frowning brow, but the mouth amid its gray/brown fringe of beard and mustache quirked in a half-smile.

Daniil let out a huge sigh of relief. "Pashka remembered." He crossed the cell in three strides and kissed his father on both cheeks. "It's good to see you, Papa."

Nikolai enclosed him in a bear hug. "Not Pashka," he said. "A courier rode in from Kasimov yesterday morning. I settled the matter then, but word of your arrival just reached me."

"Kasimov? Ogodai? But he was the one who reported me."

Nikolai's half-smile turned into a full-blown grin. "So the courier said. Reported you, then dispatched him at top speed to warn me. I think you annoyed him, son. Tell me you didn't punch him again."

Daniil shook his head, then remembered he had. "Well, yes, I did. I mistook him for an intruder. He understood. I did annoy him plenty, though, and he me." He slapped the wall as the truth hit. "Devil take him! He wanted me out of Kasimov. To keep that wretched eyewitness away from me. He must have seen the arrival of the troops as a heaven-sent opportunity."

Nikolai still looked amused, if a bit puzzled. He beckoned to Daniil. "It's clear you have a tale to tell. Let's go home."

A few harsh words from Nikolai to the officious captain produced Daniil's horse and a promise to deliver his baggage in the morning. He and Nikolai were soon riding down the hill.

First things first. "Is Irina well?" Daniil asked, remembering with difficulty to use his wife's Russian name. In his month away he had thought of her only as Nasan.

"Your mother has no complaints." Nikolai's eyes narrowed. "None concerning Irina, in any event. She filled my ears with stories of you and Grusha. What were you thinking, son?"

"Not what everyone seems to believe." Daniil flushed. "Someone attacked her, Papa. Grusha, I mean."

"*Attacked* her?"

"Yes. She had a bruise on her cheek and chafing on her wrists. Mama didn't notice?"

Nikolai frowned. "If she did, she said nothing to me. What happened?"

"I never found out. I asked her, and she burst into tears. So I tried to calm her. I didn't know what else to do. Irina misunderstood."

"We all misunderstood."

"I'll straighten it out," Daniil said. "First chance I get."

"Do. Odd, though. Attacked. By whom?"

"She wouldn't tell me," Daniil said again.

Nikolai nodded before abandoning the subject for one even more awkward. "Tell me about your trip."

Daniil's tongue tangled. The road to the estate stretched interminably.

"Come, son," Nikolai said. "I can take it. Did Boris kill Bulat's boy?"

The blunt question settled Daniil's nerves. "I don't know," he said. "I don't think so, but he was there. He lied to us, Papa."

"Lied to us. He didn't go to Trinity, then?"

"He did." Daniil filled in his father on what he'd learned in Kasimov—Boris's journey with Semyon, the tavern, the peasant hut, and the use of Boris's name there.

Nikolai slapped his saddle, startling his horse. He steadied it. "You think Semyon wanted Boris blamed for the ambush."

"Yes," Daniil said. "Which is not typical of Semyon. He does care for his family."

"Usually." Nikolai twisted his horse's mane in one hand. "I suppose it would be too much to blame a stranger."

Daniil grimaced. "I did, but I can't make it stick. The descriptions, the names. Boris and Semyon."

"And you have no idea what happened to Boris while Semyon was staying at this hut?"

"None. I ran out of time when the troops arrested me."

"Hmm," Nikolai said. "A pretty problem, indeed."

They rode for a while without speaking. Daniil broke the silence. "I wish Ogodai had introduced me to that eyewitness."

Nikolai's eyebrows rose, and the satirical twist returned to his mouth. "Well, son, we do have *one* eyewitness. It's too late to approach him tonight, but in the morning you and I will interview your cousin Semyon. After all, we know he visited Kasimov, so he can explain what he was doing there and why, when I asked him before, he fed me a barrel of lies."

Of course, Semyon knew what happened. As Ogodai had pointed out in Kasimov. Daniil should have remembered that. His investigation had not ended in failure after all. Ahead of him, the lanterns marking the Kolychev gates glowed in the dark.

"We're almost there," Nikolai said. "And in good time. Natasha will have the household in an uproar by now. With luck, we can prevent an assault on the Kremlin. Your wife and mine—the mind shudders."

Your wife and mine. My wife. Nasan. Despite their difficult parting, Daniil felt his heart lift.

They rode through the gates. Pashka, descending the stairs, let out a yell. "Saints be praised!"

Daniil dismounted and grabbed Pashka's outstretched hand in both of his. "Indeed. The soldiers didn't mistreat you, I hope."

The servant shook his head. "Not us. They knew we couldn't stop you."

"Good." Daniil gestured at the stairs. "And my mother?"

"Better get to her fast, Lord. She's about to rouse the house."

"You did well, Pashka." Nikolai joined them. "Go home and rest. Report in the morning." He slapped Daniil on the shoulder. "Reassure your mother."

Daniil took the stairs two at a time. In the hallway he hesitated. The house seemed even more engulfed by silence than the cathedral. Then he saw a sliver of light under the door to his mother's sitting room and headed for it. His father's footsteps sounded on the stairs.

Is Nasan waiting for me?

But the room contained only his mother, already on her feet. She flung both arms around his neck. "Daniil, what a relief! Pashka said you had been *arrested*. How did the bailiffs make such a mistake?"

"Not bailiffs, Mama. The army." He untangled her arms and held her hands in his, staring into her troubled brown eyes. "Irina's brother—"

"Irina! I was on my way to tell her when you came in."

"I'll tell her myself," Daniil said. "Her brother reported me for ignoring the muster. As soon as Papa explained, they let me go."

"Irina's brother? But why would he do such a thing? I thought you were friends."

Daniil loosened his grip. "Not since the feud started. But in this case, I think he wanted me out of Kasimov. He sent a courier to Papa the same day."

Nikolai walked in. Natalya subsided onto a sofa, her brows drawn together. "He reported you, then arranged for your release? What is in Kasimov that he doesn't want you to see?"

"The person who identified Boris." Daniil took the seat next to her. From the corner of his eye, he saw his father perch on the armrest of his favorite chair.

Natalya's chin dropped. "That's impossible."

"Why?" Daniil gazed at her, transfixed by her certainty. His mother left the house two or three times a year, if that—yet she could comment on events in Kasimov?

"Because the person who identified Boris is here," she said. "I found out a few days ago. I haven't even told your father, he's been so busy. Irina is the one who saw her brother die."

Irina. His wife. His delicate beauty. He recalled Ogodai at the wedding, raging about the Russians slashing his brother's throat as if slaughtering a pig. Nasan had witnessed *that*, then married into the clan she believed responsible? Coherent questions escaped him. "How?" He gulped, tried again. "How did she witness it?"

"I don't know, Daniil." His mother's gentle voice irritated nerves already raw. "She'd seen a pattern in the embroidery that reminded her of her brother's blood on the snow. She sobbed until I could barely understand her. Her Russian is poor, even at the best of times, and this was not the best of times."

His mind reeled. Nasan crouched on the bed, knife at her shoulder, terror on her face. Nasan half-fainting in the church, weeping uncontrollably after they made love, muttering into his shoulder about bad dreams. She looked at him and saw her brother's murderer. Whom she thought was Boris.

Nikolai rested his elbow on the chair's headrest and frowned. "How did she know his name? Were they lovers? Did Bulat foist her on us to hide her sin?"

"No," Daniil said. "I would stake my life she was a virgin." His father's face relaxed, and Daniil went on. "A frightened virgin. *Gospodi*, she tried to stab me."

Natalya gasped. "Stab you?" She bit her lip, then spoke as if rearranging a picture in her head. "But of course. The tears. She cared nothing for Maria's spite. It surprised me at the time, but I had no acquaintance with her then. Her mother told me what they wanted me to hear."

"Exactly," Daniil said. "And I treated it as bridal jitters. Damn that brother of hers." He stood. "Excuse me. I should talk to her."

"Be gentle," Natalya said. "Don't startle her. She has nightmares."

He stopped. "Nightmares?"

"So she says. I have no reason to doubt her."

Well, his arrest had one benefit. It had brought him home. "Then let me go to her."

He murmured good night to his parents and strode down the hall to his room. Nasan, tormented by nightmares. They needed to heal things between them, and soon.

He pressed his hand against the door and encountered resistance. Odd. He knocked. No answer. He knocked again, with greater force. "Nasan, open the door."

Maria, wearing a capacious nightgown and a shawl, emerged from her room. "They let you out already," she said. "Even the bailiffs don't want you."

Daniil was not fooled. He had stopped Mama before she could waken Nasan; she would not have confided in Maria before she told his wife. "Eavesdropping again, sister?" he asked. "A nasty habit. It'll get you in trouble."

"Much you know," she retorted.

"Back to bed, Maria," his mother snapped. "This is no business of yours." His parents had left the sitting room and stood just behind him.

Maria, pouting, retired. Daniil imagined her with her ear pressed to the keyhole but could not make himself care. "Irina has shut us out," he told his mother.

"Shut us out?" she asked. "Why?"

"I can't imagine." Nightmares were one thing, but what caused his wife to bar the door?

A harder shove opened a small gap between jamb and portal, and he heard scraping from inside the room, the sound a piece of furniture makes against a floor.

His father appeared at his elbow. "Can I help, Daniil?"

"I have it." Daniil applied his shoulder to the door. With a mighty heave, he forced it open and walked in.

Nasan might suffer from nightmares, but bad dreams alone did not account for her lack of sleep. Even in the moonlight that shone through the unshuttered window, Daniil could see at a glance that his wife was not there.

Chapter 20

"WHERE IS SHE?" HIS MOTHER STOOD IN THE DOORWAY, staring wide-eyed around the silent bedroom. Personal belongings lay, neat and orderly, as if Nasan had stepped out for a moment: comb on the dressing table, clothes tucked away. A rolled-up rug lay next to the wicker basket that held her cosmetics. A bizarre doll about the length of Daniil's hand—made of wood and fully dressed, with a head almost as large as its body and eyes of black bead—sat next to the basket. He had never seen it before.

A light breeze blew into the room. A quick search of the courtyard revealed no absent bride—no one, period, other than the distant sentry. He turned. In the bed he saw a lump crowned with long, dark hair. Wool hair. A dummy. A fake.

This new deception was the last straw. After weeks of clambering over obstacles, defending a brother whom every passing day revealed to be less worthy of defense, fighting his way past lie after lie, Daniil had returned prepared to forgive and move on. And now this?

He stalked to the bed, threw back the covers, and shook the bolster at his mother. "I have no idea where she is." He bit off each word as it left his mouth. "But I intend to find out."

His father came in, and Natalya clung to him, worry in her eyes. Daniil strove to control his temper long enough to reassure her. "Go to bed, Mama. Irina's my problem."

Papa understood, as usual. "Come, wife, let the boy handle it," he said as he drew her away. "Good night, son."

"Thank you, Papa." Daniil clasped his hands behind his back. His wedding ring pressed into his flesh. Anger formed a red haze before his eyes. His wife had sneaked out of the house. But where had she gone, what was she doing, and, perhaps most important, with whom was she doing it?

Yes, Nasan had misinterpreted the scene between him and Grusha. Everyone had, according to Papa—the price of Daniil's three years of self-indulgence. He had to accept responsibility for that and correct it. But whatever he'd done, Nasan did not have the right to flit about the town consorting with whomever she pleased.

If his wife was having an affair, his parents would force him to divorce her. They would send her to a nunnery, and he could go back to the old, carefree life. A life he no longer wanted.

His parents' footsteps faded into nothingness, taking the vestiges of Daniil's restraint with them. He ripped his room apart, searching for evidence to support his suspicions. Shifts, tunics, veils, caftans, nightgowns, headdresses flew from their chests and fell in soft, rumpled piles against every available surface. Clouds of jasmine rose from the textiles as they drifted past his face, adding to his fury. A handkerchief too hideous to exist dropped onto a book filled with the looping curves of Arabic script. Light summer jackets, heavier fall ones, hats of various types joined them without revealing a single item that did not belong. He caught a marble inkwell just before it mingled its contents with Nasan's discarded makeup.

His anger ebbed as he surveyed the mess. He reached for the closest shift, intending to fold it and return it to its place. A flash of light from the hall outside caused something to glitter amid the piles of fabric. Daniil's eyes narrowed. He bent, rummaging through the clothes he had tossed on the floor. His hand closed on a slender chain and pulled it free. A stylized lynx, formed of pure gold, swung from the chain.

⚔

Grusha halted in front of the open doorway. Startled, she forgot to guard the candle flame that provided her sole source of light in navigating the passageway. Daniil gave no sign he'd noticed her presence.

She had no business being in the family section of the house at this hour, but what she'd discovered at Semyon's estate this evening had shaken her to the point where she no longer cared about Kolychev rules. She wanted to grab her possessions and run. Semyon's threats paled against the reality of what he'd talked her into. She still felt the shock that had ripped through her when she heard that child announce, in a piping treble, that he was the grand prince of all Russia. The ruler they had to obey. She still heard Semyon's unheeding guffaw. The knell of doom. Her own. If Semyon didn't kill her to protect his secret, the prince's mother would do it for him.

In desperation, she'd thrown herself on the mercy of the guardsman Stenka, who had overheard the little prince's declaration. Stenka had been kind to her before, and he came through again, convincing Semyon that she needed to collect her belongings before she could complete her task. When Semyon at last released her, she'd fled, determined not to return. Had she thanked Stenka for his help? She hoped so. The child's voice befogged her thoughts.

But here, at the edge of disaster, the saints had sent her Daniil. If anyone could save her, Daniil would.

She couldn't tell him what she'd done. If he rejected her, she would die. But he would give up his wife. He had to. With him at her side, Semyon could not touch her. She would be safe.

"May I help you, Lord?" she asked. "Perhaps you've misplaced something?"

⚔

A wife.

Grusha. It would be Grusha who found him. As if his last encounter with her had not caused enough trouble. Here was his opportunity to tell her in words she could not mistake that their affair was over. But that required coherence, and he didn't trust himself to speak.

"Unnecessary." He kept his answer curt in a feeble attempt to convince Grusha that her time had passed.

The maid hesitated, glanced around the room. Words tumbled from her mouth. "The young mistress. She's not here. You'll hate me for telling you, but…" She stopped, wringing her hands.

"What?" He tried to sound casual.

"A man." She drew out each word as if she hesitated to speak. "Twice, returning from the kitchens late at night, I've seen him at this window." She gestured at the open shutters while Daniil stared at her, horrified, then caught the chain in her fingers.

"The Golden Lynx," she said. "Where did you get this, Lord?"

"It belongs to my wife."

She smiled—not a pleasant smile. "That explains much."

Daniil pulled the lynx from her hand. "It means nothing, I'm sure. I expect she brought it from Kasimov."

"Unlikely, Lord. You were away. You have not heard. Moscow has a new hero. People call him the Golden Lynx. I saw him myself, climbing this very wall."

Daniil's fragile composure shattered in a roar of pain. Grusha skittered from the room like a frightened spider.

Nasan crouched behind her bush. She had forgotten to calculate the phase of the moon when she made her plans. It was almost full, forcing her to edge toward the storerooms by a circuitous route. From her current location at the far side of the courtyard, she could see one building that sported a large guard: ten men at

least. That became her goal. Moving with extreme caution, she circled the grounds, staying close to the shadows. Where the bushes
met the open logs of the courtyard, she stopped. The distance of
three horses, standing nose to tail, separated her from the armed
men; only a fool would get closer. She settled in to wait.

A child's cry pierced the silence, followed by tramping feet and
a girl's shrill voice. Nasan peered from behind her shrubs to see
Semyon Kolychev dragging a young woman by the upper arm.

Not Grusha. Why?

Semyon nodded to the guards. One pulled a large key from
the ring that hung from his belt and unfastened the padlock that
secured the door. Semyon flung the girl into the building, ordering,
"Shut that brat up, but without laying a finger on either of them.
Understood?"

The door slammed behind her, and the guard snapped the
padlock shut. Nasan studied him: stocky, with brown hair and
gray eyes, simple leather armor, a stolid, pleasant face. She didn't
remember him from the raid on Kasimov.

A voice spoke from the shadows, a sibilant hiss too low to identify
as male or female. "What happened to your other nursemaid?"

The guardsman glowered. Semyon gave a sarcastic laugh.
"Blame him." He pointed at the scowling guard. "He convinced
me the girl needed her belongings. His neck's on the line if she
doesn't show up."

"Take no chances," the voice in the shadows said. "Confine
her as soon as she returns."

Semyon waved a lordly hand in the guard's direction. "Stenka
will see to it."

"She means no harm, Lord." Stenka stepped forward, as if
speaking to the person hidden in the dark. "She's a simple girl. No
need to force her."

"You see?" Semyon asked. "I think he's sweet on her."

The voice made no response. After a few moments, Nasan
saw Semyon head for the gates, a figure as dark and elusive as the

Golden Lynx at his side. While she waited for an opportunity to edge around the fence and go home, her mind raced.

Semyon had a partner. Somehow their plans revolved around two stolen children, whose identity Nasan didn't know and whose significance she had yet to determine. And from what she had heard tonight, Grusha did have a potential sweetheart at this estate, but it was not Semyon. Grusha might not even know this Stenka cared for her, but if Nasan saw a chance to throw them together, she would.

Meanwhile, she needed more information about what Semyon and his co-conspirator had in mind. Because the more she learned, the crazier the scheme sounded.

The grandmothers were testing her, for certain. She could only hope she would pass the test.

Daniil picked up the lynx pendant and studied it. A pretty thing, to hold such devastating significance. A new hero. The Golden Lynx. His wife betraying him with a stranger. How had they met, with her in seclusion? Yet the pendant told its own tale. It was too much of a coincidence that Nasan owned a piece of jewelry that matched the name of Moscow's newest hero. Whom Grusha had seen at the window to this room.

He felt sick. He might have walked in on them.

As Nasan had walked in on him and Grusha. For the first time, he understood why his wife had reacted so strongly. Not that his behavior excused hers. But he could imagine why she might have decided that she needn't worry about what *he* wanted.

Daniil dropped the lynx onto the dressing table and went to wander the streets of the trading quarter. He had no real expectation of finding Nasan and no idea what he would do if he did discover her with her lover, but the need to move consumed him.

An hour later, he returned to his room. The exercise had dispelled much of his rage, although he experienced a spark of renewed anger when he saw the window still ajar, the bed empty, the piles of clothing strewn on the floor. He stripped off his outer clothes, picked up the golden chain, lay down on the bed, and swung the lynx like a pendulum between his fingers as he waited for his errant wife.

Nasan reentered her home with her usual ease, avoiding detection despite the full moon gleaming overhead. She huddled in the shadows next to the stables to catch her breath and surveyed the silent buildings, plotting her best route back to the main house.

Her visit to Semyon's estate had paid off in some respects. She had verified the children's presence and entered and left Semyon's compound undetected. Padlocks, guards, hissing voice in the dark: everything indicated her enemy had taken the children by force. Semyon had protected the children so far, but she didn't trust him to continue. If the hissing voice ordered, he would slit the babies' throats as he had Girei's. She must return, and soon.

Even so, she had questions. Grusha had not appeared, and Nasan didn't know why. The villains' goals remained unclear. The clue must lie in the identity of the children, but she lacked that information, too.

If only she had someone to talk to. How she yearned for Girei, ready for any adventure.

She was dreaming, of course. That life had ended with Girei's death. It would have ended anyway, with marriage and adulthood.

Adulthood stank.

Throughout her review, she had been watching the courtyard. Other than the watchman, half-asleep at his post, she saw nothing out of the ordinary. Steering clear of the betraying moonlight, she made her way to the wall that led to her bedroom window and scaled it. She had one leg over the sill and had pulled off the scarf that covered her face when a familiar voice spoke. "So that's how you do it," Daniil said.

Her heart leaped into her mouth as she toppled backward. By instinct, her hands gripped the sill. Dressed in an open-necked shirt and light-brown trousers, her husband lounged against the crimson bed coverings as if he had never left. From his fingers dangled the golden lynx pendant Ogodai had intended for him.

Every chest had its lid open, and her possessions lay strewn in heaps about the floor. She wouldn't have imagined it possible to create so much havoc with such limited resources; he couldn't have ignored a single shift or hairpiece. Yet in contrast to the chaos around him, Daniil looked calm and relaxed. Nasan wrapped one arm around her middle, where a million butterflies struggled in wing-to-wing combat, and clung to the window frame with her free hand.

"Who is he?" His voice suggested idle curiosity, but she heard a harsh, raw undertone that disturbed her.

"Who?"

"This man, this Golden Lynx, you slip out to meet."

"Man? No man!" Did he think her morals as shaky as his own? Her hard-won Russian darted into a mouse hole in her brain, only occasionally poking its nose out to sniff the air. "How dare you?"

"Well, it's not the first time, is it? You didn't befriend Boris in the harem." The way he looked her up and down made her want to hit him. "You're an attractive piece, and you go in and out of the house at will. I had no idea you had so many hidden talents."

With difficulty, she puzzled out what he'd said, then tackled the most incomprehensible point first. "Befriend Boris in the harem?"

"Yes, Boris. My brother. Remember him?"

When she stared at him, confused, he used simpler words. "Mama said you saw your brother die. Your family killed Boris based on what *you* told them, so you must have known him."

She shook her head. Bad enough that he had shamed her with a servant, then left without warning. Had he no sense that witnessing Girei's murder had hurt her? He was as callous as his cousin! "Not so," she said. "I tell what happened. No names."

"So you don't deny that you saw him," Daniil said. "Where?"

Nasan clamped her lips shut. His tone set her teeth on edge.

"You won't say? Because it's a lie, like the other lies you've told?" He swung the lynx on its chain. "You have a lot of explaining to do, Nasan. You might start with this pretty trinket. You didn't get it from me."

He sat up, slamming his bare feet against the floor. "Do come in, wife of mine," he said, the edge in his voice stronger than before. "You don't look very comfortable there."

He wanted an explanation. After letting her catch him with Grusha, running off who knew where, returning without an apology, and accusing her of infidelity, he had the nerve to demand an accounting from her. And in the same sarcastic tone his detestable cousin affected!

Nasan swung her left leg into the room. "The lynx came from Ogodai. He gave me two. That one's yours." She pulled the matching pendant from under her shirt and watched in satisfaction as his eyes widened. "I am the Golden Lynx. No man."

His eyebrows rose. "You. A woman."

"Yes." She slipped into Tatar without noticing. "And if you could forget your ridiculous suspicions for a moment, you might notice that your miserable cousin Semyon is about to wreak greater havoc on your family honor than I could manage in a lifetime. And if anyone stops him, it will be me, not you."

Daniil threw the lynx across the room. She flinched as it skimmed past her face. "I didn't understand a word. Why don't you try speaking *Russian?*"

The pendant hit the dressing table and dangled from the grandmother's pointed headdress. "My grandmother! How could you?" She ran to cradle the spirit doll in her arms and murmur apologies.

"Stop that." Daniil smacked the bed frame. "Put that cursed doll down and talk to me."

He was Russian. Christian. He did not understand. With great self-control, Nasan plucked the lynx from the grandmother's hair and placed pendant and ancestor side by side on the dressing table. She faced her husband, challenging him with raised chin. "That *doll* is my grandmother," she said in her very best Russian. "She shows me the way."

"You take orders from a doll? Are you out of your mind?"

When she glared at him, stunned by his disrespect, his mouth compressed in a grim line. "Well, from now on, wife of mine," he said, "you take orders from me. That means you stay in the house. My honor demands it."

A gasp of fury escaped her. "And if I refuse?"

"Don't defy me, Nasan. I'm your husband. You promised to obey me, remember?"

That did it. With one well-aimed kick, Nasan hooked Daniil behind the knees and upended him, spewed a flood of Tatar invective over his head, and fled down the wall.

Daniil stared at the ceiling. He felt like a man who'd stepped into a whirlwind. His wife—had he really thought of her as a delicate beauty?—had knocked his feet out from under him. As if she grappled with men his size every day. How had their conversation dissolved into this?

His head was spinning. If he got his hands on Nasan, he'd throttle her. The gall—sauntering in here whenever it suited her, refusing to reveal what had taken her from the house, attacking him when he asserted his authority as her husband, then dashing off again as if he'd never spoken.

After a while, he realized that Nasan had, in fact, said quite a bit. She just hadn't said it in Russian. Her words reached him as a cascade of names: Grusha, Semyon, Boris. What they had in common he couldn't guess, any more than he could imagine why his wife called a doll her grandmother—or what caused her to run around town, for that matter.

But one thing she *had* said in Russian: that she was the Golden Lynx. The "man" whom Grusha had seen climbing the wall to this room. Was that possible?

He considered Nasan as he'd last seen her—dressed in men's clothes, her hair concealed by a scarf, the lynx hanging from her neck. Masked, when she first came through the window. No one who observed her exits or entrances would guess he saw a Tatar khan's daughter instead of a man with mischief on his mind. Grusha had misread the situation.

Or exploited it. Much easier to believe that she had manipulated him than that a young girl from a sheltered background, even one able to come and go as she pleased, would encounter a stranger and start an affair within a month of her marriage.

He'd let his frustration with Ogodai and his shock at Nasan's absence blind him. In brief, he'd mishandled the situation.

Determined to do better, Daniil sat up. His eye caught the grandmother, sitting on the dressing table. Only then did he absorb what Nasan had said earlier, that she had not identified Boris by *name*.

He gaped at the spirit doll. Nasan, the eyewitness, had not named Boris. The evidence against his brother amounted to supposition, deduction. No one could prove Boris had slain that boy.

No, that was wrong, too. As both Ogodai and Papa had noted, Nasan had never been the only eyewitness. Semyon knew what he and his cousin had done.

Semyon, whose name Nasan had mentioned more than once. Why?

Wondering what else he had missed, Daniil pushed himself to his feet and thrust his arms into a clean caftan. In the morning, he would have the fun of interrogating Semyon. But before then, he should search for Nasan. Who, while he lay dazed, had built up a significant head start.

No matter. He would try.

And try he did, without success. Eventually, he decided to lie down for a moment—not to sleep, which was a ridiculous idea, but to sift through what he'd learned. As soon as he had a clue where to start, he'd go after her. At worst, he would enjoy wringing the truth out of Semyon a few hours from now. *Then* he'd go after her.

Nasan crouched in a corner of the Kolychevs' stables. Her fight with Daniil had shaken her. Trembling, she collapsed onto a pile of straw.

The roan mare who occupied the stall regarded her visitor with gentle brown eyes. Nasan addressed her in Tatar. For the moment, they shared the stables only with other horses, but she couldn't expect more than an hour before the grooms arrived. She had to decide on her next step, and soon.

"Oh, horse, what have I done?" she asked. "So much work my family put into arranging this marriage and ending the feud, and here I have tossed it away. Will the Russians kill me for dishonoring them? Will Daniil divorce me?"

Her voice caught, but she forced herself to continue. "It doesn't matter. Better if he does divorce me. He accuses me of infidelity. Bullies me. Orders me to stay inside his house. To protect his honor. As if he had any. Who needs such a husband?"

The mare regarded her sympathetically. No doubt she had her own views on the trustworthiness of stallions.

"My family matters, though. Have I betrayed them, horse?" Nasan pleated the fabric of her jacket. They had ordered her to marry Daniil, and if they found out what she was doing, they would condemn her just as he had. They, too, thought that women belonged inside the house.

But the ancestors had other plans, as Nasan explained to the horse. "The grandmothers have made their wishes clear. They brought me here to save those children. I cannot refuse. And they will help me. I can't count on Daniil, that's for sure."

She glanced around the stall. It had no windows, but through chinks in the wood she could see signs of approaching day. The stars' obsidian setting had faded to charcoal gray.

She must go. But where? She could not stay at the Kolychev estate. If Daniil found her, he might lock her up. Then no one would rescue the kidnapped children.

If Girei were here... She closed her eyes, searching for the ancestor, for her brother's spirit. Instead she heard Daniil, cursing the grandmother. A tear scoured her cheek. She felt alone and vulnerable.

"I need a friend," she told the horse. "A refuge, just for today. But where will I find one?"

The horse nuzzled Nasan's cheek as it bent to grasp straw. Nasan rubbed its nose, and it breathed into her neck. Its lips touched the golden chain, tightening the lynx pendant around her neck as her opponent had done the night she first ventured outside the Kolychev estate.

The spirits had spoken. Nasan pushed herself off the straw. "Horse, you're right. That old man promised to help me, no questions asked! And he showed me where he lives." She embraced the startled mare, wrapped her mask around her face, and slipped from the stable.

Chapter 21

KOSHKIN HAD ASKED HIS DAUGHTER TO SPY ON HER IN-LAWS, but only because it seemed like a convenient way to keep her occupied while he completed his plans for their family's advancement. As a result, he was not best pleased when his steward announced her. However deep his affection for Maria, her arrival offered a distraction he didn't need. He had enough troubles. He'd jerked at the steward's knock as if it meant discovery.

Besides, the bells had rung for prime not long before. What brought the chit out at this hour?

His daughter clearly could not imagine herself less than welcome. She bustled into his receiving room, dropped her veil on the floor, and treated him to the briefest of hugs.

No point in alienating a person necessary to his scheme. "Well, kitten," he said, "you look full of news. Has something happened?"

A domestic disaster? Another squabble with your sister-in-law? Do not *beg me to let you come home.*

Maria clutched his hand. "Oh, Papa, you wouldn't believe the excitement we've had. Daniil was arrested! For refusing to muster, Pashka said, but I don't believe him. Daniil loves soldiering, the brute. It was something else, and I know what."

Koshkin retrieved his hand and used it to clasp her elbow. He guided her toward the winged armchair she had occupied during her last visit. "Breathe, daughter, before you expire at my feet. Let me pour you a cup of watered wine. And don't tell your mother-in-law that I did."

Maria gulped for air, then calmed herself enough to sit. She accepted the cup he handed her, although she drank no more than a few sips.

"Begin at the beginning." He took the chair opposite her. "And slow down, so I can follow you. Daniil was arrested. Where is he now?"

"At home," Maria said. "He arrived late last night."

"No one took the charge seriously, then."

"His father got him out."

He didn't have time for this. He had a conspiracy to run. Forty-eight hours after a flawless abduction, the princes had become as much a liability as an asset. Koshkin had to convince the boys' mother to free their uncle, a task that required consummate skill and the most delicate negotiations. His daughter's petty problems could wait.

"Lamentable, my dear." He patted her hand. "But please excuse me. I must secure our future."

Maria leaned forward, her eyes intent. "Papa, listen to me. Daniil's arrest had nothing to do with the muster. He is the Golden Lynx!"

"Golden lynx? What golden lynx?" Koshkin plucked the cup from his daughter's grasp. It must be the wine talking.

"You don't know?" She looked astonished. "A hero who aids those in need. We hear new yarns every day. Fantasies, I thought. But last night I heard Daniil talking with Grusha. His lover. I peeked and saw him swinging a pendant. The girl said it belonged to the Lynx. When they left, I sneaked into his room—the Tatar had gone, too—and confirmed it. A lynx!"

"Servants' gossip? A pendant? Maria, I'm disappointed in you. And what do you mean, your sister-in-law had gone?"

"Run off. Disappeared. Maybe Daniil murdered her to keep his secret."

Murdered her? What nonsense was this? "Even though he was under arrest?"

She released a long, irritated breath. "All right, maybe he didn't murder her. But you can't imagine she's the Golden Lynx, so the pendant must be his."

He burst out laughing. "No," he said when he could speak. "I don't think she's the Golden Lynx, if such a creature exists. As for her husband, I'll investigate. Go home, daughter. I swear, I will send for you soon."

Maria stalked from the room, leaving him chuckling at the thought of a woman hero. In truth, her absurd tale had brightened his day.

Nasan waited in the square near the old man's house until the skies lightened, although not so much that the street filled with people. When she heard signs of movement, she edged forward and slipped her mask into her belt. The presence of a masked visitor would cause talk.

The gate opened. A young boy emerged, driving the family cow to water. Small-boned and towheaded, he looked about the same age as Nasan herself. She asked to speak to the master and, when he hesitated, swung her pendant in front of his face.

"He said to meet him here," she announced. Better to exaggerate than to leave the impression of vulnerability. From what she remembered of the old man, he would back her story.

The boy gulped, his Adam's apple jumping in his throat.

"Fetch him, please," Nasan said. "It's important."

It took effort not to fidget as the boy dropped the cow's halter into her hand and darted toward the main house. Nasan had time to wonder if she had made a serious error before the old man emerged, bleary-eyed, belting his caftan around his waist. He shuffled toward her, slippers flapping from his heels, wispy gray hair flying in the early morning breeze.

He stopped a few feet from her. Without emerging from her place beneath the gate overhang, she released the halter to the servant boy. He departed promptly with the cow.

Nasan stepped forward and clasped the old man's hand in both of hers. "You offered help, Uncle. Did you mean it?" She had practiced the Russian words over and over while she waited. Apprehension tinged her voice; her lips felt numb with tension. Suppose he refused? She could not go home until she caught Semyon.

The old man's watery blue eyes widened, and a delighted smile spread across his face. The hand she clasped drew her across the threshold, past the gate. "Of course, Sir Lynx, of course. Whatever you require. Such a tale to tell my grandchildren!"

Ignoring Maria's snit, Koshkin shepherded her into the courtyard and watched her carriage leave. His amusement died as he thought about what she'd said. That he, who prided himself on maintaining contact with every informant in Russia, required enlightenment from a chit barely old enough to wed galled him. His people had some explaining to do—starting with that oaf Semyon Kolychev. If there was any chance Maria had told the truth, the man should thank his saints if his immediate future involved nothing worse than a stint in the meanest garrison on the southern frontier.

Of course, he wouldn't put it past Maria to make the story up. So he had scotched any hopes she might entertain of coming home right away; whether she knew it or not, she was safer among the milksop Kolychevs. But either way, he had to investigate, and fast. He was already juggling more balls than a traveling player at the market. He did not need another complication.

Heading toward his quarters, Koshkin passed his steward, Dimka, standing near the stairs. Another person who should have kept his master informed. Koshkin beckoned Dimka to join him, then shut the door behind them. "Tell me about the Golden Lynx. He sounds like a tale for children. Why does my daughter think him a real man, walking around Moscow?"

The steward stopped and scratched his head. "Master, have you not heard? You, who hear everything?"

Sometimes, silence provokes response better than speech. Koshkin did not reply.

"No, you would not hear," the steward muttered. "The Lynx aids the downtrodden, not the great."

"A rabble rouser?" This was worse than he'd thought. Russia dangled like a rattle from the fingers of a babe, and the land lay dry as tinder. The least spark could start a conflagration. He'd dawdled, trying to anticipate every contingency, but that had to change. For the country's sake, not to mention his own, he must get Yuri on the throne as fast as possible. "How far has this gone? Will peasants murder us in our beds?"

"No uprisings, Lord. The Lynx prevents robberies and assaults. He does naught but good."

Koshkin grimaced. "Yes, so it starts. Good deeds, then armed rebellion. I have no patience with heroes."

"You have it wrong, Master." The steward clapped his hands, his face filled with mindless delight. "Why, the man saved my brother Vanka. A thief attacked with a cudgel—Vanka had the receipts from the market, so his bag hung heavy from his belt, and he risked a beating if he lost it. But an arrow flew from a dark corner and hit the thief in the arm. He screamed and ran. Vanka caught a glimpse of his rescuer, the lynx pendant hanging from his neck. He tried to thank him, but the Lynx only asked if he was well, then vanished into the night."

"Tall? Short? Come on, man, you can give me more detail than that. What was he like?"

"Tall, Master, as befits an epic knight. Strong as a giant, swift as Tatar cavalry on the move. The dogs do not bark when he passes. The clouds hide his shadow. One senses his presence. One does not see him. A voice in the night, a shape glimpsed against the moon. He appears to those in need. It is uncanny, how he knows."

Folktales and legends, but a man at the heart of them, threatening well-laid plans. Koshkin dealt Dimka a blow that sent him staggering. "Get me Semyon Kolychev."

Dimka set off at a speed impressive in a man of middle years. Koshkin paced the room, pondering what he'd learned. Stripped of its embroidery, the description read tall, strong, swift, smart—yes, that fit Daniil Kolychev. Others, too, but there Maria's information became relevant. Presumably not every warrior owned a lynx pendant. And someone had aided Dimka's brother Vanka, whether dogs barked at his passage or not.

Would Daniil rally the poor against the prince his own father supported? No, probably not. Most likely, Dimka spoke the truth, and the boy amused himself, spurred on by a bunch of credulous fools. That kind of adventure appealed to hotheaded young men.

In the end, though, the Lynx's goal didn't matter. Hold out promises of a deliverer, and before long the poor *would* be murdering nobles in their beds. Freed of the lash, the downtrodden established their own rules. Then Russia's enemies would pour in from all sides.

Daniil. Son of Nikolai, Koshkin's bitterest enemy.

Bring down Daniil, and Nikolai would fall. His fall would weaken Grand Princess Elena, which would in turn aid Koshkin in freeing Yuri. A freed Yuri could dispatch Elena and her brats, then reward Koshkin by marrying Maria.

And Daniil didn't have to *be* this Golden Lynx for Koshkin's scheme to work. If he presented the idea to the grand princess in the right way, emphasizing the Lynx's potential for unrest, he could undercut Nikolai by the power of suggestion. Maria had given him a gift, indeed.

Another knock jangled Koshkin's nerves. He called to the person on the other side to enter.

The door opened to reveal Semyon Kolychev. "Your steward sent for me."

About time he showed up. "Get in here."

Semyon recoiled, then entered, looking wary. He clasped his hands behind his back and stood straight.

Koshkin let him have it. "I hear from my daughter—and not from you, my trusted assistant—that Moscow has taken to sheltering a vigilante. Maria believes—I feel certain you will appreciate the joke—that your cousin Daniil masquerades as the Golden Lynx."

Semyon bristled. "Daniil left Moscow weeks ago. He's no vigilante."

"Forgive me if I don't take your word for that."

Semyon shrugged. "Ask him, then. Though I don't know where he is."

"He came in last night. Fresh from jail, Maria says. Find out where he went, what he did, who imprisoned him, and why. We're ready to act. I don't want your clan tripping us up. Understood?"

Semyon challenged him, arms akimbo. "Ready to act. When? So far, I've done the work, and you've risked nothing. Prince Yuri's no closer to freedom than the day we started."

"Patience. Do as I ask, and I won't forget."

Semyon took a step toward him. Koshkin stopped him with a glare, but Semyon did not back off. "Easy to say. When do you take those brats off my hands? The danger increases daily, and you sit here at your fancy estate twiddling your thumbs."

Koshkin narrowed his eyes. Semyon's red face and aggressive stance reminded him of an angry bull. "You underestimate me, my friend. Go. Make preparations to move the children at my signal. And send your man Stenka to me."

Semyon, silenced, departed. Koshkin addressed the door. "Oh, yes, my Kolychev ox. Our game draws to a close. You will go where I drive you. Pray you don't wind up in a ditch."

He glanced at the spot where Semyon had confronted him, fists clenched. At the armchair where Maria had made her cataclysmic announcement, the table still holding her cup, the icons in the "beautiful corner."

He spoke to the saints, his voice hushed, his anger drained by the realization of the great scheme he had undertaken, the odds against his completing it, the many lives that hung on his success or failure. "Guide my words, Holy Ones," he said. "Russia is an infant, unaware of what serves her interests. Let me sway the grand princess with my eloquence and triumph over my enemies." His hands clenched. "Especially Nikolai Kolychev."

Daniil stood at the edge of a forest clearing, like the one that bordered Sveta's cottage but more menacing. A lynx perched near his head, its paw flicking past his cheek. Talking.

"You don't matter," it murmured over and over, like a chant. The voice sounded like Nasan's, but the Russian was perfect, the accent pure Moscow. "He loves me. He'll keep me safe. I put this away, as he will put you away."

"He?" Daniil frowned at the animal. Wide dark eyes stared into his. The black tufts at the ends of the ears lengthened, sweeping down over the sides of a face metamorphosing before his eyes. Brown-striped gold fur transformed to porcelain skin, the black-tipped nose flattened, the fangs dissolved into red lips and human teeth.

Daniil lay still, disoriented as much by the dream as by the belated realization that he had fallen asleep. Despite his good intentions, he'd succumbed like a youth on his first sentry duty. After four uncomfortable days followed by a long night, true— but he was a cavalry officer, wasn't he? He could handle a little discomfort without crumbling.

Right about then, he noticed that although the Nasan-lynx had vanished with the forest clearing, its muttering continued. Without the distraction offered by the dream, he had no trouble identifying the voice as Grusha's.

Which didn't make sense. How had the night ended with Grusha in his room? He remembered her approaching him earlier, but he hadn't told her to return, had he? No, he felt certain he hadn't.

He sat up. Grusha knelt before one of Nasan's chests, folding one veil after another. As she restored each to its place, she repeated her strange incantation. The rest of the room had recovered its pristine appearance. Which explained Grusha's presence. Mama must have told the maid to clean up, assuming she would wait until Daniil woke, and Grusha had chosen to come in while he slept. If challenged, she could claim she had misunderstood.

He needed to clear this situation up right away. Last night he'd failed to take advantage of his opportunity. He could not afford another mistake.

"Grusha," he said. "Where's my wife?"

She jerked as if he'd slapped her. The lavender veil in her hands fell in tumbled folds across her beige skirt, its gauzy cloud incongruous against the coarse linen. Jasmine perfumed the air. "How you startled me, Lord. I don't know."

"You haven't seen her?"

With mechanical precision, she refolded the veil and placed it in the chest. "Not today. Natalya Vasilyevna says the young mistress went to church to confess, but no one spends all morning confessing, do they, Lord? A few sins revealed, a penance, and you're done."

She stood and walked toward him, her smile belying the rancor he'd heard in her voice. He fended her off with a raised hand. She'd thrown herself at him last time he tried to talk to her, and here he was in bed.

Wait. Bed? Am I covered?

A quick glance down reassured him. Of course, he hadn't undressed last night. He'd never intended to fall asleep.

Grusha stopped an arm's length away. "You don't need her, Lord. She's played you false. Won't you let me make it up to you?"

He heard desperation in her voice, although he couldn't imagine why. Instead he focused on her allegation. Let it stand, and Grusha would spread the lie throughout the household.

"My *wife*," he said, underlining Nasan's importance, "did not play me false."

Anger flickered in her face. "You're wrong, Lord. I could tell you things about her."

For an instant, he wavered. Yesterday's suspicions smoldered. He quenched them, determined not to repeat his mistake. "No, Grusha. I enjoyed our time together. But those days are past."

A fair statement, clean and to the point. She had not forgotten, surely, that he had offered pleasure, not commitment. Only a cad would remind her of that fact.

"I love you, Lord," she said. Her pale blue eyes brimmed with tears.

Oh, no. Even if he believed her—and he didn't—how should he respond? It would be cruel to admit that he'd viewed her primarily as a convenience. With disturbing clarity, Daniil realized how casually he'd accepted Grusha's gift of her body, the gift of so many bodies in the years since Anastasia rejected him. He had used her, as he had used those who came before her.

How many women had he hurt? Women who did not complain, because he was a lord and they were servants, barmaids, peasants, soldiers' wives.

"I'm sorry." Hateful to descend to platitudes, but he saw no alternative. "I said we could continue, but we can't. I can't."

Grusha's lips trembled. "I'm sorry," he repeated. "I'm Irina's husband. You must understand that."

It would only confuse her if he tried to console her. He needed to confront Semyon, then find Nasan. Daniil patted Grusha's shoulder and left, feeling like a complete heel.

Grusha watched the door shimmer through her tears. Daniil had abandoned her in the midst of her incantation. Was Tatar magic so powerful that it could enchant a man no matter what?

Panic gripped her. If not for Semyon and his schemes, she could accept that Daniil had moved on. It hurt, but she would cope. He had left his bride too, right after the wedding. And next to the exquisite Irina, Grusha felt like a three-legged goat.

Perhaps Irina's beauty, not her magic, explained Daniil's change of heart. But that didn't matter either. Semyon made acceptance impossible. Daniil might be fickle, but he was not cruel. Not crazy enough to abduct the grand prince. She had to win him back. She had to.

Suppose she told the truth? If he believed her, he would confront his cousin to protect his clan.

But nobles stuck together. She'd witnessed that her whole life. If Semyon convinced Daniil that she'd lied, she'd end up worse than before.

Better to rekindle Daniil's interest. Which meant counteracting the Tatar's magic with more potent spells of her own. She must visit the witch who lived down by the city walls, spend her hard-earned kopecks, and trust time to erase the blotch on her immortal soul.

She shivered. Hellfire and damnation for sorcery. But what hope was there for her soul if Semyon kept her entwined in his wicked scheme? Visit the witch first, confess her sins later—it was the only way. New tears slid down Grusha's face at this dreadful thought.

A knock sounded at the door, and she froze. Another servant poked her head into the room. Anna, a slender cook whom Grusha disliked, not least because Anna had once spent as much time in Daniil's bed as Grusha herself.

"What are you doing here?" Anna asked. "Where's the young lord? Why are you crying?"

"None of your business." Grusha patted her cheeks with the hem of her skirt until her skin burned. "He left."

"He's not for the likes of us," Anna said. Her eyes conveyed a sympathy that should have comforted Grusha more than it did. "It was fun while it lasted. Forget him."

Grusha nodded. Anything to make Anna leave her alone. But the words hardened her resolve. She needed Daniil. She couldn't forget him. Tonight she would visit the witch.

Chapter 22

KOSHKIN STUDIED THE VAULTED CEILING OF GRAND PRINCESS Elena's reception room near the Church of St. Lazarus in the Kremlin. From the elaborate paintings on the walls to the intricately patterned red carpets and silk-covered benches for the grand princess's ladies, today mercifully absent, the room proclaimed emergent Moscow's claim to imperial power. Even the iron chandeliers conveyed majesty and wealth.

A discreet cough interrupted his appraisal. Koshkin returned his attention to the person occupying the carved ivory throne. Grand Princess Elena, mother of Russia's ruler and as of this month her son's regent in all but name, had the high cheekbones and pale coloring of her Lithuanian ancestors. The face of a Nordic goddess, haughty and forbidding—long and narrow, with regular features and a firm chin, pale blue eyes, a straight nose. Beautiful, undeniably—at the height of her powers at twenty-three—but chilly. That tendency to cold calculation explained, no doubt, how Elena had managed to circumvent the council of guardians appointed by her husband before his death and even her own family, who had dared to challenge her.

Koshkin would have preferred to meet Elena one on one, with a chaperone of his choice to prevent any hint of impropriety. Although a mere woman, Elena had a raw intelligence that Koshkin appreciated. He could rely on her sense of self-preservation to keep the information about her sons' abduction under wraps. She recognized, no doubt, that without three-year-old Ivan to lend her legitimacy, the wolves of the court would hunt her down and destroy her.

Unfortunately, Elena had fulfilled Koshkin's hopes only in part. Her elaborate robes and full regalia indicated her desire to treat this audience as a council of state. She had invited both Ivan Telepnev, her favorite, and her staunch supporter Nikolai Kolychev. As well as Telepnev's sister, Agrafena Cheliadnina, who served as the princes' nurse. Standing with arms akimbo on her massive hips, Agrafena made a good substitute for the guards stationed outside the doors.

Elena *really* did not want this information to leak, if she barred her ceremonial bodyguard from the room.

A heartening thought. Starting rumors of the boys' disappearance raised the stakes, compared to a nice friendly negotiation. But if Elena proved difficult...

Telepnev rose or fell with Elena. The nurse had lost ground for failing to guard the children. And thanks to the Golden Lynx, Koshkin might at last have Daniil's father where he wanted him. Maneuver his chessmen well, and he would take the game.

Having assessed his opponents and his chances, he moved his pawn. "Prince Yuri Ivanovich, yes. I think his release is essential to protecting your sons and your land."

"Are you mad? Who benefits more than Yuri from this assault on my children?"

Agrafena hissed in agreement. Telepnev emitted something closer to a growl. Kolychev, as usual, concealed his thoughts.

"Many people." Koshkin bowed. "Anarchy serves the brutal and the ambitious." Her mouth tightened. Good. He needed to rattle her. "Two days since the boys went missing. Who better to take the reins than Prince Yuri, their uncle? If nothing else, we must present a united front to the Lithuanians. Despite our recent successes in the west, they have not retreated."

Elena's face did not alter, but her hands gripped the armrests. "You speak truth there. Our enemies—our relatives!—act as if the ties of blood make my son's throne their own. But Yuri, no. He is a rival, not a protector. And I have generals galore. The court overflows with men of war. Prince Andrei, too, has returned to service."

"As you say, My Lady." Koshkin spoke to the grand princess, but he watched Nikolai Kolychev. Koshkin hated that self-contained alertness. It reminded him of his days as a raw recruit, when Kolychev—already a commander—used to order Koshkin about.

He forced himself to concentrate on Elena. "That's the problem. We have too many generals, each determined to outstrip the others. What we need is a prince—an adult prince—to direct them. In short, Prince Yuri." Before she could remind him again that Andrei, her other brother-in-law, could fill that position if needed, he added, "He has the most experience. He can command the most loyalty. Release him, and he will safeguard Russia for you and your sons."

Elena narrowed her eyes to slits. Only the tapping of her slippered toe against the parquet floor suggested anxiety. "Safeguard? When miscreants creep into the women's quarters and walk off with the grand prince and his brother? Unmask the enemy within our gates, then babble to us of Yuri."

"We are investigating what happened. With care, to prevent gossip, but we have made progress." Remind her of the need for discretion. Play on her fears. It was working: every tap of that toe proved his effect on her. Koshkin bowed again to hide his smile. "As for the enemy within, three sentries failed to report the next day."

"Three guardsmen failed to report. And you did not inform us at once. Where are they?"

"To answer that, I have to find them. With the children, I presume." Untrue. Semyon Kolychev had orders to bury the three men in a gully somewhere. Much too dangerous to leave flapping tongues alive. Semyon swore he had obeyed. Koshkin concentrated on the present and tried to ignore Nikolai, regarding him with the look most people reserve for week-old fish.

"But the guards didn't concoct such a scheme on their own," the nurse said. "A messenger called me away. Someone stands behind this conspiracy."

Of course, someone had called Agrafena away. Koshkin himself. He had guarded the message's origins, passing it through a chain until no one could trace it. He hoped.

Telepnev moved to stand at Elena's back. Nikolai's piercing gaze became unnerving. Koshkin reiterated the stakes—his power, Maria's future, Russia's survival—and pondered when to introduce the Golden Lynx and Daniil. He couldn't blurt out the news without a context.

"Agrafena speaks truth," Kolychev told Elena. "A noble arranged this crime. Someone who wishes you and your children ill. A man with the power to order guards who themselves spring from the most ancient lineages."

Elena emitted a wail, and Kolychev bowed, hand over his heart. "I apologize, Grand Princess. I too wish to save your sons. You can't accept the idea of troops on the street?"

"No. The court must not find out." Her voice sounded strangled.

Koshkin opened his mouth, ready to mention the Lynx, but Nikolai forestalled him. "Then let us conduct a discreet search," he said. "House to house, looking for a stolen object. We needn't say that it comes from the Kremlin."

Koshkin bit his tongue to keep from cursing. Trust Kolychev to find the worst possible action and implement it.

Nikolai was still talking. "But here in this room let us not mince words. We've received no demands for ransom. This criminal does not seek gold. If he kills the children, Prince Yuri takes the throne.

We can't prevent it; he is next in line. You will end your days in a convent."

"I agree to the house to house search," Telepnev said.

"Yes," Elena said. "But with the utmost discretion."

"Very well," Nikolai said. "Meanwhile, releasing Yuri doesn't benefit the princes. I suggest we gather information with all speed. And appoint another man to head the investigation: Koshkin's support for Prince Yuri alarms me."

"You dishonor me?" Koshkin shouted.

Telepnev caught his upraised arm. "Control yourself, man. You laid this trap yourself."

"So you did, Fyodor Mikhailovich," Elena said. "What has Yuri promised you in exchange for his release?"

Disaster threatened. Koshkin mastered his temper before replying. "You misunderstand, Grand Princess. I serve only Russia."

"You serve my son," she said. "Or I have no use for you."

"Always." He produced his most ingratiating smile. "You could send Yuri to the front. If the Lithuanians don't kill him, you can clap him in irons again when you no longer need his services."

"Hmm," Elena said. "And what do you think of this plan, Telepnev?"

Whew. Danger past.

"I dislike it," Telepnev said. "Let's not sow the seeds of future conflict by releasing Yuri. Appoint a general to lead while we search for the boys."

Profanity filled Koshkin's head as water swamped his boat again, driving out caution. "Yuri won't contest your Ivan. He has lived too many years and has no heirs. And he has sworn fealty to you and yours."

Kolychev reentered the fray. "Oaths of fealty can be broken. As you know, Fyodor Mikhailovich."

At last, the opening he needed. "You impugn my character, Nikolai Borisovich, but your own bears investigation. What have you to gain by keeping Russia weak? Or should I say, what has your son to gain? The Golden Lynx may stand behind this abduction."

"My son?" Nikolai sounded astonished. "The Golden Lynx? Will you distract us with tales for children?"

"Yes, your son Daniil. Who goes masked among the poor, luring them away from their lawful rulers." Nikolai blinked and shook his head. Koshkin pressed his advantage. "When Russia goes up in flames because of your Golden Lynx, the blame will not lie at my door—or Yuri's."

"What are you talking about?" Elena asked. "What golden lynx?"

Koshkin offered her a highly colored account of the Lynx's adventures. "My own steward, Grand Princess," he finished, "swears to the man's existence. And I have information that the Lynx belongs to Nikolai Borisovich's household. His son, surely, is the most likely suspect."

"Daniil has not spent the last month in a hermitage," Nikolai snapped. "His escort can confirm his movements. His brother-in-law, too."

The devil take Maria. Would nothing go Koshkin's way today? "His brother-in-law. The one Daniil punched at his wedding?"

The infernal gray eyebrow rose, and Kolychev's mouth twitched. Koshkin wanted to spit.

"That very one," Nikolai said. "So if Ogodai supports Daniil, he's telling the truth, don't you think?" He faced Elena. "My son traveled to Kasimov, Grand Princess. To discover what part my older son played in the feud between my clan and the Tatars. Daniil returned last night. Any number of witnesses can swear that he is not this Golden Lynx. If such a person exists, he does not operate out of my household, I assure you."

"And I assure you he does," Koshkin said, determined to sow suspicion. "Naturally, Kolychev denies it. He and his son concocted this story together, I don't doubt."

Elena studied one man, then the other. Koshkin almost pitied her—young, anxious, inexperienced, deprived of her sons, threatened with usurpation, watching her closest advisers point fingers at one another, uncertain whom to trust. Sternly, he repeated the stakes: his family's future, his own ambitions, Russia's survival. Elena and her sons were means to an end.

Telepnev touched Elena's shoulder. She covered his hand with her own. Koshkin saw her chest rise and fall. "Leave us," she said. Her voice shook. "We have much to consider."

Nikolai bowed and withdrew. Koshkin followed, weighing the results of their exchange. Awkward to have his attempt to divert Elena's suspicions so neatly countered, and disheartening not to have won any commitment for Yuri's release, but one did not expect victory from an initial skirmish. He had forces in reserve. Elena had no choice but to pay the price for her sons' release.

Back home, he found Stenka waiting. He ordered the man to remove the boys from Semyon Kolychev's questionable care tonight and transport them to a safe location outside the city. With Nikolai Kolychev launching a house to house search, there was no time to waste. Tomorrow negotiations could begin in earnest.

He would have to handle the talks himself, of course. Underlings could do only so much. Especially ignorant brutes like Semyon Kolychev. Useful for jobs that required a blunt instrument but not for any task demanding finesse or discretion.

Semyon. A Kolychev. Koshkin had another brilliant idea. Nikolai had defended his son, but Koshkin knew his Elena. The hint of duplicity would worry her. A perfect time to throw her Semyon Kolychev. Koshkin would clear his name while discrediting Nikolai and his clan.

On balance, not such a bad day.

Daniil grabbed a passing servant and sent him for a bowl of water and a comb. Once clean and presentable, he sought out Nikolai. The gleam of the sky indicated mid-morning. Why had Papa not woken him?

His mother called out as he passed her sitting room. Daniil paused to greet her, hoping for news of Nasan. Mama was embroidering, as usual. The black-caped Virgin pressed a beige cheek against a sketched-out blank destined, he guessed, to become the Christ Child. An altar cloth, perhaps: the piece looked about the right size. Next to her sat Father Job, fingers counting the knots in his prayer rope as he muttered his devotions.

"Good," she said. "You're awake. Did you sleep well, my dove?"

"Yes." He walked to the window. "Has Irina returned?"

Natalya stilled her needle and rose to her feet, setting the cloth aside. "I haven't seen her. Then Maria ran off at dawn without a word—to visit her father, she said. Those girls! I don't know what the world is coming to." She treated Daniil to a searching look. "Where did Irina go, Daniil? I'm concerned about her. She has no family in Moscow, does she?"

"I'll find her, Mama. Papa gave me a job to do first."

"That's another thing," she said. "Your father's at the Kremlin. Some crisis at the palace. He left you a message. I sent a girl to fetch you, and she reported you'd already left." Her piercing gaze intensified. "She found Grusha there, weeping."

Did *no* information escape her? "Because I told her I would be true to Irina, Mama."

"Lord, have mercy." Father Job dropped the prayer rope and ran across the room. "My son, have you found the path to virtue at last?"

"Yes, Father," Daniil said. It seemed like the simplest answer.

The priest looked as if he might weep for joy. He patted Daniil on the head.

Natalya's eyes danced. "Saints be praised, indeed. Daniil, Kolya asked you to talk to Semyon by yourself. What's going on?"

Where to start? Through the open window, Daniil heard hoofbeats. The gates opened, a horse entered, his father dismounted. "At the palace—I have no idea. But Papa's here."

When he turned back, his mother had resumed her seat. Her needle, poised above the fabric, trailed scarlet thread. Next to her, the priest in his long black robe and white cassock radiated paternal pride. Who would have guessed his scoldings masked genuine concern? It was touching, in a way. "As for Semyon," Daniil said, "he lied to us. He swore he went nowhere near Kasimov, but I found out that he and Boris traveled there together."

Natalya cried out as she pricked her finger, leaving a splotch of red on the fabric vivid as the thread. "Daniil, you can't believe my Boris slashed that boy's throat!"

"No, I don't." As the words left his mouth, he realized he spoke the truth. "Last night, Irina told me she didn't identify her brother's killer by name. That's why Papa and I want to talk to Semyon." He gave her a rueful smile. "I hope Papa comes with me, though. Semyon fears him much more than he does me."

"Boris went to Kasimov?" Father Job interjected. "But he swore he did not!"

"Excuse me?" Natalya and Daniil said in concert. "You knew that Boris intended to go to Kasimov?" Mama added.

"But of course," Job said. "He discussed it with me, although when he returned, he said he stopped at the Holy Trinity."

Daniil, too stunned to speak, stared at the equally baffled priest. The crash of a door against the wall jerked him back to the present.

Nikolai caught it with a murmured apology. "Success?" he barked at Daniil—referring to the interview with Semyon, Daniil supposed.

"Kolya!" Mama's embroidery frame tumbled to the floor. "He hasn't had time."

Daniil retrieved the cloth for her, then gestured at the priest. "I haven't left yet. I'm waiting for Father Job to tell us about Boris's journey."

"What?" Nikolai said. The priest twitched at his tone. "Boris confided in you, and you said nothing? Even after his death?"

"He assured me he had no secrets from you." Father Job frowned. "He never lied, so I trusted him. It was not my place—"

"I understand, Father," Nikolai said. "But tell us now. What took Boris to Kasimov?"

"I didn't know he went to Kasimov. But he said he might, if it would stop the violence." Job's face creased in distress. "He thought it meet, and I agreed. He intended to find out his cousin's plans and prevent him from carrying them out. But when he said he didn't go, I thought he had seen the futility of trying to soften Semyon Pavlovich's stubborn heart."

Daniil slammed his hand against the window frame. So he'd guessed right. Boris—that virtuous, lovable *dope*—had believed he could dissuade a brute like Semyon, bent on murderous revenge.

"And what then?" Nikolai asked.

"That's all I know," Father Job said. "He said he wanted to stop the killing. He didn't say how."

But the plan had failed. Or had Boris lied about his goals, too?

That was the trouble with lies. Once they began, you couldn't tell where they ended. And one big question remained. Why had Boris insisted that his journey ended at Trinity? He had no reason to conceal his trip to Kasimov once it was over.

Perhaps Papa had some ideas. Daniil looked at his father. "Could we talk about this in private?"

"Of course," Nikolai said. "Come with me."

They left Natalya stabbing her needle into the cloth, muttering, "If that boy let my Boris die, he'll rue the day he was born." Daniil heartily agreed.

Nikolai spoke first. He dropped onto the room's one chair and rested his elbows on the desk. "Boris went to Kasimov to prevent violence. And failed. Not surprising. No one else would even conceive of such a plan. But why did he lie about it? We still don't know."

"Semyon does." Daniil settled on a bench.

"Yes, Semyon holds the key. You must talk to him. But before you do, there's more. I just got back from the palace, where Koshkin announced before Elena that you are some rabble rouser he calls the Golden Lynx. I defended you, but where did he get such a story? He hates us, he's a sneak, but an intelligent sneak. Not a man who'd circulate an unsupported story, even if he had to create the evidence himself."

Daniil fidgeted. Nasan had claimed she was the Golden Lynx. Should he tell his father, even though he hadn't understood half of what she'd said to him last night and had no independent confirmation of her story? She was his wife, and ratting on her to Papa seemed wrong. He wouldn't treat a comrade that way.

Yet protecting her felt awkward, too. Boris, Ogodai, Nasan: surely the family had heard enough lies without him adding to the number.

"I am not the Lynx," he said, stalling for time. "That I swear. I did journey to Kasimov. Our men can vouch for me. Ogodai, too."

Nikolai crushed one of the scribe's quill pens against the desk, lifted it, and studied the shattered tip. "Yes, so I told the grand princess. You have no idea why Koshkin fixed on us?"

A direct question. Lie or truth? Daniil chose honesty. "Why he picked me, no. The household, maybe. I heard a rumor last night. I'd rather not say more until I investigate."

"Rumor? That ties the Lynx to this household?" Nikolai smacked the desk with the feather. "Mother of God, what did I do to deserve this?"

"Even if what I heard is true," Daniil assured him, "the Lynx poses no threat to Elena. No rabble rousing." Nasan had said a great deal he hadn't understood, but there had to be limits on what one girl could do. "Koshkin wants to discredit us, that's all."

"Discredit us—well, that he does." Papa's mouth quirked in a bitter smile. "My own fault, I suppose. I hit him pretty hard."

Hit? Papa and Koshkin had disliked each other for as long as Daniil could remember. They saw the world in different ways, and no marriage between their children could erase that. Yet physical violence seemed extreme, even for them. "Because of the Golden Lynx?"

"No." Nikolai leaned forward. "We have another problem. I do want to know about the Lynx, but this one's even more urgent. And just as dangerous to us, if we can't resolve it. Check that door for eavesdroppers—my charming daughter-in-law, for example. *Bozhe moi*, I wish I hadn't made that match."

Surprised (and rather pleased) by Papa's uncharacteristic frankness, Daniil went to check.

No one lurked outside. When he returned to the bench, Nikolai spoke just above a whisper. "The grand prince is missing. And his baby brother."

Daniil jerked back. His father's finger touched his lips. He gulped, nodded. "How?"

"Stolen away two nights ago. By their guards, who have also gone. I suspect Koshkin. Gut instinct, mostly. And because an hour ago he was arguing with Grand Princess Elena that she should release Prince Yuri Ivanovich."

"Release Prince Yuri." Shock muddled Daniil's thoughts. "And then what? Kill the children? That's treason. But if Koshkin has the princes—this sounds terrible—why not kill them right away? Elena would have to release Yuri then." For no reason he could determine, his mind produced an image of Nasan, defiant in black, fists on her hips, incomprehensible syllables pouring from her mouth.

Nikolai peeled a long strip from the quill. "Koshkin prefers to keep his hands clean. He knows that if Yuri usurps the throne, sooner or later the children will die. Elena will die—or be forced into a convent. But so long as he can convince himself he didn't kill them, he can keep his self-respect. I confronted him, pointing out that reality in the harshest terms. You could see the truth shocked him. Then he recovered, alas." He waved the mangled feather at Daniil. "That's why he accused you. I should have realized. To undercut me with Elena."

"Did he succeed?"

"Hard to tell, with Elena. She's likely to conclude 'no smoke without fire.' Although I cast doubt on his motives, and Telepnev backed me. I'd say we're safe for now. But whatever you uncover about the Lynx, tell me without delay."

Good. He had time to find Nasan.

Nikolai went on. "It's the children that worry me. Elena refused point blank to launch a proper investigation. No one must guess that she's lost the boys. We're reduced to sending men house to house under a pretense. But if we find the children and expose Koshkin, our clan has nothing to fear from the Golden Lynx."

"So you want to look for them ourselves?" Daniil felt as befuddled as a newborn chick.

"Why else would I tell you?" Nikolai flicked the feather in front of Daniil's face. "Wake up, son. This is serious."

"All right," Daniil said. "So I forget Semyon and—do what?"

The much-abused feather hit the desk again. "Semyon. No, let's not forget Semyon. Semyon has had guard duty the last six months. I don't care how watertight this scheme is. It'll spring a leak somewhere, and Semyon's in a perfect place to notice the puddles. He's family. If we go down, so does he. Remind him of that, and ask him what he's heard. Don't give him any more information than you have to. And if he explains what happened to Boris, so much the better."

"Yes, sir," Daniil said, as if taking orders from a general—which he was, in a sense. He headed for the door.

"Good lad," Nikolai said. "And Daniil?"

He glanced over his shoulder.

"Don't waste time," Papa said. "I got your muster orders this morning. Morozov's expecting you in Smolensk this time next week. That gives us a couple of days, at the most, to find the boys."

The servants had cleared the noon meal before Semyon noticed that Grusha hadn't returned. A flick of his finger summoned Stenka and Timoshka, stationed on either side of the hall. They stalked toward him like tomcats reacting to the presence of a rival: two stocky frames, about the same height and girth—one neat and stolid, the other broken-toothed and in need of a bath. Semyon, who found their mutual dislike amusing, entertained himself by calculating how he would wager if they fought. On the whole, he'd back Stenka. Timoshka's thuggishness could not offset Stenka's cool-headed application of science.

The two men stood before him, three feet apart. The wooden table between them and Semyon did not stretch wide enough to mask the odor of garlic, onions, and cabbage. Semyon leaned against the wall and picked his teeth. With Solomonida away, the cook had slacked off, and today's beef would have benefited from another two hours in the stewpot. The fibers had buried themselves in crevices of Semyon's mouth and resisted extraction.

"Have the cook flogged," he told Stenka. "Today's dinner was an abomination. And where is that wretched girl from my uncle's house? I let her go for an hour last night. At your urging, Stenka. Have you seen her since?"

Stenka acknowledged the order regarding the cook and said, "No, Lord. She promised to return at dawn, but she hasn't yet. I expect her to arrive before dark."

Semyon sensed disapproval. How dare he? Stenka stared at the wall, his face expressionless. Semyon frowned, more than ever convinced that Stenka lusted after Grusha himself. He could have her, too, when Semyon finished with her.

But where had the girl run off to, and why? It couldn't be an accident that her abrupt change of plans occurred on the day his cousin Daniil reappeared in Moscow.

Koshkin wanted full details on Daniil. Where he'd spent the last month, mostly. But why? Not because he believed Daniil had turned himself into some local hero. Even Koshkin couldn't be that daft. More likely than not, Daniil had lost patience with the virgin bride and loped off after more rewarding entertainment. That's what Semyon would have done.

Forget it. He had better means of occupying his time than pestering a wenching cousin. Koshkin valued himself too high, as if he didn't need Semyon more than Semyon did him. Because Semyon held the children, without whom Koshkin's scheme would fizzle.

Speak of the devil and he appeared, the country folk said. Raised voices sounded in the hall outside, then Daniil shoved aside two of Timoshka's finest and entered the hall.

Had Grusha already blabbed? Stupid to let the chit go without verifying how much she knew. That brat Ivan announced his name to anyone who would listen.

No troops in the courtyard, though—unless they moved like mice. Daniil couldn't know about the children, if he'd come alone. Something else had brought him here. Grusha, perhaps, complaining of mistreatment. But if the bitch thought Semyon wouldn't follow through on his threat to undermine her with her lover, he'd take pleasure in proving her wrong.

"Cousin." Without rising, Semyon gestured at the table. "I'll send for more food. The beef, in particular, rewards a hungry man." He chuckled at his own wit.

Daniil sat. Timoshka passed him a cup, but he waved it away. "A word with you, cousin, in private."

Semyon dismissed his men. Normally he didn't take orders from junior cousins, but this time he agreed with the need for privacy. A few too many sins on his conscience of late. "What do you want, Daniil?"

His cousin laughed and relaxed, his uncharacteristic grimness dissolving in a smile. Not Grusha, then, and definitely not the children.

"Did I alarm you?" Daniil asked. "Sorry. We don't chat often. I didn't see any need for the glowering guards. I'm assigned to Smolensk. Weren't you stationed there last year?"

Smolensk. Daniil had come to talk about Smolensk. He knew nothing about either Grusha or the brats. "It's a rathole," Semyon said. "Dull as ditchwater. Who's commanding?"

"Morozov. Have you served with him?"

No, saints be praised. "A stickler for detail, I hear. I've no direct experience with him."

Daniil nodded. "Papa likes him. How about you? Are you heading west?"

"No, I'm stuck in Moscow for the present. Haven't you heard? Koshkin made me his assistant. I got off guard duty a few days after your wedding."

Daniil placed his foot on the bench. His knee pointed at the ceiling. "I hadn't heard. What kind of assistance do you provide?"

"Run errands, carry messages, the usual. You know."

"No, I don't. I ride around shooting things, mostly. In the vanguard. Or the left wing. At the front, in any case."

Was that a slap? Russia had many fortresses and many types of military duty, but no service carried as much prestige as that on the front lines.

Daniil shrugged. "Except for six months last fall. Excruciating job, guard duty, don't you agree? Standing around looking noble with a whacking great silver pike and a fur hat, thanking the saints it's November and not July. Even drill's an improvement. Anything exciting happen while you were standing watch?"

"Not a thing," Semyon said, with a heartfelt sigh. "I leaped at Koshkin's job when he offered it, figuring nothing could be worse. But I was wrong. Another high-and-mighty boyar ordering me hither and yon while he lolls around making 'policy.'"

"Why not transfer, then? Papa would help if you asked."

Right. Uncle Nikolai invariably pegged his assistance to demands for Semyon to reform. He could live without that. Wasn't that why he'd allied with Koshkin in the first place?

"Koshkin's all right," he said, contradicting himself. "He promised me a better position if I hang on for a bit. Odd that you didn't hear, though. Uncle Nikolai's usually on top of court appointments."

"I just got back from Kasimov. Where I was asking about Boris. And guess what I discovered?" Daniil's air of bonhomie vanished. His foot hit the floor, and he leaned forward. "That he went there with you, *cousin*. Why didn't you tell us the truth?"

Damn. So Daniil did have an ulterior motive, and it wasn't Grusha. Semyon swung away from the wall and thumped both elbows against the table, his face inches from Daniil's. "What are you implying?"

Daniil didn't back down. "That you lied. Despite swearing you went to Trinity."

"I did go to Trinity. To meet your precious Boris. Should I have ratted him out? Dig your own dirt, *cousin*."

"Boris died in the Tatar raid. Yet you didn't come forward. You attended the wedding, took part in the fight, didn't say a word." Daniil smacked the table. "Oh no, that's not true, is it? You defended Boris when Ogodai insulted him. And why not? You knew he had nothing to do with that boy's death. You left your own family hanging on the line like so much laundry. You could have warned us."

"I didn't expect the raid." It sounded weak. Semyon fished for a better answer.

"You thought you could go into Bulat's land, kill a member of his family, and walk away with no one the wiser?" Daniil's face creased with disgust. "You expected Bulat to wash his hands of the whole thing and say, 'Oh, too bad. I have other sons'? *Bulat?*"

"What makes you so sure I killed him? Why not your precious Boris?"

"Because, you dolt, my brother didn't believe in vengeance."

"He said he did."

Daniil rocked his bench back until it slapped against the wall. "He said he did. And what happened when he got to Kasimov, Semyon? Did he believe in vengeance then?"

Semyon lost his temper. What gave Daniil the right to show up uninvited and interrogate him? "I thought so. Up to the last moment, when he turned coward. And that, *cousin*, was your precious Boris."

Daniil came off the bench in a rush, overturning the table. Semyon had no time to react before his cousin's fist slammed into his jaw.

Chapter 23

DANIIL SWORE AS HE HEARD SEMYON'S GATE CLOSE BEHIND him. In two days he had to leave for Smolensk, and despite Papa's orders, he hadn't unearthed any useful information about the missing princes. Because he'd let his anger over Boris get the better of him.

He slapped a passing fence in frustration, realizing that he'd knocked his cousin out. Semyon wouldn't be answering questions for a while—especially from Daniil. Semyon had been opening up, until Daniil mentioned Kasimov. He might have found out more.

If Semyon knew more. He said he'd left guard duty to work with Koshkin. Daniil turned a corner and stopped dead, gaping at the Kremlin ahead of him.

Koshkin. Whom Papa suspected of engineering the kidnapping. Who hated the Kolychevs but had nevertheless recruited Semyon as his assistant. And who had Semyon running errands, carrying messages, and … kidnapping princes?

No. That was insane. His imagination had run riot. Even Semyon must realize how short a future he could expect if he involved himself in so desperate a scheme.

Daniil took off down the street like an arrow from a bow. With any luck, he'd reach home before Papa left for the Kremlin once more. It seemed as if his interview might have yielded better fruit than he'd first thought.

Semyon lay on his back, rubbing his jaw. Wooden panels swung around his head in a graceful arc. He squinted at them, trying to reconstruct what had happened.

Daniil had socked him. Over that lily-livered, lying Boris. Who had spent the whole trip to Kasimov drinking and whoring and acting like a man for once, only to explain at the last moment that he'd been stringing Semyon along, coaxing him to reveal his plans so that Boris could scotch them. Of course, Semyon had dumped the traitor on the road and taken care of the business himself. Even then, he tried to protect his cousin, making up a fake name so that the Tatars wouldn't retaliate against Boris.

And yet Daniil had socked him. Was it Semyon's fault the Tatars had killed Boris anyway?

He pushed himself to a sitting position. His head rang, and he grabbed it. His jaw ached. Young Daniil packed quite a punch. Bastard.

He grimaced at the wall, which although not circling had acquired an overlay of bright spots. He rubbed his forehead and blinked. He didn't have time for this.

"Are you all right, master?" The voice was Stenka's. Semyon peered through the gold spots and saw his assistant on one knee. Stenka held out a damp cloth, and Semyon pressed it to his jaw.

A pair of dirty leggings hove into view. "Let's get him on his feet, then," Timoshka said. "Stenka, you take that arm. I've got this one. One, two, three."

Semyon, hauled to standing, subsided on the bench vacated by Daniil and regarded his two chief henchmen. Composing his thoughts took effort, but he managed.

What was most urgent? Daniil had left. Forget him. He hadn't learned anything important.

Focus on the boys. And Grusha. She hadn't sent Daniil to champion her cause, as Semyon had thought. But she hadn't shown up, either. "Stenka," he said. "Koshkin asked for you this morning. What did he want?"

"He ordered me to accompany the wagon. It will arrive tonight to pick up the cargo."

Cargo. The princes. Stenka had discretion, even if he did have a soft spot for Grusha. And it sounded as if Koshkin hadn't lied when he'd promised to take the brats off Semyon's hands. Good. The endgame couldn't come too soon. Just thinking of what he'd done made Semyon itch.

"How do we get the 'cargo' onto the wagon? Did Koshkin have a suggestion for that?" It was the weak point in their scheme. Semyon hadn't appreciated how weak until he heard Grand Prince Ivan ordering all and sundry to bow down and kiss his feet, but he knew better now.

Stenka pulled a small flask from his belt. "Tincture of poppy. A little in their evening gruel, and they will sleep like the babes they are."

Tincture of poppy. Harmless enough. Of course, once Koshkin freed the brats' uncle, they wouldn't have much time left on this earth. Still, Semyon preferred not to be the one tipping poison down a royal throat. He had taken enough risks on Koshkin's behalf.

In fact, this would be a good job for Grusha. The more he involved her, the less incentive she'd have to tattle. Send a man for her, bring her to his uncle's estate by force, supervise her as she dosed the boys, then lock her up until Koshkin got the brats out of there. The perfect solution.

But whom to send? Stenka's attraction to the girl would encourage him to hunt her down—but Semyon didn't trust him to deliver her as ordered. He needed a less scrupulous servant. "Timoshka," he said.

Timoshka slouched to attention. His lips widened in what some people might call a smile.

"Find that girl," Semyon told him. "Bring her to my uncle's estate. Don't rough her up more than you have to—"

Stenka emitted a groan, small but audible.

"You have a comment?" Semyon clenched his fist and held it up, lest this servant forget the penalty for insubordination.

"No, Lord." Stenka stood rigid, hands clasped behind his back.

Semyon waited until he squirmed, then addressed Timoshka once more. "Don't rough her up more than you have to"—he glowered at Stenka, who did not react—"but deliver her as soon as you can."

"Yes, Lord." Timoshka grinned, obviously relishing his task.

Semyon dismissed them both. Alone, he sipped beer to pull himself together. He would leave as soon as possible to monitor the situation at his grandfather's estate. That would stave off any further visits from irate relatives. And while there, he could amuse himself by imagining punishments for Grusha.

Nasan woke, much refreshed, in a bed not much bigger than a cot. Linen sheets, coarse compared to those at home but clean and smelling of sunshine and violets, pressed against her cheek. The slanting light of late afternoon brushed her face.

The unfamiliarity of the room puzzled her until she recalled the events of the previous night. Daniil's return, their quarrel, her flight, her early morning arrival at the old man's house, her fear that he would have forgotten her, her joy at his welcome. He had fed her a simple meal of bread and fish, brought her to this room, bid her sleep. And he had asked no questions, a concession for which she would forever thank him. His conviction that in her he saw a mythical hero had served her well.

She couldn't tell if he had identified her as a woman. Most likely not, for he had cared for her himself, although he had a wife—Nasan had seen her bowing in the shadows. So her secret remained safe.

She still had to decide how to extricate the kidnapped children from Semyon's power without implicating herself or putting the three of them at risk. Her enemy's strength alarmed her. The grandmothers would aid her, but...

If the ancestors thought she needed human assistance, they would send it. Until then, she must muddle along as best she could.

She rose and washed in the basin the old man had left her. The water reflected her face, and she studied it, planning how to proceed. Her women's clothes remained at the Kolychevs'. Nor would she have wanted her host to see her in female garb.

Her scarf covered her hair. Her black tunic, jacket, and full trousers, tucked into her boots, looked odd—her people did not usually shrink from color. Add a cap, though, and she could pass for a Tatar boy in mourning. No one would consider her a man, because she had neither beard nor mustache, but by carrying a sword she ensured that no one would imagine her a girl.

Too bad she had left her bow and quiver at the house. They could prove useful when she returned to the small estate, but she had forgotten them in her anger at Daniil.

Too late for regrets, though. She tucked her lynx pendant under her tunic and went downstairs to bid a grateful farewell to her host.

The goodbyes took a while, but crowds still thronged the market when Nasan reached it. She wandered from one stall to the next, listening for snippets of information. Moscow was larger than Kasimov, meaning it had more people to spread rumors: more slaves happy to discuss their masters, more merchants supplying the royal household, more peddlers spreading stories they had picked up along the roads.

And Nasan did overhear plenty of tales, not a few of them scurrilous, about the high and mighty of the capital. She gleaned far more information than she wanted about backaches, headaches, stomachaches, and bad bowels. Within an hour, she could have taught her mother-in-law remedies for a half-dozen ailments and an equal number of charms and potions (assuming Natalya exhibited any interest in such things). She did catch more than one whispered speculation that the young grand prince and his brother had died, because no one had seen them recently, but none came with the specific detail needed to convince her that it had a foundation in truth. Even a direct question to one particularly garrulous shopkeeper drew a blank.

As the afternoon wore on, Nasan began to doubt her own senses. Why put herself and her family at risk for a phantom? The sensible course, surely, was to go home, apologize to Daniil, and effect a reconciliation by whatever means came to hand.

Except that she could not. What kind of person would abandon two innocent children to appease a faithless husband? She had not saved Girei, but she would save them.

Return in triumph or die trying. Her family's honor required no less.

And since she had already burned her bridges, she might as well visit the small estate that evening. With luck, she could rescue the children tonight.

Daniil returned to his room after hours of frustration. One day almost gone, and little to show for it. Time spent dealing with his cousin's misdeeds had gobbled up his chance to search for Nasan. The setting sun, gleaming in his wife's brass mirror, revealed only his own face.

Tired but restless, Daniil paced the room. The ugly wooden doll Nasan called a grandmother drew him as he approached the dressing table, and he sat on the bench to observe it.

It had a creepy, half-human appeal—blackened face and large eyes, the suggestion of features, a disproportionately large head. Someone had put effort into carving it, sculpting not only nose, mouth, and ears but fingers, even fingernails. Rough horse hair adorned its head under a beaded headdress, and it wore layers of loose silk robes. When he picked it up, it felt warm and heavy in his hands. Heavier than expected, given that in length it stretched from his fingertip to his wrist.

He stroked the wood, wondering how many generations had sought the doll's assistance. The idol had a comforting heft, and despite its weird appearance it did convey a sense of grandmotherliness. He couldn't figure out how.

The doll sparked memories of his dream, the lynx that had metamorphosed into Nasan. Of Ogodai talking of wood spirits and messengers, a world of connectedness beyond Daniil's ken.

Superstition. But the doll showed him how profoundly he and his parents had misunderstood the stranger they had brought into their house. The mistake lay there, in his hands, in the wooden idol of an ancestor who directed his wife's actions, unbeknownst to the family that had not once asked who she was or what she needed, presuming that she would conform to their expectations because she could have none of her own.

He no less than the rest. Daniil reviewed his brief acquaintance with his wife and discovered that he liked the idea of a woman who wielded a bow like a man and fought for what she thought was right, even if it meant defying her husband. They had interests in common: he could talk to her. Extraordinary in a world where men and women interacted, on the whole, only to produce children. And there, under the grandmother's approving eye, Daniil made his choice: to build a partnership with his wife as strong as his parents'.

With her agreement—and for that, he had to find her. Mama was right. Nasan had no relatives in Moscow and no opportunity to make friends outside the household. Where had she gone?

He restored the grandmother to its place and walked to the window. In the courtyard below, Grusha passed by on her way to the kitchen.

The kitchen? At this hour? The sky had darkened while Daniil communed with the ancestor. Dinner had ended long ago.

Thoughts clashed in his head. Grusha claimed she had information about Nasan. Last night, Nasan had included Grusha's name in her incomprehensible list. Suppose he had again missed the clue right in front of his face, and Grusha knew where Nasan went and for what purpose?

As he watched, Grusha glanced over her shoulder and scooted into the shadows. Odd.

After their confrontation this morning, he had no desire to talk to her. Better to follow her, especially if he could keep her from seeing him. He knelt and rummaged in one of the chests, pulled out a set of dark brown trousers and shirt, squinted, shrugged, put them on.

He saluted the grandmother, who in the flickering light appeared to be smiling. A glitter caught his eye. The second lynx pendant—intended, Nasan had insisted, for him. He clasped it round his neck, letting it hang outside his shirt. From a black silk bag lying nearby he fashioned a mask, tied it around his head, and checked the effect in Nasan's brass mirror.

"A regular vagabond," he told his reflection. "Greetings, Golden Lynx. Let's see where your adventures take us tonight."

He returned to the window in time to spot, in the last rays of the setting sun, Grusha slipping out of the estate. The hunt was on. Daniil grabbed his bow, quiver, and dagger and ran for the courtyard.

Grusha hurried through the town. Fear drove her forward even as it stayed her feet at every cross-street. If she didn't pick her route carefully, she would pass too close to the small estate that Semyon had adopted as his lair. The place where he kept the child who had identified himself as the ruler of Russia. The place she hoped to avoid for the rest of her life. Remembering the snake pit Semyon had dumped her in made her shudder.

She hated being out so late. The streets near the estate had significant traffic even at this hour, but as she progressed down the hill, the roads narrowed and emptied. Every so often she glanced over her shoulder, convinced she heard footsteps behind her. No one.

Move fast, finish quickly. Night served her purpose best, despite its terrors. During the day the wise woman traveled the streets, peddling her medicines and herbs. But the witch did not visit the Kolychevs. Natalya forbade it. The servants always slipped out of the compound and bought what they needed after dark.

It was the Tatar's fault. If she had not enchanted Daniil with her beauty and her magic, Grusha would not be rushing through dark streets fearful of losing her way and stumbling over Semyon and his men. She cringed at the memory of Daniil patting her as if she were one of his faithful hounds. But fears of what she could expect without his protection loomed larger.

Grusha reached her destination without anyone accosting her and rapped on the wise woman's door. The tiny hut looked more like a shed than a house, and an ill-kept shed at that. A shutter hung from one hinge, and the door didn't fit true. The garden contained more weeds than vegetables. The house reeked, even from outside: urine and manure, unwashed clothing, rotting timbers. Grusha breathed through her mouth and blocked thoughts of how bad the inside must smell.

The old woman had a good reputation, though. Grusha's fellow servants had used her potions to prevent conception, start or protect a child, or abort an unwanted infant. Anna, the cook who'd alternated with Grusha in Daniil's bed, had tried the abortion medicine. It made her sick as a dog in clover, but she lost the baby. The witch's spells worked.

The door creaked open, revealing a pair of dark eyes in a round face creased with age. Wispy white hair escaped tightly pinned double braids. The wise woman wore a patched linen shirt over a threadbare shift. Slippers constructed from birch bark enclosed her feet.

The urine and unwashed-body smells came from her. Grusha strove for charity. One day *she* would be old and unwilling to spend her limited strength fetching water from the river. But she would not live alone, if she could help it. The desire to avert that fate had brought her here.

Since she needed the witch's help, she forced her nose not to wrinkle. "Do you remember me, mother?" She offered the woman a day-old loaf and a hunk of cheese that she had stolen from the Kolychev kitchens to sweeten the witch's humor. "I apologize for the lateness of the hour."

The crone captured the food in her narrow hand. "Come in, come in. And I thank you. Yes, I know you, child. From the big house near the marketplace, no?"

Grusha inclined her head and followed her hostess into the tiny hut. Bunches of dried herbs hung from the ceiling, requiring visitors to duck as they passed. A branch scratched her cheek, releasing the bright tang of sage. The witch waved at a rickety stool. Grusha sank onto it and clasped her hands.

"So, child, what can I do for you?" The wise woman placed the loaf in a covered wicker basket and sat on a bench next to a rough-hewn table.

Grusha looked around, fighting repulsion. The hut lacked a chimney, never mind a stove. A small fire burned in the center of the room. Soot clung to the walls, and smoke curled around the herbs as it made its way to the hole in the center of the roof. A crumpled blanket tossed on a straw pallet in one corner suggested recent occupancy, and a pair of shelves housed a few clay cooking pots and implements, as well as the mortar and pestle that the wise woman used to prepare her potions. Two chests held, Grusha assumed, the rest of the woman's possessions.

The life Grusha was going to such lengths to avoid. She leaned forward. "I need a love spell. I can pay."

The old woman smiled, exposing blackened and missing teeth. "A love spell. Charming. Well, who can argue with passion?"

*

Daniil trailed Grusha to a broken-down hut near the city walls. She walked fast, almost running, although she stopped at every intersection before continuing on. After a while, he became accustomed to her frequent pauses. He didn't think she detected him, but he ducked into the shadows every time, just in case. When she reached her destination, he couldn't believe the evidence of his own eyes. What brought her to this ramshackle dwelling? The guilty glances she cast over her shoulder didn't enlighten him. The hut, if poor, did not suggest any nefarious purpose.

But maybe guilt wasn't the right word. The atmosphere in this part of town would unsettle anyone. The silence seemed imbued with menace, and the decrepit buildings added an aura of sorrow and decay. Daniil had cast more than one backward glance himself. Even now he would swear a malign force had him under surveillance, although repeated checks revealed only himself and Grusha, who had vanished into the tiny shack and seemed intent on staying there.

Which meant that he had again wasted his time. Grusha had brought him no closer to his goal. He would have to start his search for Nasan anew.

Grumbling, he retraced his steps.

The crone frowned. "You can't give this man food or drink? And you have nothing that belongs to him, not even a hair from his head? That makes our task more difficult." Her blackened teeth flashed again. "More expensive."

Grusha shook her head. She *could* tamper with Daniil's food, but she wanted a surer method. It wouldn't do for him to hand the dish to someone else at the last moment, leaving her to fight off another man.

But she did own one object of Daniil's: he had given her a linen shirt to wash the day before his wedding, and she had kept it and worn it next to her skin, a keepsake to treasure until he returned to her. She pulled back the sleeve of her gown and held her arm out to the old woman. "His," she said, pointing to the linen.

"Ah, this is better." The woman stroked the shirt.

Grusha flinched, tempted to drag her arm away from that filthy, caressing finger. How could she share Daniil, however briefly, with this disgusting hag?

"Fine linen," the wise woman said. "You love a boyar? You're a fool, girl."

Grusha pulled her arm away and hugged the sleeve to her chest.

"One grivna," the woman said. "And you'll have to learn the spell by heart. Have you a good head for memorization?"

"Good enough." Grusha released her sleeve to dig coins out of her pouch and hand them over. The avaricious gleam in the old woman's eyes made her shiver. Again she wondered if she had made a mistake in coming here. But if the wicked Tatar had enchanted Daniil, only a counter-spell would free him.

"Repeat after me." The wise woman dropped Grusha's coins into a clay cup. "I will leave the courtyard not by the gates, crossing the open fields to the ocean-sea."

"I will leave the courtyard not by the gates, crossing the open fields to the ocean-sea."

"On the ocean-sea stands an iron hut, and in that hut the stove is copper, and there burn aspen branches, flame on flame."

Grusha repeated the first phrase, then added the second.

"So let burn the body and soul of your slave—give his name here—for me, your slave—add yours."

Grusha parroted the entire phrase, except for the names. Something about the wise woman's avid curiosity made her hesitate.

The crone's beady eyes misted with disappointment, but she went on. "Let him ache for me by day and by night, at noon as at midnight, sunrise and sunset, new moon and old moon—forgetting father and mother, kith and kin, yearning only for me."

Grusha had practiced the spell twice when a knock sounded on the door, echoing amid the hut's cool, dark silence. As the wise woman went to answer this new summons, Grusha muttered the spell under her breath, entangling Daniil's sleeve around her fingers and including their names this time. The spell had cost her entire savings; she wanted it to begin working as soon as possible.

The wise woman returned. No one accompanied her. She gestured at Grusha as she crossed the room to drop more coins into her cup. "You must go, child. My next guest desires privacy. You have learned the spell?"

"I have. Thank you, mother." Grusha stumbled to her feet, anxious to leave now that she had concluded her business.

The crone waved her narrow hand. Again she treated Grusha to her grisly smile. "Excellent. May you experience happiness with your young man."

Grusha shivered without knowing why. Not until she walked out of the hut and right into Timoshka's arms did she realize that she had not imagined the malice on the witch's face. Semyon's man had paid the old woman off.

"Well, well, my pretty," he said. "A fine dance you've led me, to be sure."

Grusha struggled, but although he stood only the width of two fingers taller than she, she could not match his strength. He pinioned her arms behind her back and held her close enough to kiss, laughing at her efforts to free herself. For a horrible moment she thought he *would* kiss her, but instead he said, "His lordship has been waiting a full day for you. Do you want to anger him even more? That boyar you had trailing you has gone. So stop that and come quietly."

"Boyar?" Grusha gaped at him. Daniil had followed her? Could the spell work that quickly? No, surely he had *not* stopped caring for her, whatever he'd said. She could have stayed safe at home, waiting for him to summon her. She hadn't needed the spell!

"Yes, boyar." Timoshka sounded annoyed. "Why do you think I didn't grab you an hour ago when you left the house? Big blond fellow, our Semyon Pavlovich's cousin. Who visited earlier today and left him flat on the floor." He grinned, an expression even more hideous than the wise woman's. "And no, I don't know why. But he took off after you went into the witch's hut, so you come along with me. Our master's waiting."

Stunned by her rapid and incomprehensible change of fortune, Grusha submitted to Timoshka's grip on her upper arm. As he dragged her through the streets, she brooded on this latest twist of fate. Daniil had followed her. He must love her. But he went away when she entered the hut, and Timoshka was hauling her back to Semyon—who had committed a terrible crime, dragged her into his coils, and foiled her escape. An angry Semyon, with punishment on his mind.

Hope flickered as she pondered Timoshka's other bombshell: Daniil had knocked out his cousin earlier today. Why?

Not on her behalf, surely. She hadn't mentioned Semyon. But Daniil had returned only last night, too soon to learn about the children. So the fight couldn't have had anything to do with them, either. In any case, it didn't matter: he couldn't help her now. Because while she risked her soul for his sake, he had lost patience and left.

Without question, she was the unluckiest girl in the world.

Chapter 24

NASAN APPROACHED THE ESTATE WHERE SEMYON HELD HIS captives. From the end of the street she saw no signs of life. No lights split the gloom. No rolling cartwheels or clanking weapons suggested a human presence. No soldiers' challenges, no grunts or coughs, no children's cries. No smell of food—although that shouldn't surprise her. The supper hour had long since passed.

Still, she had expected some signs of habitation. On every previous visit, Semyon had guarded the gate. Had she arrived too late?

He could have moved the children, but after risking so much, Nasan would not slip away without finding out. Keeping to the shadows where possible, she ran for the overhanging tree and scaled it.

From the branches she surveyed the courtyard below. Dark, silent. None of the usual guards. But that could be a glimmer of candlelight from the house. Nasan dropped to the ground behind an abandoned outbuilding, possibly a stable. She peered through a chink in the wall, but the moonlight, although strong enough for her to navigate, did not penetrate the gloom within. She shrugged and crept toward the courtyard.

When she reached the far corner, she peeked around it, trying to gauge the distance to the next sheltering wall. A voice spoke right next to her left shoulder, causing her to jump. "Where is that blasted

Timoshka? Every task I set him, he blunders. Even an oaf like that shouldn't have trouble laying his hands on one wretched girl."

The lordly arrogance of that voice permitted no mistake. Semyon Pavlovich, in person. But where was he?

When a thorough survey did not reveal him, Nasan recovered her calm enough to realize he must be inside the building to her left. She pulled her head back, hunkered down to make sure she attracted no unwanted attention, and prepared to eavesdrop. Here, with her head pressed to the wall, the sounds of horses' hooves pawing the ground, the occasional whicker or snuffle, were clearly audible. She had guessed right: a stable.

She heard a mumbled protest from a voice she couldn't identify. A man's voice. One of Semyon's soldiers, probably.

"Don't try to plead for the wench," Semyon said. "She disobeyed me, and sending Timoshka after her is the least she can expect. If I want servants who argue with me, I'll hire them. That includes you, Stenka."

Stenka. Nasan remembered him. The stocky warrior she had seen on her previous visit, the guard who had defended Grusha. And Grusha, for two nights in a row, had not shown up, even though Semyon expected her. Odd.

No, not odd. Obvious. Daniil had returned to Moscow. Lying Daniil, who could do what he liked with Grusha in Nasan's absence and apparently was. No wonder Grusha stayed home.

Grusha and Daniil together. The thought made Nasan's teeth ache. At the same time, a fierce pride flooded her. She hadn't abandoned two babies in distress to satisfy her disloyal husband.

Stenka was speaking. "Yes, Lord. What should I do with the children until she arrives?"

Semyon snarled. "The brats will be safe enough in the storeroom till the wagon appears. If necessary, you can dose them yourself."

She had guessed correctly, then. Semyon did plan to move the children. But dose them? To keep them quiet, probably. It didn't sound safe.

She had no opportunity to find out more. A creaking door signaled Stenka's departure, then Semyon's. Crouched behind the stable, Nasan watched the two men cross the courtyard and climb the outside staircase. The moment they entered the main house, she darted for the next outbuilding.

Daniil turned a corner, his third since leaving the ramshackle hut where Grusha had, for whatever bizarre reason, decided to spend the night. He recognized this part of town. His grandfather had owned an estate nearby, although no one in the family had lived there in twenty years. Daniil's father had shown it to him when he was eight, and for a while he and Boris had turned it into their private castle—until Boris fell out of an ill-kept tree and broke his arm. Papa had forbidden the boys to play there afterward, although once in a while they defied him.

Strange how he'd forgotten that. Boris as an adult had radiated such an aura of piety that the moments of childhood disobedience slipped from view. Was that the key, then: that Boris had never been as good as he seemed? Semyon had described Boris as cowardly. But that was untrue. Boris hadn't enjoyed war, but he'd behaved well on the battlefield. Semyon twisted everything. Daniil could imagine the Boris who'd climbed those forbidden trees lying as part of a misguided plan to set Semyon straight. It felt like having his brother restored to him, without the halo.

Sounds of scuffle interrupted his reverie. Daniil followed the noise to the next cross-street. A middle-aged man—a peddler or artisan, Daniil deduced from his dress—struggled in the grip of two burly shadows, while another man calmly searched the victim's pack, ignoring his sputters.

Daniil grinned. His chance to play the hero.

Three against one, although the artisan appeared solid enough to provide some aid once Daniil distracted his captors. The man searching the pack looked short and scruffy—probably a dirty street fighter, like most of his kind, but within Daniil's means to overpower. The other two would offer a bigger challenge, but with the artisan's help, Daniil thought he could succeed. Difficult to tell, when he could see only shadows, but worth the attempt.

Bow or dagger? He could shoot from where he stood and hit his target, even in this light. But the knife gave him more options, including sheathing it unblooded. And it would raise fewer questions if he did use it.

That decided, Daniil propped his bow against a nearby building and pulled his dagger from its sheath. In the spirit of pure mischief he tugged on the golden lynx pendant, making sure no one could miss its gleam.

See what these thieves make of that!

He ran toward the trio. His boots padded against the wood. The looter was still intent on his task when Daniil knocked him out with a fist to the temple, felling him with a single punch.

He dropped into a crouch, assessing the two louts. Not as burly up close—layers of loose shirts expanded their underfed frames. From here, he could see their collar bones pressing against the skin of their necks. A quick feint, and he'd have them.

He gripped the dagger, preparing himself to lunge. But as he began his rush, the taller lout noticed him. The color drained from the man's face, and he gasped, "The Golden Lynx." He and his companion released their victim's arms and dashed down the street away from Daniil, whose mouth dropped open. His beautiful wife could inspire that kind of panic? What *had* she been doing?

The artisan was trying to hug him. Daniil fended the man off with assurances that he'd been happy to help. After a while, he extricated himself, returned his dagger to its sheath, slung his bow and quiver over his shoulder, and resumed his journey.

Two streets away, recalling the expressions on the louts' faces just before they ran, he burst out laughing. Two hardened criminals in desperate flight from a sixteen-year-old girl—what a story that would make.

He turned yet another corner, and the desire to laugh left him. Halfway down the street he saw his grandfather's estate. A villainous-looking thug strode purposefully toward it, dragging Grusha by the upper arm. She staggered at his side. Even from this distance Daniil could hear her weeping.

Despite having ended their affair, Daniil retained a certain fondness for Grusha—and besides, she belonged to his father. He wasn't going to stand by while some miscreant hauled her off to an unpleasant fate.

Miscreant? Daniil frowned. This man wasn't a stranger. Daniil had seen him this morning, in attendance on Semyon.

Semyon again. Everywhere he turned, he tripped over his cousin. Although where Grusha entered the picture, Daniil had no clue.

But he intended to find out. He juggled the dagger in his hands as he moved to intercept them.

Nasan took advantage of Semyon's and Stenka's retreat into the house to inch as fast as she could toward the storeroom where, she believed, her adversary held the kidnapped children. She had not forgotten the huge padlock she saw affixed to the door on her last visit. Without the key—or a handy cannon—she had no hope of opening the door. That meant she had to find a window. Or, in the likely event that the storeroom had none, a loose plank.

With Semyon's exit, the estate again fell into intense silence. The servants and soldiers Nasan had seen on previous nights gave no evidence of their presence. As she slid from one shadow to the next, she marveled at that lack of sound.

Circling the estate while hugging the outside wall helped her keep track of the warehouse she sought even as it prolonged her journey. At last, she stood behind the padlocked storeroom. A careful survey revealed no window in the back or sides. She did not bother to check the front of the building, which she had observed before. Instead she searched for a chink or weakness in the wooden panels.

Someone had repaired the storeroom, and not long ago. The outside wall—indeed, most of the estate—bore the air of neglect that characterized this entire region of the town. In contrast, the planks here came in two tones: gray and light brown. More evidence, if she needed it, that this warehouse served a special purpose.

As an experiment, she pressed a few of the older planks. It did not surprise her when they failed to yield: whoever had repaired the building must have tested them.

She checked the corners. Nothing. The boards, as high as she could reach. Still nothing. She had almost resigned herself to knocking on the door and running for cover when a knot in the wood caught her eye. About the width of her palm, it lay knee height from the ground. If she could remove it without breaking the silence, she might gain a peephole.

Nasan crouched and applied her dagger to the knot, working to pry it loose. Her hands trembled as the need to move fast warred with the desire to escape discovery. When at last the knot fell into her hand and she could peer through the rough oval she had created, she had to bite her lip lest an unwary gasp reveal her presence.

Light from a dozen lamps cast its glow over thick coverings of brocade and velvet. A bed piled high with pillows stood to one side. Nasan saw neither children nor yesterday's nursemaid. Booted feet, dangling swords, and leather jerkins obscured her vision.

She had found the missing guards.

Although Daniil ran at top speed, two houses still separated him from his goal when he saw the gate of his grandfather's estate open. Semyon's man shoved Grusha through and followed her.

Daniil heard the gate slam and the bar fall into place. He bent over, gasping for breath.

A heartrending wail split the air: "Master, save me." Apparently, Grusha had noticed him. The words unleashed a cacophony of pounding feet, crashing doors, and clanking that sounded like nothing so much as a troop of armed men.

More than anyone would need to subdue a single servant. Daniil didn't wait. He had no desire to end up captured, like Grusha.

A tree stood nearby. Its unclipped branches overhung his family's estate. He shinned up the trunk just before the troop burst onto the street.

The silence exploded, as if blasted by lightning. A distant slam preceded a woman's wail that set off howls within the warehouse. Nasan hadn't seen the children, but they were there. Through her knothole, she watched booted feet run out, leaving the door ajar. No padlock, after all.

Her chance had come. She darted around the building.

The sight in the courtyard would have daunted a less resolute heart. Eight fully armed men rushed the gate. The soldier Nasan remembered from Kasimov—Timoshka, the man she had kicked—stood over Grusha, who knelt amid the soldiers keening, "Master, save me." Nasan assumed the slave must be pleading with her god—unless she called to Semyon, who had reappeared, Stenka at his side, at the top of the outside staircase.

Too far away to hit with a thrown knife. If she had brought her bow...

But she had not, so she would worry about him later. Nasan drew her sword and raced for the half-open storeroom door. A shout from Semyon alerted the guards to her presence. Two turned to face her. Each of them, individually, would make a formidable opponent: taller than she by a head, with broad shoulders and powerfully muscled arms. Their flat faces menaced her.

Nasan retreated, sword at the ready, hoping to draw one of them into battle. The men approached from opposite angles, converging as they advanced. She retreated farther, projecting fear while forcing them into a tighter space. When she reached the point where they would have trouble swinging their weapons in a full arc, she smashed her sword against one man's helmet. The force of the blow set the weapon reverberating in her hands. She fought to stay upright, then silenced the steel by thrusting the sword into her second opponent's right arm.

He yelled and grabbed at the wound, but unlike his comrade, downed by her blow, he kept coming. She parried the dagger he held in his left hand, sliced him again—across the ribs this time—and danced away. He was bleeding heavily from her first strike. If she forced him to chase her, he would soon collapse from loss of blood.

It was a good plan, and it worked—until an arm closed round her waist from behind. The reek of sweat filled her nostrils, and a hated but familiar voice sounded in her ear. Before she could stop him, her captor ripped the scarf from her face and twisted her to face him.

"*Gospodi*, see what I have here," Timoshka said. "If it isn't the trooper's brat from Kasimov. How I have looked forward to running into *you* again."

For an instant that felt like a lifetime, Daniil, secure in his tree, stared in shock at the scene below. He had expected to see one villain dragging Grusha off to a deserted barn, presumably with the intention of raping her—a plan Daniil intended to foil. The addition of eight soldiers and his cousin Semyon forced him to recalculate.

Semyon. Soldiers. The unauthorized use of a family property. And those sounded like children's cries. Could Daniil, against the odds, have stumbled onto the kidnapped princes?

A devastating blow to their clan, if Semyon had arranged the abduction. Papa had blamed Koshkin, but Daniil saw no evidence of anyone but his cousin and his cousin's men.

The surprises had not ended. Light spilling from the half-open door of a warehouse illuminated a slender figure identifiable only by its outline. Sword in hand, the figure ran for the door, then veered off as a shout from Semyon sent two of the armed men after it.

As Daniil watched, the figure, clad entirely in black, its head swathed in scarves, lured two hulking soldiers into a trap, disabled them with its sword, and escaped without a scratch.

Then Grusha's captor released her, grabbed the figure from behind, and ripped off its mask—revealing the face of Daniil's exquisite Tatar wife. Grusha had led him to Nasan after all.

And Nasan fought well—how well amazed him—although she was lucky he had arrived when he did. No one could defeat so many opponents on her own. Never mind Semyon, whom Daniil could see descending the staircase at a leisurely pace, the other guard from this morning at his heels.

Semyon barked an order, and four soldiers scurried back to the warehouse. Grusha's keening intensified. Nasan struggled and kicked in her captor's hold, to no avail, although her attacks on his shins had him cursing.

Daniil pulled himself together. From the far end of the street, he heard the rumble of wagon wheels, but his wife's safety took precedence. While everyone else focused on Nasan, he dropped into the courtyard. Watching her writhe in the grip of Semyon's henchman, he pulled his bow from its case and an arrow from his quiver. As he moved toward the henchman, he was already calculating his line of attack.

"Give him here." Semyon hauled Nasan out of Timoshka's grip and shook her. "The boy from Kasimov! As if I'm not sufficiently cursed with troublesome brats. Well, you'll be sorry you crossed my path again. I'll see you in hell before the church bells ring."

To distract him, she spat Tatar insults while she plotted her escape. Her feet touched the ground and she could maneuver, but she would get only one chance. He was taller, heavier, and stronger than she. She couldn't afford a mistake.

Semyon spoke to Timoshka. "Shut that girl up. Where did you find her?"

"At the witch's house. About to run for the woods, I bet." Timoshka reached for Grusha, but she threw herself forward, arms outstretched against the dirt.

"He lies, Lord. I swear I meant to arrive before now."

Nasan moved her right foot a few inches, then her left, giving herself some purchase. When Semyon didn't react, she increased the distance between them by the width of several toes.

Semyon nudged Grusha with his foot. "Yes, yes. You and your excuses. I'll discipline you later. For now, get to work."

But the mention of discipline sent Grusha into renewed paroxysms of apology. She wept and pled while Nasan took advantage of each precious moment.

"Grandmothers, aid me," she mouthed to the dark.

Against the side of the warehouse, she saw a hint of movement, an alteration in the shadows, a hint of blond hair, a familiar face. She blinked, and the phantom Daniil disappeared.

Semyon lost patience. "Is this a bad joke? First we have this mischief maker creeping in." He shook Nasan for emphasis. "Then that miserable rainspout can't finish the job. Stenka, come and get the silly wench. Put her in the warehouse, hand her the vial, and watch her while she doses the boys. Can't you hear the wagon? We've no time to waste."

Timoshka hauled Grusha off the ground. Stenka moved toward them. Nasan braced herself, digging her booted toes into the mud. The spirit that had filled her in Kasimov flowed into her, revealing the crystalline structure governing the natural world. She opened her heart to the ancestor. Once again, the grandmothers had sent one of their own to assist her. Time slowed, and Nasan saw the path unroll before her. She took a deep breath.

The crunch of wagon wheels against wood grew louder. Daniil, masked, stepped from the shadows, bow loaded and one finger pulling the string to its fullest extent. His blond hair gleamed in the moonlight, as did the pendant around his neck. Unlike Nasan, who had dressed for stealth, he wore his lynx in full view. With a sensation akin to horror, she felt the ancestor retreat. Stenka said, "The Golden Lynx!"

Nasan muttered under her breath in Tatar. Semyon laughed. "Dolt. Don't you recognize my cousin? Daniil, stop playing games. You can't shoot me. I'm family, dammit."

Grusha wriggled in Timoshka's hold and stretched pleading arms toward Daniil. "Save me, Master. I love you."

Semyon's laughter turned into a guffaw. "Devil take you, girl, for the liar you are. *Love* him? You, who came to me of your own free will?"

Grusha slumped in Timoshka's hold and sobbed, "That was a mistake. I never wanted you."

With Semyon focused on Grusha and Daniil, Nasan saw her chance. Daniil's arrow had not wavered. Quick as thought, she twisted, kicked Semyon in the stomach, tugged herself free, and chopped her hand across his throat as he fell backward. She heard the twang as her husband loosed his arrow, but she kept running. Halfway to the warehouse, knife at the ready, she heard him call her name. Her birth name. She whirled.

Daniil raised a hand. His teeth flashed in the moonlight. Feathers protruded from Semyon's hip. Her adversary writhed on the ground, yelling in Russian. She didn't understand a word.

Shock froze her in place. Daniil had shot his own cousin to help her!

"Stop swearing," Daniil said to Semyon. "You'll survive. If I'd intended to kill you, you'd be dead already."

Semyon subsided to a grumble. Daniil pulled another arrow from his quiver and aimed it at Timoshka. The six remaining guards, two behind Timoshka and four between Stenka and the warehouse, regarded him with a wariness that did not speak well for their devotion to duty but heartened Nasan considerably.

"*Molodets!*" Daniil called to her. "Good work."

He couldn't disarm six men at once. Nasan hefted her sword and ran toward the two soldiers lurking behind Timoshka. She had almost reached them when she realized that the brown-haired warrior, Stenka, was heading in the same direction.

Chapter 25

DANIIL FOCUSED HIS ATTENTION ON THE APPROACHING guards. Somewhere in the back of his mind, an astonished voice remarked that he was counting on a girl to keep a pair of armed men at bay. He pushed the thought aside.

Two of the men were edging toward him. They had enough sense to move apart, making it more difficult for him to hit them both before one attacked him. But they underestimated Daniil's skill with the bow. He shot the first man in the fleshy part of his sword arm, forcing him to drop the weapon. The second man broke into a trot. Daniil grabbed another arrow, targeted the unprotected space between helmet and mail shirt, and eliminated his attacker.

The first man, swordless, tugged the arrow from his arm, causing a river of blood to gush down his sleeve. Bad move. He'd have done better to leave the arrow in place. He headed for Daniil with a lopsided stagger. It wasn't even a challenge. Daniil shot him in the leg, and he collapsed.

He targeted the remaining two guards, raising an eyebrow, daring them to fight. Anything to keep them from going after Nasan. But facing Daniil's withering fire and with their leader down, the guards ran. Daniil followed their progress with his bow until they passed through the gate.

Again he heard children crying. Semyon had mentioned boys, and it seemed ever more likely that he held the little princes. The wagon wheels Daniil had noticed earlier rumbled toward the gate. Grusha had subsided into watery sniffles. He couldn't see his wife, but the clanking of swords told him where she must be. Bow at the ready, he headed in her direction. Whether she wanted it or not, Nasan was about to get backup.

To avoid Stenka, Nasan altered her run. She came up behind the two guards while they were still staring at Daniil, placed her sword on the ground, pulled the scarf from her head, and jumped on the back of the man closer to her. While he turned in a circle, trying to buck her off, and (as planned) made it impossible for his companion to get a grip on her, Nasan twisted the scarf around his neck.

Ogodai had shown her this move long ago when they lived on the steppe. Wrapping one arm around the man's neck from behind and using it to twist the scarf, she felt for the great arteries that ran along both sides of his throat and compressed them. She didn't want to kill him, if she could help it—only to knock him out so that he couldn't hurt herself or Daniil. Stop the blood flow, and she would render him unconscious within moments.

It worked. The soldier went limp under her fingers. With a mental salute to her brother for insisting she practice, Nasan leaped away. She stuffed the scarf into her belt and swept her sword from the ground in time to parry the blow that the one remaining guard aimed her way.

He lunged, and she withdrew, then approached from a different angle, feinting at the last minute. The blades clashed, and she retreated again, assessing his skill.

He was good, the best opponent she had faced tonight. Controlled, knowledgeable. He hung back, evaluating her, too. He moved in, out—quick and steady, with a panache that spoke of solid training diligently applied. She became wary. Her warrior's crouch protected her midsection, but she needed more than defense. Victory demanded she identify flaws and exploit them.

The ancestor returned, directing her mind, showing her where to look. Her opponent lacked patience. Probably he underestimated her because she was small. Men often made that mistake. She had learned to turn that overconfidence to her advantage: he moved fast, but she outpaced him; his agility did not equal hers. She allowed him to drive her backward, as if he overpowered her—a tactic popular among Tatar warriors, who had long lured armies into the borderless steppe. This Russian soldier should have recognized the ploy. Instead he pursued her, exactly as she had hoped.

She drew him toward the corner where the walls met, eliminating his one advantage: a more powerful swing. The instant her back touched wood, she pushed off, hurtling toward his face with one booted foot extended, the other bent beneath her, her sword arm parallel to the leading leg. She let loose a mind-splitting shriek, the kind her people used in battle to intimidate the enemy.

For a crucial instant, her opponent went rigid. Nasan's foot connected with his jaw, and she slammed the blade of the sword against his skull. The force of her leap carried her over his tumbling body, and she hit the ground on the other side. The impetus sent her into a series of somersaults. The sword flew from her hand, and she ran back to retrieve it. Tightening her grip on the hilt, she raced for Timoshka. Halfway there, a thought occurred to her, and she spun on her heel to ensure no one was chasing her.

No need to worry. The fallen guardsman lay in a heap where she'd left him. Nasan pulled her scarf from her belt and wrapped it around her hair, then headed into the fray.

Expecting to see Nasan engaged in combat, Daniil drew up short and stared at the scene that met his eyes. The stocky guard who had followed Semyon from the house appeared to have switched sides. He was looming over his former comrade—the one who'd captured first Grusha, then Nasan, then Grusha again. Timoshka, Semyon had called him. Timoshka didn't cringe before the other man's clenched fists and scowl. He had Grusha in a choke-hold and his dagger at her throat. Her sobs had subsided into the occasional whimper.

An unearthly shriek split the air, and everything happened at once. Timoshka let go. The stocky guard grabbed Grusha with one hand and dragged her free. With the other he aimed a punch at Timoshka's chin. It didn't connect, because in the intervening instant Daniil fired, and Timoshka crashed to the ground, an arrow through his heart.

Daniil swiveled, aiming at the remaining guard. But he didn't shoot, because the man had both arms around Grusha and was patting her back, consoling her.

Nasan skidded to a stop beside him, then picked up the mask Timoshka had pulled off her earlier and tied it around her face. "What happened?" she asked.

"I don't know," Daniil said. "Did you hear that ungodly yell?"

She giggled, an oddly girlish sound under the circumstances. "I make ungodly yell."

He would have loved to find out more, but the wagon wheels had reached the gate. Daniil caught Nasan's arm with his left hand. "Keep an eye on the man with Grusha, and stay out of sight. That cart's about to enter." She nodded. He released her, and she slipped into the dark.

From her viewpoint outside lantern range, Nasan watched the cart trundle through the gates. It might have been the one that had delivered the children a few days before; she couldn't tell, since she hadn't had a clear glimpse of the driver then, and most wagons looked alike.

She could hear Stenka crooning to Grusha. They seemed oblivious both to her presence and to the approaching cart. "Come with me," he whispered. "I'll take care of you. No more Semyon Pavloviches. The games of princes aren't for you and me."

Grusha's reply was inaudible. Nasan listened with one ear but focused her attention on the wagon. The sturdy carthorse was not the same. Farmers and merchants generally owned only one. A different cart and different drivers, then.

That made sense. If they had come for the children—and what else would bring them, right when Semyon expected them?—then the man in charge would want to preserve his anonymity. He wouldn't use the same driver twice.

She checked the vicinity. To her right stood Daniil, bow in hand, a menacing outline in the dark. To her left and much closer, Stenka held his hand over Grusha's mouth. The slave made no sound; her rigid stance revealed her fear more clearly than words. Nasan gripped her sword, glad that *she* didn't need a man to defend her.

The wagon pulled up. A sturdy carter jumped from the seat with an oath. "What happened here?" He gestured at a scrawny tuft-haired youth climbing down from the wagon bed. "You, boy, help me check these bodies."

But the carters had not taken two steps before Daniil loosed a shot over the young man's head. The boy cried out and turned toward the source of the arrow, but Daniil had already cut across Nasan's line of sight and dispatched another. It skinned the driver's nose.

No fighters these. The carters dropped to the ground, faces buried in their arms. The carthorse charged across the courtyard, attaining an improbable speed for such an ungainly beast. Nasan, ignoring Daniil's orders to remain hidden, ran to stand over the carters. Confronted by a masked figure with drawn sword, they cowered.

The horse staggered to a stop, blown, just inside the gate. Edging around the carters, Nasan moved toward it. With so many bodies to transport, and the unknown children to return, she could imagine many uses for a horse and cart. She wanted to ask Daniil to watch the two cowering men but didn't know what to call him. She couldn't say "husband" under these circumstances.

She decided to think of him as Ogodai, for the moment. "*Aby*," she said, then recalled the Russian. "Brother, watch these men while I speak horse?"

"Brother!" Daniil laughed, and she flinched. Surely he would not reveal her identity to everyone in the courtyard.

He didn't. Instead he saluted her with the tip of his bow. "Dear comrade-in-arms," he said. "You honor me."

Ai, eni, no one should have that much charm. Especially a faithless husband.

The carters posed no obvious threat, but Daniil headed their way regardless. He had promised Nasan, who, in her own words, had gone to "speak horse." Indeed, it seemed an apt description. She stood patting the animal, addressing it in her native tongue. He could see that like Ogodai—like most Tatars, in fact—she had an almost magical rapport with horses. In no time, she gentled the massive beast and guided it toward him and his quarry. Semyon, who had lain quiet for a while, began mumbling again.

The mumbling sounded feverish. Daniil had seen enough wounds on the battlefield to guess that this one, although not life-threatening, might induce shock. He fended off a flash of guilt with the assurance that Semyon deserved worse. With luck, he'd be able to answer questions, of which Daniil had many.

He watched Nasan release the horse to munch whatever grass straggled through the ill-maintained logs that lined the yard. As she rejoined him, the carters raised their heads. The youth pointed at Daniil's pendant and poked his companion in the ribs. "Look, Granddad, the Golden Lynx."

Nasan hissed, and Daniil smiled. "Let them fool themselves, love," he murmured in her ear. "Best if the Lynx keeps her secret, don't you think?"

Her mouth dropped open. Daniil patted her rump, enjoying the effect of his statement. The men's awe fed his sense of the absurd.

Alas, in a courtyard littered with bodies, his cousin groaning on the ground, and even basic questions unanswered, personal concerns took second place. Reluctantly, he took charge once more.

Years of military service paid off. He spoke to the townsmen, infusing his voice with the same note of command he used in the field. "The Golden Lynx indeed. And I need your help, men. Are you with me?"

Nasan caught his sleeve. "Bad men. Work for enemy."

"We need them to drive the wagon," he said. "To transport Semyon, if nothing else. Trust me. They won't betray us."

"Semyon nothing," she said. "Transport *children.*"

Yes, the children. Well, that question he could ask. No answer mattered more. "The children. Where are they? *Who* are they?"

"There." She pointed at the warehouse. "Two. Small. I came to save."

Daniil stared at his cousin, mumbling on the ground. "Semyon has lost his mind. See to the children, sweetheart. We'll decide how to handle him later." Nasan ran for the warehouse, and he spoke to the townsmen. "You. Where were you heading?"

They hesitated. Daniil grabbed the older man by the collar and shook him. "Fight me, and you'll regret it."

His threat had the desired effect. "Dmitrov, Lord," the driver said when Daniil released him. "Those were our orders: pick up a load and take it to a cabin on the Dmitrov road. Someone will meet us there. No questions, no delays. No one said anything about children."

"The Dmitrov road," Daniil mused. "Where on the Dmitrov road?"

"Not quite sure, Lord," the driver said. "A turnoff marked with a red ribbon, about one-fourth of the way."

"And who gave you those orders? Is he here?" Ridiculous to hope someone else had arranged this scheme. Anyone but Semyon.

The carter looked around. "Don't see him, Lord. Tough to tell, with a dozen bodies. But he gave his name as Stenka."

Stenka. The man who'd changed sides. More evidence against his cousin. Daniil surveyed the courtyard, but Grusha and Stenka had gone. No wonder, if the carters could identify him.

They couldn't escape. The Kolychevs would have to track them down. Daniil's view of Grusha as an unwilling victim had dissolved in the face of Semyon's obvious familiarity, his assumption that he need only order the girl to do her part.

Another point to consider later. Although he and Nasan had eliminated the immediate threat, solving the problem posed by the children couldn't wait. And as the carters had noted, the courtyard contained an array of bodies, some living, some dead. Four guards, Timoshka, Semyon himself. Daniil ordered the carters to bind any guard able to move. He kept an eye on them while he went to examine Semyon. No point in letting them disappear as well.

He found his cousin flat on his back and looking distinctly pale. No need to bind him. At his approach, Semyon raised his head and spat in the direction of Daniil's boots. "Whoreson. What kind of man shoots his own cousin?"

Not as incapacitated as he looked, then.

Daniil did not respond in kind. That Semyon could remain truculent after what he'd done defied belief. "What have you been up to, Semyon?" he asked. "Begin with the children."

But as the words left his throat, Nasan emerged from the warehouse. She raced across the short distance that separated them and dragged at his hand. "Come quick. Must see!"

Chapter 26

NASAN TUGGED HER HUSBAND TOWARD THE WAREHOUSE DOOR. "Children here. Big one tell she is grand prince."

Daniil stopped short inches from the entrance. "So it's true." As he reached past her, his hand slipped and the door hit the inside wall with a crash. The baby howled. Nasan went to comfort him. The child screamed louder, and she ripped off her mask. She should have realized it would frighten a baby.

"You expect this?" she asked over her shoulder. Daniil removed his mask too.

"Papa told me they were missing." He sounded dazed. "We've been looking for them. And you found them."

"Semyon take them."

"Yes, Semyon took them. I'm trying to get used to the idea." He kicked the door jamb with the toe of his boot. "He's endangered us all. Even you. Papa will turn into smoke and fly up the chimney when he hears."

Unsure how to comfort him—or even whether she should try—Nasan knelt on the rug. Life in the harem had given her some experience with screaming infants. Deciding that picking the baby up would only upset him further, she patted his back. After a few moments, the three-year-old who had identified himself as the grand prince clambered into her lap. The baby quieted and stuck a thumb in his mouth. Daniil's next words reverberated in the silence.

"We can drive them straight to the Kremlin, but Papa will never forgive me if we don't warn him first. So let's stop at the house and see if he's there." He glanced over his shoulder. "Good work, men," he called. "Put that big blond in the wagon, please. Lay the others in a row. We'll collect them later."

"Man near fence," Nasan said. "I send sleep with foot. And another." She grabbed her neck and imitated strangulation.

Daniil raised an eyebrow but relayed the information. "I should monitor them. They haven't much reason to help us, and we need the cart."

"Grusha sees children," Nasan reminded him. "Talk, maybe."

"Grusha left. So did that man she was with. He hired the cart, it turns out."

"Stenka. He say her go with him."

"You couldn't stop them?"

Nasan shook her head. "Leave when I not see."

"Of course. I didn't see them, either."

"You sad?" Nasan bit her lip, wishing she could recall the question. But if they did not solve these issues now, when would they? Better the truth, however painful.

"No." He took two quick steps toward her, then stopped in the doorway. "You misunderstood, that day. I felt sorry for her, that's all. Someone had hit her. I can't imagine how she let herself get entangled in this plot, but I'm glad she's gone."

"Oh," Nasan said. Images clashed in her head. She had thought he loved Grusha, but he had only pitied her. He didn't care that Grusha had run away. And he had fought by her side like a comrade. The contradictions left her feeling young and confused.

He turned away, and she remembered her unspoken confession. "Husband, wait. Must tell." She stopped, afraid of his reaction.

"What, sweetheart?"

"Semyon," she stammered. "Who said cousin."

"He is my cousin. What of him?"

Better the truth, even a bad truth. "*He* kill Girei. My family—mistake. Not Boris. Cousin. No need to marry."

His hand clenched on the door jamb, and she choked, anticipating rejection. Resolve it now, she told herself sternly. No more secrets between us.

"When did you find out?"

"After you go. Here. Think him dead before."

Daniil bit his lip and glanced over his shoulder once more, then crossed the room and clasped Nasan's left hand. Her right encircled the grand prince, who stared woodenly at the stranger. His baby brother had fallen asleep, exhausted by crying.

"Our fathers would have married us anyway, love," Daniil said. "If Semyon had died instead of Boris, I would still have been the only unwed male in my clan. But I'm glad you can vouch for Boris. That's where I went, to find out what happened. I never believed he could murder—not a boy your brother's age. Not for revenge." He bent and kissed her, hard.

A huge weight lifted from her heart. Nasan said, "Oh, Daniil."

"Yes." He studied her as if he wished to say much more. "We need time alone. But the children come first. And the clan: we must undo the damage Semyon has caused. Can you bring the grand prince?" He scooped up the baby and headed for the warehouse door.

Nasan struggled to her feet and stretched out her hands to Grand Prince Ivan. "My Lord, permit? We take you home." He held up his arms, and she lifted him, balancing him on her hip as she had seen *Ana* do a thousand times. As quickly as she could, she made her way across the floor.

Daniil had not traveled far. She caught up with him near the wagon. Inside the cart, bound feet kicked the air and the occasional groan sounded. "I ride with you?" she asked.

"To our house. Then I want you out of it."

"But—"

Daniil cut her off. "Think, love. Semyon already named me. I have nothing to hide, so let me handle this. You can keep your secret."

He had said as much earlier, yet she still had trouble believing it. It contradicted everything her parents had taught her. "You won't fight me?"

"There's a price, wife of mine. But yes, if you agree to my terms, I won't fight you about the Golden Lynx." He flicked a finger against her cheek. "The men are ready. Let me see if I can find a pair of horses. The grand princess must be frantic. Let us reassure her."

Wordlessly, Nasan pointed to the stables where she had heard Semyon talking with Stenka.

Daniil beckoned to one of the carters. When the man came running, he handed him the sleeping child. "Change of plans," Daniil said. "We're heading for the marketplace, then up the hill. The man who hired you, Stenka, what did he promise you for this job?"

"A Novgorod ruble each."

What insanity was this? A Novgorod ruble, worth twice a Moscow ruble, paid a carter's bills for a year. Stenka didn't command such resources, either on his own behalf or as Semyon's representative. Someone else must hold the purse strings.

Daniil's heart lightened. True, Semyon's involvement reflected badly on the Kolychevs, whoever else had taken part. But Daniil and Nasan's role in saving the children might offset Semyon's villainy, especially if the family could prove that its one bad apple had been corrupted by an outside force.

Fortunately, Daniil's branch of the clan commanded greater wealth than its most disreputable member. "Serve me well," he told the carter, "and I'll match his fee."

The man panted like an enthusiastic hound.

"Good," Daniil said. "Hold that babe for a moment while I saddle the horses. And don't try anything." He waved his bow at Nasan for emphasis. "My colleague here will watch you."

"No trouble here, Lord." The carter looked surprised at the very idea. "It's an honor to help the Golden Lynx, so it is. And I want my Novgorod ruble, too."

Daniil slapped his shoulder. "Good man. I won't disappoint you."

Daniil returned with two saddled horses, his lynx pendant no longer visible. Nasan mounted, and he lifted the grand prince to sit in front of her. He wrapped the baby in his jacket and held him. He nodded to the carters to set off; then he and Nasan fell into place behind them. Only the clopping of hooves and the trundle of cartwheels broke the silence.

Nasan, one arm cradling a sturdy waist, relished the heavy weight of the child's head against her ribs. Here in this moment between one resolution and another, with Daniil riding at her side but not speaking, she let herself imagine bearing a child. Their child. What would motherhood be like? She refused to live like the harem women, but Daniil had said he would not object to her remaining the Golden Lynx. If she accepted his terms. Whatever they turned out to be.

Could she accept, though?

An important question, but it could wait. In the wagon Semyon rolled from side to side, emitting the occasional groan. A deep sense of satisfaction flowed through her as she let herself feel the defeat of her enemy. She had won!

Her contentment communicated itself to the little prince—or perhaps he liked the thought of going home. Either way, when they reached the lighted gates of the Kolychev estate, the plan to leave Nasan there suffered a major setback. "I command you, slave," Grand Prince Ivan told her in his piping treble. "You, not these others. Take me home at once. What is your name?"

Nasan conquered her urge to laugh at his arrogance. Khans, even ones as small as this, did not appreciate people laughing at them. "Girei, Lord," she said with as much solemnity as she could muster. Over the child's head, she looked at Daniil, sure he could see the mischief on her face. "She say. We do."

"You must obey me," Ivan announced. "I am ruler of all Russia." He added, "My mama says so," which rather spoiled the effect. Nasan watched her husband's teeth flash in the lantern glow.

"Indeed you are, My Lord," Daniil said. He glowered at Nasan, who could not suppress the smile tugging at the corners of her mouth. "Very well, Girei, you may accompany us."

But the child's voice had drawn the attention of the Kolychev guards, and one of them fetched Nikolai. Or so Nasan concluded when the oak gates swung open as rapidly as anything that heavy could, revealing a father-in-law standing with crossed arms and an irate expression. His appearance led to the second change of plans.

"So there you are, you young rascal. You've worried your mother half-sick," Nikolai said in greeting. He looked at Nasan, and one eyebrow rose. "*Bozhe moi*, what have we here? Damn it, Daniil, you swore to me…" His gaze traveled down to the child she held, and his second eyebrow joined the first. He stepped back and ushered them in with one sweeping gesture. "Please."

Nikolai would not hear of them taking his nephew to the Kremlin, whatever his crimes. "He'll end up there soon enough," he told Daniil. "But bad or good, he's family, and I can't let him go to jail with that wound untreated. Your mother will care for him while I talk to the grand princess. As head of the clan, I have to answer for his behavior." He scowled at his recumbent nephew.

Semyon had lost the power to argue. He lay silent as servants lifted him from the cart and carried him to a storeroom so that

Natalya could remove the arrow. "There are four more wounded at Grandfather's estate," Daniil said. "Two dead."

That set off another round of paternal swearing on the theme of ingrates who used family property in their nefarious schemes, but Nikolai eventually calmed enough to order a pair of his own servants to accompany the carters while they retrieved the injured and dead with their now-empty wagon.

Natalya appeared at the top of the stairs. Daniil nudged Nasan and her horse into a dark corner and kept her there, using his own mount as a barricade. She didn't resist. He assumed she had no more desire than he did to reveal her escapades to the rest of the household.

The grand prince grew restive. Nasan murmured to him in a mixture of Tatar and Russian. It sounded reassuring, whatever she said. But they had to resolve this soon. A three-year-old's patience doesn't last long.

"Papa," he said. Nikolai looked round. The servants had crossed to where Natalya stood at the foot of the stairs. She pointed to the open door, waved an acknowledgment at her husband and son, then followed the servants into the storeroom.

"We need to return the princes," Daniil said. "What of Semyon? How can we leave him here?"

"I'll set guards," Nikolai said. "And come with you. I must stand surety for him. As if he has not already cost me enough, that one. But your *companion* should stay."

Daniil didn't miss the stressed word or the protests it elicited from the shadows behind him. "That was my plan," he told his father, "but my other companion refuses to allow it. Girei must accompany us, I fear."

Nikolai grunted. "Very well. Then let's not delay." He gestured to a groom, who ducked into the stables and returned with a saddled horse and a sash. Another command sent two sentries from the walls to guard the storeroom. Nikolai secured his robes, placed his slippered foot in the stirrup, and mounted. A jerk of his head summoned them to follow as he headed for the street. Daniil nudged his horse away from Nasan's, and the procession— minus one miscreant and the cart—resumed its journey toward the Kremlin.

They had only a short distance to traverse: across the wooden street that cut the marketplace, empty at so late an hour; through the main gates and over the moat. Daniil wondered what Nasan made of the fortress. He doubted she'd ever seen the inside— he hadn't taken her there since their wedding, and he didn't think she had visited Moscow before. He really needed time to ask her a few pertinent questions.

Nasan regarded the reception area with a mixture of awe and astonishment. How could anyone create a room so magnificent yet at the same time so tasteless? Although richly decorated, the palace lacked the harmony of Muslim architecture—its lightness, its grace, its perfect proportions. Here no opaline swirls of marble refracted with lunar subtlety the rays that pierced filigreed walls, no turquoise tiles glowed more intensely blue than the sky above them, no looping black-dotted calligraphy captioned brilliant miniatures of everyday life. Here squat pillars and arched ceilings extinguished any stray moonbeam that managed to struggle through the tiny panes. Hanging iron chandeliers radiated golden circles that offset the gloom only in their immediate vicinity. Glittering paint and crimson carpets conveyed an oppressive opulence. And holy images, everywhere—saints, angels, monks, princes, the Son and His Mother loomed over her wherever she looked: gilt on gilt, scarlet alternating with sky-blue and green, pearls competing with gemstones. Yet this was obviously a throne room, not a church. A lifetime would not be long enough for her to understand these Christians.

She did not share her thoughts with the elegant blonde, ethereal in sky-blue silk, who sat on her carved throne, her hands clutching the arms of the ceremonial chair as if contradicting her expressionless face. Other than the grand princess, the only occupant of the room was a handsome, brooding man of about forty. From what Daniil had told her as they crossed the marketplace, she guessed that the man, dramatic in green velvet with a sable collar, was Prince Ivan Telepnev, whom the gossips dubbed the grand princess's lover. Tall, well formed, with dark brown hair frosted with silver and green eyes, he stood at Elena's side, occasionally leaning over to murmur in her ear.

More guards had met them before they entered the room. Nikolai ordered them to collect Semyon's bound and wounded soldiers when the carters arrived. Nasan wondered how many of Semyon's men would see the morning, only a few hours away. The kidnappers of khans could expect a painful and dishonorable death, but it seemed harsh to punish the servants when the master lay in relative comfort under Natalya's care.

Grand Prince Ivan wriggled in Nasan's arms. When she put him down, he ran to the throne, shouting, "Mama, I'm back. These people saved me. Yuri, too."

Grand Princess Elena's austere face crumpled into a mixture of laughter and tears. She scooped Ivan onto her lap. Chubby arms encircled her neck as she kissed him. "Well, my dove, Mama is very, very glad to see you. What an adventure you've had. Are you well?"

"Yes, Mama," he said. "A bad man took me, and I missed you. Yuri cried a lot, but I was brave as could be. Then Girei came, and he and his friends brought me back to you."

"You were brave, indeed, my child. And which one is Girei?"

Daniil clasped Nasan's hand as the child pointed her out. From the strength of his grip, she could guess he was anxious. He wanted her part in this rescue kept secret.

Perhaps she, too, should feel anxious. Unlike her father-in-law and her husband, she had no personal acquaintance with Russia's royal family, and the tales one heard of their intrigues did not inspire confidence. But Nasan had one asset denied to her in-laws. She had grown up a Tatar khan's daughter, a descendant of Genghis, raised to rule a state even more cutthroat in its politics than this one. Her birth made her Elena's equal. In response to the grand princess's summons, she freed her hand from her husband's, walked forward, and bowed.

Elena regarded her critically. "They call you Girei? Who is your father?"

Nasan studied Elena. Her haughty expression could not conceal the strain she had suffered: blue circles shadowed her cheeks; small lines creased her full mouth. Strain caused by Semyon, who had killed the original Girei.

Elena couldn't know that the man who had abducted her children had slaughtered a fourteen-year-old boy without compunction or regret. But she must have guessed that their lives hung by a thread. Only by chance had Nasan discovered the children in time to save them, and even that plan might have failed had Daniil not intervened.

She thought of her mother, keening over her son's dead body. Of herself, her false calm shattered by the sound of a kettle drum breaking. Of Ogodai and Bulat, roaring in fury and sorrow. And of Daniil and his family, also caught up in Semyon's drive for revenge.

She had sought vengeance, too, but she found it in restoring these two children to their mother's arms so that Elena would not grieve as Nasan and Daniil and their families had grieved. The ancestors had shown her the path to salvation, allowed her to atone for the death of Girei.

Allahu akbar. God is great. Despite her conversion, the words came in Arabic first.

Nasan made a decision. Her father-in-law might hate it. Her husband certainly would. But whatever happened, even if it cost Nasan her cherished freedom, it was the right thing to do.

"Grand Princess," she said, in her very best Russian. "Please be so kind as to listen, and I will tell you the whole."

Chapter 27

DANIIL WATCHED AS TELEPNEV BENT TO WHISPER IN THE grand princess's ear. Elena's grip slackened, and young Ivan slipped from her lap and ran to Nasan, who picked him up and hugged him. "Not tired, My Lord?" she asked.

As if reminded of the late hour, Elena beckoned. "You. Daniil Nikolaevich. Were you not among the guardsmen last fall?"

"Indeed, My Lady." He inclined his body as much as he could while cradling Prince Yuri in his left arm.

"Then the layout of the palace should be familiar to you. Find the children's nurse and bring her here." Her harsh features softened once more. "But first, give Prince Yuri to me. I would assure myself that he has suffered no harm from his confinement."

Daniil placed the child in his mother's arms. His own ached after almost an hour of baby tending, yet he felt an unexpected reluctance to relinquish his charge.

He was getting soft. As he went to perform the task laid on him by his sovereign, he hoped Nasan could keep herself out of trouble until he returned.

He didn't have far to go. As he reached the door, a rotund noblewoman rushed in, a swirl of lawn scarves and rose silk. A girl in a high-waisted robe trailed her. The noblewoman—Agrafena Cheliadnina, the children's nurse—paid him no heed as she sailed past.

"Is it true?" she asked. "Have my dearest falcons returned to the palace?"

Nasan placed the grand prince on his feet. The boy raced, arms outstretched, toward Agrafena, but she, despite her bulk, moved faster. He had crossed just one section of carpet when she swept him up in her arms. A flurry of baby talk ensued, mingled with giggles and cooing.

Eventually, Agrafena retreated with the child clutched in her arms. Elena beckoned to the girl, who accepted the gift of a sleeping infant and followed her mistress from the room. Only then could Nasan begin her tale in her odd, halting Russian, which Daniil had to help her sort out if any of them were to follow her story. He, no less than the grand princess, had questions he wanted answered. How had Nasan discovered the kidnapping? What set her on Semyon's trail in the first place?

First, she explained how Semyon had ambushed her and her brother in Kasimov, her own escape and Girei's death at Semyon's hands, her family's error and the raid and marriage that followed. Elena shuddered. Daniil, too. Terrible to think of his bride witnessing such a scene.

The story switched to Moscow, with Nasan following a surreptitious someone from the Kolychev estate, only to discover that her brother's killer still lived.

Hmm. A few points missing there. How she slipped from the estate at night. Where she obtained men's clothes and weapons. Which surreptitious someone?

Grusha, probably. Daniil did not ask, reluctant to increase the burden on Nasan, whose shock at learning the truth was audible. He understood *that*, too. Princesses usually married strangers, often hostile ones, but to survive such an assault, think yourself safe, and sacrifice your future for peace, only to discover the villain alive and as rambunctious as ever—where had his wife found the courage to continue? Yet Nasan had not only gone on but brought the battle into enemy territory. One had to admire her.

Elena, too, seemed captivated. At first incredulous when "Girei" identified himself as a woman (a glimpse of Nasan's bound hair solved that problem), the grand princess slowly warmed to her unconventional guest. As the story progressed, she leaned forward. Her clasped hands tightened and released as the tension in the tale rose and fell.

Nasan ended her account with a flourish, emphasizing the help Daniil had provided while avoiding mention of the Golden Lynx. But just when he thought the story finished, she produced a surprise. "I heard another. Who gave this Semyon orders. Not there tonight."

"You can't identify him?" Elena asked.

"No. Hide in the dark."

"Someone wealthy," Daniil interjected. "The carters' fee was exorbitant. More than my cousin could cover."

"Koshkin," Nikolai exclaimed.

"Nonsense," Elena said. "Why him, and no other? Your nephew bears the blame here, Nikolai Borisovich. Don't cast aspersions. Why, Koshkin himself offered to find my sons."

"An easy promise to make," Telepnev noted, "if he arranged the abduction. He did argue for Yuri's release—quite fervently, too—just yesterday."

"Perhaps," Elena admitted. "Summon him, Telepnev. But I would hear Nikolai Borisovich explain his reasoning."

Telepnev relayed her orders to the troops standing at the door. Nikolai stepped forward, hand over his heart, and bowed. "Alas," he said, in tones that bespoke great self-control, "the answer lies with the character of my nephew, Semyon Pavlovich. You know him, Grand Princess."

She frowned. "I do. Semyon Pavlovich. He stood guard here. I have not seen him in weeks."

"Because Koshkin recruited him as an assistant," Nikolai said. "Yet Koshkin has no love for my clan, despite the match that bound his daughter and my son. And, may the saints forgive me,

Semyon lacks both scruples and intelligence. I find it difficult to imagine a man as clever as Koshkin recruiting Semyon for any lawful purpose."

"Then we must question your nephew. Find out what Koshkin required of him. In which jail did you place him?"

"We have him at my estate, for the moment."

Elena emitted a yelp of outrage, and Nikolai hurried to explain. "Under guard. Daniil shot him to prevent him from hindering the rescue of your sons. My wife tends his wound. We will question him for you or surrender him, as you direct."

"Question him, then surrender him." Elena's hauteur had returned in full force. "A patrol will call for him. A man so base cannot remain free. You disappoint us, Nikolai Borisovich!"

"My apologies, Grand Princess." Nikolai's flush darkened until Daniil feared for his health. "I don't excuse his crimes."

"No," Elena said. "For your own sake, I hope not. As the head of his clan, you answer for his misdeeds."

So much for their efforts. Right then, Daniil would gladly have strangled his cousin Semyon.

Nasan forced herself to stand straight. With her grand tale told, she experienced a letdown. She had worked hard, risked much, and succeeded. With Daniil's help, she had rescued the children, thwarted Semyon. Grusha had run away, and Daniil said he didn't care. She was not an outcast. Her husband supported her. The grandmothers had aided them both.

It was too much to take in. Words sang in the back of her head, begging for her attention, while the present unrolled before her, demanding with equal firmness that she keep her wits about her.

Danger threatened once more. Daniil and Nasan had rescued the princes, but suspicion lingered in Elena's eyes. Nikolai stood stolid as the massive beeches of the Kasimov forest, whatever anxiety he felt invisible to the eye. "Semyon didn't confide in me, My Lady," he said. "He walks his own path. He lied to me about killing the Tatar boy. He let my older son die for his crime. He almost reignited the feud at the marriage of these two"—he indicated Daniil and Nasan—"as we were making peace. I don't consider him a credit to my line. But I will stand surety for him."

Nasan knew about surety. Natalya had explained the practice to her. So she could imagine Nikolai's anger. No one wanted to put up a large sum of money to guarantee the good behavior of a man he despised, but as head of the clan Nikolai had no other choice.

"My son and I do not accept surety," Elena said silkily. "Not in this case. You have already proven you can't control him. We will order him knouted—we have no doubt of his guilt, since your son and daughter-in-law caught him redhanded. Ask him about the voice in the dark. If he answers, good. We will take that into account when we sentence him. If not, the bailiffs will question him, and he will pay the price of defiance."

"Agreed," Nikolai said. "But if he survives the knouting, may I suggest a monastery? In the Far North, perhaps?"

Nasan, standing shoulder to shoulder with Daniil, heard him choke. He turned it into a cough when Elena turned her elegant brows in his direction. Nasan, thinking of Solomonida airily describing her husband's exploits with servants—and what a delicious revenge if Semyon, who had threatened to immure his wife in a convent, ended up tonsured!—had to admit that a monastery would constitute, for Semyon, an inspired penalty. For herself, though, would tonsuring and exiling Semyon be enough? Could it satisfy her family? The grandmothers?

As Nikolai had noted, Semyon might not survive flogging with the knout, a heavy knotted whip that could kill if Grand Princess Elena chose to order it so. And if Nasan explained that Semyon would rather die than suffer the fate his uncle planned for him—no fine food, no women, nothing but fasting, work, and prayer—her family would accept the sentence as a fitting retribution. Nasan decided she could live with it, too.

The grand princess had yet to respond. She frowned at the painted saints on the walls, studied the Kolychevs as if debating whether she could trust them. Nasan tried not to fidget, conscious she had nothing to hide but less certain that Elena believed her. She felt as taut as her own bowstring by the time the grand princess spoke.

"It may suffice," Elena said, "if you select the most stringent hermitage you can discover."

"I thought of Pechenga," Nikolai said. "The monk Trifon built a few cells there last year. He wishes to convert the Lapps to Christianity. They say the sun never rises in winter nor sets in summer, that beyond the shores lie only walruses and white bears. Even Semyon must discover remorse in such a place."

Elena nodded. "Very well. If he survives. But first, the interrogation. Find out what you can. In the hour after noon, our patrol will remove him from your home."

"I will see to it," Nikolai said with a bow. "If you will excuse us."

But Elena did not excuse them, because at that moment Telepnev returned, alone. "Where is Koshkin?" she demanded.

"Last seen heading for the Dmitrov road."

Nasan, hearing an echo of her own satisfaction in the favorite's voice, wondered. It sounded as if the Kolychevs might have a high-placed protector—and Koshkin a powerful enemy.

"Dmitrov," Elena said. "That is indeed suspicious."

"Yes," Telepnev said. "Will you permit me to send a patrol?"

Elena nodded. "See to it. Lead it, and include this young man." She gestured at Daniil. "Set everything up and return for him."

Telepnev left, and Elena beckoned. "Nikolai Borisovich." Nasan's father-in-law stepped forward. "You have not hidden your nephew's guilt. For that act of courage, we absolve you. Although we will be watching you—and your clan." His cheeks turned faintly purple, but he thanked her.

Her clear gaze swept over Nasan and Daniil. "Your children have earned a reward. You, whom they call Irina."

"Yes, Grand Princess," Nasan said.

"You are a Tatar. From Kasimov, you said."

"I am Bulat Khan's daughter."

"Daniil Nikolaevich," Elena said. "I relieve you of your current service assignment and appoint you to accompany my next diplomatic embassy to Kazan."

As Daniil thanked her, Nasan saw the grand princess's haughty face, until now relaxed only when she greeted her children, dissolve into a smile of pure mischief. "I have but one condition," Elena said. "You must take your wife. I know that is not usual, but her knowledge of the local customs and language will be an invaluable asset to you."

Nasan gripped her elbows. Go, not home exactly but to a place so like home as to make no difference? Hear the muezzin call once more, surround herself with familiar smells and tastes and, more precious still, the sounds of her native tongue? See her birth family, live among their ancestral lands and spirits? And with a husband who had given *some* evidence that he appreciated her true self? The grandmothers loved her indeed.

Daniil caught her right hand in his left, and together they faced Russia's regent. "It would be a great honor, My Lady," he said. "And if my wife may accompany me, a great pleasure also. We will serve you to the best of our ability."

Elena, restored to gracious condescension, tipped her head a few inches toward them. "We expect no less. And now, my Kolychevs, you may go. Telepnev is waiting for you, Daniil Nikolaevich."

Telepnev met them in the corridor. "Come with me, Daniil Niko-laevich. Your father may leave. Does your companion ride with us?"

"No," Daniil said.

Nasan tugged at his sleeve. "You are tired, too."

He brushed her cheek with his finger. She knew he wouldn't kiss her here, in the royal apartments, with her dressed as a boy and people surrounding them, but she could tell from the way he licked his lips that he wanted to. She leaned toward him, then drew back when she realized what she was doing.

"You have been more than valiant, Girei," he said. "But please, let me finish this task alone. Papa needs your help. This ride is nothing. We find Koshkin and question him. You can stand aside without dishonor."

Nasan hesitated, but Daniil's phrasing acknowledged her as a partner. And he'd been most generous this evening—treating her as an equal, praising her skills, hinting that she could remain the Golden Lynx with his blessing.

For a price. Again she wondered what price he had in mind.

No doubt she would find out soon. Here she didn't need to prove herself. "Yes," she said. "I do as you ask." She gripped his forearm. "But please, Daniil, take care."

His fingers closed over hers, and he bent to whisper in her ear. "Don't worry. I have every intention of coming home to you unscathed."

Telepnev signaled, and Daniil released her hand and moved to join him. Nikolai, who had waited silently, caught Nasan's elbow and ushered her through the door.

"I don't think we should tell your mother-in-law about this," he said as they reached the courtyard. "Of course, we can't hide Semyon's foolishness and Daniil's part in preventing disaster." He flicked Nasan's black shirt with one finger. "But—and don't think I am less than proud of you, Irina—your running about the town in men's clothes might be better concealed."

Nasan had her doubts, but she didn't argue. Nikolai knew Natalya best. If he believed she couldn't accept the Golden Lynx, Nasan was in no hurry to confess. "I go home as usual," she told Nikolai. "Dress as woman. Then talk."

He agreed with enthusiasm, so, a few streets from the Kolychev household, Nasan waved goodbye. Stopping to retie the mask around her face, she saw his head turn, searching for her, and laughed soundlessly. She could still, if she wished, elude pursuit.

Leaving him behind, she ran lightly through the few remaining streets between herself and the Kolychev estate.

Chapter 28

THE POUNDING HOOVES OF TWO DOZEN STEEDS, THE CHILL OF the dawn breeze against his face, the intermittent odor of horse dung, the clank of armor and weaponry—Daniil, riding amid the small contingent of troops, felt himself back on campaign. His current journey was a campaign of sorts, an attempt to right a wrong and bring a villain to justice while redressing the injury done to the honor of his clan. If the rulers of Russia couldn't rely on those who swore fealty to them, how could they govern? That the present ruler had yet to attain maturity meant nothing. If every man abandoned one leader for another who suited him better at a given moment, the system would revert to the chaos of the past. Koshkin should know that.

Semyon, too. Yet his cousin had not cared how much damage he inflicted on his family. The tangle of murder, revenge, plots, kidnapping, and betrayal undercut Daniil's sense of how the world worked. The faith that had carried him through his nineteen years— already tested by his discoveries about his brother—crumbled on that isolated stretch of dirt road, meandering like a river through the forests that ringed the Russian capital.

The troops led by Telepnev were traveling due north from Moscow. Men carrying lanterns on long poles rode on both sides, but the need to avoid stray stones, tree roots, and depressions in the soil constrained the troops' speed. As the sky above the rustling birches shaded from black to gray, they could progress faster. Already Daniil could detect the thinning branches that indicated a peasant hamlet, past or present. One glimpse of a nobly caparisoned saddle horse, and they had found their quarry.

If Daniil had charge of the mission, he would have commandeered the wagon and used it to trick Koshkin into revealing himself. If he had served with Telepnev before, he might have suggested that course. As things stood, he kept his mouth shut, followed orders, and kept an eye open for the slightest sign that a nobleman and his party had recently passed this way.

The Kolychev household showed no more activity than was normal for this hour of the night. Nasan glimpsed the faint glow of dawn against the horizon. If she had already returned to the Tatar lands—she could hardly wait for her journey to Kazan—she would be anticipating the morning call to prayer.

A cluster of lanterns marked the storeroom where she had last seen Natalya and Semyon. The guards had collapsed into their usual slump. Nasan climbed the fence and scaled the wall to her room. No one challenged her. No outraged mother-in-law or inquisitive sister-in-law popped out to scold the prodigal bride. Grateful for the reprieve, she slipped inside and shut the window.

Someone had propped the spirit doll against the brass mirror. Nasan rushed to the doll and cradled it against her chest. After murmuring her thanks, rubbing grease across its lips, and promising to burn incense for it tomorrow, she returned the doll to the dresser, then changed clothes as swiftly as she could. Unwinding her double braids, she left them uncovered, grabbed the first veil she saw, and tied it around her waist, in case she had to hide her face from Semyon, then made her way to the corridor. She wanted to know what was happening.

When she reached Natalya's sitting room, Nasan stopped. No flicker of candle flame hinted at a human presence. Maria's door remained closed. The strengthening sun, etched in stripes across the floor, made it possible to walk without bumping into walls, but Nasan could see only outlines of slippered feet beneath her robes. It seemed unlikely that anyone occupied the silent sitting room. She headed for the stairs.

The bells rang, harsh and clear, for prime as she reached the courtyard. The creak of a gate, the blast of outside air, and the shuffle of slippers on wood signaled the arrival of Daniil's father. He beckoned to her as she entered his line of sight—just as if they had not spent the last few hours together—and set off for the storeroom. Nasan lifted her long skirts and ran to catch up with him.

Natalya met them at the door. She wore a full robe over lace-trimmed sleeves; and her hair, like Nasan's own, was confined in double braids that dangled to her hips. As if forgotten, a linen towel, stained dark at the edges, draped over her right arm.

When she saw Nasan, she dropped the towel and rushed to embrace her daughter-in-law. "Irina, my dearest, where were you? I thought you had run away. I was sick with worry."

"Sorry," Nasan said. "I did not mean to worry. Daniil was angry. I hide but safe." Squeezed, kissed, and petted, she writhed at this warm welcome. Should she not tell Natalya the truth? But Nikolai had insisted otherwise.

A groan from Semyon interrupted such thoughts. Natalya released Nasan and handed her a fresh rag from a pile on a nearby barrel. "It's good you arrived," she said. "You can assist me. I sent Maria away when Semyon started babbling. I couldn't figure out half of what he said, but it troubled me. The last thing we need is that girl spreading rumors." She frowned at Semyon, who thrashed on a bed that looked oddly familiar.

Only then did Nasan realize that the servants had placed her enemy in the storeroom previously converted for her wedding night. It made sense to use this empty space with its easily assembled bed. Yet she could not help feeling uncomfortable at the thought of

Semyon, wounded or not, lying on the mattress where Daniil had initiated her into adulthood.

Her husband had come home. He had kissed her. He would want to do that again. She shivered in anticipation.

Natalya tapped her arm. Nasan hesitated. Would it seem odd if she veiled herself under these circumstances? But she soon realized Semyon could not see her. He had scrunched his eyes shut. Sweat beaded his brow, and the clench to his jaw suggested intense pain. If he were anyone else, Nasan would have sympathized.

Nikolai followed the women in and sat on a bench near Semyon's head. "Will he live?"

"Unless blood poisoning sets in," Natalya said. "The arrow missed the artery. And he's wearing silk, so I can pull the arrowhead out without causing further injury. Who shot him?"

"Can he talk?" Nikolai asked.

"We'll know soon." She pointed to the pile of cloths near the door. "See those rags, Irina? Put them somewhere you can reach them easily."

Nasan fetched the cloths, piled the extras at the head of the bed, and held one at the ready. "Good," Natalya said. "Kolya, sit there in case I need you. Irina, the moment I pull this arrow free, clamp that rag onto the wound and bear down as hard as you can."

Nasan nodded. Natalya gripped the shaft and the fabric beneath it and tugged. As the shaft came free, blood welled from the wound right below Semyon's left hip. Its acrid scent added to the room's odor of sickness. Nasan pressed with the cloth. The crimson stain spread into a circle under her hands.

It was tempting to release the pressure, to watch her enemy's life blood spurt as Girei's had onto the snow. But the grandmothers had spoken, back when Nasan first learned that her enemy lived. And in his present condition, Semyon would not survive the knout. One way or another, she would see justice done. Let the ancestors decide the means.

Natalya dropped the arrow in a bowl and swapped Nasan's cloth for a clean one. "Keep the pressure on," she said. "I must stitch that wound, but we need to slow the bleeding first." She spoke to her husband over her shoulder. "What happened to him, Kolya?"

This time he answered her. "He let Koshkin talk him into a scheme to abduct the grand prince and his brother. He almost brought down our entire clan. Daniil stopped him."

"No!" Natalya said. Nasan heard a matching gasp and a rustle of skirts from the region of the door. Her in-laws didn't react, and no one entered the room. She must have imagined the noise.

"He did what?" Natalya asked. "Who shot him?"

"Daniil," Nikolai said, provoking another gasp. "He found the children in Semyon's possession. At that old estate of my father's near the palisade. Meanwhile, Koshkin has run off. Telepnev went to hunt him down and took Daniil with him."

He stared long and hard at Nasan, who bit her tongue and said nothing. Natalya, knocked off-balance by his revelations, didn't notice.

"Daniil?" she stammered. "How did he find out? He hasn't been home more than a day."

"I'm as much in the dark as you, Natasha," Nikolai said. "That's why I need to question Semyon."

"Well, you can't question him yet. He's fainted." Natalya reached for a lacquered bowl holding a threaded needle and a pair of embroidery scissors. "Lift the rag, Irina, and let me see."

Nasan lifted the rag. The wound, ugly and raw, oozed rather than spurted.

"Not bad," Natalya said. She handed Nasan another clean cloth. "You'll find a bowl of mint and vinegar on that table. Soak this in it and bring me the cloth. The tiny cup, too."

Nasan did as she was told. She knew from Sumbeka that mint prevented infection, and vinegar cleaned. But what did the tiny cup hold? Ah, a spider web, for healing. Of course.

When she handed the requested items to her mother-in-law, Natalya daubed the wound with the cloth but set the cup aside. She took Nasan's hands in hers and placed them on either side of the wound, pushing the edges together. "Hold it right there. Good girl. I'm going to stitch." She applied the threaded needle with grim efficiency.

"I must talk with Semyon as soon as possible," Nikolai said. "While his defenses remain weak. Do you think the grand princess's guards will treat him with loving kindness? Before they arrive to interrogate him, I need to know how much damage he's done."

Natalya, intent on her sewing, did not look up. "Understood. Stay if you like. Otherwise, I'll send for you when he recovers enough to speak. But if the grand princess's troops arrive first, Kolya, you will have to stall them."

In the end, a dog tipped off Telepnev's troops to the correct turn-off. An ordinary coursing hound—brindled, with the alert ears and slender legs of his type—sniffing with great interest a deposit of horse droppings visible against the dew-laden leaves that littered the path into the woods alerted them to the presence of a red ribbon half-concealed amid the briars. The ribbon in turn pointed to a trail ending in an isolated cottage. Telepnev wasted no time in directing his cavalry unit down the trail.

Daniil, glancing up, saw the sun douse the pearl-gray sky with streaks of rose. Past dawn, if not by much. Although lack of sleep set the world shimmering around him, he had ridden this route often enough to estimate that, as the carters had promised, the troops had traveled about one-fourth of the distance between Moscow and Dmitrov.

The men tethered their beasts in a circle around the cottage and moved in from all sides at once. At first, their caution appeared excessive. Nothing disturbed the silence: no crackle of burning logs, no breath. The shutters stood open; the frames lacked the panes that protected wealthier homes from the elements.

A wakening bird chirped in the woods. Wings flapped; a horse whinnied. Other horses, not from the circle tethered among the trees, replied. A harsh voice exploded in a curse. At Telepnev's signal, Daniil readied his bow. Soldiers charged the door.

And stopped, mid-rush, at a command from inside. Telepnev said, "Mother of God!"

Daniil stared as Koshkin, dressed for a court ceremony, strolled through the doorway. A half-dozen men-at-arms followed him, their leather armor and set faces a grim backdrop to his suave elegance. The gold chain around his neck would have ransomed a prince. Only the boots visible beneath the satin hem suggested he might have ridden here. What game was the man playing?

"Well met, Telepnev." Koshkin, impossibly urbane, waved a hand at the cottage. "Please, come in." His eyes swept the company. "I fear your men will crowd the hut. If you could select one or two, and leave the rest outside?"

Telepnev tapped Daniil and another young nobleman on the shoulders. "You two. Keep those bows handy, but don't shoot unless I order it." He turned to Koshkin. "Your men stay outside, too. Mine will ensure their comfort."

"And their good behavior, no doubt," Koshkin said in tones that made Daniil think of butter in mid-June. "I see you picked young Kolychev. How apropos. Please, come in."

Following Telepnev into the hut, Daniil considered his options. Not hard to figure out that Koshkin had some trick up his sleeve. Daniil had to guard his family's interests, but carefully. Junior members of illustrious patrols like this one were supposed to listen, not to act.

Telepnev surveyed the interior with disdain. Unlike the hut that Daniil had visited outside Kasimov, this one showed little evidence of recent care. A lopsided table and a single bench, a pile of banked embers with a kettle dangling over them from a makeshift frame, a trio of cots with coarse wool coverings thrown over straw mattresses, six saddles heaped in a corner, and several piles of straw, one still with a military cloak draped over it—the contrast between Koshkin's surroundings and his court dress could not have been starker.

Telepnev noted as much. "An odd hostelry for one of your standing. And, if you will permit my candor, a poorly timed journey. What sends you flying to the woods at such an hour, when the grand prince of Russia remains at risk?" He moved his foot, pressing down the toe of Daniil's boot. Daniil stepped back, acknowledging the unspoken message: don't tell him we've recovered the children.

Not that he had any such intention. Telepnev, an old hand at these games, clearly had the skill to match Koshkin's duplicity.

Koshkin spread his hands, the epitome of aggrieved innocence. "You misunderstand. I seek to recover the princes. By now, my man Stenka will have removed the children from the hands of their kidnapper."

He pointed at Daniil. "Semyon Kolychev, cousin to your young assistant."

Daniil realized he had taken a hasty step forward when Telepnev's arm blocked his way. Reminded of his resolution not to interfere, he retreated. Koshkin had a nerve, double-crossing Semyon!

Koshkin, with a smile that made Daniil long to punch him, continued. "I set Stenka to watch Semyon weeks ago, after certain comments of his made me wonder. His father, you know, was Yuri's man."

Which, God help them, was no more than the truth. Daniil's uncle Pavel had served Yuri in Dmitrov—during the old grand prince's lifetime, when such service implied no disloyalty to the central throne in Moscow.

"Stenka reported yesterday that Semyon planned to move the children," Koshkin said. "I told him to hire a cart and accompany it when it left the estate. If we caught them on the Dmitrov road, we could prove not only who had taken the boys but why."

"A complex scheme," Telepnev said. "So complex that it seems to have failed. You are here, without cart or children. No Stenka either, unless he waits among the men outside."

Daniil, about to confirm the absence of Stenka, clamped his lips shut.

Koshkin laughed softly and raised his hands once more. "Alas, you have uncovered my weakness. I love indirection. Whereas you charge the estate with cavalry archers."

Telepnev looked as skeptical as Daniil felt. But Koshkin had woven enough truth into his story to obscure the falsehoods. And with Stenka gone, it would be Semyon's dubious word against Koshkin's. Without proof of Koshkin's involvement...

"You, too, served Yuri in Dmitrov," Telepnev said.

Koshkin's laugh sounded louder this time, less forced. "Once upon a time, yes. But I switched my allegiance to Vasily when he married Elena. So young and beautiful a bride would naturally produce heirs. As, in fact, she did. Elena knows whose fealty she holds." He gestured toward Daniil again. "And whose she doesn't."

Damn. Had he just *said* that?

Telepnev grabbed Daniil's arm and hissed into his ear. "Stand down, boy. He's trying to provoke you."

Grumbling under his breath, Daniil stopped, gritted his teeth, and waited.

Telepnev tapped a boot toe against the dirt floor. "How enterprising of you, Koshkin. You appear to have considered every contingency." Was he surrendering?

But he had not finished. "And given your unwavering loyalty to Grand Princess Elena, you will be delighted, I'm sure, to learn that we have recovered her sons unharmed, together with Semyon Kolychev and several of his men. I'm sure we can persuade them to tell us what we need to know." He bowed and, pushing Daniil and his companion ahead of him, left the hut. As Telepnev shoved him through the door, Daniil sneaked a glance over his shoulder and saw Koshkin's urbanity dissolve into a mask of pure fury.

He mentioned it to Telepnev as they remounted their horses. "I know," the older man said. "He's guilty as sin. But powerful. Without more proof of his involvement, we would be unwise to arrest him. Instead, we will assign him to a post far from Moscow. Prestigious enough that he can't complain of dishonor but isolated, so that everyone will know he has fallen into disgrace."

Daniil nodded. Such assignments were standard when a nobleman raised doubts that could not be proven. It would serve. Koshkin's standing would fall fast once people learned of his new posting.

Telepnev slapped Daniil's shoulder and signaled to those who had ridden with them. "And now we return to Moscow. Protecting the grand prince and his brother must become our chief concern."

Moscow. Home. Nasan. If nothing else, Daniil decided, he could hope for a few hours with his wife. Although the way things had gone since he returned, stars would fall from the sky before they had a moment alone.

Natalya finished her sewing. She daubed the wound with a more intense mint-based compound, then supervised as Nasan laid the spider web over the closed wound. The neat bandage constructed from another strip of cloth drew a nod of approval. "Your mother trained you well."

"Thank you." Nasan dipped her hands in a nearby basin and watched Semyon's blood redden the water. "I like medicine." Better than mushrooms and soap. She decided not to add that part.

"Do you? Then I will teach you more."

Nasan replaced the soiled water with fresh, and Natalya washed her hands and arms. "Good girl," she said, as she had earlier. "Tell Pashka to replace the linens."

Nasan did. Watching two husky servants strip the soiled sheets from the bed, she had time to wonder about Daniil, on his way to Dmitrov.

Which was where, exactly? Hours away? Days? No one had said.

And when he did return, what then? He wanted to kiss her today, maybe, but soon others would take Grusha's place. Or his heart would remain forever fixed on the pattern card Anastasia, leaving no room for Nasan. Which was too bad, because a man who agreed to fight at her side, to accept the Lynx—such a man she could love, given half a chance.

The servants finished changing the bed and left. Semyon lay on his back, eyes closed and breathing stertorous, oddly pathetic stripped of his usual swagger. In this guise, he bore little resemblance to the brutal man who had ambushed two teenagers in the forest, murdered one of them in cold blood, and held a pair of royal children to ransom.

"He's in God's hands now," Natalya announced. "We can only wait." She sat on the bench and patted the cushion next to her. Nasan obeyed. Nikolai, a ferocious scowl on his face, paced beside the bed. "Do sit down, Kolya," Natalya said. "Or go away. Your roaming will not revive him."

He stopped, giving her a rueful smile. "Sorry, Natasha. I'll wait in the house for Daniil. Should I alert you when he returns?"

"At once," she said. "And when you do, please send someone to sit with Semyon."

His eyes sparkled. Nasan, startled, recognized for the first time the resemblance between Nikolai and his younger son.

"Yes, General," he said.

Chapter 29

BY THE TIME DANIIL REACHED HOME, THE NOON SUN DASHED from cloud to cloud, as if playing a game of heavenly tag. The gates to the estate stood open. Servants passed to and fro, engaged in a variety of tasks: caring for animals, visiting the market, tending the orchards, sweeping the courtyard, making repairs. The storeroom where the men had carried Semyon had no traffic in or out. Daniil decided to search for his wife, then his parents. Somewhere along the way, he would obtain news of his cousin.

Nasan was not in their chamber, nor in his mother's sitting room. Daniil stood at the end of the hallway, debating whether to try the warehouse that held Semyon or to look for his father first. Then he saw Maria creeping down the corridor, clothed for the outdoors, with a veil over her hair and a velvet bag hanging from one shoulder. Behind her trailed an unhappy Pashka carrying a cylindrical trunk. From the bend in Pashka's shoulders, Daniil concluded that the chest weighed enough to contain most of Maria's worldly goods.

Three strides brought him close enough to grab her arm. "Where are you going, sister?" He made no attempt to moderate his voice.

Pashka, startled, dropped the chest, which sprang open as it hit the floor. The crash brought Nikolai out of his study. He sized up the situation with one comprehensive glance and addressed the servant. "You, Pashka. Find Natalya Vasilyevna. Tell her our son has returned."

Pashka fled. Nikolai turned his attention to his son and daughter-in-law. "Bring her in here, Daniil." He indicated Natalya's sitting room. "Your mother and your wife will join us soon. I'm glad to see you safe. Did your mission succeed?"

"We met up with Koshkin."

Maria interrupted him. "Papa! You beast. What have you done?"

"So you caught him?" Nikolai asked. "*Molodets!*"

"We found him." Daniil dragged Maria into the room. "And left him. I'll tell you the rest later. How is Semyon?"

"He lives," Nikolai said. "I wish I could be sure that's a good thing. For him or for our clan."

"Who cares about Semyon?" Maria demanded. "How dare you chase my papa?"

Natalya arrived, Nasan in her wake. While his mother exclaimed over him, Maria, and the mess in her hallway, Nasan ducked around her and regarded Daniil with a solemn expression. He reached for her with his left arm—the one not restraining Maria, who fought to haul herself out of his grasp.

"Let me go, you great brute." Maria stamped on his foot. Nikolai nodded, and Daniil released her, so abruptly that she staggered, and clasped Nasan's fingers. The touch of her hand made his palm tingle, and he wished the world away.

"Safe," she said. "Success?"

"Safe," he confirmed. "Some success." He looked at his mother. "I hear Semyon is recovering. I knew you would heal him."

"Irina helped. The wound is clean but deep. It may yet putrefy." Her brow crinkled anew. "Did you intend to kill him?"

"Of course not." With his right arm, he barred Maria from the exit. "Has he talked?"

"He can't. He fainted when I cleaned the wound."

"He must," Nikolai said. "Before the grand princess's troops arrive. I expect them any moment."

"She's waiting for Telepnev's report," Daniil said. "We have an hour, at most."

"Very well." Nikolai gestured to the chairs that ringed the room. "Family, sit. We have not much time."

Daniil had taken four steps toward the window seat when his father glowered at Maria. "But much to discuss. Starting with you, miss. Where were you off to, pray?" He transferred his gaze to his son. "Watch her, Daniil. She's slippery as they come."

"My pleasure." Daniil dropped his wife's hand and lounged against the door. After several attempts to dodge past him, Maria gave up and took the bench opposite Natalya. Asked again about her destination, she pressed her lips together.

Daniil decided to goad her into an admission. "She likes to eavesdrop. I'd say she's heard that her father's a traitor and was running away. Isn't that so, sister?"

Maria stared at her feet. Daniil repeated his question twice before she mumbled, "I was going to visit Mama."

"With all your belongings?"

Maria's head came up then. "I wouldn't expect you to understand."

Nikolai took over. "Don't lie to us, daughter. You know more than you admit. Enough that when Daniil announces that your father's a traitor, you don't ask what he means."

"I don't need to ask, because it isn't true. My papa places Russia's interests first."

"Russia's interests. What do you know of such things?" Natalya leaned forward, her hands clasped in her lap. "No one discusses politics with a slip of a girl like you."

Maria's face contorted in anger. "My papa does. My papa loves me. You would have been sorry when he made me grand princess. I would have barred every one of you from the sight of my bright eyes." She pointed at Nasan and hissed, "Especially you."

Nikolai intercepted his wife in mid-slap. "Grand princess," he mused in a voice guaranteed to soothe a fretting infant—or throw an errant daughter-in-law off guard. "And whom did your father intend for your grand prince? Ivan has a dozen years to go before he can marry."

The ploy worked. Maria bestowed on him a gaze every bit as haughty as Grand Princess Elena's and said, "Prince Yuri, of course. He has no wife."

Nasan followed the quick back-and-forth among the Kolychevs with some difficulty, but the last comment threw her into complete confusion. For a moment, she thought Maria meant to wed the baby whom Daniil had carried back to the palace. Surely he would make an even less suitable groom than his brother.

Then she realized Maria meant the other Prince Yuri, the captive. "So old," she said. "You not hate to marry such?"

"To become grand princess?" Maria asked, still haughty, although her voice trembled.

Nikolai looked amused. "Fifty-four doesn't seem old to me, but Irina speaks the truth. What do you want with a husband your grandfather's age? Yuri is not yet grand prince, nor like to be."

Natalya broke in. "You are a silly girl, Maria, and heartless as well. We would have found you a young man, whose household you could govern, but in good time. Boris died only three months ago. You owe him a decent mourning."

"Much you know," Maria muttered. Nasan, sitting closest, recalled those earlier occasions when Maria had declared how she detested life among the Kolychevs. Perhaps Boris hadn't been as good a husband as his mother believed.

Daniil spoke from the doorway. "Do we understand the whole, then?"

"I don't," Nasan said. "Why Semyon grab children? Why Maria marry Prince Yuri?"

"Oh, you are so slow," Maria snapped.

"No need for rudeness," Nikolai said. "Irina has yet to learn our ways." He smiled at Nasan. "As I reconstruct it, the plan went something like this." He beckoned to Daniil. "You can sit down, son. I think Maria recognizes the futility of escape."

Daniil joined Nasan. Maria scrunched into her seat as he passed. Nikolai said, "Maria's father argued for Yuri's release. I think he seized the children to force the grand princess's hand."

"You lie!" Maria shouted. "What children?"

"Papa didn't tell you that part?" Nikolai's serene gaze swept over her, and she cowered again. "He has some sense, then. Semyon abducted the grand prince and his baby brother. I think he took orders from your father, who begged Grand Princess Elena to release Yuri. She refused—and wisely. Let Yuri go, and he'd grab the throne, then dispose of the boys at his leisure."

Daniil pulled Nasan against his shoulder. His chin touched the crown of her head. She relaxed in his hold. At the end of a long and stressful night, his warm bulk comforted her.

"What I can't figure out," Nikolai said, "is how Semyon talked himself into joining such a scheme. Too subtle for him by half, I would have thought."

"Please," Nasan interjected. "If Maria's father has boys, why she marry uncle?"

"For power." Daniil's voice reverberated over her head. "Koshkin puts Yuri on the throne and weds him to Maria, and Koshkin sets policy for the rest of his life. And his kin after him, if the dice roll his way. Like the *beylerbey*, in your world."

"Different," Nasan said. No one heard her, because Maria emitted a noise like a frustrated hen and dashed for the door. Nikolai, moving faster than anyone would think possible for a man of his years, darted after her, but she eluded him. Nasan could hear him bellowing orders in the hallway. "Pashka, pick up that mess and return the young mistress's belongings to her room."

"Ridiculous girl." Natalya had risen to her feet. "If her parents want her, they can send for her. Until then, she belongs here."

"She's in no danger," Daniil said. "Let her go. I want to tell you about Koshkin."

The telling took some time. Nasan watched her in-laws' faces, listened hard to Daniil's words. "Telepnev supports us," he finished. "He knows Koshkin lied."

"Telepnev," Nikolai mused. "Well, that's something. Can we pin this crime on Koshkin?"

"I doubt it. Admitting to hiring Stenka was inspired. We'll find it hard to prove he did anything more than trust the wrong people."

"And Stenka himself?" Nikolai asked. "Can't he testify against Koshkin?"

"He ran away," Daniil said. "With Grusha. Telepnev sent men after them. But Koshkin already claims Stenka as his own man. Stenka won't contradict that, if he values his skin."

"Grusha!" Natalya clapped her hands. "What does she have to do with anything?"

"Not sure." Daniil closed his hand over Nasan's. "I saw her sneaking out of our estate. I didn't stop her. I'd told her that morning I no longer wanted her."

Nasan yelped. She couldn't help herself. He grinned at her, and her cheeks warmed. "What did you expect?" His voice teased, but he didn't wait for an answer. "She had a reason to hide. But I wanted to find you, wife of mine, and Grusha had implied that she knew where you went. So I followed her."

He had been searching for her, not for Grusha? But Grusha didn't know where Nasan went, whatever she said. By what coincidence had he stumbled onto the right place?

"I lost her for a while," Daniil said, still talking about Grusha. He told his parents about the results of his search, ending with the maid's disappearance with Stenka.

His story sparked a memory. Not long after they discovered Grusha's absence, Nasan had told her husband the truth about

Girei's murder. Nikolai had heard the tale during their meeting at the Kremlin, but Natalya still didn't know. "Semyon," Nasan said. "Please, listen. Important." She repeated the news of her discovery.

Natalya pressed her hands against her eyes, and her shoulders shook. Nasan hovered, uncertain, before patting Natalya's arm. "Very sorry, Mama-in-law. Terrible mistake. Terrible." She had never wished harder for fluent Russian.

Natalya took a few sobbing breaths, then straightened. She brushed a trembling finger across Nasan's cheek. "Thank you, daughter. Your truth has given Boris back to me. I never believed him guilty, but I was afraid. That I had let love blind me to his faults. Do you understand?"

Nasan nodded, although not certain she did understand. "Sorry Boris die," she said. "I too live sad."

"Yes," Natalya said. "I'm sure you do, poor child."

And there, watching Natalya wipe away her tears, Nasan realized in her bones that *these* Kolychevs were not her enemies. She could stay with them. A burden slid from her shoulders, and she sighed.

"For what it's worth," Daniil said, "Grusha wanted out. Thanks to Semyon, we're already implicated. If we have to hunt for her, we will. But I'd prefer to let her go."

"And Stenka?" Nikolai rose and went to the window. Tromping feet sounded from the courtyard. "Answer quickly. The grand princess's patrol has arrived. We must interrogate Semyon before they take him."

"Would finding Stenka help?" Daniil asked. "When he's likely to confirm Koshkin's story?"

"Very well," Nikolai said. "I'll see what I can do. Let's tackle Semyon."

He left the room at a trot. Natalya sprang to her feet. Daniil stood, more slowly, and his mother regarded him with a worried frown. "I have questions." He sounded tired. "I want to hear the answers from Semyon."

He held out a hand to Nasan, and she moved to his side. They were all tired. Who wouldn't be, after a full night spent riding and running and shooting, being quizzed by a relieved but embattled grand princess, and tending an injured villain? But Daniil had ridden farther and fought longer than any of them. She didn't protest when he put his arm around her waist. With Nikolai in the lead, their strange cavalcade lurched down the stairs to confront Semyon.

Nikolai bullied two royal guards until they allowed him to enter the warehouse. Inside, the family found Father Job praying in a corner and their quarry feverish, awake, and—judging by the scowl with which he greeted them—defiant. The one servant in attendance scuttled off at a jerk from Nikolai's head. Father Job followed at a slower pace, promising to return when needed. Only members of the immediate family remained.

Daniil shielded Nasan with his body, blocking her from his cousin's view. To reassure him, she unwrapped the veil from her waist and covered her face. He settled onto a bench in the corner and pulled her down to nestle at his side. Natalya bustled forward, Nikolai at her heels. She dampened a cloth and pressed it against Semyon's forehead. She sat at his left side, Nikolai at his right. When he spoke, his brusque tone startled Nasan. "Speak. You don't have long."

"Am I dying?" Semyon said.

"No." Natalya set the cloth to one side.

"Thanks to your aunt," Nikolai said. "The grand princess's troops are at the door. Start talking—fast. Elena minced no words. You confess to me or to them. Your choice."

"Charming ruler you serve." How Semyon managed a sneer in his condition, Nasan couldn't imagine, but sneer he did. "Do you enjoy bowing at her feet, Uncle?"

"Begin with Kasimov," Nikolai said. "What went awry between you and Boris? Daniil discovered you traveled together."

"Daniil." Semyon gazed blearily into the corner. "Whoreson, shooting your cousin over a Tatar brat."

Daniil surged to his feet. Nasan caught his sleeve and pulled him back, and he subsided with a thump. Natalya, her face as calm as if she were offering bread and salt, picked up the cloth she had just discarded, placed it over Semyon's wound, and said, "Language, nephew."

Semyon's bluster collapsed in a yowl. Natalya lifted the cloth. "Answer your uncle, and mind your manners."

Semyon looked at her as if he would like to turn himself into a were-tiger and eat her. She smiled at him with terrifying serenity and waved the cloth.

"Find your own answers," he said. "Why should I make your life easy, when you never did anything for me?"

"Never did anything? You ungrateful swine." Natalya poked his hip for emphasis.

"Not when it counted. Bulat's men killed my brother. You stood back and let them get away with it. I defended our honor."

"And Boris?" Nikolai's voice held a hint of strain.

"Don't get me started on your precious Boris." Semyon closed his eyes, until Natalya revived him with a wet cloth to the brow. He responded with another were-tiger glare.

"Get on with it," Nikolai said. "We have a lot of ground to cover in a short time. Where was Boris when you killed Bulat's boy? And we know you did kill the boy, so don't try to deny it."

Semyon grunted, but another round of encouragement from Natalya proved effective. "Boris didn't have the guts to kill anyone. He pretended he did, but it was a ruse. About a mile from the river, he tried to talk me out of it. And when I laughed in his face, he rallied his men to overpower me and my troop. I had to clout him on the head. Knocked him out, then gave him the slip—the sneaky, yellow-bellied peacemaker."

He spat out the last words as if they were a curse, which to him they probably were. Nasan focused on Daniil, bent double next to her. "What a waste," he muttered. "My poor brother. I lost him for nothing."

Nasan patted his shoulder in silent sympathy. He said in a louder voice, "Maybe Boris didn't lie, then. If Semyon knocked him out, he may not have remembered what happened. I saw that once: a man standing next to me on campaign took a blow to the head, and when we dragged him off the field and revived him, he thought he'd missed the battle altogether."

"Yes, I've seen that, too." Nikolai sounded relieved.

"I wouldn't know," Semyon said. His voice implied he didn't care, either. "His men carried him off, I assume."

"We can trace their movements," Daniil said. "If necessary."

"You wouldn't know." Natalya smacked her cloth across Semyon's cheek. "You didn't try to find out. You left my Boris unconscious on the road. You let him and his men die. And you didn't warn us. Better we had harbored a serpent than you."

Semyon flailed an arm. "Wake up, Auntie. Your son dragged our honor in the dust. Why defend him?"

"Have you ever heard the like?" Daniil whispered. "Steam will pour from Mama's ears if Semyon says one more word." Nasan suppressed a highly inappropriate giggle.

The guardsmen rapped on the door, and Nikolai went to answer it. A brief conversation followed, out of Nasan's earshot, before her father-in-law returned.

"All right, enough about Boris for the moment," Nikolai said. "Let's discuss the kidnapping. I talk, you listen. You'll be charged with these crimes, so set me straight if I make a mistake." He recapped the series of events that he and Daniil had constructed earlier.

Semyon didn't interrupt until he heard Maria's revelation that her father had intended her to become Yuri's grand princess. Then he exploded. "That two-timing snake! He used me to secure his own power. Left me with the risk while he arranged his reward." He grabbed Nikolai's sleeve. "Tell them, Uncle. I'll cooperate. I'll answer any question you ask. Just don't let them kill me. He was the ringleader. The scheme was his."

Nikolai shook him off. "Help you? After what you did to my son? I owe you nothing."

Semyon flinched. Nasan, disgusted, stared at him. No wonder the grandmothers opposed him. He had no honor!

"I have a question," Daniil said. "How did you get the children out of the Kremlin?"

Semyon laughed, a harsh, curt sound. "Easy. The guards used to dice and drink with me on watch. They knew I could expose them. I suggested they make themselves scarce."

"And what happened to them?" Nikolai asked.

"Guess, Uncle. They met with an untimely end. Koshkin's orders." Semyon grimaced at Daniil. "That cheating servant of yours made the perfect nursemaid. Terrible bedmate, though. What did you see in her? Silliest wench I ever had."

"You let my son die." Natalya applied her bandage weapon with sufficient force to make Semyon scream. "You abducted the two baby princes. You killed Irina's brother and three hapless men. You endangered and dishonored our clan. *And* you seduced my servant. What kind of demon spawn are you?"

"Indeed," Daniil said. "You have much to answer for, cousin."

Semyon's eyes rolled back in his head. Natalya threw down the cloth and stood. "I hope you were finished, Kolya. He's fainted again."

Nikolai patted her back. "Quite finished, my dear. Unless you have other questions, Daniil?"

"No," Daniil said. "I've heard enough." Nasan couldn't agree more.

"Very well," Nikolai said. "Go back upstairs. I'll speak to the guards. They can watch him here or take him wherever they like. I'm done with him."

Daniil and Nasan had reached the top of the stairs when Pashka materialized in front of them. "Lord," he said. "A pair of carters await below. They ask to speak to the Golden Lynx. I told them no such person resides here, but they insist he gave them this address. One word, and I will send them about their business."

"Show them up," Daniil said. "Alert my father." Pashka departed. Daniil ushered Nasan into his mother's sitting room. He pulled her onto the bench near the window and pushed her veil aside. "Tired?"

"Very." A frown appeared between her perfect eyebrows. "You ready fall down. Must be."

He kissed her, a brush of lips against lips. "Just about. Care to revive me?" He laughed at the face she made. "Don't scowl. It was a joke. I'm exhausted." His father's boots sounded in the hallway, and Daniil whispered in her ear, "That will change."

Her virginal blush looked so adorable it threatened to revive him in truth. He reached for her, but before he could act, his parents arrived. The carters would appear any moment. "Did Pashka explain?" he asked.

"Carters," Nikolai said. "The two who returned the children, I assume. What do they want?"

"Their pay," Daniil said, grateful for Papa's quickness. "Koshkin promised them a Novgorod ruble each."

"Daniil!" Natalya said.

Nikolai waved her down. "A small price to preserve our honor. You offered to match his fee, of course."

Daniil leaned forward, elbows on his knees. "Yes. We needed the cart, and I thought it better to keep the men occupied than to send them off to spread rumors around Moscow. You see how ready they are to embrace this idea of the Golden Lynx."

Nasan shifted position at his side, and he reached for her hand. Mama lived by the rules. Better to hide the truth that she harbored, unawares, Moscow's newest hero.

"A tale for children," Natalya said. No one contradicted her.

"Not if men can swear they have seen this Lynx in person," Nikolai said. "Withdraw, Daniil, and let me handle this."

"No. They would spin the tale, say they saw me in person, then followed me here, only to have me vanish without a trace. We must convince them I'm an ordinary boyar, not this hero they seek."

The carters' arrival cut off Nikolai's response. Nasan covered her face once more.

Here Daniil caught his first real glimpse of them: two nondescript townsmen, one scrawny and young, the other broad of shoulder, square but not fat, his face worn and lined. Wispy hair, brown and gray, peeked out around their leather caps, hastily doffed as they recognized the exalted nature of their hosts. Eyes the shade of robins' eggs teared in the light. You might see a hundred such men in the Moscow streets any day of the week, dressed in homespun, aprons protecting their clothes.

"Kvass," Nikolai told Pashka, "and my money bag."

The servant bowed and departed, and Nikolai turned to the two men. "You realize, of course, that this tale of the Golden Lynx is nonsense." He gestured at Daniil. "This is my son, who detected his cousin in a crime and sought to prevent it, to guard the honor of our clan."

The carters twisted their caps in their hands and shuffled their feet. "Yes, Lord."

"I wore the pendant for its effect," Daniil said. "I am no hero."

"You will not spread this about," Nikolai added. "I should be most displeased to hear of it."

"No, Lord," they chorused.

Daniil didn't believe them. Who could resist so fascinating a tale? The story would not only spread but grow, becoming indistinguishable from legend. But the more fantastic, the better. Any link to the Kolychevs would be lost.

"The troops didn't rough you up, I hope," he said.

The older townsman raised his head. "Not much, Lord. They sought bigger game."

Pashka returned with cups of dark liquid and a pouch. He handed the bag to Nikolai and cups to the townsmen. When he extended the tray to Daniil, Daniil refused with a raised hand. After the night he'd had, he would indeed fall over if he drank.

Nikolai accepted a cup, toasted the townsmen, and with one final admonition handed each of them a large silver coin. Their eyes brightened, like sunlight viewed through ice. They thanked him profusely, downed the cups in one gulp, and left with a brief farewell. The steward followed, removing both bag and tray.

"Which leaves only Semyon," Daniil said. "Did the soldiers agree to go without him?"

"For the moment," Nikolai said. "He will talk, although I doubt Elena will take his word against Koshkin's. Perhaps it will encourage her to order him tonsured and knout him less. More than ever, the Pechenga hermitage sounds like the right destination for him."

"I pity the Lapps," Daniil said. "They'll have to lock up their daughters."

"Pechenga hermitage?" Natalya asked. "Semyon a monk? By all the saints. Well, at least Solomonida will be happy."

Daniil puzzled over that, but Natalya did not enlighten him. Instead, she reached forward to pat Nasan's hand. Her lips pursed, and she shook her head. "As for you, give us a babe, that's all I ask. And no more running away to hide. My dear Anastasia…" Nasan flinched, and Mama stopped mid-sentence. "Well, never mind. Anastasia is dead and gone."

"I'll visit the Kremlin later today," Nikolai said. "Let's meet again before I do. First I'd like some rest." He held out his hand to Natalya. "And you, my dove?"

She went to him at once. Daniil stood and pulled Nasan to her feet. "I need sleep. Come, wife. Haven't you kept me waiting long enough?"

Daniil collapsed onto the bed and lay there staring at the ceiling, arms flung out to the sides. Nasan, hands on hips, regarded him from her post near the door. As tempted as she felt to tumble onto the bed next to him and sleep until tomorrow, too much had happened since their wedding, and they had negotiated none of it.

Not to mention that Daniil shouldn't sleep in his boots. It was a wife's duty to remove them. She pushed away from the door and tugged at her husband's right foot.

The boot came off without difficulty. She removed the left one and dropped it beside its mate. She was deciding what to do next when Daniil surged into a sitting position, captured her with his right arm, and dragged her onto the mattress beside him. "Hah," he said when she wriggled. "You thought I was asleep."

"Let me go!"

Instead, he propped himself on his elbow and draped his arm around her waist. "I told you before, I don't force women. No one's checking the sheets now. We'll do what we both want when we want it. You didn't hate it, did you?"

Nasan shook her head. She hadn't hated it. Daniil's caressing hand on her waist hinted at pleasures unexplored. For some reason, her mind fixed on the idea of kissing him.

"Where did you go?" he asked. "When you ran away."

"To an old man. And his wife. He make story about Golden Lynx, I think. He say help me. So when nowhere to go, I ask."

Daniil's arm tightened around her. "Nowhere to go? This is your home. You belong here. With me."

A gulf opened beneath her feet. For her parents—her brother, her ancestors, her clan—agreed: she did belong with him. Yet he remained a man whom rumor linked with many women and who, worse, loved a dead bride. She could not dodge the confrontation any longer. She wrestled her skimpy Russian into complete if simple sentences. Here, more than ever before, he had to understand. "But that's the problem, Daniil. I am not Anastasia. And I don't want to be like *Ana*, one of many."

"You are not one of many. You are my wife." He brushed the stray wisps of hair back from her forehead. "I would like to build a marriage like my parents'. Have a wife I can talk to. Won't you trust me?"

But... "You love Anastasia. Mama-in-law says it. Every day. Be a good woman, Irina. Speak low, walk slow, do not argue. Anastasia did not act so. Only I am not quiet. I will make you sad."

Daniil's shoulder jerked under the hand she had placed there to hold him at bay. "Are you joking? *Mama* loved Anastasia. I didn't."

Nasan stared at him, stunned. All those tales Natalya had told were a lie?

Daniil placed a finger under her chin and looked deep into her eyes. "Listen to me, wife. Anastasia had no use for me. Every time I touched her, she shivered like a frightened horse. After a while, I left her alone, but by then she was pregnant—and she died bearing my child. I felt guilty. So I swore to keep my distance from women."

Nasan felt her jaw drop. "Distance? But Ogodai, Maria, everyone say you have dozens... Stop laughing!"

He swallowed, hard, but he did stop—almost. "I pleasured them, sweetheart. I didn't let them get close."

"Even Grusha?"

"Especially Grusha."

He sounded sincere. Maybe she *had* swallowed Natalya's assurances too easily. When had Daniil himself ever mentioned his first wife? And Grusha—whatever he felt for her, she had left, and he'd asked his father not to hunt for her. It was not trust, exactly, but Nasan decided to let the past die. She and Daniil had to start somewhere.

One last obstacle to surmount. But they had made enough progress that she didn't prevent her fingertips from straying across his cheek. "And the Golden Lynx? You agree that I continue?"

"Ah." Daniil tapped her nose. "I'm glad you brought that up. Let's talk about that. What makes you want to continue? Isn't it exhausting, racketing about the streets every night? Dangerous? Semyon might have killed you tonight." He caressed her cheek. "I can offer more appealing ways to spend your evenings, at least while I'm here."

Nasan blushed. That again. Yet he made a good point, and he hadn't forbidden her, which as her husband he could if he chose. "It's what I always wanted," she explained. "To become a heroine, like those in the old tales. To help those not strong enough to help themselves."

"You're already a heroine to me," Daniil said. "You saved the princes. Who knows what other adventures may await? Your legend will live on without the nightly patrols. Why not keep your skills in reserve until the next emergency presents itself?"

Nasan considered this idea. By rescuing the princes, she had atoned for Girei's death. Daniil's family had accepted her, and she them, so she no longer needed the refuge of the streets. And soon she would leave for Kazan with her husband. His suggestion made sense. "May I practice?"

"Of course. We'll practice together. Mount the next rescue together, if need be. Just promise me you won't fight alone."

A concession, indeed. Natalya would protest, but if Daniil gave his wife permission to ride and shoot, his mother had no right to object. It would be like having Girei restored to her, only better.

Daniil shifted position on the bed, revealing the grandmother sitting serenely on the dressing table. Nasan's mouth opened, but no sound came out.

Daniil shook her gently. "Have I turned you to stone? Will you promise or not? I'm only concerned for your safety."

The grandmother's beady black eyes gazed steadily at her descendant. Nasan would have sworn she saw one of them wink. A cloud of happiness engulfed her, as if the ancestral guardian rejoiced at having lured, prodded, or shoved her to the destination the spirits had always intended her to reach. She recalled her pleas for assistance as she faced Semyon and how Daniil had arrived soon thereafter, as if dispatched from above. And how long she had yearned for a man who would play hero to her heroine, as in the epics she had adopted as her guides to life.

Nasan kissed her husband. "I promise," she said. "We fight together from now on. And we will give this marriage a chance."

Thus the legend of the west concludes with the princes restored to their mother's arms, one villain apprehended, another compromised, peace concluded, and the balance of the universe temporarily restored.

Meanwhile, in the east, a new storm gathers its forces.

Tengri readies another messenger. The lynx has fulfilled its task.

Historical Note

THE KHANATE OF KASIMOV EXISTED FOR MORE THAN TWO hundred years within the religiously conservative Orthodox Christian grand principality (after 1547, tsardom) of Russia: a Muslim polity, autonomous in its internal administration and economic matters although subordinate in foreign relations, in its obligation to supply troops to the grand prince's campaigns, and in the appointment of its rulers by Moscow. It took its name from its first Tatar ruler, Kasim, a younger son of the house ruling Kazan. As Nasan notes, the Tatars called the town Khankirmän (Khan's Fortress). The Russians often used its original name, Meshcherskii gorodok (Meshchera Fortress). For simplicity's sake, I refer to it as Kasimov throughout. "Tatar," too, is a later designation for people who would have identified themselves primarily as "Muslims."

Although the Kolychevs and Koshkins were real (related) boyar clans from this period, most of my characters, including all the main characters, are fictional. The Russian royal family—Ivan Vasilyevich and his brother, their parents and uncles—as well as Prince Telepnev, whom rumor portrayed as Elena's lover, are historical. So are the two men described as Nasan's uncles, Shah-Ali and Jan-Ali. We know almost nothing about any of these people as individuals: usually just their names and rough details about their ages, military careers, and (sometimes) deaths. So in that sense the historical characters are just as much my invention as the fictional ones.

There is, of course, no evidence that anyone attempted to kidnap the child ruler Ivan and his infant brother. Such an attempt would have been highly unlikely to succeed, although their uncle Yuri's incarceration and the boyar politics surrounding support for him versus his nephew did consume much of 1534 and 1535. Fyodor Koshkin represents one side in the debate, and Nikolai Kolychev the other.

As for whether Nasan would have striven so hard to save the baby prince if she had any idea what he would become in adulthood … well, we can only speculate.

Sixteenth-century Tatars generally used only one name, although the various khanates sometimes distinguished themselves by adding a second, unvarying personal name. The Crimean khans, for example, were Mengli-Girei, Devlet-Girei, Sahib-Girei, and so on. To minimize confusion, I generally did not adopt the Crimean custom for my fictional Tatars.

Tatar words are usually accented on the last syllable, so Boo-LAT, Na-SAN, Gee-RAY, etc. Sumbeka is the Russianized form of the Tatar Söyëmbike (Suh-yem-bee-KEH).

Many Russian nobles already employed the system used by everyone in Russia today: first name, patronymic (father's name with one of several different syllables added, ending in -ich for a man and -na for a woman, although wives often used their husband's names instead of their father's), and clan name. Clan names were not set in those days; one branch of the Koshkins eventually achieved fame as the Romanovs. Women's family names end in -a: Daniil Kolychev, Irina Kolycheva; Pyotr Sheremetev, Darya Sheremeteva; Mikhail Glinsky, Elena Glinskaya.

People changed their first names after baptism, ordination, or tonsure. So one person might have several names throughout his or her life. My Nasan becomes Irina after baptism and would be addressed by inferiors as Irina Bulatovna (Irina, daughter of Bulat). Use of the patronymic expresses respect.

Russians also make ample use of nicknames, which I have largely avoided except in reference to characters from the lower classes, who use only nicknames. Peasants, artisans, and slaves were usually addressed by a short variant of their given names, often one ending in -ka. Stenka, Dimka, and Timoshka are examples of "lower-class" names. The differentiation of names by status explains why Nasan recognizes immediately that "Semyon Pavlovich" must be a nobleman.

A word, too, on the women portrayed in this book. Throughout Eurasia in this period, women's roles were constrained, their intelligence and moral judgment questioned, and their value linked to the number of sons they bore. In Russia and Tataria, unlike in the West, women retained certain property rights, but except among the nomads, elite women lived in seclusion. Young girls, in particular, had little or no contact with men outside their families, because the nobles arranged the marriages of their children to secure political alliances, and they didn't want personal attachments to interfere with their plans. Those lower on the social ladder typically had arranged marriages as well, for different reasons, although non-noble brides and grooms often had some acquaintance before the wedding, whereas aristocratic couples met at the altar—more accurately, at the betrothal preceding the wedding. In the Turkic world, khans and sultans maintained harems, which their rivals sought to raid and capture, although less prestigious Tatars usually had only one wife. On the whole, though, the Turkic peoples placed a greater value on daughters (while still preferring sons) than Russians did. They also had a long epic tradition featuring women warriors, including *The Book of Dede Korkut*, which inspires Nasan.

Regarding the Tatar words sprinkled throughout the book, most of them express relationships, which Tatars even today often use in preference to names (the custom, now largely confined to older women, of showing respect by avoiding a husband's name is an extension of this practice). The terms given here—*ata* (father), *ana* (mother), *aby* (uncle or older brother), and *sengel* (younger sister, with the "g" as in song)—may not be exactly those common in the sixteenth century, but they are close. Fictive kinship—expressed in the institution of sworn brotherhood (*qarïndashlar*, sing. *qarïndash*), among other things—was one of the organizing principles of steppe life. Khans, who were always descendants of Genghis, retained their high status in Russian society into the 1530s, where they were addressed as tsar. The Russian equivalents of the other Tatar titles listed in the Cast of Characters were *tsaritsa* (*khatun*), *tsarevich* (*sultan*), and *tsarevna* (*khanim*). The Russian titles translated here as "My Lord" and "My Lady" for the royal family and "Lord," "Master," or "Lady" for the nobles are *gosudar´* (male) and *gosudarynia* (female), often translated as "sovereign" although the true meaning implies something closer to ownership.

In the sixteenth century, Russians did not measure distances or even count the years in the same manner as Western nations, which themselves had far from coherent systems. Standard measurements of time, space, quantity, and the like developed with industrialization and the introduction of railroads; before then, hours varied in length from winter to summer, and a German mile did not necessarily correspond to an English one. Tatars observed the Islamic calendar, Catholics and Protestants the Julian calendar. Russians used the Byzantine calendar, which year to year matched the Julian but began with the supposed creation of the world in 5508 BCE. Hence I have avoided giving specific distances and times as much as possible. Islamic dates come from the online conversion program available at www.oriold.uzh.ch/static/hegira. html.

Acknowledgments

My list of debts for this novel begins in graduate school and extends to all the many wonderful scholars whose work I have used and, no doubt, distorted in the service of fiction. Thank you especially to the members of the Early Slavic Studies Association List, who graciously answered my questions about such diverse subjects as the physical appearance of Kasimov in 1534 and whether Russians and Tatars would have branded their horses. Thank you also to Sandi Sonnenfeld and Anna Isozaki of *The Lyon Review*, which published a chapter from the first edition of this book in August 2011.

My warmest gratitude to Ariadne Apostolou and Courtney J. Hall, who read every word at least three times; to our fellow writers at Five Directions Press for their support; and to all those who made comments on the first edition before publication. Couldn't have done it without you, ladies!

In a class by themselves are my husband, my strongest supporter; my son; and my two Siamese cats, who ensure I do not run the printer too often or work past their dinnertime.

Last, a special thank you to my readers. If you are encountering Nasan, Daniil, and their families for the first time, I hope you have enjoyed the book enough to want to find out more.

The Author

AS A CHILD, C. P. LESLEY THOUGHT EVERYONE MADE UP STORIES while falling asleep. It never occurred to her that anyone would pay her for them, and for a long time, she was right—no one would. But after years of producing horrible prose, reading books about novel writing, and pestering hapless fellow writers and friends to read her drafts, some of the advice stuck, and she finished *The Not Exactly Scarlet Pimpernel*, then *The Golden Lynx* and its sequels: *The Winged Horse*, *The Swan Princess*, *The Vermilion Bird*, and *The Shattered Drum*.

She is currently working on a new series, Songs of Steppe and Forest, featuring secondary characters from the Legends series who never had the space to tell their stories.

When not thinking up new ways to torture her characters, Lesley edits other people's manuscripts, reads voraciously, maintains her website, and practices classical ballet—an interest reflected in *Desert Flower* and *Kingdom of the Shades* (Tarkei Chronicles 1 and 2). She also hosts New Books in Historical Fiction, a channel in the New Books Network. You can find out more about her and her books at www.cplesley.com.

The Winged Horse

LEGENDS OF THE FIVE DIRECTIONS 2

East of the Don, 5 Muharram 941 A.H. / 17 July 1534

THE RUSTLING OUTSIDE THE FELT TENT STILLED AS THE SUN set over the grasslands. Even the lambs hushed. An owl hooted; a wolf howled in the distance. The guard dogs barked in response, but the high, keening wail drifted away on the wind. Bahadur Bey, head of a nomadic Tatar horde, relaxed against the embroidered cushions that placed him north and center relative to the other diners and reached for the quail leg he had dropped when he heard the howl. One wolf, far away, could not threaten a community of forty or fifty households—nor even its sheep and goats, penned for the night.

The quail leg disappeared in a bite or two. Bahadur licked his lips and savored the lingering richness on his tongue—molten fat flecked with salt, gaminess mixed with herbs.

A few too many herbs, in fact. That tinge of bitterness, although not unpleasant in itself, could easily be overdone. A point to bring up with the cooks tomorrow morning.

Platters of food, stripped almost bare, dotted the felt mats laid over the rugs that protected the diners from the thin grass of the steppe. Elaborately decorated, many of the felts bore the stylized form of the winged horse, Bahadur's banner. His camp, his home: here among family and friends, even a bey could lay down the burdens of leadership at the end of a long day.

In addition to the quail, always a favorite, the platters held braised venison and flat bread, hard and soft cheeses, pomegranates and nuts. Bahadur had drunk deep from pitchers filled with frothy mare's milk and shared cups from a cask of wine, warm with the sunshine of the Crimean hills. One good thing left behind by that scoundrel Tulpar. Its taste lingered on the tongue in happy marriage with the quail.

He considered eating more, but his sash already felt tight to the point of discomfort, and the light slanting through the smoke hole reinforced the message delivered by the quieting of the herds. In the steppe, the midsummer sun hid itself for so short a time that if he did not retire to his private tent to sleep as soon as night fell, he would find himself on horseback again before his muscles ceased to ache. Once he had caroused the night away, as his son Jahangir did, but no more. The counsel of age and wisdom told him he had eaten enough, drunk enough. Time to rest.

Outside, the wind was picking up. "Hear that?" he said to his chief herdsman, seated not far from the door. "Better get the lambs and the weaker animals under cover. It will storm before morning. Check the pens, too."

The herdsman bowed in acknowledgment and ducked from the tent without more ado. A good man, knew his business. Always placed the needs of the animals first, aware that the tribe depended on the herds.

Time for Bahadur, too, to go before the weather changed.

With a sigh, he pushed himself upright. His right knee gave way under his weight, and he staggered. The reception tent rocked as he grabbed at the trellised frame for support. Woven hangings released puffs of dust as they shushed from side to side, setting off a flurry of coughs.

"We must change them," Diliara, his chief wife, said from the women's side of the tent. She pointed at the hangings. "I will order it done tomorrow. After six weeks in place, they have picked up a lot of dirt."

"Yes, do." Bahadur smiled at her. "We have at least another month here before we need to move the herds." Against the fading light, the rich reds and golds of the cloth softened her features, recalling the beauty he had known in their youth. Diliara had once been the jewel of his harem, her physical gifts enhanced by a sweet and generous spirit. These days, she hid the signs of aging with a plethora of veils, but graying hair and a thickening body could not conceal the loveliness of the soul within. Of his many wives, Diliara occupied a special place in his heart. She had raised his twins after his first wife's death and never complained, even when her body failed to produce children of its own.

A silvery gurgle drew his attention in another direction. Roxelana, his concubine of the moment, wrestled playfully with his eldest son, Jahangir, seated on the cushion next to her. Her long brown legs thrashed in their flimsy rose-colored trousers, narrowly missing Jahangir's goblet. A servant dashed forward and wrenched an endangered pitcher off the table, earning a kick from an embroidered royal-blue slipper for his pains.

"Stop tickling her, Jahangir," Bahadur said. His knee gave way again, adding to his irritation. "What are you, an infant?"

Jahangir sputtered half-concealed laughter into his goblet as the four clan leaders who together constituted Bahadur's council stood to bid the bey goodnight. The leaders frowned. Roxelana rallied enough to deliver a smart slap to her tormentor. Jahangir subsided, although an occasional snort escaped him.

A strong young arm caught Bahadur's elbow. "Here, *Ata,*" his daughter Firuza said. "Let me help you."

She had noticed the problem with his leg and come to his aid. Bahadur patted her hair to show his gratitude. She blushed, eyes on his boots, ignoring the byplay between her brother and Roxelana.

Out of innocence, perhaps. Or an awareness of her own shortcomings. Although eighteen, only a year younger than the concubine, Firuza could not match Roxelana for allure. No slinky elegance or sultry mystery here. Firuza was nothing if not straightforward—open, generous, and competent, with an air of untouched purity appropriate for a maiden destined to become a khan's chief wife. Slender, tall for a woman, with the dark hair and eyes of her Mongol ancestors, Firuza had a mind like a general, a face that spoke of intelligence and character, and a trim, compact body. He had never known her to shirk a burden, even one posed by a well-fed, somewhat inebriated father with a gimpy knee.

Indeed, the girl needed to stand up for herself more. Stop protecting that worthless brother of hers. Look at him—drunk and flirting with his father's woman!

Bahadur flexed and straightened the knee and found only a lingering weakness and a slight, persistent ache. "Send for the shaman," he said. "Tell her I need her potion—and make it strong. Not that namby-pamby pap she offered me the last time. What's the point of a medicine too weak to do any good?"

"But, *Ata*," his daughter protested. "She said you must not take too much."

He reacted without thinking. "Ah, what does she know, the old fuss-budget? It's not even her potion. Tulpar brought the recipe from Crimea. Fetch her to my tent, girl, and accept no nonsense."

http://www.fivedirectionspress.com/the-winged-horse

This book was typeset using Garamond, a body font dating from the early days of printing, with headings in Tangerine, chosen for its Arabic lines, evocative of Tatar script. The ornaments come from Type Embellishments One LET.

www.ingramcontent.com/pod-product-compliance
Lightning Source LLC
Chambersburg PA
CBHW031054260626
47172CB00001B/56